I0771752

also by fae

SPOOKY BOYS SERIES

Bite Me! (You Know I Like It)

Possess Me! (I Want You To)

Hunt Me! (I Crave the Chase)

There's a Monster in the Woods

PNR/OMEGAVERSE

The Devil Takes

King of Hollywood

CHRISTMAS DADDIES

Let Your Hearts Be Light

You Can Count on Me

FAE QUIN

Editing by Angela O'Connell

Cover Art and Interior Artwork by Fae Loves Art

WWW.FAELOVESART.COM

Typography and Interior Formatting by We Got You Covered Book Design

WWW.WEGOTYOUCOVEREDBOOKDESIGN.COM

A full list of content warnings and tropes

is available on my website:

WWW.FAELOVESART.COM

Dedicated to my husband,
for always making me feel safe.

For anyone who needs a
little extra Holiday magic.

one

ROBIN

YOU KNOW YOU'RE FUCKED UP when the best thing to happen to you in years is falling asleep while leaning on a stranger's shoulder. I know what you're probably thinking, "That's fucking sad, bro". And you would be right. It *is* sad. *Pitiful,* probably. Stupid? Maybe. Rude, *absolutely.*

I mean, *who does that?*

Just fucking commandeers another dude's bicep?

Me, motherfucker, that's who.

In my defense, it was a *very* nice bicep.

And we were on a long flight—economy—across the whole country.

And if you understood just how *tired* I truly was, you'd get why the second that sandalwood and blossom scent hit I was motherfuckin' done for, motherfucker.

For context, you have to understand that I'm the kind of guy who travels often. I'm always on planes. Always crossing time zones, oceans, and over countries so quickly they blur together in a liquid smear of farms, cities, and mountains. I've been to so many places that half the time I can't tell which city is which. It's only the fucking teleprompter that keeps me straight, and Nancy's painful—but well-meaning—tongue-lashing in my dressing room to hype me up before each show.

Touring is brutal, I'll be honest.

It's go-go-go till you drop-drop-drop.

That's all my life's been for longer than I can remember. At least— until this last year. When the go-go-go stopped drop-drop-dropping. And instead, after the adrenaline had settled, and my sweat had dried, I found myself staring blankly at the nondescript wall of whatever hotel we'd booked that night. Or the floral—because they're always fucking floral for some ungodly reason—comforters of B&Bs, or the sloped, claustrophobic ceiling of the tour bus.

Covered in glitter, with eyeliner old enough it should have its own driver's license, I'd just kinda…die. Shut down.

Staring, staring, staring.

And that staring *never* stopped.

Didn't stop till the world woke up around me, and my eyes were grainy, but the stress remained. I could feel eyes on me, even when no one else was around. Could feel the weight of expectations, heavy on my shoulders.

For a while, I got used to pretending. Pretending that all was well, popping sleep pills when the grittiness became too much. Listening to the audiobooks from my favorite author, and hating the fact that even those couldn't lull me into blissful slumber anymore.

I tried everything.

And when trying everything didn't work, I kept pretending, until the moment I couldn't anymore.

Till my body chose for me, the lights went out, and I woke up one day—lying flat on my back on the stage at one of my performances, with Nancy—my assistant—fucking staring down at me like I was the goddamn antichrist.

"That's fucking it, Robin," she said like I'd shat in her cereal.

She was so far up my ass after that I hadn't needed to get laid. Not that I could, considering the state my dick and body were in. Apparently, you needed proper blood flow to get hard—and sleep was…kinda fucking important?

Not that I'd tried to get laid, or even *wanted* to. I mean—you ever try to drive when you're operating on two to three days with no rest? The world's a fucking *mess*, you can't see straight, your body's full of pins and needles, and left isn't left anymore.

Imagine trying to *fuck* like that.

No fucking thanks, man.

And that's without adding in the extra drama of the paparazzi, the press, or the assholes that treated me like a trophy fuck to shine and display on their mantle. Robin "Trashmouth" Johnson, a motherfuckin' ace in the hole.

I was *always* an ace in the hole.

Even when I wasn't.

But that was better than being one of those famous dudes that simply sneezes and pisses people off, so it's not like I could complain. Even though, after a certain point, I started to wonder if one day I'd stop being a real person at all. I'd wake up shiny and plastic like they thought I was, and not even realize I'd changed.

So yeah.

The bicep-stealing, sleep-falling incident was pretty monumental for me.

Especially because I happened to be nervous as hell.

This was my first time going to visit Miles—my baby brother—for longer than a few days. At least…since I'd left him in my early twenties, bright-eyed and bushy-tailed, certain I was gonna fucking change his goddamn life. And now, I was returning with my tail between my legs, years of neglected text messages between us and frown lines around the corners of my lips.

My publicist said they made me look *rugged*. But I caught her telling the media dudes to photoshop them out, so I wasn't all that optimistic about them. Not that I could be assed to care about that right now. Not when I was sleepy, well-rested, and had a face full of man meat.

Bicep smelled *good*.

Because that's what *he* was, in my sleep-addled state. Not a fully grown, mountain of a man with dark auburn hair and a frankly sexy-as-hell stank face—he'd stared at me with a constipated expression when we'd taken our seats on the plane. No. *He* was simply a lovely, tight bicep—soft now because he'd finally relaxed.

He smelled like the cologne booths that populated the closest mall to where I'd grown up in North Carolina. Booths where the salespeople would accost you on your way to the food court and convince you to let them show you whatever fancy-ass-manufactured-money-in-a-bottle they had on hand.

Expensive.

Cultured.

Like *he* was important, not because he'd fought tooth and nail for it—like a rabid raccoon like I had—but because he was simply the kind of man who'd always mattered.

He didn't make me move.

Maybe because he could feel the way I sunk into him. And see the way my phone fell to the carpet where it remained abandoned because I was too damn tired to pick it up. I didn't even pause the latest raunchy werewolf book I was listening to. Just let the narrators croon in my ears as I drooled on man-muscle, and thanked whatever god that had goddamn listened, that I was here—on this flight—with the best fucking pillow I'd ever had.

It was a long flight.

L.A. to Vermont.

Eight hours, give or take a storm or two.

And I slept the whole fucking time.

At the end of the flight, I stirred, too groggy to care that I was drooling, but more than a little pleased to find my phone in the pocket in front of me, and the stranger's quiet snores rumbling beside me. He'd fallen asleep too, and his warm breath ruffled my hair in a weirdly soothing way.

Kinda like a metronome.

Puff, suck, exhale.

Puff, suck, exhale.

Puff, suck—

"Welcome to Vermont," a woman's voice echoed through the cabin, and both of us startled awake. Stranger made this loud snorting sound that should not have been cute, but totally fucking was.

He straightened, on high alert, his toffee-colored eyes blazing.

His irises were too light to truly be called brown. They were the color of melted caramel, or the toffee Nancy always bought me for my birthday. I'd call them hazel, but there wasn't an echo of green inside them. Could eyes be hazel without green? I wasn't sure. Either way, they were...*seriously* pretty. I'd been too tired earlier to really appreciate him, but I certainly did now for a few brief, sleepy moments.

I tried not to stare, I really did. But he was impossible not to stare at.

All broad shoulders, lean frame, and a resting bitch face that was as hot as it was intimidating. A dark dusting of stubble coated his cheeks—like he'd shaved earlier and it was already growing back. It clung to what had to be the sharpest cheekbones I'd ever seen, and an upper lip that was maybe too thin, but somehow perfect anyway.

There was something...calming about him, grumpiness aside. A soothing energy that when paired with his devastatingly sharp jawline and the gray at his temples was like fucking catnip to a starved man like me.

I couldn't remember the last time I'd been this attracted to another person. Maybe never? And that thought was sobering as it was intimidating.

I peeled my head from his arm, embarrassed once again to find that I'd left a drool spot there.

Godammit, Robin.

I didn't look at him again. *Couldn't.* My cheeks were way too hot, and the humiliation was finally settling in. Especially after I realized just how goddamn hot he was.

Now that I was no longer exhausted to the point of incoherency I could admit how fucking weird what I'd just done was.

Even weirder though? The fact he hadn't pushed me off.

He could've been sneaky about it too. Could've told me he needed to use the bathroom and then made sure his armrest was down when he came back so I couldn't snuggle into him a second time. It would've been easy to turn me down.

But he hadn't.

Why hadn't he?

I got the impression that he wasn't the kind of guy who voluntarily let strangers cuddle him.

Maybe it was the way he wore his black turtleneck sweater, all prim and tight and proper. Or maybe it was the way he held his head high, back ramrod straight—staring around the plane like he expected the worst to happen and was prepared to face it the moment it did.

I booked it off the plane the moment I could, head down, heart in my throat.

The airport was a small one. It was as close to Belleville as I could get, though I knew from experience there was still a decent drive ahead of me to reach the quaint mountain town where my brother had settled.

Autumn in Vermont was gorgeous. I'd visited a few times since Miles had moved here, and it always hit me like a punch to the face every time I saw it. Passing by the large open windows that faced the tarmac, with my heart in my throat, even the fall leaves couldn't fully distract me from the man I knew would be exiting the plane after I did.

Silently, I willed the handsome stranger to walk by me.

A myriad of colorful red and orange leaves spread out like paint strokes across the skyline at the edge of the airport. It looked like a Bob Ross painting. Like someone had taken a brush and artfully crafted each tree, one swipe at a time. Our plane sat sentinel in front of the wall of the forest as the rest of the passengers filed off and the crew prepped for the next flight.

My pulse thrummed.

He's not going to follow you.

He's not going to get mad at you.

It was just a nap.

Not the end of the world.

Thud, thud went the footsteps behind me, and I prayed that the stranger wouldn't stop. That the *one* awkward glance we'd shared would be it. That I'd never have to acknowledge just how weird I'd acted again.

My cheeks were hot enough to boil eggs on.

A throat cleared behind me and my shoulders rose even higher, my shame obvious as I took in a steadying breath and swiveled to—

"Are you "Trashmouth"?" It wasn't him. My stranger.

Thank god.

"Ah—yeah. That's me." I cleared my throat, offering the woman—because it was a woman speaking, not a sexy silver fox—a friendly smile. Beside her, a little boy stood, his dark hair sticking up in all directions, his eyes wide as he stared at me like he wasn't sure he wasn't imagining things.

"Oh my *gosh*!" the woman gushed, her eyes bright. "We were at your concert last fall."

I nodded along like I remembered where that concert had been. "Ah. Thanks for coming!" *That was a good thing to say, right?*

Personable?

Mom had raised us to have manners, but situations like this always made me uneasy. It'd been years, but I still wasn't used to being recognized out in public like this. At least the paparazzi hadn't found me here. This was uncomfortable, but not in a bad way.

I'd always loved talking to fans.

It was my favorite part of my job, even if I sucked at it.

Felt like I had to play a game. Like they saw me as something other than a dude who wore too much eyeliner. And because of that, whatever I said was important and needed to be *perfect*.

I didn't want to let the people who supported me down.

"Bobbie's a *big* fan," the woman shoved her son forward. He looked… miserable. Totally fucking embarrassed that his mom was doing this to him. And that *killed* me.

"*Moooom*," Bobbie grumbled, cheeks about as red as mine were two seconds ago.

"He's got the biggest crush on you!" She continued to chatter, way too fucking friendly, throwing her kid under the bus without realizing it. *Poor kid, oh my god. Was this lady oblivious or what?*

I grinned, ducking my head, catching his gaze with a conspiratorial wink. "I'm flattered."

He relaxed a little, relieved when he realized I wasn't offended. "You're old but you—" he fidgeted, "I really like the way you play guitar."

You're old.

Damn kid, goin' right for the kidneys.

"He wants to be a musician when he grows up," she gushed again. "Do you have any advice?"

People did this all the time, treated me like I was fucking Jesus of music or some shit. Like I knew the secret to success in the music industry. Unfortunately, the truth was that *I* wasn't even sure how I'd made it as far as I had. I'd simply been in the right place at the right time.

Knew the right person.

Got lucky.

But you couldn't say *that* to a fucking kid. Even if it was true.

"Don't give up, even when things get hard," I said instead, swallowing the lump in my throat. "Find out…what inspires you." I scratched my temple, embarrassed this was happening, a sick pit in my stomach because I felt like a fucking hypocrite. "And cling to that. No matter how hard it gets—or who tells you that you can't. Don't let *anyone* tell you that you need to change to achieve your dreams."

Projecting much?

"That's a good point," Mom grinned. Her expression softened.

"And *practice*," I added, making eye contact with the kid again— because I was *trying* to be uplifting. "Because one day someone might come knocking on your door, and if you're not ready, that's on you."

Well, that was dark.

Jesus.

Bobbie, to his credit, nodded along. His eyes lit up, a little grin spreading across his lips, like what I'd just told him was pure gold. "Okay," he said, cheeks still pink. "*Okay*," he repeated, more determined this time.

"You're already ahead of me, kid," I shrugged, my smile softening. "Seriously. When I was your age I had no idea what I wanted to do. So keep trying and just…" I swallowed the lump in my throat. "Hold on to the parts of music that make you happy."

I wish I could say I'd done that.

"Could we get your autograph?" Bobbie's mom asked, and I nodded, already reaching for the pen I kept in my backpack for moments just like this.

I signed the kid's baseball cap and made sure to make eye contact. He smiled shyly at me, ducking his head, his chubby little hands shaking. I hated that I made him nervous, but I didn't know how to fix it.

So I just let his mom take a pic of us together, and then watched them walk away, feeling like somehow…I'd fucked that up.

Like I could've been more *profound* or motivational or some shit.

But that had never been my strong suit.

Slumping a little, I turned back around—only to see that apparently, I'd had an audience. Immediately, my pulse skittered to life, and my hands grew sweaty.

He's not going to yell at you, I tried to convince myself.

But I wasn't so sure I believed it.

Because the sexy stranger from the plane was behind me. And judging by the fact I hadn't heard footsteps for quite some time, he'd been behind me the whole fucking time. He looked pissed off still, his brow twitching as he stared at me. I wasn't sure what to make of his face. It was the same face he'd given me when I'd boarded the plane and taken the seat next to him.

Unfortunately for me, if he hadn't recognized me—which I was kinda doubting was the case—that meant he was waiting for me because of the arm thing.

Fuck my life.

"Look," I started, cheeks hot. "I'm sorry for molesting your bicep, man." Fuck. Now that he'd seen me interact with the kid he was bound to assume I had money—maybe he'd want compensation?

Nancy would be *pissed* if I ended up on the news again.

She was still beating reporters away with baseball bats. Fucking assholes wanted to know all the nitty-gritty details about my medical condition. About why I'd collapsed on stage. Like I wasn't a fucking *person* who was struggling, but a piece of entertainment.

Not that I thought sleeping on someone's arm was newsworthy, per say.

But fuck if I knew what made money nowadays. The press was full of vultures.

"That was nice of you," the man said simply, watching me with those oddly warm eyes as he jerked his head toward the mom and son who were now out of earshot.

Mr. Sexy had a *deep* voice, slow and sweet and even, like he said every word with purpose. Like he was ten steps ahead already. Like he knew *exactly* what to say and how to say it. Except that his eyes widened after the words popped out, like he was surprised.

I was so distracted by how hot he sounded that I nearly forgot what he'd said. And when I remembered, it took me a second to even process. Because that had not been what I was expecting.

At all.

I blinked.

Huh.

My mouth clicked shut, my ire and anxiety fading away and replaced by confusion. "Wh—"

"Goodbye."

Before I could respond, tall, gorgeous, and apparently awkward-as-hell, turned on his heel and strode as fast as he could, as far from me as he could possibly get. His long muscular legs ate up the distance quickly. I tried not to watch his ass as he moved, and failed.

What the fuck just happened?

Somehow, I thought, I must've fucked *that* up too. Probably by ogling him. Fuck.

At least I'd never have to see or talk to him ever again, right?

Which should be relieving.

So why was there a pit in my stomach?

two

BEN

I HAVEN'T HAD A LOT of regrets in my life. I mean, yes, I was an angsty teen with a chip on his shoulder. Yes, I had secrets. Yes, I hogged the bathroom. Yes, I was an asshole sometimes—most teens are, which in turn bred mistakes. But since I'd become an adult and moved away from home to pursue my medical degree, I could count on one hand the number of times I'd cared enough about something to feel any sort of true regret.

The kind of regret that eats you from the inside out.

That makes you question things in a way you never had before.

Pins and needles buzzed at my fingertips as I finished washing my hands in the airport bathroom. Regret tasted bitter as the burnt coffee I'd had for breakfast. It clung like a film to my body, clogging my pores, and making my movements feel more sluggish than usual.

Because while I often acted like an asshole—and I was fine with that—

for some reason…the idea that the small blond man I'd met on the plane might think I was one was…uncomfortable.

Ah. There was that pesky *regret* again.

I wasn't normally the kind of man that ran away from things. I was stubborn and stalwart. *Sturdy*. I said what I meant. And I always did what I said I would. Promises were vows that were kept. And problems were meant to be dealt with when they arose. Not that the man had been a "problem", because I certainly didn't mean that.

The problem was my reaction to him.

My very visceral reaction to him.

This wasn't who I was.

This wasn't who I'd been raised to be.

So why had I run from him?

I wasn't naive enough to think it was because I'd recognized who he was. It was something deeper than that. Something I wasn't sure I was equipped to face right then, standing in the airport bathroom, my hands sweaty with anxiety.

So instead, I replayed our encounter.

When he'd stepped onto the plane it was like a bucket of icy water had been doused all over me. I had *not* been prepared for all that…*gorgeous* in high definition. *And who could blame me?* Seeing photos on the album I bought the girls for Christmas last year was not the same as seeing those pale green eyes up close.

Framed by bruises darker than the eyeliner he wore, smudged and grungy—like he'd done his best to cover them up. Like he was *ashamed* of his own exhaustion. Chapped lips, under-plucked eyebrows, a tiny, almost invisible scar on his chin. Frown lines by the corners of his lips that looked particularly kissable.

He was all sharp edges and harsh lines when he was awake. But the moment he'd fallen asleep, so sweetly, that changed. Slow and steady, he'd leaned more and more against me, tipping into me with each warm puff of his breath, his walls eradicated.

I'd been scared to move.

Terrified I'd wake him when he so clearly needed the rest. In a way, he reminded me of a sculpture I'd seen at a gallery in New York. Immortalized in glass, a crushed flower petal had sat on display for the world to ogle. It had been delicate once. Before its destruction had been celebrated. Perfect from a distance, in the way only the truly manufactured can be, but when you moved in close, its history became evident.

When he was asleep, he was vulnerable. Walls down, armor gone. Like he was an entirely different person than the man who had sat stiffly beside me, his head down, like he was afraid of being seen. Like the glass had melted away, and the petal was bare once again, bruised edges on display.

Truth be told, I'd had a lot of time to stare.

Eight hours.

Eight hours to admire the way Trashmouth's hands were a little large for his frame. Eight hours to admire the veins that danced atop them. The broad swell of his knuckles. His chipped black nail polish—fresh still, like he'd painted them right before the flight and somehow chipped them anyway.

The moles on his throat, the insides of his wrists.

And the freckles that scattered across the bridge of his nose.

I'd never seen *those* in photographs.

Maybe he wore makeup to cover them? Or maybe they were photoshopped out. Treated like imperfections when they were anything but. The little flaws that the magazines edited away were the things that made him devastatingly perfect.

And…in a way, that perfection made him *terrifying*.

Because he made my pulse thrum like it never had before. He made my belly fill with butterflies. He made my palms slick with sweat. Made me want to pull him to my chest, tuck a blanket around him, and let him take a nice long nap.

He certainly looked like he needed it.

He must've been *exhausted* to fall asleep on a stranger's shoulder.

What if I'd been a creep?

Something protective flickered inside my belly at the thought.

I wasn't sure if I should be offended or grateful that my book had put him right to sleep.

I'd been prepared to walk away the moment he escaped off the plane, running as far and as fast from me as he could. I'd been prepared to write off my feelings as a passing crush—but then…but then…The nail in the coffin had been the way he'd talked to that damn kid.

I'd seen him.

And while Trashmouth hadn't looked comfortable in the slightest, there was no denying how *careful* he'd been when he encouraged the child. He'd been rudely stopped while out in the wild—which had to be annoying, my god—and yet…he'd still been so *gentle* with him.

Just like when I'd seen him enter the plane I'd frozen, unable to look away. Unable to get my feet to move. Unable to follow the plan that I'd made—to let this be an odd chance encounter, and leave it at that.

I shouldn't have stopped him too—I *knew* that.

Especially after the way he'd run off.

But the second we were alone again, my mouth had opened before my brain could catch up. And then I'd run—just like he had. Which, again, was not like me. Not at all. And now…I needed to figure out what to do. Because I didn't want to seem like a total creep, but it also didn't sit right with me—the way we'd left off.

Not when I kept replaying the confused, almost hurt look on his face, over and over in my mind.

No, no. He most definitely deserved an apology for that.

He was a *person*. And I'd been less than kind by walking off when he was mid-sentence.

"I'm sorry for molesting your bicep, man."

He'd looked so…defeated when he said those words. Paranoid almost. Like he expected me to get mad at him for borrowing my shoulder. To be fair…if it had been anyone else I would've found a way to politely excuse myself from the situation.

I'd never liked being touched as a general rule.

I'd always thought I had very few exceptions.

My daughters, Rosie and Jane, my mother—because she'd always been my closest confidant—and begrudgingly, my best friend, Trixie—the mother of my children. And on the very rare occasion I left town for a medical conference or to visit my publisher, I would sometimes tolerate the hands of the random men I'd pick up.

Though, admittedly, it had been years since I'd felt inclined to scratch that particular itch—despite having just arrived home from a conference today.

Apparently, I'd been wrong—about my limitations, that is.

Because…while my bubble remained small, today I had learned that it was still large enough to accommodate a tiny, black-clad emo twink.

An emo twink that I was going to need to find, so that I could properly apologize. And perhaps…maybe thank for reading my book. Which I still couldn't believe had really happened. It felt surreal at best.

Drying my hands, I sighed and pulled the men's bathroom door open with my foot using the lever near the floor. I wasn't about to touch the handle. Absolutely not.

Speak of the devil.

Apparently, I didn't need to hunt him down to apologize, after all.

"Oh," Trashmouth stood outside the door, his hands raised like he'd been about to reach for the handle. His movements were clearly sluggish, another hint at the sleep deprivation I could see written all over his face. He had to tilt his head back quite a ways to meet my gaze, the difference in our heights even more obvious up close. "Bicep guy."

Bicep guy?

Now I was met with a very awkward situation. I could…wait for him to use the bathroom so I could apologize for acting rude. Or…we could have this conversation in the doorway of a public restroom.

Neither option was good.

But which choice would frighten him less?

Best to rip the Band-Aid off now.

I had no idea what kind of people he interacted with back in California— or why he was here in Vermont at all, but I didn't want to frighten him by lurking.

"I'd like to apologize to you," I said, the door still awkwardly positioned on my foot.

"Apologize…to me?" Trashmouth—god, that was an awful name—

looked confused, head cocked to the side as his eyes narrowed. "For what?"

He had a scratchy voice, lower than one might expect. Almost like he was a smoker, even though I was fairly certain—given his career—that he wasn't. There was something effortlessly sexy about it, all low, crackling amusement.

"I'd like to apologize for running away," I clarified.

"What?" He stared at me like I'd grown a second head.

"I was embarrassed," I added on because I wasn't sure—at this point—he even realized I'd been running. He deflated a little, shrugging a shoulder as he nodded along.

"I tend to get that reaction from people," the light in his eyes dimmed, closing off, and I—

"No." I stepped out into the hallway, letting the door swing shut behind me. "I just…" I ran a hand through the back of my hair, cheeks heating. Damn. I couldn't remember the last time I felt this…off. "You were reading my book."

And you're gorgeous.

Really fucking gorgeous, I thought but didn't say.

"Reading your…" Trashmouth's brow furrowed. His eyebrows were darker than his hair, maybe dyed? Or maybe naturally that way. I wasn't certain. One unruly hair near the front of his right brow was off-kilter, sticking slightly to the left, and I had the oddest urge to reach out and stroke a finger over it. "What?"

Stop ogling him, Ben, and answer the question.

"My book," I shrugged, uncomfortable—the butterflies in my belly rioting. "I enjoy your music. I wasn't expecting to see you reading my book."

"As in…you're the *author* of the book I was reading?" he asked, staring at me like he was ready to call bullshit.

"Unfortunately."

There was a pause as Trashmouth's guard wavered, threatening to fall. His eyes were wide, like he genuinely hadn't expected me to say that. Which was fair, I hadn't *meant* to say it—it had just slipped out.

It was like when he was around, my body and mouth betrayed me.

"*What?*" He laughed, clearly surprised. "What does *that* mean?" I'd apparently done something right because the warmth bled back into his gaze. "Why *unfortunately?*"

Only I was glad I'd slipped up now, because he'd laughed.

I made him do that.

I got the feeling he didn't laugh often.

"I'd be happy to tell you when you're finished," I jerked my head toward the bathroom, figuring I'd monopolized enough of his time. "If you have time, of course."

Trashmouth stared at me, head cocked, a thoughtful hum buzzing in his throat.

He has a lip ring.

I wasn't sure how I hadn't noticed before.

But I certainly did now.

After a moment of serious deliberation, he seemed to decide that I was, in fact, not a threat. Maybe it was the awkward way I was standing, staring at him. Or maybe it was the sweat on my upper lip? I'm not sure.

"Yeah, sure. My ride's not supposed to be here for another forty minutes," Trashmouth replied. His lips twitched up at the same time that his pale green eyes narrowed playfully. "How do I know you're not fucking with me?"

How odd, my ride was due to arrive at about the same time.

"I guess you'll just have to find out." I hadn't really meant to flirt. I mean, I had. Of course I had. He was fucking adorable. But it just kind of slipped out?

Trashmouth snorted—amused. And I made a mental note to find proof of who I was before he returned so he'd know I wasn't lying. So that I could put him at ease once and for all. And as I stepped aside and let him through, I tried to tell myself that the butterflies would fade. That this was a fluke. It had to be.

Talking to him would prove that.

Only…that felt like a fucking lie.

Robin—because after a quick Google search, it was easy enough to find his first name—returned from the bathroom, looking marginally better than before. His hair was a little damp, like he'd washed his face and gotten it wet. The pale, nearly white strands dripped onto his forehead before he brushed them out of the way, only for them to fall back down again.

He stood awkwardly for a moment, eyes guarded, shoulders hunched as he hunted the empty terminal for me.

The moment he spotted me he relaxed a little, taking a few strides my way, his black combat boots thudding with every step. Right now, there wasn't a thing about him that wasn't on guard. He wore his clothing like it was armor, carefully picked so you couldn't see the chinks.

The sleepy-soft cuddly man from the plane was notably missing.

If it hadn't been the strangest, most surreal, most rewarding moment of my life I would've thought I had made it up.

Fortunately for both of us, I was a doctor and a father, which meant I'd grown pretty adept at reading body language over the years.

I saw right through that prickly exterior.

Robin was hiding, and I couldn't blame him.

He was in uncharted waters.

I gestured for him to take a seat beside mine. While he'd been splashing his face, I'd settled at the gate across the hallway. We were in the middle of the airport so we'd have some walking to do to get to the pickup zone, but I figured we had time. Plus, it was a small airport.

Coincidentally, our rides were coming at the same time, which meant if this went well we could chat while we walked.

And if it didn't…well, I'd already planned for that too.

I'd pretend I dropped something at our original gate and politely say my goodbyes to give him a head start so he'd never have to see me again.

I'd already apologized—which had been the original plan.

So I wasn't sure what I wanted from this.

Only that…it had been a long time since I was simply excited to talk to someone else. And despite my best efforts, the butterflies were still rioting in my belly.

Robin sank into the seat that I'd indicated. He crossed his ankle, left over his right knee, closing himself off—a clear sign that while he was willing to chat he still hadn't decided whether he could trust me or not.

I didn't blame him.

So I pulled up my phone, cheeks hot, and offered it to him.

He accepted it, black polish flashing, his brow furrowed as he stared down at it, probably trying to figure out why the fuck I'd handed it to him.

"I took the liberty of gathering some proof," I told him, ears burning as he scrolled through the photo album on my phone, expression pensive. "So that you would know that I am who I say I am."

Robin scrolled past photos of me with my publisher. Photos of me signing at book conventions. Screenshots of a few contracts that had both my written name and my pen name upon them. I'd blacked out the confidential bits while I'd been waiting, and hoped that this was enough to set him at ease.

"Huh," he said, handing me back my phone. His legs remained crossed. He scrubbed his ring finger over his eyebrow, humming thoughtfully, expression far away for a moment. "You put this together?" He blinked, staring at me, eyes searching mine. "Just now?"

I nodded.

"Why?" Robin looked confused. "I mean, I believe you—" *Oh, thank God.* "But why go through all this trouble?" His cheeks flushed. "You like…a super fan or something? Not to be an asshole, but like…dude. That's a *lot* of work to put in for a stranger."

He wasn't wrong.

"You like my books," I settled on, burning from the inside out. "It's not often I…" God, I wasn't sure how to say any of this. I felt like an idiot. I probably looked like one too. This wasn't like me. I always knew exactly what to say.

I felt wrong-footed, tripping over myself to get him to like me.

He was so damn pretty it was distracting.

"You…" I tried again, annoyed when my hands began to shake a little. They hadn't done that for years.

"Okay," Robin said, ending my suffering. His legs uncrossed. The pensive expression on his face bled away, replaced instead by a sunny but wicked grin. "I'll stop torturing you."

I laughed—*way* too loud. My shoulders relaxed. I hadn't realized I'd gotten that tense—fuck.

"Sooo…" Robin ducked his head, meeting my gaze. That pale lock of hair stuck to his forehead. I had the weirdest urge to lean down and lick his eyebrow. It was right there. Right there. And it looked very lickable. Just like the rest of him. This was way worse than the eyebrow-stroking urge. And way harder to ignore.

"So?" I countered, skin hot.

"This is weird," Robin confessed, shrugging a shoulder.

"It is," I agreed, because it was. "I'm fucking it up."

If Rosie had been here she would've made me put a dollar in the swear jar. And that thought made me crack a smile. Robin smiled back, and while it was still a little guarded, it was far warmer than before.

"You're not fucking it up," he disagreed, eyes crinkling at the corners. "You're just…super fucking awkward dude. But in a cute way. I mean… the photo album was pretty extra, but I super appreciate it."

"I don't want to be creepy."

"The fact that you don't want to be creepy majorly helps toward the not-creepiness," Robin laughed—all scratchy soft—and it was the prettiest sound I'd ever heard.

"Ugh." I covered my face with one hand, embarrassed, and then I dropped it—because if I was only ever going to have this one conversation with this stunning, beautiful, *talented* man, I wasn't about to block my view of him while I did it.

"Why'd you say being an author was unfortunate?" Robin asked, repeating my earlier words. My cheeks burned even hotter. I'd always been an ugly blusher, and I was certain it was that horrible splotchiness that made Robin take pity on me.

"That is a…recent development," I admitted.

"Care to elaborate, big guy?" he asked, obviously amused.

"I don't," I shook my head, face still blazing. "Because it's *horrible*."

"Is it?"

"You'll laugh."

"I like laughing."

I cracked a smile. "My mother's book club started reading one of my books," I confessed. I hadn't told a single soul about this. I was more than a little surprised at how easy it was to talk to Robin.

"*Supportive*, that's not a bad thing." Robin's lips looked very soft.

"She doesn't know they're mine."

"Oh?" Robin blinked, head tilting curiously to the side.

"She…" Oh no. "This is too awful to say."

"Say it anyway."

I laughed, unable to help it. "She and her group of rowdy, knitting buddies have all decided my books are…" I couldn't help but die a little on the inside, "*tantalizing*."

"Oh my god," Robin's eyes widened. "No way."

"Yes."

"Which is why…you said it was *unfortunate*."

"It's been on my mind, yes," I admitted, though all of this felt slightly less terrible now that Robin was laughing because of it. "Every day. All the time." I laughed, unable to help it. "She texts me."

"Oh, dear god."

"She wants me to read them."

"Oh my fuck," Robin cackled. "What do you even say to that?"

"I told her I'm too busy," I replied, more than a little shocked that this conversation was going so well. Especially because we were airing out the most embarrassing thing that had ever happened to me.

"And she…?" Robin waited.

"Bought me the audiobooks."

"This is gold," Robin's eyes were dancing. "Sorry, not to be an asshole or anything. But—shit dude. Look at you! Indoctrinating a bunch of old ladies into your gay-werewolf-porn cult."

"I know."

Robin slid a few inches closer. Close enough I could feel his heat, his thigh only a few scant centimeters from mine. "Your books are my favorite," Robin confessed after a second, voice dropping low and personal and sweet. "For the record."

"Thank you," my voice cracked a little. "They bring me joy," I frowned. "*Brought* me joy," I corrected. "Before my mother ruined them."

"That's good." Robin's eyes flickered dark for only a moment before the light bled back in. "Joy is good."

"It is." I swallowed the lump in my throat, sure that now that my humiliating story was over, the easy camaraderie would end. I'd never just…conversed with someone else like this. Effortlessly. It felt like a fluke.

"Music used to do that for me," Robin told me, a sad little twitch to his lips.

"Yeah?" My heart ached for him then, as I watched a metaphorical shadow flicker over his face. The dark crept forward before flitting away just as quickly.

"You know that part when Beckett left his pack?" Robin changed the subject deftly, obviously not ready to delve deeper into the topic of music. "In your last book," he added, in case I didn't remember my own books. Which I thought was…adorable.

I didn't mind the question. It wasn't often I got to openly talk about my characters.

Now that my mother and her friends had decided my work was hot shit, I had made myself a vow that I would *never* reveal my identity. It was far too late for that. Old women—that I'd known since I was born—were getting off on my werewolf porn.

I would die before I let anyone know that "little Ben Montgomery" was responsible for the epidemic of primal kink in Belleville.

Last week, I'd seen Martha Berry—one of my mother's friends—*growl* at her husband while I was at the grocery store. Playfully yes, but…no. *Nope.* I was still doing my best not to think about it.

And that wasn't the first time either. Trent, my younger brother, had told me that he'd had to chase a few college-age kids off of the tree farm he ran because they'd been playing wolves in the woods. Just the *thought* of that made my face hot all over again.

"Yes," I replied to Robin, hoping I hadn't paused too long—remembering Martha and the horrors that my mother's book club had bestowed upon our small mountain town. "I do."

Beckett's story was near and dear to me. While it wasn't exactly what had happened to me, I could relate to his need to leave. To provide for his family while he kept them safe from a distance. Because that was what he'd done. In the next installment of the series, I planned to let Beckett meet his end. It'd be a noble death, and a fitting end for a character drenched in tragedy.

"He gets to go back, right?" Robin asked, voice oddly small.

"What?" I blinked, surprised.

"In the next book?" He waited patiently, green eyes beseeching. Like he wasn't asking for insider information that literally no one, not even my agent, knew yet. "He gets to go home?"

"I…" I didn't want to tell him I planned to kill Beckett. So instead, I just winked and shrugged, doing my best to play it cool—even though the movement felt odd and unnatural on my face. "You'll see?"

"*Bitch*," Robin thwacked my arm. I was so surprised all I could do was laugh. "Tell me right now or I swear to god I'll—"

"You'll what?" I asked, cheeks hurting from the force of my grin. "Paint my nails?"

Woah. I had not expected something so smooth or flirty to come out of my mouth.

"Yes." Robin looked as surprised as I felt by my words. "I will. I'll fucking paint your nails. And that's a *threat*."

"Uh-huh," I agreed, hot all over. "To be an effective threat it'd have to be *frightening*."

Robin cocked his head. "Most men that look like you would be terrified," he tried to convince me.

"Of nail polish?"

"Yes," Robin nodded.

"I have two little girls back home. You'd have to do a lot more than paint my nails to frighten me."

"Is that a challenge?" Robin puffed up, looking oddly excited. We were never going to see each other again, so I figured there was no harm in agreeing to his little game.

"Yes," I agreed.

"Deal." Robin held a hand out, waiting expectantly. I hesitated for only a moment before taking it within my own and giving it a tight squeeze. He was cold. That was the first thing I noticed. Poor baby needed gloves or a warmer coat if he was going to survive Vermont.

Maybe this was just a layover for him?

No, no. He'd mentioned a ride.

Still. Maybe he was only spending a night here before heading off somewhere with brighter lights, and fewer men in flannel.

"If you can scare me I'll tell you what happens to Beckett," I promised, still holding his hand. I could feel the calluses from his guitar where they pressed to my skin, and that gentle scratch made my pulse thrum. I licked my lips, trying not to stare too hard at his collarbone where it peeked out of the sloped collar of his black, half-sheer shirt. His overcoat—over *jacket*, really—slid open a little, enough that I caught a glimpse of his nipples.

And god…fuck.

They were pierced too.

Made me want to pull on them just to make him yelp.

Which was not…a very appropriate thought to have when one was making a deal, but still.

Robin nodded seriously, accepting my terms. "And if I can't scare you?" he asked, obviously waiting for the other shoe to drop. A pessimist, the way I'd always thought I was.

"You owe me a cup of hot chocolate."

"Hot chocolate?" Robin blinked, clearly shocked. Then he laughed, eyes crinkling. "Yeah, biceps. Fine. I'll buy you cocoa, you big weirdo."

I dropped his hand, not because I wanted to, but because I didn't want to be a creep.

My phone buzzed, signaling that Trent was here more than likely, which meant our time was up…unfortunately. It seemed there wouldn't be much time for Robin to scare me, after all. I patted my shoulder to make sure my satchel was still in place, and Robin did the same with his backpack.

Regret—a new flavor—simmered in my belly as I rose to my feet and offered Robin a hand up. "Anyone ever told you that you have gigantic hands?" Robin asked, accepting the help. His guard went back up a little, but this time, the armor wasn't aimed toward me but toward the rest of the airport as we made our way down the hallway. He ducked his head toward me, like he was hiding from the scattered families that littered the different gates as we passed by them.

"Yes," I admitted, because it was true. Men often made comments about my hands when I had my fingers inside them. Not that I thought that was an appropriate thought to share.

"Bet they feel real good inside somebody," Robin mused thoughtfully.

I choked.

"I'm just saying," he shrugged. "Bet your cock's big too."

"Jesus Christ." I pinched my eyes shut, face bright red.

"Bet it blushes just like your cheeks do," Robin was clearly having fun at my expense again. And I couldn't even be mad about it. "Bet you walk in a room and the first thought anybody has is, "Woah, that dude looks like a ride and a half.' Especially size queens. You ever heard of size queens? You're like a size queen's wet dream."

I realized what he was doing a second too late.

"Are you trying to scare me?"

The doors that would lead out of the airport were fast approaching.

"Maaaaybe?" Robin grinned, and I glanced down at him. Quite far. Because he was incredibly short. Barely came up to my rib cage, actually, when we were both standing. "Is it working?"

"No," I replied because it wasn't.

He blinked, eyes narrowed. "So you're not afraid of nail polish or size queens," he nodded playfully. "Hmm."

"Gay sex of any kind doesn't scare me." I stared down at him as we reached the doors. "You'll have to try harder than that."

It took me a second to realize what I'd just admitted, but Robin took it in stride easily.

"What about spiders? You afraid of spiders?" There was approval written all over his face, like I'd passed some sort of unspoken test.

"No."

"Snakes?"

"No."

"Needles?"

"I'm a doctor, so no." A brisk breeze assaulted us the second we stepped outside. I could see Trent's truck at the end of the procession, slowly approaching. Relaxing a fraction, I twisted to look at Robin. Took him in, every last beautiful detail because I knew our time together was coming to an abrupt end.

"A doctor?" Robin grinned. "Big hands, big dick, not afraid of gay sex, would wear nail polish, writes smut, and is a *doctor*." His cheeks grew a little pink, like it took him repeating what he'd said out loud to realize how blatantly he was flirting—if he was even flirting at all. Maybe he simply didn't have a filter? "Your wife is very lucky."

"No wife," I corrected as Trent's truck pulled even closer.

"Husband?"

"No husband."

"Boyfriend?" Robin's eyes danced. "Girlfriend?"

"No and no."

And then, because he was apparently gorgeous *and* a shithead, loud enough to frighten the birds hopping along the sidewalk, Robin shouted, "Commitment!"

I stared at him, flabbergasted.

Trent pulled up, the truck parking as he moved to hop out. I only had my backpack on me, so I didn't need help carrying anything. But I couldn't do anything more than stare at Robin as I tried to figure out what the fuck he was doing.

"Still not scared?" He frowned. "Damn, thought that would've gotten you for sure."

"Oh my god." I couldn't stop staring.

Had he been trying to frighten me with the word *commitment*?

Who does that?

Robin, apparently.

"Ben," Trent addressed me with a grin. Trent was my little brother—but not by much, at least size-wise. Wider than me, and only slightly shorter, Trent towered over Robin as easily as I did. It wasn't until Trent said my name that I realized I hadn't properly introduced myself.

"You must be Robin," Trent said, turning his attention to my small companion.

How did he know—?

Was he a fan of Robin's music too?

Trent's easy smile was welcoming, and it took me a solid ten seconds to get past my shock and realize that there was a second reason Robin looked so damn familiar.

Oh.

"I'm Trent," Trent said, holding a hand out to him. "It's so great to meet you. Miles has been so fucking excited you're coming home to visit."

Oh my god.

It was taking me a bit, but yes, my brain was finally connecting the dots. *Wow. How the hell had I missed this?*

"Nice to meet you too, man." Turning his shit-eating grin away from me, Robin took Trent's hand and gave it a shake. His hand didn't linger like it had when we'd touched. When he dropped Trent's hand, he even went as far as to take a half-step in my direction.

His shoulder brushed my arm.

My heart fluttered.

"Commiiiiiiitmeeeeeent," he repeated again, low and spooky, like a platform-wearing ghost. It was honestly nice that Robin wasn't acting any different now that Trent was here. But I was too shell-shocked to properly respond.

"I see you've already met Ben," Trent laughed, eyes crinkling. "Ignore his face. He's got a permanent stick up his butt. I promise he's a secret softie." A dark lock of black hair slid across his forehead like it always did, and as the sun lit him up from behind I had a weird urge to reach over and mess it up. He looked too good. It pissed me off. I kind of wanted to strangle him.

"There is *not* a stick up my butt," I glared at Trent, cheeks hot all over again. I didn't deny the "softie" comment. Because that was true.

Robin cracked a grin, obviously noticing that. I suppose I had betrayed myself by apologizing and immediately making a photo album to set him at ease.

"And I'm *not* afraid of commitment," I told Robin directly because for some reason, I needed him to know that.

"Damn," he shrugged a shoulder, eyes dancing, tone mockingly disappointed. "What a *shame*." He batted his lashes up at me playfully. He did not sound disappointed by this at all, even though it was obvious he was teasing.

"So, you…know my brother?" Robin added, watching me curiously. If he was as shocked as I was by this turn of events, he didn't show it.

"Yes." My cheeks were hot. "I'm his brother-in-law." Oh, dear god. What had I gotten myself into?

"And you're from Belleville," Robin added.

"Yes." My cheeks burned and burned and burned.

"Cool." Robin looked pleased, and that made me…well… That made me super fucking happy. "Cool, cool, cool. Small fucking world, am I right?"

Relief, unlike anything I'd ever known flooded my system as I finally processed what this meant. Because if Robin was Miles's brother…we'd get to play this "scare" game again.

I'd get to see him.

A lot, apparently.

And I was…embarrassingly excited about that.

three

ROBIN

IN MY DEFENSE, BEN MONTGOMERY was a total *snack*. Not that I'd tap that, because I wouldn't. Family, duh. And I was only here temporarily. I'd be leaving right before Christmas Eve, so there was no reason to shake the foundation that Miles had painstakingly built. But still—I could *look* at him and think that, couldn't I? In the privacy of my own head.

It wasn't illegal to want to climb him like a tree.

Ben glared a lot more now that we were in the car with Trent. Kept glancing at him like he was Satan incarnate and I couldn't help but find that fucking hilarious. I could see where Trent's "stick in his butt" comment had come from. But I got the feeling the "softie" descriptor was more accurate.

My amusement, however, was dampened by the fact that Miles wasn't here.

He hadn't come to get me.

When his text had said when Trent would be arriving I shouldn't have assumed they'd be coming together. But I had. And messing with Ben was the only thing that had managed to keep me distracted enough not to negatively react when I realized that Trent was alone.

I mean…sure, I was happy to meet him.

Of course I fucking was.

I'd have to be an asshole not to be.

If there was anyone on God's green earth who deserved Prince Charming, it was my baby brother. He'd always had a heart two sizes too big for his body. Always been as nervous as a long-tailed cat in a room full of rocking chairs, despite being tall as a mountain himself.

He carried the weight of the world on his shoulders.

Was sweeter than sweet.

And I was so fucking glad he wasn't alone anymore that it made me ache. But that also didn't mean I wasn't a little, tiny, itty-bitty bit devastated to realize I'd have to wait till we arrived in Belleville to see him. That picking me up hadn't been a priority. Despite the fact we hadn't seen each other in almost two years—the longest we'd ever gone without seeing one another.

I'd wanted to come out for his wedding but it'd been in the middle of one of my concerts—and while Miles had offered to reschedule when he found out, I hadn't wanted to disrupt his big day.

A little part of me hadn't wanted to go at all, so I'd been grateful for the excuse.

Not for a shitty reason or anything.

But because even though I was Miles's big brother, that wasn't what most people saw when they looked at me. I was "Trashmouth". And I didn't want to outshine him on the biggest day of his life. Figured he was better off without me, you know?

Wanted to give him his moment, 'cause Lord knew he deserved it.

Which was *why* this was my first time meeting Trent.

And why I had…naively expected Miles to be here for that.

Because he'd been sending me texts telling me just how much he wanted me to come home—and here I was, "home"—his, not mine—and where the fuck was he?

Maybe it had been all talk?

No, no.

Miles wasn't like that.

He had to have a damn good reason for not being here.

"Where's Miles at?" I asked, casually interrupting Trent and Ben's bantering. They'd been biting each other's heads off since the second they got in the car. Brotherly shit, you know? Nothing weird. So I'd tuned it out until now.

I had my own brotherly shit to worry about.

"Isn't that the same outfit you wore when I dropped you off?" Trent laughed. He jabbed at Ben's chest, and Ben slapped his hand away with an unhappy grunt.

"It's *comfortable*," Ben sniffed.

"I hope you washed it," Trent snorted, reaching for the radio, only for Ben to beat him to it. Immediately country music filled the car and Ben groaned, turning it off. Meanwhile, Trent dramatically sniffed the air, and Ben glared bloody murder his way.

"Of course I fucking washed it."

"You better watch that mouth of yours or Rosie's gonna empty out your wallet," Trent hummed gleefully, eyes dancing. Ben didn't have a reply to that—and I only had a second to wonder who Rosie was before Trent was finally turning his attention to me and answering my question. "Miles is at home waiting for us," he said, his smile turning tender.

My stomach churned.

So…he *hadn't* had a reason for not coming.

What did that mean?

Maybe he was just…tired?

"You look just like Bubba," Trent said—staring at me in the rearview mirror for a moment before he turned his attention to the road ahead. It was stop-and-go pulling out of the airport, the cars packed like sardines toward the single exit.

My cheeks heated and I grinned, "I know."

I *did* know.

It would be hard not to miss it.

"Like his older, evil twin," Trent added, with a snort.

I cracked a smile but it felt forced.

When I glanced Ben's way, I saw him watching me. His eyes were the same shade as Trent's, but there was nothing similar about them aside from that.

His eyes said, *you okay?*

And I shrugged a shoulder in response.

Of course he'd noticed the stark difference between our play-fighting in the airport and my silence now. Hell, I did too. Wasn't often I met a person that I got on with like I had with him. He'd seen my chaos as charming. At least…I *assumed* he had—based on how many smiles he'd flashed my way, and the sudden lack of smiles now.

Like he'd saved that sunshine just for me.

He was different now, just like I was.

His body language was stiffer.

I mean, sure he'd been a bit uncomfortable earlier, so had I. But there was a looseness to him that was missing now. Like he had walls up that hadn't been there before. Still though, he'd recognized my own discomfort despite that. And that was…fuck, that was pretty fucking sweet, you know?

Made me want to reciprocate.

I'd been surrounded by enough strangers, been in enough unrecognizable places, that I'd grown pretty good at reading people.

Came with the territory.

And Ben Montgomery liked me about as much as I liked him.

Therefore, there was no harm in a little flirting.

Not when it wasn't going nowhere.

Not when he was a dad—had a whole-ass family—and was Miles's brother-in-law to boot.

"I dunno about *evil*," I smirked as evilly as I could, then licked my lips as I glanced Ben's way, before turning my attention back to Trent. "Naughty, maybe."

"Jesus *Christ*," Ben coughed, and Trent cackled, delighted.

"I see where Miles gets his sass."

That comment alone made me feel a thousand watts brighter. Because the only two people in my entire fucking life that I'd seen Miles sass were me and Gram—and that meant…well—

That *meant* that my assumptions had been correct.

And Trent was a good man.

Good enough he'd made Miles drop his guard.

I relaxed, pushing aside my earlier hurt adeptly and instead, putting my new brother-in-law to work. I wanted to flirt with Ben more but wasn't sure he'd welcome the extra scrutiny from Trent. And besides…I was curious about the guy who had stolen my brother's heart.

"Miles said you have a dog?"

"We do," Trent agreed. "Two. Tucker and Barb."

No fucking way.

Miles hadn't mentioned the new dog—only the one that Trent had already owned when they got together. "*Two?*" I blinked, surprised. I'd never expected that. I mean…not that Miles wasn't an animal person—'cause he totally fucking was. But after Margie, our childhood dog had died, he'd sworn to me he'd never willingly go through that again.

I couldn't help but feel blindsided.

"Fun names," I said as chipper as I could even though I felt like I was cracking right down the middle.

"Barb's short for Barbara," Trent added.

"Obviously," I nodded seriously. He snorted.

"Tucker's named Tucker on account of his missing leg. You know. 'Cause it looks like he tucked it in."

"*Dark*, I like it," I laughed, cheeks heating when I realized Ben was still watching me. Maybe I'd offended him with my "naughty" comment? I hoped not.

"You can blame Bubs for that one," Trent added and my heart warmed. I *loved* that fucking kid. "Said Tucker should own what made him different. Wear it like a badge of pride."

"Smart kid."

"The smartest."

I liked Trent Montgomery.

I decided that immediately.

For the next forty-five minutes, because damn—Belleville was in the middle of fucking nowhere—I grilled Trent as sneakily as I could. Figured out how he and Miles had met. Figured out all the lost little details I'd missed when I'd been too blinded by exhaustion to be able to process the texts Miles was sending me.

After a solid eight hours of rest I felt like a fucking machine.

My brain was sharper than it'd been in months.

I learned that Miles and Trent had moved—which I'd already known, but it was nice to confirm—because they wanted to be closer to Gram and Miles's work. Learned about the tree farm the Montgomery's ran, and spent a solid five minutes fantasizing about Ben hacking trees down— forearms rippling.

Hadn't seen his forearms yet.

But…looking at him, I sure fucking bet they rippled.

By the time we arrived in Belleville I'd almost forgotten I'd been sad about Miles not showing up.

Almost.

The town looked the same as the last time I'd visited. All picturesque mountain beauty. Picket fences. Old, homey looking buildings lining Main Street. There was a pride display in a bookshop across from a bakery that had a line out the door, and some sort of sale going on.

Pumpkin bread?

Maybe.

At least, when I squinted, I thought that was what the paint on the window said.

An old man stood on a ladder outside the hardware store, hanging up Christmas lights despite the fact it was only a few days past Halloween.

Shit, had he no shame?

"Damn, y'all work quick over here, don't you?" I asked, my North Carolina accent sliding in thicker than before. I'd been training it out of my voice for years—but sometimes when I was relaxed it slipped right back in, smooth as butter.

"Work quick?" Trent echoed, confused.

"He's talking about the Christmas decorations," Ben explained, sexy ass mind-reader—because of course, he'd seen exactly what I had. What a *babe*.

"Exactly, Benjamin." I joked, pointing at the man on the ladder as we pulled to a stop at the light. "You skip right over Thanksgiving." Ben did not react to me fake full-naming him. Which I thought either meant Benjamin was *actually* his name or he hadn't noticed.

I'd have to up my game.

"Everyone knows Thanksgiving is just "First Christmas," Trent shrugged. Ben nodded along, which surprised me, and also made me snicker. I sobered, however, eyes widening curiously as Trent pointed toward one of the buildings across the street from the hardware store. It was two down from the bookstore and had a big sign that read Montgomery Family Practice in the most practical-looking font I'd ever seen.

Like it'd been hacked up and thrown together in Microsoft Word.

Red brick, white trim. The place looked friendly as hell despite being a doctor's office. I avoided doctors like the plague usually. I'd been to enough over the last year that I'd started to associate them with stark white and bad news. But this place was…*nice*-looking.

Friendly.

Way less intimidating than any of the places I'd visited back in L.A.

"That's Ben's place," Trent said, eyes twinkling as he glanced between the two of us. "God forbid—if you ever find yourself in need of medical care." He winked—and I flushed. "He lives right above it. Pax, Becca, and I built the place last year."

"You built the building?" I stared at him, flabbergasted.

"They renovated the upstairs apartment." Ben leveled Trent with a glare, then his eyes softened as he turned to look at me. "He's not *that* cool."

"I wasn't *trying* to be cool," Trent huffed—the first sign of true annoyance. "I'm just *saying*, it wasn't livable until we got in there. *Therefore*, we built it."

"You *renovated* it," Ben doubled down.

I cracked a grin, leaning back in my seat and letting them continue to fight good-naturedly as I watched dappled orange and red trees blur alongside the jolly buildings that made up downtown Belleville. Those buildings and businesses quickly melted into houses, and with a happy hum, Trent stopped arguing with his brother for long enough to pull into the driveway of an adorable little home right in front of the Belleville Elementary School.

I knew it was Miles's house immediately.

There was chalk on the sidewalk, Halloween-themed—like he and Bubba had spent hours out here decorating. Some of it was smudged, but most of it remained intact. A few carved pumpkins—five to be exact—sat on the front stoop, half-sagging, though the chill in the air kept them from outright rotting too soon.

I've never carved a pumpkin before.

It looks fun.

I jolted the second the chill bit into my skin, turning toward my now-open door with surprise. Ben waited there, cheeks bright red. He looked… fucking cute, I'm not gonna lie. Embarrassed and traditional, awkward, in his tall frame like he didn't know quite what to do with himself as he held my door open for me.

Beneath that, however, there was a confidence to him that I couldn't help but admire.

Like he knew exactly who and what he was, and had never questioned that for a minute.

He wasn't thick like his brother, all brawny and stocky.

He had a leaner frame, though no less impressive. Ben Montgomery was the kind of man that looked incredible dressed to the nines in a tux. Sculpted thighs, thick enough the muscle only accentuated their length. And broad shoulders, simply because he'd been born that way. A waist that was trim and tight, and made it clear that he was probably very conscious of what he put in his body.

When I could get myself to eat, I was a human garbage disposal, so I could not relate.

The second I stepped onto the driveway—avoiding squashing one of the ghosts that had been painstakingly drawn there—my nerves came rushing back.

Because this visit was different than any of the others.

I was here for longer than I'd ever stayed.

I was *here* because Nancy had banished me—and told me in no uncertain terms that I was not allowed to speak to her until I was boarding my flight to L.A. for the dress rehearsal.

Things were different because Miles wasn't staying in the house I'd bought him anymore. He had a whole-ass family of his own now. A life. A husband. *Two* dogs.

I wasn't sure how there could possibly be room for me too.

And maybe…he knew that? Maybe *that* was why he hadn't come out to greet me yet. Maybe *that* was why he'd sent Trent to go pick me up.

Because he knew as well as I did that I didn't belong here.

"You okay?" Ben asked, because he was observant as hell. I had no idea how he'd realized I was freaking out when my face hadn't changed a bit, but he had.

"I'm fine, biceps." I patted said bicep, to emphasize just how fine I—and it—was.

Damn, it was just as nice as I remembered.

I leeched strength from it, before letting go and turning to face the front door.

It was red. Cheery looking. Had a Halloween wreath on it and everything.

Dread curled tight in my belly.

Does Miles not want me here?

I hated that I was having that thought again, but the longer I waited for that damn door to open the heavier the thought became. Till it weighed me down, made me feel sick to my stomach. Made my hands shake and my heart skip a beat.

Ben's hand lay on my shoulder, as if he could sense my panic despite my brush-off. He gave it a squeeze and I melted a little. It was huge, honestly. And warm. Super fucking warm. Like—molten levels. It'd been warm at the airport too, like he naturally ran a few degrees hotter than he should.

Which was kinda fitting, considering how hot he was.

Trent cleared his throat, and Ben's hand quickly left my body, like he'd been burned. The look Trent leveled the both of us was *curious* as he cocked his head, eyes narrowed, and headed toward the porch steps.

I followed after him dutifully, my shoulder super cold now that Ben wasn't touching it.

"You first." Trent gestured for me to cross in front of him.

Which…in hindsight I should've thought was weird.

But I was kinda too panicked to do anything other than clomp my way up the front steps. My shoes offered me a few additional inches, but I still only felt a centimeter tall as I knocked on the front door and waited with bated breath to see what would happen next.

When it swung wide and Miles's broad frame filled the doorway I only had a second to process what was happening before my feet were off the ground and I had a face full of giant-little-brother-chest. He squeezed me so tight I felt my back pop.

"Jesus fuck—" I gasped out at the same time a loud cry echoed behind Miles.

"Surprise!" At least a dozen voices cheered. Voices I didn't fucking recognize—and couldn't see because—again, I had a face full of little brother.

"Robin!" Miles shook me like a dog toy, toting me around like I weighed less than a soaked blanket, his big frame quaking with excitement. Behind us, Trent was laughing his ass off like they'd planned this whole thing— and Ben was quiet.

That was kinda his thing.

Tall, dark, and serious.

Miles set me down on the porch, and I groaned, shoving at his chest playfully with a grin. "Fuck, I think you broke my back."

"Yeah, right." Miles rolled his eyes and grinned at me. Easy as that, all my doubts fell away, and I couldn't believe for a single *second* that he hadn't wanted me here. I could see it all over his face just how happy he was. "I made cookies!" Miles grabbed me by the shoulders and marched me right into his house. "*That's* where you put your shoes," he said, but didn't give me time to take mine off before he pushed me toward the kitchen. "*That's* the living room." He didn't give me time to even look at the living room, or all the random strangers currently occupying it and staring at me. "Up the stairs is where the bedrooms are."

"Uh-huh, woah—" Miles shoved me through an open archway and into a seat at a dining table. Then promptly decided that apparently breaking my back once wasn't enough times, because right after pushing me down, he picked me right back up again and gave me another shake-hug.

"I missed you!" he breathed into my hair, smelling like cookies and Christmas and home.

"I missed you too," I replied, my voice cracking. Miles's grip relaxed enough I could finally hug back, legs still hanging off the floor.

I couldn't believe I'd let doubt almost ruin this for me.

Miles was *Miles*. Didn't matter how many years passed. Didn't matter how many texts I left unanswered. He forgave me as easily as the tide cleared sand.

"*Welcome home.*" Miles gave me one last, tight squeeze before he set me down again. Suddenly my skin no longer felt too tight, and my heart was light as I settled into the spot at the table he'd designated as mine and let him ply me with treats.

He was a chatterbox when he was excited. Told me all about how he'd planned my surprise for me, then started panicking because he realized he was taking me away from the surprise he'd planned, and "oh lord, you haven't even met everyone yet!"

And then he spent the next half hour introducing me to all his new brothers-in-law and his mother-in-law, who was a fucking riot and a half now that I knew she read werewolf porn for fun. I met Jason, the grocer. Met Leanne, the woman responsible for the pride display on Main Street.

I met Baxter—who apologized for his son Nathan's absence, because apparently he was the one manning the line at the bakery. I didn't get *why* he was apologizing, seeing as I didn't know who the fuck Nathan was, but I appreciated it all the same.

I met a girl named Becca—she looked suspiciously like Baxter—who took one look at my outfit, gave me a thumbs-up, and told me I was— and I quote—"Hot shit. No cap."

Maybe I was getting old, but I had no idea what the fuck half of that meant. So I just nodded and told her she was too. Which made her incredibly excited.

All the while, I searched the crowd for a familiar little blond head, only to find Bubba suspiciously missing.

By the time I was full of sugar and squashed between Miles and Trent on the couch, I felt two seconds from bursting. This was…a lot of people. Nice people, yeah. But they were still people. And I needed a break.

"Where's Bubba?" I asked, two man-shoulders smushing me.

Jesus fuck, I was surrounded by giants.

Across the room I caught a glimpse of Ben talking to his mom. He looked visibly uncomfortable, and I had no doubt she was trying to tell him about his own books again. Which was so fucking cute, what the fuck.

"He's comin'," Miles assured me, grinning down at me. "He's still getting ready."

It'd been at least an hour since I'd gotten here.

What the hell was he doing?

As if he had read my mind, a parade of tiny feet thundered down the stairs loud enough to be heard over the low rumblings of the party. Four kid feet, and seven dog feet thumped their way into the living room as Bubba—and a kid I did not fucking recognize—burst into view.

Bubba had a poster in his hands, glitter sliding off of it and sluffing onto the floor as he held it high above his head. His head whipped around as he searched the crowd for me aaaand—the second he *saw* me his entire fucking face lit up.

Like Christmas.

I was off the couch in seconds, cheeks hot and uncaring of the spectacle I made launching myself across the room like a bat out of hell. Ben paused mid-conversation with his mother, his attention on me once again, and Miles looked like a fucking kid with a jar full of cookies—but all my attention went to my favorite kid in the whole fucking world.

"What's up, pipsqueak?" I teased, sliding through the crowd and across the floor. I'd taken my shoes off at one point, and my socks offered no traction. Vibrating with glee, I paused only a foot or so away from him, my gaze caught on his familiar—and now older—face.

He was taller than the last time I'd seen him. Less baby fat too. The poster lowered down by his chest, as Bubba tipped his head up to stare at me.

"Nothing much," Bubba waited for a beat, face scrunched up as he tried to think of a comeback. This was our favorite game. We played it every time I saw him. "Uncle…" His face pinched even more. "Idiot."

I laughed, unable to help it, before tilting my head to admire the poster he'd made at the same time a grin split across his face.

"Welcome home!" Bubba shook the poster at me, and I did my best to cover my mirth as I read what it said.

Welcome back Uncle Dad Robin.
Dad Uncle Robin. Duncle Robin. Robin the First.
Duncle Robin the 1st. Duncle Robin the 1st,
the coolest duncle in all the land.

It'd never been a secret that I was Bubba's bio dad. He was even fucking named after me. And while I'd never been present in his life the way Miles was, I'd done my fucking best to provide for him in whatever way I could.

The way my dad never had.

"I didn't know what name to call you so I called you all of them," Bubba declared, looking shy and excited all at the same time. "Is that cool?"

"Fuck," my eyes burned a little. "That's super cool. Put that poster down, you little shit, before I break it trying to hug the fuck outta you." Laughter burst through the room, reminding me that this wasn't a private moment at all as Bubba set the poster down carefully, commanded his tall friend to watch it, and then held his arms out expectantly.

You can bet your ass I squeezed the fuck outta the goddamn kid.

And all the while, I felt the heat of Ben's eyes on me.

Warmer than his hand had been.

They *burned*.

I was more than a little glad for my nap with Ben on the plane because, without it, I had no idea how I would've survived the party Miles had planned for me. There were so many people and names. So many stories that I got them all jumbled up in my head.

No one seemed to recognize me, which was relieving and a bit flabbergasting.

The first time someone called me over, saying, "I know you!" I had a genuine moment of panic, only to be shocked and grateful when the man added, "You're Miles's brother. My kid loves his class."

For once, it was nice to be recognized for something more than the music I no longer enjoyed making. I had what felt like a dozen encounters like that, over and over, till it was really hammered home that here—in Belleville—I was a fucking ghost.

Ben seemed to be the only person who knew who I was.

And therefore, flirting and scaring him was pushed to the back of my mind as I did my best to ward off the well-meaning townies and their many sugar-laced treats.

And by the time the party was winding down, the spiked eggnog had been emptied, and my belly was full of Christmas-flavored booze, I was more than ready for some alone time.

Which was why I was relieved as hell when Miles gave me the information for the room I'd asked him to book for me at the B&B downtown. Because he knew me—the little shit—he hadn't tried to offer me his guest room. Which I appreciated a lot.

We both knew I needed space sometimes.

Not that I was looking forward to another sleepless night staring at floral, but still.

As I was wandering toward the back door to head outside for a breather—after my last shot of the night—I was chased down by a small cherubic little girl in black.

She stood with Beatrice, Miles's mother-in-law, and her little blonde hair was in piggies. Her honey-colored eyes narrowed as she looked up at me, tiny hands clenched into fists.

"You swear lots," she told me sagely. I nodded because I did. "You owe me lots of monies."

Ah. So *this* was Rosie.

Ben's daughter.

I had the most ungodly urge to bite her chubby lil cheek 'cause she was cuter than shit, but didn't. "How much, Al Pacino?" I asked, pulling out my wallet, my movements a little sluggish from the booze.

Beatrice laughed, her dark eyes dancing as she stared at me appraisingly. "You don't need to pay Rosie," she said, amused.

"Yeah, I do." I shrugged a shoulder, flipping through the black leather, looking for cash. I didn't have a ton of options. A hundred dollar bill. A couple twenties. "How much, short-stop?"

"Short-stop?" She squinted up at me, face pinched. I licked my finger, wiggling through the bills with an eyebrow waggle. I waited patiently, curious to see what she'd say. She eyed the twenties, little lips pressed into a thin line.

"Yeah. 'Cause you're short."

"You're a *bigger* short-stop," she countered like the two-foot-tall badass she was.

What a comeback! Vicious as hell.

"Right in the kidneys," I mock-gasped, still waiting. I don't think she *actually* expected me to be willing to pay her because she looked pretty shocked. However, she got over that pretty quick, and her eyes started to glint like a dog watching a treat, set on my money.

"You swore thirty-seven times." She blinked, her curly blonde lashes fluttering.

"I didn't know babies could count," I muttered under my breath, amused as I grabbed both my twenties and handed them over. She very carefully took the bills, folding them and shoving them in the front of her dress like she expected me to take them back. "Keep the change."

"I'm *not* a baby," Rosie told me, her brow furrowed and eyes full of the fury of a thousand suns. "I'm four."

"My bad." I held up my hands to placate her.

Beatrice stared at me, amused. "You are a *wild* one," she decided after a moment as Rosie grinned evilly down at her money, like a fucking black-frill-wearing Scrooge. She seemed happy now that she'd robbed me.

I'd known very few toddlers in my life. I'd only gotten to see Bubba like twice when he was that age, and I'd been half comatose after a tour both times. My retention of that time was not great.

Maybe all toddlers were maniacal bankers.

"Where's your sister?" I asked, before she could walk away. Ben had mentioned having two daughters.

Instead of answering, Rosie simply stared up at me with those huge fucking eyes and said, "no."

And then they both walked off.

While that had been an endlessly amusing experience, I was officially overstimulated and way too drunk to try to people anymore. So I said my goodbyes and headed outside like planned. I knew Miles would've tried to drive me if I hadn't literally bolted out of the house, so I worked quickly, ducking out the back door and into the yard to avoid the worst of the indoor crowd.

It was fucking cold out.

The stars glittered between the black drooping branches of a large maple tree. An abandoned but well-maintained grill sat in the back corner of the leaf-strewn grass, and the shed in the other corner of the yard was padlocked shut. I had no doubt that the Johnson-Montgomery household had some picturesque lawn furniture locked away in there.

Something perfect and wonderful for the summer months.

Making a beeline to the darkest part of the yard, I sat on the edge of the fire pit, took a steadying breath, and tried to process the last five hours. Coming here was…a lot. Made me happy, yeah. But it made me sad too.

Mostly it just made me feel grateful.

To see that despite all my fuck-ups and our shitty upbringing, Miles had gotten exactly what he wanted.

He was so…happy here.

I was terrified of ruining that.

Like poison, I tainted everything I touched.

My nipples were hard and cold and uncomfortable, but I ignored that, curling into a tighter ball, the alcohol in my system making my movements feel sluggish and disjointed. My backpack felt impossibly heavy, everything that mattered to me packed neatly inside. Tingling tingles lit up my limbs as I closed my eyes and breathed.

I was only here for the holidays.

This wasn't my home.

I knew that.

But what if…what if it could be?

Was there room for me here?

"You okay?" A familiar, deep voice echoed through the dark, lighting me up from the inside out. My eyes opened, and to no one's surprise—especially not mine—Ben Montgomery was standing just a few feet in front of me. I hadn't even heard him approach. His silhouette was lit up gold from the lights still on in the house behind him.

He'd disappeared for a while there.

It was only the presence of his children that had cued me in to the fact that he was still around. I hadn't expected to see him again, but I was unsurprised that he'd come looking for me.

It's like I summoned him with my mind.

"I'm fine, Benjamin Button," I reassured.

He didn't respond to this nickname either.

Which was…fun.

And also a fucking *challenge* if I'd ever heard one. Ben was full of challenges.

"You don't *seem* fine. It's cold. You're barely dressed." He stood there, awkwardly towering over me, and my heart gave a weird little flutter. "And you're out here alone in the dark."

Don't hit on him, Robin.

Don't do it.

"It's just…loud in there, you know?" I offered the truth easily. "Lots of people. Not that that isn't great, because it is. But my brain just—" I made a fizzling motion beside my temple. "And I'm…"

"You're…?" Ben waited, as patient as I'd been with his daughter just a few minutes prior.

"I can't think when you're towering over me. Come sit." I patted the stone beside mine and Ben frowned but strode my way anyway after a moment of deliberation. He sat beside me, still towering. He couldn't help that he was a goddamn giant.

"Better?" Ben asked.

"Not really. You're still fucking huge, dude."

Ben laughed, and the sound lit me up all over again. It was weird. I didn't often like people, not like this. He was…nice. Which wasn't usually the kinda person I found myself drawn to, but I didn't fight it. Why would I? When he smelled like a department store cologne and he chuckled like that?

"You were telling me why you look sad," Ben reminded me as if I'd forgotten.

"I'm not *sad*," I told him, staring up at Miles's perfect house, and his perfect family inside it, and the perfect world he lived in.

"Bullshit."

"*Careful*, Rosie might hear you," I joked, shrugging a shoulder. "She already emptied out my wallet. She'll come for yours next."

"*What?*" Ben's eyes widened. He was obviously surprised I'd met Rosie. Or maybe he was surprised that his daughter was a four-year-old mob boss. Either way, the surprise was real. And looked really fucking cute on his face. Thick brows drawn high and together, a little tick in his jaw, his lashes as dark and fluttery as fucking Bambi.

"Sorry, I deflect when I'm nervous," I admitted, my mouth suddenly dry.

Ben softened, his surprise melting away as he nodded. "Me too."

"Miles is happy," I told him, finally answering his question because he'd asked. I'd learned throughout my life that people didn't ask unless they cared at least a little. And maybe sometimes they only cared because they wanted to hurt you. But when I looked into Ben's eyes I didn't see any ire at all.

And I figured…even though I'd already decided I wouldn't climb him like I wanted to, it wouldn't be a bad thing if I left Belleville after the holidays with a Ben-shaped friend.

"He is," Ben agreed, patient as ever.

"I'm not *sad*," I repeated, even though my eyes burned and a tear slipped down my cheek.

Ben frowned at me, calling bullshit without even having to open his mouth. He shifted a little, though the movement was awkward, betraying how uncomfortable talking about feelings must make him. His shoulder brushed mine. I melted.

"I'm happy." I sniffed, the alcohol getting to me. Or maybe it was the sleepless nights. The loneliness.

"You look *super* happy," Ben deadpanned sarcastically. He reached out and gently scrubbed a thumb across my cheek. I imagined he did the same thing for his toddlers, and that should've ruined that for me, should've made me feel small and babyish. Should've filled me with shame, but it didn't.

Instead, I felt warm and safe and cared for.

"Shut up," I snorted, brow scrunching just like his was. I reached up to bat him off, but realized halfway through the motion that I didn't want to. So I dropped my hand back to my lap, thumb picking at the chipped polish on my pointer finger instead. "I'm just…"

We were back to this again.

An annoying loop I'd caused, but I couldn't seem to stop.

"I'm just worried I'm going to ruin it."

"Why do you think you would ruin it?" Ben asked, dropping his hand from my face and taking its comfort with him.

It was only because I was drunk that the next words slipped free.

Normally, when I was well-rested my mind was a steel trap. But the eggnog had whittled away my walls. Or maybe that was Ben's influence. Ben and his observant, gorgeous eyes. Ben and the fact that he was quiet enough to hear me, even when I whispered.

Inhibitions be damned, my darkest secret spilled from my lips to a total stranger.

"I'm poison. That's just what I do."

four

BEN

AFTER ROBIN'S CONFESSION AT HIS welcome party, I hadn't expected to see him up close again. He'd looked miserable the moment the words came out, like he hadn't meant to say them at all. And when I'd offered to drive him home, he'd refused.

He'd very clearly wanted to be left alone, and I respected that—even though it felt inherently wrong to leave when he looked as sad as he did.

I mean, sure, we were technically something family-adjacent. I knew he'd be there at Thanksgiving, and probably during Christmas too. We'd awkwardly pass by each other, maybe share a nod and smile—at Mama and her book club's expense—but that would be it.

There would be no more games.

There would be no more flirting.

At least…that's what I'd thought.

Until Robin showed up at my office two days later with a plastic femur in one hand, sunglasses on, and his cheeks pink from the cold.

My receptionist, Lynda, let him in, looking far too amused as Robin clomped his way through the open door to my office like a pint-sized goth avenger. He walked like he had a purpose, a purpose I found I was more than excited to be made privy to.

"You didn't tell me the book club was hosted at the B&B," he accused me, instead of a proper greeting. The door slid closed behind him with a click, and I swallowed the lump in my throat, suddenly oddly self-conscious of my space. It felt far too small with him in here. Too plain. What I'd once felt was a practical room, now felt bland.

"I didn't know you were staying at the B&B," I countered. Then, raising a brow, I glanced over his skin-tight black ensemble—and again, the too-thin floor-length black jacket—and back up to his face. "That wasn't a very polite way to greet someone, Robin. Now, was it?"

Robin paused, femur in hand. He lowered the bone, his sunglasses slipping down his nose a little as his mouth closed with a quiet click. He seemed to agree because his eyes widened, and then softened. "I...guess not?"

"Would you like to try again?" I asked, not even sure what the fuck was coming out of my mouth right now, only that seeing him in my office was making me feel like the world as I'd known it was shattering apart.

Robin stared at me for a beat, like he was deciding whether or not he did. He ultimately seemed to come to the conclusion that he could've been more polite, however—probably the same Southern manners his brother seemed to possess coming to the surface—because he relaxed, pulled his sunglasses off, shoved them in his pocket, and beamed at me.

A big, sunny smile that lit up his whole face.

The smile made the dark circles under his eyes look even more out of place.

"Hi," he said, grin turning sly as he glanced at the coffee mug on my desk, "Ben-nilla latte."

It was close enough, so I ignored the ridiculous nickname and smiled right back. "Good morning, Robin." I hardly recognized my voice, it was so warm. "Why do you have a femur in your hand?"

Robin stared down at the bone like he was surprised it was still there, and then he laughed. "Did you know the B&B is run by the cutest old lady in the world? Total fucking grouch. Wears a pinstripe suit every day and swears like a sailor."

"Matilda Deed," I hummed, eyes crinkling in amusement.

"She's *so* cute, man." Robin laughed, then flushed. "Is that rude to say? I hope not."

"She is cute," I agreed, heart fluttering like crazy as Robin crossed the distance between us and sat right on the corner of my desk like this was a totally normal and not at all invasive thing to do. I scooted my chair back to see him better, and he graciously offered me a turn with the femur. With a quirked brow, I shook my head, and Robin happily kept the bone to himself.

"Anyway—your mom was there. At the B&B. Because she and Matilda run the book club."

"Right."

"On Mondays."

"Yes."

"And she told me—"

"Who? Matilda or my mother?"

"Your mom," Robin grinned, eyes dancing. "Keep up, Benmantha.

Really. It's like you have the attention span of a goldfish."

"Two nicknames within five minutes, really?"

"So you *are* paying attention!" Robin crowed in triumph, wiggling happily, his cute butt shifting my papers over. He didn't even notice, which made my belly fill with even more butterflies despite the fact that he was mussing my desk. My hands felt sweaty, his close proximity lighting me up all over again.

I'd thought I'd made that up.

My reaction to him.

But I hadn't.

"Of course I'm paying attention," I countered, suddenly self-conscious of the slacks I'd chosen to wear to work today. I didn't have any clients scheduled. Today was the day I reserved for admin, and aside from the occasional walk-in, it was usually quiet.

Not with Robin around though.

Why is he here? This was the last place I expected him to go after what he admitted to me.

"Anyway—" Robin began again. He had eyeliner on again today, just as smudgy as the makeup he'd been wearing on the plane. Smudgy? Was that the right word? I wasn't sure. "Your mom told me that your kids were sick on Halloween."

"Yes." I had no idea what this had to do with the femur, but I couldn't wait to find out.

"And that the B&B puts up a haunted house every year, and your kids love to go, but they couldn't this year because they were sick." Robin was thrumming with excited energy now, so I didn't interrupt him because I could tell he had to get it all out. "So I asked her if we could set up the haunted house again! Matilda—not your mom. And she said that it was still up. But it'd just need, like…electricity and shit. I dunno. And I told her I'd handle it."

Still hadn't explained the femur, but I could be patient.

"So I went to check it out. Thing needs major repairs. Maybe some paint? Anyway, I accidentally knocked a skeleton over—" There we go. "But when I was fixing it, I couldn't figure out which bones went where. So I figured I'd come over here and ask you." He blinked. "Because you're a doctor."

I nodded.

"Therefore you probably know a lot about bones." Robin blinked again, seemingly realizing too late what he'd just said. "Not *that* kinda bones." His pale green eyes raked over my shoulders, down my chest, and to my crotch. "Though I bet you know about those too."

My cheeks grew hot, my cock twitching as Robin's lovely pink tongue flickered out to wet his lips.

To be completely honest, I had no idea what was going on right now.

I mean…I knew *why* he was here. He'd just explained his thought process. And his need for my expertise. But it felt, in a way, like I'd accidentally adopted him. Like he was a duckling that had imprinted, and was finding any excuse to come see me.

And I wasn't sure how to feel about that.

You find it adorable, Ben. Don't play coy.

"So," Robin waited, though I wasn't sure what he was waiting for. "Are you coming?"

"Coming?"

"To the B&B! C'mon, keep up." He waved the femur impatiently. "We gotta get the thing up and running so your kiddos can come."

And *that* was when it clicked.

All of it.

His disjointed rambling. His evil plan. The fact that he'd marched over here on foot—luckily it was only a few blocks away—wearing nothing more than cotton just to enlist me. There was a manic glint in Robin's eyes, exhaustion apparent all over his face.

He's lonely.

"*Robin*," I said gently, and he deflated immediately, wilting like a popped balloon.

"You're too busy?" He frowned, biting his lip. When he twisted his head to the side, no longer looking in my eyes, his lip ring glinted. "That's cool. I mean… You're probably elbows deep in doctor-y shit, right? Got better things to do."

"That's not what I was going to say," I countered, reaching out to grab his chin. Gently, I tilted him back to look at me. His skin was surprisingly soft.

"It isn't?" Robin's tongue wet his lips again, and I internally groaned.

God, being friends with him was going to be a lesson in patience.

"I think it's incredibly sweet that you want to do that for my kids," I said, watching as Robin's cheeks pinked up from something other than the cold. He was so expressive, even when he didn't mean to be. It was addicting.

"You do?"

"Yes," I released his chin reluctantly, and he stiffened right back up, like my touch had been what was holding him together. "*Thank you.*"

Robin blinked, surprised. Like he'd expected the worst and didn't know what to do now that he hadn't gotten it.

"I'm poison."

His earlier words fluttered around inside my head, making my heart ache for him as I chose my next words very carefully.

He looked like he needed a nap. Fifty naps. A hundred naps. There was something wild and slap-happy about the way he was moving, like he wasn't entirely in control of himself. But his pupils weren't abnormally dilated, so I knew he wasn't high, and I could tell based on looks alone that it had to have been a while since he rested.

Maybe the B&B made it difficult?

Hell, I had a hard time sleeping when I was in an unfamiliar place.

Add on the fact that Miles was still in school, as was Bubba—and that meant that for most of the day, Robin was left on his own in a foreign place with no friends, no car, and nothing to do—and yeah. I could see why he'd latched onto me.

Why he'd have a hard time resting.

Despite the fact we'd only had two conversations—three now—I was more familiar than anything else here.

"I have a few things I can't push back," I lied gently, speaking quickly enough it wouldn't give him time to get disappointed again. "Why don't you lie down on my couch and take a nap while I finish up? Then I can come help you."

He needed to rest, and I hoped I could trick him into it.

"A nap?" Robin looked dubiously at me. "I'm not a little kid." The longing when he glanced at the buttery soft, red leather sofa in the back corner of the room spoke volumes, however.

"Believe me, I know that." I glanced at his chest, and the nipple piercings that poked through the fabric, my pulse thrumming. "Humor me? I'll drive us over when I'm done."

Robin squinted at me, like he was trying to get a read on me but couldn't. When I didn't give in, he simply sighed, slid off my desk with a thunk and wandered his way toward the couch.

"You can take your shoes off," I told him, turning back to my papers, even though there was no way in hell I'd be able to get anything done with him here with me.

He set his femur on the floor, flopped onto the couch, and reached for the many, many buckles on his combat boots. *Click, click, click,* he slid them open.

"There's a blanket in the cupboard to your left."

"A blanket," he mumbled, confused. After tugging his boots off, Robin rose to his feet, socked and far shorter than he'd been before. He looked kind of vulnerable like this, and I let myself stare as he turned his back to me and rifled through the cupboard looking for what he wanted. "*Crows?*" He pulled a blanket out, the pink fabric splattered with cartoon crows.

"Jane's favorite animal."

"Cool, me too." He grinned back at me and climbed back onto the couch. Rolling onto his back, the blanket clutched close, Robin sighed.

"You'll need to unfold it," I teased him, and Robin flipped me off with a snort before doing just that. Snuggled down, he stared up at the ceiling. His cheeks were bright pink, but there was a pleased little curl to his lips as he twisted his head to look at me. Already, his eyes were drooping.

"You like Christmas shit?" Robin asked with a yawn. He stared at me, waiting expectantly.

"Of course," I lied. I'd never been big on Christmas. I celebrated because it was something we did, and after I'd become a father I hadn't wanted my children to go without. I knew I was somewhat of a Scrooge, and I didn't want that to ruin the holidays for everyone else.

"Really?" Robin perked up, some of the sleepiness fading. He blinked rapidly, trying to force his eyes open. "Because they do these matinees down at the theater—with Christmas movies. And I thought it might be fun to go."

"That does sound fun."

It did not sound fun. I did not watch movies unless my children insisted. It wasn't something I'd ever enjoyed.

"And there's like…a market thing too? I thought that might be fun." Robin yawned again, then frowned, betrayed by his own sleepiness. "And *sledding*." His words were syrupy and slow. "Holy fuck. I *always* wanted to go sledding."

"Do you want me to go with you to these things?" I stared at him, curious.

"I mean…" he shrugged a shoulder—what I was coming to recognize was his signature move. "Do *you*…want to go to them?" He bit his lip. "With me?"

Instead of answering his question, because it felt quite loaded, I asked, "Why me?"

Robin frowned, snuggling his blanket closer to his chin as he stared at me. He looked young. Which wasn't hard—because he *was* young. Far younger than I was at forty-five. He was probably still in his early thirties. Probably not a day over thirty-three.

Why he'd want to hang out with a grouchy, boring man nearly ten years his senior I did not understand. He wasn't asking to date me. I understood that. But even wanting to spend time together as innocently as he'd just proposed made zero sense.

At least…until he spoke again, and shattered my walls completely.

"I like you," Robin said simply.

And I figured that was answer enough.

five

ROBIN

BEN MONTGOMERY WAS HILARIOUS. ALL bossy and tall with one eyebrow that wouldn't stop twitching whenever he was annoyed. After my nap and thanks to my daily dose of Ben-a-dryl—damn, I should not be thinking about Ben and drilling at the same time—I was feeling sooo *much* better.

He was obviously a genius.

And also knew how to purchase a badass couch.

It'd been another two sleepless nights between the time I'd blown Ben off—not in the way I wanted, dammit—and the time I showed up half out of my mind at his office. And those two nights felt like a living hell.

The only thing I had in my stinky-old-lady room to keep me company at the B&B was yet another yellowing floral comforter, and my own existential dread.

Miles was back at school. He was an art teacher, which I found super fucking cute and very fitting. I loved picturing his giant frame standing at the front of a classroom full of leaky-nosed-crayon-wielding-hobbits. Bet he was the best damn art teacher they'd ever had, lucky little shits.

I sure as hell had not had a teacher like him growing up.

The only exception was maybe my music teacher.

She'd been pretty cool.

Damn, I hadn't thought about her in a long time.

I was thirty-three now, and that may not have been old, but I sure wore my years that way. Wore them like each one weighed a thousand tons, because sometimes it felt like they did.

Because I didn't want to be a sad sack and I wanted to make Ben's eyebrow twitch again, I smacked his ass with my femur. He startled, glaring over his shoulder at me. He was bent over the pile of bones I'd accidentally toppled, on his knees, because he'd said crouching was uncomfortable on his back.

I wasn't sure why he'd told me that, but I appreciated it all the same.

"*Robin.*" Ben said my name like it was a sentence, irritation and amusement laced in his tone.

"Has anyone ever told you that your ass is stubborn?" I asked, smacking said ass again. The plastic bone made a very satisfying hollow thud sound. I was careful not to whack too hard. Now that he'd mentioned his back, I was wary of hurting him.

"No." He paused. "Why?" Ben's question was dry as hell, like he knew what was coming before I even said it.

"Because it just won't quit."

Thwack.

Damn. It even jiggled.

"If you hit me again you aren't going to like the consequences." I could hear his laughter, so I didn't take him too seriously.

"Yeah, yeah. Promises, promises." I thumped the bone into my palm, leaving him alone for now as he painstakingly began notching all the little plastic pieces together again. He was halfway through and I didn't want this to end.

Maybe if I smacked him more it'd buy me time?

I didn't want to go back upstairs alone. Didn't want to curl into a ball on my mattress, counting down the hours till Miles was off work and he could spend time with me. Didn't want to think too hard about the impending doom that always seemed to hang over me nowadays.

I'd flown across the country and still hadn't moved far enough to escape the shadow of dread that clung inky black to my heart. My contract was up in less than two months, and the idea of renewing it made me want to die.

The truth was, I hadn't told Ben what had *really* happened before I'd visited him at his office.

Figured he didn't need to know that I'd seen black spots. That the world had swum and swum. That my knees had buckled while I was admiring what was left of Matilda's aged Halloween decor, and I'd woken up covered in dust with a plastic skull staring at me.

I'd picked myself right up off the ground as quickly as I could before someone could see—I had no doubt the rumor mill would eat that shit up here. Maybe for different reasons than the paparazzi would back home, but still. Last thing I wanted was to be *pitied* while I was here. I wanted this to be the best Christmas ever.

Needed it to be the best Christmas ever.

Unlike any Christmas I'd ever had before.

Besides, my doctor had told me that getting away from the stress of my life in the city would more than likely help. Which made sense. Stress-induced insomnia was apparently a thing? And his theory made sense.

Except…I'd been here three days now, and *still*…couldn't fucking sleep.

Unless I was in Ben's personal space, that was.

Sure…smacking Ben's ass was a detour from my "Best Christmas Ever" plan, but it was a good one—good enough I figured I might even add it to my official itinerary. "Robin's Perfect Christmas To-Do List" had officially gotten one item longer. Besides, I was still whole-heartedly on the path to the nice-list, despite my dalliance with those thick-ass glutes. And *this* was still working toward my goal.

I definitely wasn't trying to distract myself from my feelings. Nope. Totally not. Nooope.

Thwack, I slammed the bone into Ben's ass again.

Just to see what he'd do.

Because he'd threatened me. And I kinda wanted him to follow through.

Maybe he'd get up and chase me around or something. I dunno. Grab the bone back and smack my ass till it was red? That sounded fun too.

But he…didn't.

Instead, he made good on his promise—and did something I definitely didn't like.

He *ignored* me.

"Ben," I tried after a solid minute of silence and four more booty smacks. "Ben." *Smack, smack.* "Ben." *Goddammit. Goddammit. Fuck. How did he already know me so well?* It didn't make sense. He was a fucking stranger. I hated this. "Ben?" I tried again.

This time I did not smack his ass.

This felt mean.

I hated it.

The bone fell to the ground with a hollow thump and I shivered, the cold feeling colder all of a sudden.

"Are you going to behave now?" Ben asked, finally breaking the silence. I knew realistically it hadn't been *that* long. Maybe two minutes at most. But my skin felt like it was crawling, and my chest felt too tight, and my hands were shaking.

Sick and unhappy, I nodded, curling my arms tightly around myself. I didn't look down at Ben, figuring it didn't matter if he saw my nod or not.

This wasn't fun anymore.

"*Oh,*" Ben's voice flooded with warmth, low and rumbling and soft. "I'm *so* sorry."

I couldn't look at him.

Or I'd probably do something stupid like cry.

I was too tired for this shit.

"*Robin,*" Ben rose from his spot on the ground with a quiet groan. He stretched his back out, grimacing as I peeked at him through my lashes. "*Come here.*" He didn't even brush the dirt off his knees as he held a hand out to me.

And because I was fucking pitiful, it only took me two seconds to latch onto it, despite my hurt feelings. Ben's hands were larger than mine, and warmer. I'd thought that before too—when we'd shook hands at the airport. He had piano hands. Fingers long and dexterous and careful.

Mine were rougher, by comparison. Guitar calluses definitely didn't help.

"Look at me," Ben's voice was gentle and my lips wobbled as I did as I was told—finally, *unhappily* meeting his gaze.

His eyes were liquid caramel, warm as a bonfire.

Looking into them sent a shiver up my spine, even though I still felt small and miserable and cold.

"I'm sorry," he said again, even gentler this time, very obviously sincere. His dark lashes fluttered, casting shadows on his cheeks. The grumpy eyebrow twitch was missing. He wasn't annoyed, despite how I was freaking out. And he really did look sorry. "I shouldn't have done that."

"It was mean," I told him, voice hoarse. I hadn't meant to say that out loud. He seemed to inspire honesty out of me, even when I didn't want him to.

"It *was* mean," he agreed, squeezing my hand tight. "I won't do it again."

I nodded jerkily, the tension in my body settling a little.

"Why'd you do it?" I asked, because I knew him giving me the silent treatment had to have been intentional. "If you knew it was mean."

Why are you doing this?

He's going to think you're annoying.

Why are you making such a big deal about this?

He was kidding.

Ben tipped his head to the side, a dark lock of auburn hair falling across his forehead. The sun lit him up from behind, dancing across his jaw and painting him with a halo, kinda like an angel. It was setting now, the autumn cold creeping in as the sun sank below the trees at the back of the B&B's unkempt yard.

Didn't look like anyone had taken care of this place in years. Paint peeling on the fence. The shed where the decorations were normally housed half-rotted. I wasn't stupid. I knew Matilda Deed hadn't always run this place alone, and judging from the photo frames that lined the mantle in the lounge downstairs, Mr. Deed's death had hurt more than just her heart.

There were empty holes everywhere. Things he used to do probably. Things she couldn't do anymore without thinking of him. Like how I couldn't eat lemon cookies without thinking about my mom. About the only time she'd ever smiled at me, when I'd been too little to realize she hated me.

Ben was quiet as I mused, seemingly waiting for the moment my eyes connected with his again and he had my full attention.

I hadn't meant to space out.

I'd warned him earlier that I had a tendency to deflect, and apparently the same could be said for my thoughts.

Ben's eyes said, *there you are.*

They said, *it's okay.*

They said, *forgive me?*

And when he was looking at me like that…it was kinda impossible not to.

"When we were younger we often played juvenile games to keep each other in check," Ben explained, his palm warming mine. He hadn't taken his hand away, and I didn't remove mine either. Being touched felt so fucking good. "I responded to your teasing the way I would've if Trent had been the one hitting me."

I nodded because that made sense, even if it made me feel *weird* he was treating me like his little brother.

Why does that make me feel weird?

"I shouldn't have done that," Ben added, voice soft. "I didn't realize it would upset you the way it did."

My heart fluttered.

"Do you forgive me?" Ben asked, holding my hand tight.

I nodded, the heavy weight that had hung over me falling away. "Next time just call me an asshole," I told him. "I really…" I sucked in a breath. "I really, *really* hated that."

"Noted."

Ben looked reluctant to let me go, and I didn't know why.

Except…fuck, if I was being honest, I did.

He could probably see how bad I wanted him to hold on.

"I'm sorry for hitting you," I added because I was.

"It's okay," Ben replied, tone just as soft. "Were you testing me?"

"Testing you?"

"To see how I would respond?"

I…hadn't realized that was what I was doing. Maybe in a way, it was. Maybe I'd been burned enough in my life that I'd wanted to suss out if Ben would do it too, early on.

"Maybe?"

"Ah." Ben's voice was a quiet rumble, and his expression was fond. "I hope I passed."

"You did."

I hadn't liked being ignored. But the fact that he hadn't raised his voice or his hands meant a lot to me. Made me feel safer now that I knew he wasn't likely to act rashly—as odd as that sounded.

Belleville was like an alternate dimension. People were…nice here without knowing my net worth. They smiled at me. They greeted me. They threw big-ass parties and brought snacks and treats—taking the time to bake, to dress up, to leave the goddamn house just to meet a stranger.

It was no wonder Miles fit in here.

But I…well… I wasn't so sure I did.

Ben and I seemed to have a lot in common.

Like no matter how hard he tried, he was an outcast just like I was. Never quite sized to fit the cookie cutter this picturesque place expected. This encounter proved that. He may be soft like the other Bellevillians, but he had a backbone too. And he was odd—in a good way.

He *liked* me.

Even after I'd freaked out at him for doing something totally normal—smacked his ass over and over and over—and followed him to work like a lost puppy.

Fuck, why did I hit him with the bone?

It was a testament to how much better I was feeling after my nap on his couch that I was even able to feel remorse at all. Usually it wasn't till days later that the mortification would set in and I'd realized just how odd my behavior had been.

Aaaaand now I'd been weirdly quiet again.

Goddammit, Robin.

How did Ben not realize I was a walking red flag?

How could anyone put up with me for an extended period of time?

I was "too much" on a good day, and I hadn't had many of those lately.

"Robin," Ben's voice was a quiet hum that broke through my spiraling thoughts. Something warm brushed my cheek and I jolted, startled. "Did you…" Warm, warm, warm, Ben's hand pressed against my cheek, fingers brushing along my temple. Fucking Bigfoot hands, goddamn.

"Did I, *what?*"

Ben sounded hesitant.

Slowly, my mind came back to the present. Focusing on Ben's toffee-colored gaze and the way the setting sun lit his hair like Christmas ribbon, snow-laced pine trees framing the sides of the artfully styled strands.

"Sorry, I realized what I was about to ask was incredibly invasive."

"Oh."

"It's the psychologist in me. That was my favorite part of school. I have a hard time turning it off."

"Like Hannibal Lecter," I replied without thinking. Ben blinked. Then his serious expression cracked and he laughed, shaking his head.

"Yes," he agreed. "Like Hannibal Lecter."

"The NBC one or the *Silence of the Lambs* one?"

"NBC, obviously."

"That's a very gay choice of you, Ben," I teased, warming up all over again.

"Is there any other choice?"

"I mean, Anthony Hopkins is a total snack," I countered. Then my cheeks warmed when I realized I'd had that very thought about Ben earlier that week. His palm never budged from my cheek, his fingers tracing these very distracting patterns on my skin while he grinned down at me. He was going to hurt his back if he kept bending down like that.

"Anthony Hopkins is an incredibly talented actor," Ben agreed.

"*And* a total snack." I blinked innocently. Again, Ben's smile grew, his eyes crinkling at the corners. In a weird way, he looked his oldest then. He had kind of a baby face? Looked close to my age most of the time. The gray at his temples betrayed him, of course, but still. For the most part, the years didn't show.

They did now though, written in every gorgeous crinkle by his already expressive eyes. Laugh lines. These were laugh lines. And they were… fuck. Ben Montgomery was the prettiest thing I'd ever seen.

And he had never been more beautiful than he was then, all forty-something years of him. (Yes, I'd asked Miles how old he was. I'd asked him a lot of questions, obviously.)

"Say it, Ben," I hummed. "Say that he's a total snack."

"Please don't make me do that," Ben laughed.

"Coward," I tsked.

"I like my men a lot less…*terrifying*," Ben snorted. "And I've been told I have *very* good taste."

"Whoever told you that also probably does not think Anthony Hopkins is delicious. And is therefore also tasteless."

"Jesus *Christ*." Ben's head tossed back as he chuckled, shaking his head like he was asking the overcast sky for patience. It was the second "Jesus Christ" he'd uttered around me in that exact same tone, and it kinda felt like I'd won an award.

It looked like snow would fall tonight, covering the quiet streets of Belleville in a soft white blanket.

I was…weirdly excited about that.

It would be the first snowfall of the season. The first true snow I'd ever really seen. Like movies, you know? With the pine trees and the mountains. With the trees still painted autumn's fiery hues.

All my life I'd imagined what that would be like.

Would the snow be soft?

It looked so soft.

Would it be cold? It was hard to imagine.

I'd seen snow on occasion when I was a kid. But we weren't really allowed to go outside. And I'd always used my imagination to fill in the gaps.

All my life I'd dreamed of one of those big, winter snow storms. The kind that piled up against doors. The kind that crunched beneath your feet. The kind that was as peaceful as it was dangerous.

But now that I'd heard Ben's laugh, I had a feeling the snow's beauty wouldn't compare. Not to his laugh lines. Not to the way his face scrunched up, a miracle in itself.

"You always have something to say," Ben's eyes danced as he stopped sharing his joy with the sky and gave it back to me. He sounded pleased by this, which was another surprise.

"Trashmouth," I blurted.

"What?"

"That's what the other kids called me when I was little. That's why it's my stage name." Ben hummed thoughtfully like he was psychoanalyzing me again. Locking away memories of the grin on my face, and the tension around my eyes so he could crack it open later and get right down to the ooey gooey parts.

He looked at me like he found me fascinating.

And I shouldn't have liked that, but I did.

"Ask me your question," I urged, my hand moving up to cup the back of his, to force it to stay where it was. "The invasive one you didn't want to ask."

"Really?" Ben's eyes widened, his brows rising.

"Sure." This was an exercise in trust. Which was something my therapist had strongly urged me to do while I was over here on vacation for the holidays. Ben could take what I gave him to the press. He could twist my words and hurt me.

But I didn't think he would.

Simple as that.

"Were you often ignored when you were a child?" Ben asked, looking nervous—like he was still scared of upsetting me.

Memories surfaced, of sitting by Miles when he was sick, of combing his hair back, of waiting for help that never came. Memories of spending hours building sand castles only for the waves to knock them away before my mother ever turned to look.

"Yeah," I admitted, and it didn't hurt like it should.

Because maybe I'd been ignored then, but Ben was looking at me now.

I was here, and it was going to snow, and Ben's hands were larger than dinner plates—so there was no need to be sad.

"I'm sorry that happened to you," Ben's thumb rubbed my cheekbone. I squeezed the back of his hand in response. "No child should ever feel ignored. Especially not one as precious as I'm sure you were."

"It's old news." My eyes fell shut as something cold and wet fluttered down to my temple. It took me a second to realize what it was—lighter than rain, and softer somehow. Chilly. Snow.

A snowflake.

"Shit!" I knocked Ben's hand off my cheek without thinking as I jerked my head back to stare at the sky. "It's snowing!"

"Just because it's old pain doesn't mean it doesn't still hurt you," Ben countered quietly. "It's okay if it does. And I promise to never ignore you agai—"

"Oh my god, I'm gonna make a *snowman*." Slapping Ben on the chest in excitement, this time deflecting accidentally, as visions of what was to come danced around in my head. "*Oh my god,*" I repeated, hopping up and down in excitement. "Oh-my-god. I could go sledding!" Shit. "I need a sled. Where do you buy a sled? Is there a store for that?"

That excitement, however, was short-lived because I realized that I'd successfully distracted Ben from his job—and now it was snowing—and there was no way he was going to be able to finish the skeleton now.

Deflating, I realized that snow probably also meant going inside. And not sleds, like I'd hoped. And certainly not snowman.

And…that also meant no more Ben.

Damn.

"I forget you're from the South," Ben hummed thoughtfully, watching me with fondness. He seemed to decide he'd stared too long, however, because he dropped back down to his knees on the cold, leaf-strewn ground, and began working on the skeleton again. Like it wasn't fucking snowing. Little white blobs landing on the back of his dark red hair.

"What—"

"You don't have much of an accent. Not like your brother."

"Only when I'm horny," I waggled my eyebrows, but my sexy one-liner was wasted on him.

Doctor Ben was back.

"Have you never seen snow?" Ben asked, continuing to fit the bones together.

"I've seen it." I rolled my eyes, sticking my hands in my armpits to keep them warm. It was cold without Ben's hand on my face. A few more snowflakes melted on my cheeks. "Just not like this. Live. Actually falling.

Where I could touch it."

I did another happy jig, feet crunching on the grass.

"Have you really never been sledding?" Ben asked. Either I was going crazy, or he was working three times as fast as he had been before. *Click, click, click.* Bones notched back into place.

"No. *Pshh.* I wish. That's like number one on my 'Perfect Christmas To-Do List'."

"Would you like to?" Ben's voice was far away, like he was already plotting ahead. *Click, click, click.*

If I didn't know any better—based on his current speed—and the fact that he was still able to maintain an entire conversation, Ben Montgomery had been stalling earlier. Just like I had.

Oh shit.

My heart beat like crazy.

"Would I *like* to go sledding? Hell yes."

Ben paused, quiet for a solid thirty seconds before he spoke again.

"Every time it snows all the Montgomery's get together at Knoll park and go sledding," Ben informed me like this was a fact. *Click, click, click.* And suddenly, the skeleton was back in working order, aside from the femur I'd been toting around. It sat at my feet, and Ben twisted to grab it, lingering a little longer than necessary before he shoved it into place.

He rose to his feet, hung the skeleton back onto its stand, and turned to face me.

"That's cool," I echoed, a little too late—because holy shit. The dude was a genius.

"Would you like to maybe…come?"

"I always want to come," I joked—then flushed because I realized what

I'd said too late to stop the words. "I mean, yes. Please, Sir Bennington. Allow me to rideth your sledeths with your clan." I saluted him, then waited for orders. "I don't knoweth where Knoll Parketh is, but I will findeth out." I twisted around, like an idiot, trying to see the magical sledding park he spoke of through the trees and past the buildings that dotted the road beside the B&B.

Ben's eyes danced with amusement. "I'm feeding you first."

"Boo," I countered with a sigh.

Ah. *Boo*!

Now *that* would be a fun way to scare him. K.I.S.S. Keep it simple, stupid. And all that.

Miles told me this year was unseasonably cold. That last year, the chill hadn't hit till December. I couldn't help but be glad. Felt like the world was planning on giving me the white Christmas of my dreams. And Ben Montgomery was the Christmas elf I hadn't known I needed.

six

BEN

"GO UPSTAIRS AND GET YOUR warmest clothes on," I told Robin as I herded him toward the front door of the B&B. Matilda was behind the front counter, a book—my book—in hand. She raised her head when we entered, arching a brow our way before she huffed and turned her back to us so she could get back to her book.

"This is the warmest thing I have," Robin frowned at his floor length, cotton jacket like it had personally betrayed him.

Right.

He lived in L.A.

I doubted the man had proper winter gear at all. "You didn't bring sweaters?" I blinked, confused. Who comes to Vermont and doesn't bring sweaters?

In truth, I needed to get rid of him for ten minutes. If I didn't, there wouldn't be time to call up my family and ask for their help. The twins were with Mama, so that was easy enough. But if I was going to make my lie believable I'd need all hands on deck.

Christ, why had I told Robin that *all* the Montgomerys got together every time it snowed? Why couldn't I have said something easier to accomplish?

I'd have to use every minute I had to make this happen. And even then, I wasn't sure if any of my brothers would be available.

Trent and Miles probably. I bet they were both looking forward to spending time with Robin. But Paxton? He was a wild card. And those were the only two that still lived inside the town limits. The rest...yeah. I didn't think I'd manage that. Too many kids to wrangle.

But...Trent and Paxton were enough, weren't they?

It'd still feel truthful if two of my brothers came.

Yes.

Yes.

Perfect.

"Upstairs you go," I urged, gently pushing at Robin's shoulders.

"But I don't think I have—"

"*Check.*" I maybe lingered a little too long on his shoulder blades when I gave him another playful shove. Robin laughed, stumbling way more than he probably should've. My eyes narrowed, but my worries were diverted to my plan-making the second he did as he was told and began to clomp his way up the ornate wooden staircase.

Halloween baubles dangled from the railings. They glowed softly, though some bulbs were burnt out. Probably because these decorations were as old as I was. Or close.

"What else should I look for, your Ben-evolence?" Robin joked.

"Long warm socks." I didn't rise to the bait, though I wanted to. "Gloves. If you can't find warm sweaters, layer a few shirts. Anything is better than jeans."

"I'm not gonna find any of that," Robin laughed, but did as he was told anyway, continuing left up the staircase and disappearing toward his room.

The second he was out of sight, I strode forward, peeking around the bannister to make sure he was well and truly gone before I bolted toward Matilda's desk.

"If I'm not inside when he comes down, distract him." Nervously, I tapped on the wood, leaning over to make sure she could hear me. "Please?"

Matilda very slowly turned the page in her—my—book. She twisted to eye me dubiously over her shoulder, but her lips twitched—which I assumed meant yes.

Excellent.

Speed-walking outside, far enough away not to be overheard, I whipped out my phone. The chill hit, a snowflake landing on my cheek as I waited at the bottom of the steps, heart pounding.

"Pick up, pick up, pick up." Anxiously, my foot tapped on the cobblestone ground. There was an orange maple leaf beside my boot, and I carefully bent down to pick it up, shoving it in my pocket to give to the girls later.

The phone rang.

And rang.

And—

"Ben?" Mama's voice connected, a confused lilt to it. "Everything okay?"

Of course she knew this was out of the norm. For the last two years, every Wednesday I'd call her up at exactly seven o'clock and let her know

I was on my way to pick the girls up. We had a routine.

It was barely five. She knew me well enough to know that I very rarely, if ever, deviated from my routines.

"I need your help," I blurted. "I don't have much time, so don't ask me questions."

"Okay, honey." Her voice was concerned. "Is it serious?" She immediately asked me a question.

"What?" I frowned, confused. And then realized she'd already distracted me from my mission. "No. Nothing serious. Except that it is. *Very* serious, I mean," I amended. "Because Robin has never been sledding—and I lied and told him that we'd all be meeting at Knoll Park because it's snowing. That it's a tradition of sorts. Something we always do."

"Ben—"

"I need to call Trent and Paxton and get them on board. But I don't have time before Robin comes downstairs. I estimate I have an hour and a half to get him fed and dressed properly before I can meet you at the park. I need help organizing. Please."

Mama laughed, the merry sound warming me from head to toe. "Alright," she hummed, obviously amused. "One question."

"What?"

I wasn't sure how much time had passed, but I was terrified Robin would walk out and overhear what was going on.

"Why did you lie to him?" she asked. I didn't have time to lie again, so I simply told her the truth. Because she'd always been my closest confidant, and if there was anyone in the world I had no walls up with—okay, one wall, singular—it was my mama.

"I couldn't just ask him to go *alone* with me. Baby steps. I need to take baby steps. I don't want to scare him off. I need to acclimate him to my presence." Never mind the fact that we'd been alone for most of the day already.

What if he got sick of me?

Or I tried to psychoanalyze him again?

No, no. I needed a barrier to protect him from me at the same time I got to make him smile. He'd said sledding was on his "Perfect Christmas To-Do List". I wanted to help with that.

"Riiiight." I could practically see her grin through the phone.

"And besides—he's here to spend time with his family. He'll be more comfortable, and more excited if he can make memories with them too. I don't want to take that from him."

I just…want to be there too.

To see him light up.

To share that first with him.

"That's very…*thoughtful* of you." Mama's tone made it clear she was surprised I was using my "thoughtfulness" on Robin—a stranger.

"Please?" I begged again, glancing toward the front door and the yellow stained glass that lit up from the inside, worried I'd see Robin's figure approaching. "Bring the girls. An hour and a half. Knoll Park."

"If you'll read the books I bought you."

Oh Jesus Christ.

This again?

"Fine." I gave in because what choice did I have? Robin's Christmas was on the line. If she was surprised she didn't say, simply promised me she'd call around and get as many of my brothers involved as she could, before hanging up.

I loped back up the steps and shoved the door open—relieved when I made it just in time to watch Robin thud his way back down the stairs. I suppose with boots like those he probably didn't need long socks, but he looked incredibly proud of himself as he paused at the top of the stairs and pointed at his feet.

"Two pairs of socks, motherfucker," Robin declared, then waggled his brows and hopped down another step. He kicked a leg out, the buckles on his platform boots glinting. "Knee length," he added, like he was saying it posh like "*cashmere.*" *Thump, thump,* my heart beat as Robin stomped the rest of the way down the stairs looking proud of himself.

"I even found a sweater," he proclaimed proudly, plucking at the thinnest fucking sweater I'd ever seen. Thin enough the fabric clung to his nipples and the divots at his hips, his piercings even more obvious than normal.

Jesus fuck.

"Good job," I praised. It was a joke—to match his joke—but he lit up anyway, his eyes crinkling with delight as he beamed up at me.

Praise kink.

He might have a praise kink.

My head spun.

Stop thinking about his kinks, Ben, and feed him. He looks hungry.

"How do you feel about Italian?" I asked, doing my best not to ogle— and failing.

"Delicios-o," Robin said in what had to be the most horrible Italian accent I'd ever heard.

"Perfect-o." I offered him an elbow, like a freak—and instead of staring at me like the weirdo I was, Robin took it with mock seriousness. My pulse skittered as we headed toward the front door, his hand gripping me tight.

He groped my bicep a little.

I pretended like I didn't notice.

Matilda turned a page in her book.

When we stepped outside I realized—belatedly—just how much snow had fallen. I'd been so distracted on the phone with my mother I hadn't noticed. Thank god, I'd been standing under the awning or the snow on my shoulders would've betrayed me.

I would've been embarrassed about asking my family for help like I had, and for lying—but there simply wasn't room in my head for that right now.

Not when the look on Robin's face soaked up every ounce of attention I had. Crept into the corners of my head, filling every nook and cranny, my head buzzing, my heart warm despite the chill.

There was barely an inch of snow on the ground, and yet Robin *stared* at it like he'd never seen anything prettier in all his life.

Like this was one of the world's seven wonders.

And when he glanced up at me, grin softer than before, a private, giddy thing, I decided right then and there that I would make him smile like that as many times as I possibly could before he went back home, my dignity and dislike of the holidays be damned.

seven

ROBIN

"THIS IS THE BEST DAY of my life!" I yelled in excitement, watching Bubba slide down what had to be the biggest hill known to man. A cloud of snow plumed behind him, the sled moving so fast all I could catch in the dark was the glint of his blond head. We'd already made a few accidentally horrible snowmen, which sat sentinel behind us, watching his descent.

"It goes faster if there's more weight," Miles told me from where he stood to my left, calmly waiting for his turn. He didn't really like this. At least, not unless he was going down with Trent. But I figured that had more to do with the lumberjack behind him than the actual sledding itself.

"More weight," I hummed thoughtfully, eyeing Ben where he stood ten or so feet to the left with a sled of his own. His daughters. *Twins.* Twins, motherfucker! Were dressed adorably in little black snowsuits.

They looked like chunky lil goth snowmen, their heads tipped up as he bent low to speak to them.

I wanted to know what he was saying super bad, but didn't want to be greedy.

He'd taken me to dinner after all. Refused to let me pay. Stopped by his apartment, came down the stairs with his arms full, and forced me into one of his hoodies, a coat, gloves, scarf, and a pair of snowpants that were so fucking big on me I could hardly move.

When he'd been rolling up the hems and trying to shove them into the lips of my boots, he'd promised me he'd get me stuff that fit properly— like this wouldn't be the first and last time we were doing this.

Like it was his job to take care of me.

And I'd stared at his lovely, red head—and the little whirl of hair at the crown—and tried not to fall head over heels in love with him.

I'd always fallen quick.

It was a curse.

And just as quick, the people I fell for tossed me aside.

It was why I was glad I was only here for a few weeks. Why, despite admitting I liked Ben, I hadn't made a real move.

Also because I could tell he liked me too. And that was…terrifying. Even though it was mutual.

I'd always liked dudes as much as girls. Sure it had taken me a while to figure that out—but once I had, I'd never gone back. Dicks were hot. It was simply a fact. I loved them. Loved sucking on them. Loved touching them. Loved sitting on them. Loved the way they throbbed sometimes when the guy I was with was really turned on.

Loved when they were soft, and hard, and soft again.

I tended to like my men a little dangerous too. Bigger than me and strong enough to push me around. Unfortunately those kinds of guys were usually assholes.

So…being attracted to Ben was not this earth-shattering, horrible realization. I tried to tell myself I liked him because he *had* a dick. Because he walked kinda spread out—like his dick was big and he had to accommodate its girth. Tried to tell myself it was a sex thing.

But even *that* felt like a lie, when I knew the first thing my sleep depravation had taken from me was my fucking libido.

And I could hardly get hard most days, let alone get off.

So yeah.

Even though Ben Montgomery probably had the dick to end all days, that was not the reason I liked him.

Not at all.

It was the juxtaposition between his grumpy facade and a hidden sort of gentleness that attracted me. Like he knew how big he was but didn't want to use his size to intimidate.

"Why don't you ask Ben if you can ride with him?" Miles asked, eyes twinkling with mirth as he watched me stare down the illusive doctor man, while wearing the ridiculous getup he'd forced me into.

"Eat shit, little brother," I gruffed at him, cheeks bright red because he'd seen right through me. And then, before he could tease me some more—because apparently that's what he'd been doing—I stomped my way toward Ben and his munchkins.

Tried to stomp.

Waddled, more like.

The girls watched me approach, twin sets of eyes narrowed like they weren't sure what to make of me. Which was fair. If this was the wild, I'd be the hyena panting after their hot lion dad. Wasn't that how *The Lion King* went?

Either way.

I was a predator.

A stupid-looking predator, but a predator nonetheless.

Trying to look cool, and failing, I picked up the pace.

Only…it quickly became clear *that* had been a mistake, because my boot hit a rock—or ice?—or some other winter, mountainy shit, and I went plummeting to the snow in slow motion.

"Goddammit—"

Boom, hit the ground as quick as that, snow in my mouth and everything.

The snowsuit broke my fall so it didn't hurt.

Not the way falling earlier had.

But still—

It was humiliating as fu—

Laughter, crystalline and hysterical broke out in front of me. I lifted my head, surprised, and elated when I saw the two cherubic little girls grinning at me. Their giggles bounced around the bowl of the hill, all the way down to where Bubba was slowly but surely picking his way to the top.

Ben grinned at me, side-stepping the littles and holding a gloved hand out toward me. He yanked me to my feet as soon as I took it, pulling me in close and brushing the snow off my shoulders, expression amused.

The little shits kept giggling, and weirdly enough, rather than feel embarrassed—I kinda felt like I had won something.

"You okay?" Ben asked, voice tender.

"Just peachy."

"Good," his eyes crinkled at the corners the way I liked before he twisted me around to face his daughters.

They sobered the second I turned to face them, eyeing me critically, their arms stuck out at the sides like starfish because of the bulk of their snow outfits.

"You owe me monies," Rosie, the mob boss told me. She was the twin on the left and easy enough to distinguish. The other twin didn't have freckles on her nose.

"A dollar, right?" I laughed, cheeks hot.

"Thirty-seven," she countered, eyes bright.

There was no way in hell I'd sworn thirty-seven times since we'd arrived at the park fifteen minutes ago. Which…weirdly enough, made sense. I'd believed her at the party—and now I was realizing I might've been just drunk enough to be duped.

"Thirty-seven?" I asked, dubiously.

She nodded.

"Is that the highest you can count?" I asked, ignoring Ben—who was literally quaking with laughter beside me.

Rosie nodded again.

"You are one sneaky motherfu—," I paused, watching the way her eyes lit up like she was just waiting for me to mess up. "Mother*fudger*." Her eyes narrowed, disappointed. "Sneaky, *sneaky*," I clucked at her before turning to the other twin. "Hi. What's your name?"

This twin shook her head, watching me warily.

"This is Jane," Ben said in her stead, his shoulder gently brushing mine. "She's shy."

I nodded, because I got that.

Miles had been that way too.

"Nice to meet you, Jane." I held a hand out for her to shake, but she just shook her head again, so I retracted it. "I'm Robin." I smiled at her first, then Rosie, careful not to make the two of them uncomfortable.

I wasn't the best with kids. But I really wanted to be. Especially these two.

They were seriously cute as fuck.

Looked like grumpy lil penguins.

"You ready to go down again?" Ben asked them, tone light. They both nodded very seriously. Ben turned to me with a little smile. "Would you like to take one of them? Only two people can fit per sled."

I wasn't sure I wanted to do that.

What if I crashed the sled and launched one of them Jason-Statham-style into a snowbank? Just…*weeeee—smack,* toddler legs sticking out in the air.

"I don't want to fu—" I glanced toward Rosie. "Fudge it up," I amended.

"You won't." Ben had way more confidence than I did. He handed me the sled. "Let me ask them first, one moment." And then he bent down and whispered to the two of them.

"What do you think? Should we let Robin sled with us?" Ben's voice was a quiet, gentle whisper.

The twins glanced at each other, and then up at me. And then, as if they could read each other's minds—holy shit—they nodded at the same exact time.

"Which one of you would like to ride with him?" Ben asked. He talked to them like they were tiny little adults, and I couldn't help but find that super fucking adorable.

I'd never had a dad like that. Or a dad at all—not really. Mine was a piece of shit who'd fucked off, and only came back to screw me over all over again. This was a totally new concept to me. The only other dad I'd ever known was Miles—and that was…different.

Because he was my kid brother, and I'd never looked at him like he was a juicy steak before.

Apparently, I liked men who were good with children.

Good to know.

I figured Rosie would want to ride with me. That way she could trick me into more swearing. I was nothing but a cussing piggy bank to her. And Jane was shy. She probably didn't want to hang out with a stranger she didn't know.

However…I was more than a little surprised when Jane was the one that raised her hand.

"Alright," Ben replied, standing back up. He stroked a hand over each kid's hat, his eyes on mine. "Jane would like to ride with you."

"Cool," I said, because it *was* cool.

Super cool actually.

Except…I didn't know how to do this.

And again, Jason-Statham-level child-yeeting was not on my Christmas to-do list. Not that he'd ever yeet a child. He'd yeet people—adult people. Like that scene in *The Beekeeper*. But not kids. Obviously. Every version of Jason Statham was just honorable like that.

"Don't look so nervous," Ben laughed, eyes crinkling at the corners again. "All you have to do is sit down and hold on."

"Hold on to what?" I fretted. "The kid or the sled?"

"Jane has her own handles. She's an expert." Ben looked far too amused by this. Jane did not look concerned, even though she should. Instead, she nodded seriously—like she was, in fact, an expert.

"Is she certified?" I half-joked, because the longer I kept talking the more I could stall.

Again, Jane nodded.

Yeah fucking right. There was no way she knew what the word certified meant. Unless she was a genius. Or like—a super baby, or whatever.

Still though…Ben didn't look worried.

At all.

He took the sled back from me—like it was easy to yank it right out of my death grip, and lay it down. "Sit," he commanded.

I sat.

The snow crunched beneath my weight and my heart thundered. Jane crawled onto the sled, settling in front of me, her cute little mittened hands latching on to the handles. "Do I hold you?" I asked her, because again—no one had fucking told me.

Jane ignored me, staring resolutely ahead.

"Hold the handles," Ben's voice was right next to my ear. It tickled, warmth bleeding through the hat he'd shoved on my head. I melted a little, my nerves fading. "Relax. It's going to be fun."

I'd been super fucking excited about this—and I knew realistically he was right—it was just…hard to let go of the nerves. They stuck to me like cling wrap. I could hardly breathe, I was so tense.

An awkward beat passed.

"You know what—how about…" Ben pulled back. I twisted to look at him, but only caught the tail end of the gesture he made. The *crunch, thump* of the snow alerted me to someone approaching from behind.

"Paxton?" Ben asked.

"What?" a gruff, low voice replied. When I twisted to look, I realized I was looking at the only Montgomery brother I hadn't met yet. The grumpy one. That's what Bubba had told me.

"Would you watch the twins for a second while I take Robin down?" Ben's voice was as calm and serious as ever. "It's his first time. He's nervous."

Oh, thank God.

Embarrassed, I tried to tell him I was fine—but he didn't listen. Both brothers ignored me actually, as Paxton leaned down to yank Jane right into the air. She released a fit of giggles—not quite as loud as the ones she and her sister had made when I'd fallen, but still joyful.

"Why don't we watch, hmm?" Paxton hummed, surprisingly gentle as he grabbed Rosie too and hoisted both girls onto his shoulders. "Your daddy's made his first friend."

"Oh, fuck off," Ben muttered.

"You owe me monies," Rosie clapped back immediately.

Ben laughed.

And then he was sinking down behind me. He used his weight to keep the sled in place as he easily maneuvered me into Jane's vacant spot and settled down at my back. He was so fucking warm. Christ. And big. His lovely, cultured-looking hands wound around my body, picking up the handles and forcing them into my grip.

"Hold tight," he murmured, giving my hands a squeeze. His long legs framed my body, going way past where mine ended, feet nearly twice as large as my own. I was suddenly quite glad I was not the one in the back— otherwise my dick might've woken from the dead just to fuck with me.

"Don't you mean, hang on tight spider monk—eeeeeeee!" My screech turned into laughter as the sled pushed off and the world blurred white.

Wind whipped my cheeks, bitter and cold. It burned the tip of my nose, icy bright as it filled my lungs and the snow kicked up around us. Ben's breath was warm on the back of my neck as he kicked one leg out, digging it into the snow and sending the sled spinning, spinning, spinning.

I couldn't stop laughing. Couldn't stop for the life of me.

Those few seconds felt like years as the blurry trees along the top of the park danced.

When we finally spun to a stop I was out of breath and Ben was laughing against the nape of my neck.

"Oh my fuck," I gasped out, wiggling in Ben's grasp. "That was amazing."

"I knew you'd like it."

"That thing you did—with the leg—" I twisted around to look at him, momentarily distracted by the way he was looking at me. "Seriously inspired. You're like the Picasso of sledding."

"The girls love that. I figured you might too. That way you can impress them with my trick." Ben winked. *Winked!*

"You're high if you think my legs can reach that far."

Ben tossed his head back and laughed.

And then we were scrambling up the hill again—me, with newfound confidence. Ben's smile never died.

It didn't die when he let me go a second time in a row—this time with Jane. It grew broader after I took her for a spin and squinted up at the top of the hill after her giggles subsided. It softened when I carried her up the hill on my shoulders because the snow was too deep for her tiny legs to climb.

Up and down, over and over. I rode with Jane, Rosie, and Bubba. Giggling my ass off like a man possessed, my heart pounding, my skin hot now—despite the chill. Like my body was burning up my happiness to keep me warm.

And all the while, I wished and wished and wished that I could ride down that first time again. That I could feel Ben behind me. That his warmth could be mine, and that smile would stay forever.

Snowflakes fell.

The night grew dark.

And for the first time in years, I felt like I belonged.

eight

BEN

"SO…" MAMA SAID, CRUNCHING HER way through one of the free cannolis we'd gotten for free-cannoli night at Rudy's. Every Saturday was free-cannoli night. And every Saturday, like clockwork, Mama and I made our way here.

I was too old to worry about the fact my mother was my best friend.

Sure, if I'd still been in my twenties I might've felt some embarrassment that the highlight of my week was the time I spent with my mom, but I was well past that now.

After losing Dad, it'd become all too real, all too quickly just how fast we could lose the people we loved. And I'd made a point to call her every week after that, even when I lived in New York, or when I was still in school. I'd hardly had time to breathe, and yet I'd still found time for her.

A fact I knew she appreciated.

Now that I had moved back to my hometown, things were different.

It wasn't a harried phone call we shared. It was cannolis. And all the fun moments in between when I picked up Jane and Rosie from her house after work, and we spent a solid forty minutes telling each other about our days over cocoa.

"So…?" I echoed right back, cleaning up the last of the cream from my plate before taking a long sip of water.

A sip of water that I promptly choked on when her next words came out.

"Robin Johnson, hmm?" Her eyes slitted, lips pulling into a Cheshire-like grin. "Matilda caught you making eyes at him the other day."

"Oh, stop." I waved her off, my cheeks hot. Couldn't tell her to 'fuck off' like I could with my brothers. I was forty-five, and despite what I'd just said about being too old for those sorts of games, I would never be too old to respect my mother.

"Also—did you really think I wasn't going to bring up the sledding?" she teased. There was a dark lock of hair curling around her ear from where it'd slipped free of her updo. I reached out to tuck it behind her ear, and she smiled gratefully, though that didn't stop her from giving me more shit. "Your brothers are in a tizzy about it. Everyone is."

"It's been three days. How can that possibly be?"

"I have my ways," she tapped her nose. "The whole town's talking about it."

"No, they aren't."

"They are." Her eyes danced.

"How could *the whole town* possibly know?" I glared at her. "Unless… someone told them?" Like Jason at the general store. Jesus fuck, he had a mouth on him. And I didn't mean that in a sexy way.

"I may have *accidentally* let slip to Becca that you have a soft spot for him…"

"Oh lord."

"Who was talking to Baxter about it…"

"No."

"When he was picking up his bulk order of cocoa from—"

"*Jason*." Jesus fuck. That explained all the weird looks I'd been getting since Wednesday. And also the odd "congratulations" that had been tossed left and right at me as I walked down Main Street to get my daily dose of caffeine before my shift every day.

"What do they think is going on?" I asked, eyebrow twitching.

"Everyone in Belleville is incredibly happy that you're in *love*, Ben." Mama reached out to pat my hand. "There's no need to look so offended."

"I'm not in love—" I countered, even though that felt like a lie. "I just…I mean." My cheeks were bright red. "How could I be in love? That would make it love at first sight. Which only exists in books, not real life." I laughed, because that felt ridiculous, and also horribly on the nose. I was an author. I wrote about these things, but I'd never once thought they could be real.

"I've never even seen you have a boyfriend, Benjamin." Mama's voice grew kinder. "Never seen you so much as *glance* at another person. And yet…"

Ugh.

Why was she doing this to me?

"And yet, here you are…organizing a sledding expedition for our fancy-little-city-visitor. Going out of your way to interact with him. Buying him dinner, dressing him in your clothing—"

"I get it—" I cut her off, cheeks hot. "I get it."

At least she hadn't seen how giddy I was to hop onto the back of his sled. I'd never hear the end of it.

"He's only in town for the holidays," I added, trying to douse water over the flames of her excitement. "It's not like it means anything. It's casual flirtation. That's all."

"If I know you, Ben—" Mama squeezed my hand tight. "And I do. I birthed you after all—"

"Jesus." *Why did she always bring that up?*

"Then I know nothing you've ever done has ever been casual."

Mama's words followed me around the rest of the night. When I got home I thanked Becca, my niece, for babysitting, slipped her an extra twenty—because I knew she was saving up to buy a car—and settled onto my couch with a depressed sigh.

The grandfather clock ticked and ticked and ticked.

Annoyingly loud.

Distracting.

Why the hell had I bought a grandfather clock?

It'd seemed like a good idea at the time. Classic. Old-school. The way I liked most things. But now the steady *tick, tick* was doing nothing but pissing me off. If it cuckoo'd I was going to scream.

Against my better judgment, my thoughts spun and spun and spun.

Eight weeks. Give or take a few days.

That was as long as Robin was staying. *He* hadn't told me that. I had texted Trent to confirm, and there was very little I could do about that.

I'd blink and our time together would be up. Easy as that.

If I was being completely, brutally honest—something my therapist recommended I practice, at least in the privacy of my own head—I knew that if Robin were staying here in Belleville indefinitely things would've been different for us.

My approach would've been different.

I would've acknowledged the fact I liked him long ago. Would've asked him on a date properly. Something fancy, just so I could see his face light up when I got the bill for him again. I would've brought him flowers. Would've asked for his number. Would've already been planning our second date before the first had even ended.

"Nothing you've ever done has ever been casual."

The truth of Mama's words haunted me.

Robin made me laugh in a way no one ever had before. He was funny, sweet, and entirely too sexy for his own fucking good. Energetic and bright, he made whatever room he stepped inside fill with life. Like he was a walking ball of sunshine, and everyone else couldn't help but turn toward him.

Beneath that, though, he was…fragile.

Maybe because of the tumble he'd taken last year on stage? *Thank you, Google.* Or maybe it was simply the job itself. The fact that he'd been away from his family. I couldn't imagine living a life at the level of fame he possessed. That was an incredible amount of pressure, even when he wasn't actively touring.

If there was one thing that didn't make sense to me, however, it was the fact that Robin Johnson had left Miles and Bubba behind. He seemed more likely to be the kind of oddly doting uncle you saw in movies.

Always around. Heavily reliant on his family to make him feel seen, and appreciated, and loved.

And without that…

I wasn't sure how he'd survived.

At least, judging by the way he watched Miles and Bubba with wide, starved eyes.

The only answer could be that he left because he had to. He left because—like he'd uttered to me in the dark, his secret cracked open—he thought that he was poison.

Like Beckett, in the book I was writing. The character that he'd been most invested in.

I didn't blame Belleville for being curious. Mama had been right. I had never done things by halves. And it made sense that they'd all be fascinated that for the first time in my life, serious stalwart Ben Montgomery was actually interested in someone.

But that didn't mean that I could pursue this without accidentally hurting Robin.

And I didn't want to do that.

Hence my frustration.

Because I didn't want to spend any more time worrying about my newest tiny-black-coated shadow, I rose from the couch and headed into the twins room to check on them. The light was off, only their matching nightlights casting a glow about the tidy room. We allowed messes in our house, but under the condition that the twins were responsible enough to clean up after themselves, and that had always worked.

There were a few stains on the carpet that were never coming out—despite the fact our home was still fairly new—but the floors were always tidy, the toys always put away.

Unsurprisingly, Rosie's bed was empty.

She often did this.

Climbed in with her sister, like they were two halves of a whole, and she could only relax when they were together. Wearing separate blankets, purple and green respectively, Jane and Rosie were curled up on the left bed, their blonde curls spilling across the dark bedspread.

I'd let them pick the decor.

And unsurprisingly, they'd chosen something more fitting for the children of Gomez Addams than me.

I didn't mind, though. I liked to let them express their creativity and personalities wherever I could. Even though I was quite aware that some of their interest in the little kids' version of Edgar Allan Poe's stories, and their obsession with black came from missing Trixie, their mother.

Trixie was as soft-hearted as a person could be.

Gentle. Kind.

And I'd never seen her wear anything that hadn't been ordered from an occult catalog, wasn't blacker than the night sky, and covered in lace. I could admit seeing my children dressed the way they preferred sent a pang of longing for their mother through me whenever I let it catch me off guard.

She'd been my best and only friend when I'd moved to the city.

We'd bonded over our love for books and our aversion to public transportation. And despite the fact I'd never made a real friend before, we'd quickly—and effortlessly—become two peas in a pod.

It helped that Trixie was as gay as I was. We'd had a lot of mirrored experiences as teens, though *she'd* kept the eyeliner, and my style now leaned more toward Tom Ford.

Trixie had been the one to tell me I should contact agents. She'd been the one who read my first book and quietly proclaimed—over tea one day in her favorite tea shop, because she was a tea drinker—that if I didn't send it off to be published, *she* would.

My platonic soulmate.

In all the years I'd known her, we'd never fought once. Not even when we were planning to have children. Not even when she'd been pregnant with our twins, and I wouldn't stop hovering. Always panicking, always overbearing.

She was my biggest fan. And I was more than a little happy that she'd finally broken into her dream career in L.A., but that didn't mean I didn't miss her, especially at times like this.

I ran my hand over Jane's fuzzy head, and then Rosie's, sighing softly as I crouched down on the ground beside their bed, moving slowly to make sure I wouldn't cause my back to spasm.

Trixie would know what to do in this situation.

I wanted to ask her for advice.

But I was more than a little worried she knew Robin personally as they ran in the same circles. And I didn't want to betray his privacy like that. Not that I ever thought she'd do something as awful as spread my concerns over his health—or rumors about us.

She would never.

It was simply the principle of the thing.

As someone who was incredibly well-known, there was very little privacy Robin had left. I wasn't about to betray that, not even to my best friend.

Jane made a snorting sound, and I bit back a laugh, fingers combing through her silky curls as she snuffled against the mattress.

I didn't want to disturb them, so I remained quiet, soaking up their little sleep sounds and finding peace in them like I always did. When it was far too late to be up any longer, I rose with a pop, biting back a groan as my back twinged—just like I'd hoped it wouldn't—and I made my way to my own bedroom to do the physical therapy I'd been neglecting.

Robin was on my mind as I brushed my teeth.

He was on my mind as I set my alarm—bright and early—for Sunday, my designated day with the girls.

He was on my mind as I pulled on sweats and slid beneath the covers.

And when I dreamed, I thought of green eyes.

Chipped nail polish.

Bruises.

And laughter.

And the fact I didn't want to half-ass this thing with him at all.

"Don't forget to breathe!" I cheered, stopwatch in hand, as Rosie huffed and puffed. Her little chubby limbs worked double time, hands clutching tight to the spoon she was strangling, and the egg it balanced atop it. The snow had melted earlier in the week, leaving grainy brown patches, here and there, the soggy-soaked leaves beneath it squishing beneath her booted feet.

It'd been a lovely Sunday so far.

We'd had pancakes this morning—with chocolate chips—my specialty. We'd watched an hour of Jane and Rosie's favorite cartoon—LilPoe. It was a child-like retelling of a lot of Poe's work. Their favorite was the *Cask of Amontillado* episode with the wall. And we tended to watch that over and over and *over,* on a never-ending loop. They knew every single line and would shamelessly quote it while staring at the screen like it was hypnotizing them.

Afterward, we'd made lunch together, chicken wraps that were more cheese than wrap. And now that the twins were full of energy and dressed to fight the cold, we were at the park down the street, training.

Training…had not been my idea.

After the Pie Festival last fall and our inevitable loss during the relay race, the twins had become determined to win the following year. Sure, I doubted we would. I wasn't as fast as Paxton or Trent was, and therefore would be hard-pressed to beat them in the race. And if I had the twins roped up to my legs for the three-legged portion, we would lose for sure, but that didn't mean I wasn't going to support them when they wanted something—however misguided it was.

I figured there was a lesson in losing, just like there was in winning.

And I was proud of them for wanting to work hard toward something that wasn't a guaranteed success.

Rosie wheezed in a breath—finally remembering that air was a thing she needed—before she crossed her designated finish line and cheered happily in triumph. Except, when she cheered, she threw the spoon upward, and the egg flew and—

Yep.

Smashed right into Jane's coat where she'd been waiting at the end.

Jane looked down at the yolk, slowly dripping down her coat, pulled in a long, labored breath—and…

"Oh, honey," I knelt down immediately, pulling the wet wipes I brought with me at all times out of my coat pocket. "It's okay. It's just a little—"

A high-pitched wail filled the air, loud enough to startle a few birds out of the roost they'd made. Indignant, they squawked at the three of us like we were Satan himself.

"I'm sorry," Rosie said, her own little voice wobbling. "It was ass-dent."

"Accident," I corrected gently.

"Ass-dent," Rosie agreed, wetter this time. "I didn't mean to."

Jane stopped wailing, but by that point, all was lost. Because now that the waterworks had begun, there was little I could do to stop them. Rosie sniffled, sucked in a long breath of her own, and I braced myself for two screaming, blubbering toddlers at once.

I knew they needed to be distracted. But Jane also needed the egg off her coat, otherwise it would just set them both off again. So I moved quickly and efficiently to clean her up, all the while murmuring soothingly to both of them and using my free hand to stroke over their shaking little backs.

"It's okay, my angels," I promised, trying not to panic when the pitch of their cries stabbed directly into my brain and made me feel shaky and overstimulated myself. "I promise. See? It's gone. All gone."

I swiped a fresh wet wipe over Jane's coat, clearing the last of the yolk, my heart aching for my two favorite little people. At this age, they had such big feelings, so big they couldn't figure out how to regulate them most of the time. I tried to help as much as I could, but there were times when feelings just needed to be…felt.

"It's okay," I promised them both, settling them against my chest and placing a kiss on each of their little heads. I wasn't sure if they'd feel the kiss through their hats, but I hoped so. "Papa's got you."

The hug seemed to help for all of thirty seconds.

But then Rosie started blubbering more apologies, and Jane discovered there was egg on her shoe too—and I had to pull back to grab more wet wipes.

The last thing I expected on a sunny, brisk autumn afternoon was for Robin Johnson to appear like the guardian angel he apparently was, and save the day.

But he did.

Because Rosie sucked in another breath, ready to wail again—and instead—a peal of laughter escaped her. Wild and twinkly and bright. Jane turned to see what she was looking at and her eyes widened, a little shark-like grin lighting up her face too.

"Ow!" a familiar scratchy voice yelled. "That *hurt*."

Swiveling, I tried to see what they were looking at, only to be shocked and endlessly amused when I realized it was Robin.

Robin.

Dressed in head-to-toe black like usual.

Hopping around on one foot like an overgrown cartoon, Robin had a comically shocked expression on his face. It was obvious he was faking, and my heart lurched as he slowly, ridiculously, pretended to trip. Face-planting against the ground with an exaggerated thud, he raised both hands above his head toward us and gave us a double thumbs-up.

"I'm okay!"

The girls cackled, like watching him get hurt was the funniest thing they'd ever seen. Which…I supposed it was. He'd really put his back into that one. Something I couldn't do, all things considered.

I cracked a grin of my own, a startled laugh escaping me when Robin hopped onto his feet again, looking proud of himself. The sun doused him in dappled shadows from the trees lining the park, dancing over his body as he took a step toward us—

And promptly fell again.

But this time for real.

More riotous laughter escaped the twins, these howling little guffaws that made me light up from the inside out.

"Should we go help him?" I asked them, only to be met with twin nods and an adorable view of my babies waddling their way over to where Robin lay prone on the ground. There was no thumbs-up this time, only an embarrassed laugh, as Jane and Rosie latched on to his hands and tried to pull him up to no avail.

"I think I'm good here," he told them, muffled into the dirt. "I'd like to die a slow death please." His embarrassment was obvious. Even if I hadn't been able to see how pink his ears had suddenly gotten.

"My uncle died once," Rosie proudly told him, voice still full of giggles.

"He's okay now," Jane added, her tiny voice morose.

"Y'all are creepy," Robin countered with a laugh, gamely letting them help him out of the dirt. I could've helped. But...I didn't want to miss a single moment of this. Didn't want to ruin it. The girls hardly ever opened up to new people. They had a hard time with strangers, Jane especially. "Lucky for you..." Robin was finally on his knees again, a toddler hanging off each arm. "I like creepy."

I stepped in then, because I didn't want to be an asshole and kinda wanted my own turn with Robin. Moving forward, I helped him to his feet, brushing off the wet leaves that clung to his knees and the dirt that smeared across his chest.

"You okay?" I asked, voice low and far sweeter than I'd meant for it to be. I was always asking him that, but I couldn't seem to stop.

Robin tipped his head up, meeting my gaze, his own eyes soft. "I'm good," he told me. His fingers wrapped around my wrist, halting it as I pulled on the hem of his shirt to tug it back into its proper place. And then, low—low enough only I would hear, Robin whispered. "Did I help?"

My heart cracked right open then.

Right down the middle.

I nearly kissed him.

Nearly grabbed his sweet pink cheeks and tasted those lovely, chapped lips.

"You did," I promised, huskily. "You did so well, Robin. *Thank you.*"

He lit up.

Praise kink.

Definitely a praise kink.

And then, because I couldn't help myself, and my mouth apparently had a mind of its own I added, "You're such a *good* boy."

In response, Robin released this high-pitched, muffled whine that made my knees instantly weak. It was so quiet, I wasn't sure he'd even realized he'd been the one to make it.

Oh god.

That's the prettiest sound I've ever heard.

I cataloged every aroused detail on his body. The way his chest shuddered. The way he melted. The way Robin's pupils flooded wide and black as he stared up at me like I was nothing less than a miracle.

Robin seemed to realize at the same time I did that we'd kinda just been standing there staring at each other because he hopped back quickly, releasing my wrist like it'd burned him. Before I could even blink, he'd turned his attention back to Jane and Rosie.

"What're you guys doing out here, anyway?" Robin asked.

I wanted to ask him the same thing, but didn't, content to let this play out.

"Training," Rosie told him seriously. Jane didn't speak again, but the once had already been more than she'd done with anyone aside from Mama.

"Training for what?" Robin asked, cheeks still bright pink.

"To beat Uncle Trent's ass," Rosie told him.

Goddammit.

I covered my laugh with my shoulder, then did the responsible parent thing and asked her not to swear. To which she nodded very seriously, before immediately swearing again.

"Gonna beat Uncle Paxton's ass too," she added, faux innocently.

"*Rosie,*" I countered, because apparently she wasn't in the mood to see reason. Usually she was better about listening, but I think between the crying and the laughter, both little girls were feeling quite overstimulated. I could relate. I felt that way too. Skin jittery, heart fluttering.

Anxious.

"Sorry," Rosie immediately replied, eyes wide, because she hardly ever got in trouble, and obviously didn't want to now.

"It's okay," I promised, keeping my tone gentle. "Just don't make me repeat myself a second time, please. It's not nice."

Sometimes I had to remind her what things were "nice". It was the easiest way to get her to understand when she'd crossed a line.

Robin, because he was darling, didn't interrupt, and instead, he dutifully waited his turn. He watched me curiously, cheeks heating up when my voice dropped low again, his slick pink tongue flickering out to wet his lips.

His eyes searched mine, waiting for permission.

Which I eagerly granted, excited to see what he would say next.

"How and why are we beating your uncles?" he asked, turning his attention back to Rosie.

"In the race," Rosie replied.

"The relay race," I added because now that Robin was here, an idea was…oh yes. An idea was forming. "Every year during the Pie Festival there's a relay race," I explained, watching Robin raptly. "Last year we lost. The girls would like to win this year."

"Oh, that's cool," Robin nodded along, though he looked somewhat confused. I could understand. I'd lived in New York, after all. Though I'd had Belleville as my background, I could see why someone who lived in a large city would be surprised by the intricacies of our little town's social engagements.

"We could use another adult," I hummed, eyeing him up and down. "You look fast." Faster than the toddlers, anyway. "How would you like to be on our team?"

"Be on your…" Robin stared at me, then the girls.

I wasn't sure what I expected.

Maybe for him to laugh? To say, "Hell no." Or for a polite yes, best case scenario. What I didn't expect, however, was for his eyes to grow wet. For his lips to curl into a wobbly little smile. For a certain sort of reverence to spread across his features as he nodded his head jerkily. "You really would…you know…want me on your team?"

My heart lurched.

Oh, sweet baby.

Sweet, sweet baby.

Unable to help myself, I reached out and gave his shoulder a tight squeeze. "Of course we do," I told him, suddenly grateful I hadn't given myself time to overthink this. "We would be honored."

"*I'm* the one that's honored," Robin sniffed, smiling at me, then the girls. "I'm not really fast though," he admitted. "I dunno what really goes into these things, and I'm not sure I'll be much help. Someone else would probably be better."

Suddenly, I no longer cared about winning.

And I didn't think the girls did either, because they didn't seem put off by this at all. Their little faces were bright with excitement, bodies vibrating with glee. "That's okay!" Jane promised, piping up a second time. "We want you. Even if you're a loser."

Jesus *Christ*.

"I'll teach you," Rosie's chest puffed up with pride. "I'm the *best*." Jane looked at her dubiously, which was fair, seeing as Rosie had just launched an egg at her.

"Yeah?" Robin laughed. His eyes were still wet. I wanted to bundle him up and never let him go. What a sweet, *sweet* creature he was. "I mean… as long as you're cool with putting in the work. And know I might not be all that great."

Both girls nodded exuberantly.

Robin's eyes met mine again.

They asked, *is this okay?*

They asked, *am I really welcome?*

They said, *I'm poison, I'm poison, I'm poison.*

To which there was only one honest answer.

"We meet on Sundays around two," I told him. "You'll need warmer clothes than that."

"Okay," Robin nodded seriously.

"We'll go get cocoa and have dinner after."

"I like food."

"I'll bring water for you and the girls, so don't worry about that."

"Yes, Daddy," Robin joked—though even I could tell it was strained.

"He's not *your* daddy," Rosie countered, annoyed. "He's mine."

Robin, because he was adorable, turned *bright* red. His eyebrows shot up, and a startled laugh escaped him as he nodded. "Right. My bad. Sorry. Won't happen again." His voice cracked.

Glancing over him, I couldn't help but scan his chest for those lovely perky nipples he kept flashing. They were hard, as per usual, the cold making them poke against the fabric even worse than the piercings did.

I licked my lips, bit back a groan, and forced myself to focus.

"On second thought," I dragged my gaze back to his face. "I'll take you shopping. I don't think you know how to properly dress in this kind of weather. You'll need a guide."

"My very own Vermont-ian expert. Vermonter? Vermontian-er." Robin frowned, obviously confused by his own bullshit. "Okay." His cheeks were still bright red.

"What are you doing now?" I asked, plans already forming in my mind.

"I was just walking to the hardware store," Robin answered immediately. "You know…for paint. For the *thing*?" His eyes bulged like he was trying to communicate to me telepathically.

"The…thing?"

Oh. The haunted house.

Huh.

I was more than a little surprised he was still working on that. Days had passed and I'd assumed with his radio silence that the haunted house had just been an excuse to come see me that first day. Which…maybe it had been. Maybe now it had turned into something more.

"Oh, the *thing*," I agreed, nodding along.

"What thing?" Rosie asked, but Robin sidestepped the question adeptly.

"I don't wanna get in the way of your day," he said, biting his lip. His piercing flickered. "I just wanted to say hi." More like, he'd heard the kids crying and came to rescue me. My adorable goth knight-in-shining-armor. Not that I needed to be rescued from my own children, but still.

What he'd done had been incredibly helpful, and exactly the kind of thing that would make child-rearing so much easier if I had a partner to share it with.

"Let me ask the girls what they want to do." I sunk down low so that we could speak, the way we always did. "What do we think?" I asked them, making sure to make eye contact with them both. "Are we done training for now?"

They both nodded.

Which…thank God.

I couldn't handle any more egg-induced freakouts.

"How would you girls like to go shopping?" I asked them. They wavered, looking at each other for a moment before turning their attention back to me. Simultaneously they both shook their heads. "Okay, so no shopping."

I did my best to let them pick what we did on our special days together. I worked enough that we didn't get a lot of time together throughout the week, and because of that, these days were sacred.

I was, admittedly, a little disappointed.

But I pushed that feeling aside, turning back to Robin to tell him we'd go another time when Jane interrupted me, her little voice quiet. "Can Robin come get cocoa with us?" she asked, voice timid and higher than her sisters. "We always get cocoa after training."

That was true.

He may not have trained with us today, but the fact the girls wanted him to come was frankly adorable. I glanced at Rosie, who also nodded. "He got hurt so he needs extra marshmallows."

Any time one of them tripped during training that's what I'd tell them. And the echo of my own words made my heart lurch. *My sweet little angels.*

"Of course," I agreed, rising back to my full height and catching Robin's gaze. "How would you like some cocoa, hmm?" I asked, reaching out to gently push a stray lock of his pale blond hair away from his forehead. "You look cold."

And then, because I couldn't help myself, my other hand slid down the lapel of his jacket, tugging on it pointedly as I glanced down at his very hard, very cold nipples. I released him just as fast, but the heat in his eyes haunted me. "Next time, wear the hoodie I lent you."

It took him a second to get his head back on straight, which was… gratifying.

Robin licked his lips and nodded. "Yeah. I mean. Totally. Cocoa is good. Way good. Super good. Totally the best. Yep."

"Okay." I gave his ear a little tug before releasing him. "Time to clean up. And then we'll go."

Five minutes later, my bag was packed, the egg was cleared, and every one of our little entourage had piled into my van. Robin had done a double-take when he saw it, muttered something like, "Mom van? Holy shit, you cannot make this shit up," and then climbed into the passenger seat.

I obviously had not been thinking because it didn't even occur to me what CD was in the CD player as I flipped the ignition and Robin's latest album began to blast.

Immediately, the girls perked up in their car seats, screaming along with every word as we pulled out of the parking lot and headed toward the coffee shop across town. They had Belgian chocolate, which was my favorite. It tasted richer, and in my opinion, was far superior to Trent's powder collection, or Paxton's homemade variety.

We got our cocoa snobbery from our parents, though admittedly Mom and Dad had never been as bad as any of us kids were about it.

Robin's eyes were wide as his music continued to play. He glanced at me, cracked an amused grin, then stared at the little girls in the rearview mirror. I turned down the music enough that he could speak because I could see the words ready to burst.

"You guys like this?" he asked, obviously excited.

The girls eyed him dubiously, then each other, obviously annoyed he'd interrupted their jam session.

"This is their favorite singer," I told him, more than a little amused. After the first time they'd met it'd been abundantly clear to me that the twins did not recognize him. Which was fair, seeing as I don't think they'd ever seen any of his music videos—there was way too much nudity for that—or his photos on his albums.

"Oh?" Robin's voice squeaked. "Um. Wow. That's..." He looked flabbergasted, which was fair. I don't think he'd expected this. "That's actually super cool."

"It is," I agreed, and then turned up the music again so the girls could unknowingly boost my little bird's ego.

nine

ROBIN

BELLEVILLE FELT LIKE A SAFE haven, and because of that, it had to be the weirdest place in the world. I could hardly believe my luck most days as I wandered down Main Street, totally unaccompanied, and the only comments and extra attention I got were Miles- or Ben-related.

No one seemed interested in who I was, and I was perfectly fine with that.

Sure, when I was younger I craved fame and the attention that came with it. But I was old enough now to realize that having everyone and their aunt know your name was a cage more than it was a cushion.

I'd been emotionally immature before. A kid in a candy store full of bad decisions covered in pretty wrappers. I hadn't been ready to be serious about anything but running away. I'd had a lot of growing to do.

I wouldn't have changed the way I'd done things. Because it was moving to L.A., and all the experiences that came with that, that had shaped me into who I was now.

Which was…apparently the kinda guy who bought a gallon of black paint from a hardware store so that I could fix up a haunted house for two funny little kids.

Rosie and Jane were hilarious.

They always had something to say—even without words. Sometimes it was as simple as a scathing, chubby-cheeked look. They were terrifying in their own way, and I loved them.

I loved them a lot.

Even before I found out they loved my music—which woah. Man. That had been…fuck. That had been so fucking sweet I could hardly breathe.

Gave me a pang when I realized I probably would've loved Bubs at this age too, all chubby-limbed and grouchy. It was a shame I hadn't had the chance to really spend time with him.

I hadn't realized what I was missing back then, but I definitely did now.

Maybe…I could negotiate more time to visit in my contract moving forward?

My term was up after the Christmas party in L.A. I was hosting. Nancy was already working on drawing up the new one. I could always call her and ask. It didn't hurt. And besides, even though I was *supposed* to be on vacation—she couldn't *actually* get mad at me for calling about something work-related, right?

Ben had dropped me off at the hardware store after our impromptu cocoa not-date.

Everyone who had been at the shop had stared, and stared, and stared.

And some old lady sitting in the corner nodded at Ben with a slow, happy smile, wiped a tear, and said, "It's about time!"

I wasn't an idiot. But even I had a hard time piecing that one together.

Ben had just blushed bright red and steered us to the back corner of the room away from the eclectic mix of people—all staring. He hadn't acknowledged their attention though, aside from the blush. He simply put his back to them, blocking me from view, and spent five minutes explaining to me why Belgian hot chocolate was superior to any other kind.

Apparently, he'd stumbled upon it when he lived in New York and never gone back.

The fact he was so opinionated about cocoa was fucking cute.

I mean…

What was he? Santa's overgrown elf?

Maybe it was a Vermont thing. Seeing as the coffee shop was completely full of well-meaning Bellevillians. Maybe they *all* loved cocoa? Like a collective hive mind of chocolate devotees.

Somehow I doubted that.

It was after dodging fifty questions about "the thing"—the toddlers would not let go of that secret once they'd caught scent of it, and two cups of Belgian cocoa, which was, absolutely, the best cocoa in the world, holy shit—that Ben had driven me back to Main Street and the hardware store I currently occupied.

He'd offered to wait and drive me home, but that was stupid as hell.

He had his little kids with him, and his house was right across the street from the hardware store. So I declined.

I'd already taken enough of their day. Didn't want him, or the munchkins, to get sick of me.

So yeah. Me, a gallon of paint, and my phone were about to make the trek back to the B&B alone.

"Are you allergic to vacation?" Nancy's voice was full of ire. Apparently, she could, in fact, be mad at me for calling. She picked up on the first ring, which was good for me because it gave me an excuse to set my paint bucket down and sit on it. Right at the end of the street.

"No," I retorted. Except, I kinda was. "I just have a question."

"Jesus Christ. What part of 'get some rest' and 'do not call me for any reason other than death before December' do you not understand?" Nancy huffed.

"Nancy—"

"I will fly out there and *chain* you to a bed if I have to."

"Kinky."

"Don't start your flirty little shit with me. You know it doesn't work." Nancy sighed, a slow put-upon sound. My heart flooded with warmth, my love for her growing exponentially as a car passed by on the street. They honked at me, but it was friendly, and the driver waved so I waved back.

This was some Twilight-Zone shit.

"Are you still putting my renewal contract together?" I asked, picking at a hangnail on my thumb.

Nancy was all bark but no bite. She'd mother hen me to death if she could, even though she was probably the severest, scariest person I'd ever met.

Seemed I liked a lot of those kinds of people.

Lookin' at you, Ben Montgomery, and your tallness. Nancy was half his size but still towered over me. They could both compete for resting bitch face of the year, though I figured Nancy would probably win—simply because of her competitiveness.

Ben was more chill than she was.

"*Yes*," Nancy sighed after a long, drawn-out pause. I'd half-expected her to hang up on me but was grateful she hadn't.

"Do you think it would be possible to negotiate my time off?" I asked, moving on from picking at my nail to biting it. "You know, so I could…" I trailed off, cheeks growing hot as I realized what my question would imply.

"You're liking it there, then? In bumfuck Vermont?"

"No bumfucking has happened unfortunately, but yeah." I bit harder, voice muffled. "I like it. It's weird. People are…nice. No one bugs me. It's kinda…peaceful?"

"How much time off are we talking about?" Nancy had officially gone into business mode. "Holidays?"

"Yeah." I shrugged a shoulder, shrinking in on myself even though she couldn't see. Another car passed. Another honk. Another wave.

Damn, people here were so nice.

"Maybe summers too?" I wiggled uncomfortably. "And um, Miles's birthday. Bubba's birthday too. I'll need a week for both." My mind whirred. "Valentines too. Miles told me yesterday that he has a hard time prepping for class during the holidays. Maybe I could come back and help?"

Nancy was silent.

"Oh, and Halloween!" I blurted, still biting at my nail. Couldn't catch the damn thing with my teeth. "I need to be here for Halloween. I can't miss that."

"What about *your* birthday?" Nancy's voice was gentle—the gentlest I'd ever heard it.

"My birthday would be cool too," I agreed, already imagining that.

I could throw a party! Invite Ben and his kids. Miles, Trent, and Bubs. Hell, even Ben's grumpy brother, Paxton, could come. Actually, you know what—it would be weird not to just invite everyone, right? Maybe

Matilda would let me host it at the B&B and we could get the haunted house up and going again.

There'd be lights and food and *music*!

I could get one of those projector things and play Tim Burton movies on it. Hire scare actors. The whole shebang. Could test run animatronics with Ben and the munchkins and pick out which ones were the spookiest!

"So…you want…every holiday off. Summers off. Your birthday, Miles, Bubba, and—"

"Ben's too," I added, even though I didn't know when it was. "I bet he's not great at celebrating his own birthday. I could throw him a party!"

"And Ben's birthday." Nancy sounded amused. She didn't ask me who Ben was, which I appreciated because I knew my voice would betray me. "Robin, *honey*," her tone softened in a way it only had after my big fall last year. "Have you considered retiring?"

"Retiring?" I blinked, confused. "I mean, yeah, I've thought about it."

"I hate to break it to you, sweetie, but your label isn't going to like you not working…" There was a rustling sound in the background, like she'd been writing down my words. "Ever."

"Oh." I blinked, surprised, and then embarrassed. "Yeah…I mean. I guess I just…"

I'd thought about retiring.

If I was being honest, I'd thought about it more times than I could count.

I wasn't happy anymore.

I wasn't allowed to make the music I wanted. It wasn't part of my "brand." I was sick and tired of the meaningless parties full of people I didn't know or care about, of performing for crowds like I was a party trick my label got to throw out.

Even my last tour had been a shit show. Scalpers had bought out all the tickets, and I hadn't found out until after it was over that the people who had attended had basically been robbed just to see me perform.

I'd grown since I was a punk-ass kid, fresh out of North Carolina, looking for the attention I'd never received.

I was tired.

I was so, so tired.

And though my sleep was still mostly whack, it was getting better. At least…it had been since I'd moved to Belleville and met Ben. Away from the stress of the city, from my label, from all the things that had caused my sleeplessness in the first place.

It felt like a fresh start.

My doctor had been on to something.

"It would be okay for you to quit, Robin," Nancy said, her voice still gentle. "I mean, I'd miss you. You're my favorite boss. But even I can see you're slipping. And if you keep going down this path, you might fall too far to get back up again."

It was on that cheerful note that a familiar voice interrupted me.

"Robin?"

"Gotta go," I hung up quickly, swiveling to see my favorite human in the whole wide world standing behind me.

"There a reason you're sitting on a pail of paint in the middle of the sidewalk?" Miles asked, eyes crinkling in amusement. He was massive as always, dressed in cow print, his dark hair sticking out beneath the hat he wore.

"Just…ruminating," I told him, hopping up quickly before he could see how shaken I was by my chat with Nancy. I reached for the gallon of paint again, but Miles grabbed it before I could, hefting it easily with one arm—asshole—and slipping into step beside me.

"Ain't like you to ruminate," he countered.

I wanted to fight him for the bucket, because I wasn't a weak-ass bitch who couldn't carry my own shit. But he was also…gigantic. And I was tired. So I didn't.

"Guess you don't know me that well," I shrugged a shoulder—then immediately regretted my words because hurt flashed across Miles's face so quickly I nearly missed it.

"Guess I don't," he agreed, quieter than before.

Fuck.

"Sorry," I blurted immediately, feeling small and miserable. "I didn't mean that."

"Nah," he shook his head. "You did. You didn't mean to *say* it, but you meant it."

Tense and unhappy, I didn't know how to shove the words back into my mouth. The problem with having a trashmouth is that sometimes garbage comes right out. Especially when you're exhausted.

"That's okay," Miles lightened up, softening despite how much of an ass I'd just been—because he was sweet like that. The sugar to my sour. Most people would never believe that I'd had to pick up this ginormous angel of a man more times than I could count after he'd beat some kid's teeth in for calling him names in school. "You don't really know me either."

He didn't mean it in a mean way—his cheeky smile made that obvious—but still, I ached.

"I've been away a long time," I sighed, and Miles nodded.

We'd hung out a lot this past week. Any time he was free, really—

though again, I was doing my best not to overcrowd. The more time we spent together the easier it was to fall into the accent I'd had all my life, mirroring Miles's own.

He sounded like home, the way nothing had for years.

"You have," Miles agreed. "But you're back now." It was forgiveness, simple as that. "And that's enough for me."

I swallowed the lump in my throat, eyes burning. Had to look away so he wouldn't see.

"Why're you out here alone, anyhow?" I asked him, staring at a crack in the sidewalk while I gathered myself. I was cold. But I was always cold here, so I didn't pay it much attention.

"Grabbing pastries with Gram," Miles answered. "She told me to fuck off when she saw you out here."

"Nice lady," I laughed, meaning it.

"The nicest," Miles agreed. He hefted the gallon into the other arm, and I realized, belatedly, that we were kinda just standing here.

"Shit, sorry. I can take that back." I reached for it, and Miles smacked my hand away with a laugh.

"No offense, but you look like shit. Ain't no way I'm letting you carry anything."

"I don't look like—"

"Shit warmed over," Miles continued. "Leftover shit. Microwaved—"

"Okay, *okay*. I get it. I look bad. Fuck."

"You been sleeping at all?" Miles asked. He was the only person I'd told about my insomnia and the sleep deprivation I experienced because of it. I'd maybe left out the bit about passing out sometimes when I got my worst—and what the doctor called "micro sleeps" which were like…

eyes-open naps. But still… After Miles's panicked phone call to Nancy last year—*or maybe that was Trent?* Didn't matter, *anyway*—I'd looped him in on most of my medical…shenanigans eventually.

"My doctor says that getting away from L.A. is supposed to help," I deflected without answering his question.

We started walking, and Miles fell in stride beside me, shortening his gait so that he wouldn't totally overpower my Frodo legs.

"Is it helping?" Miles asked.

"I…don't know," I admitted. "A bit? Maybe." When Ben was near.

The sky was overcast now. It'd been sunny earlier. Sunny enough that despite the cold, I'd been sweating a bit as I walked.

"You looked better when you got here," Miles wheedled.

Better being relative, as I'd looked like shit then too.

"That's 'cause I slept on the plane."

"*You did?*" Miles's eyes widened. "Really?" He looked way too excited about this.

"Blame Ben's biceps," I said without thinking—because again, I was stupid when I was tired.

"What?" Miles blinked.

He blinked again.

"Rewind. Ben's biceps? What are you talking about?"

"Shut your mouth," I groaned, so he'd stop staring at me all shocked and appalled. "It's not that big a deal. We maybe…kinda met on the plane?"

I hadn't told him this because I'd expected this exact reaction.

"And you slept on his arm?" Miles continued to look stupidly shocked. "But you hate touching strangers."

That was true, I did.

Our mom had forced us into all manner of uncomfortable social situations when we were little. Enough that we both had our scars from it.

"I guess he's special," I admitted as we neared the gate in front of the B&B. The tall building and its picturesque picket fence loomed as we approached. My cheeks felt hot. *Everything* felt hot.

"I guess so," Miles agreed, eyeing me curiously. "Have you tried again?"

"Tried what?"

"Sleeping on his arm?"

I pushed the gate open so he wouldn't have to, and stumbled a little. "Why the hell would I do that?"

Already though, visions of leaning against Ben, of snuggling up against that bulk and taking a little cat nap assaulted my senses. He'd smell good. He always did. He'd be warm and solid. Big enough to block the rest of the world out. *Safe.*

I shook my head to clear it.

"If it worked once, it might work again. Worth a shot," Miles continued.

"As if I could just go up to him and be like, 'Hey, so you know how I creepy slept on your bicep? I should do that again.' Yeah, right." I rolled my eyes.

"Ben's a doctor," Miles countered. "If you explain your situation he might be open to helping."

"No thank you."

"He took an oath."

"How the hell do you know?"

"I dunno," Miles shrugged. His brow pinched. "Don't all doctors have to take an oath? Help the sick and needy, or whatever."

"I'm not sick. And I'm not needy." I glared at him, though even this—

fighting with him—was better than being away from him. We rounded the corner, and Miles's questions were halted as he paused, shocked all over again.

"What in the hell?" he muttered, staring at the haunted house with wide eyes. "I thought this would be gone by now."

"Cool, right?" I grinned, distracted from my own ire. "I'm fixing it!" I'd been working on this shit all week. Watched YouTube videos. Borrowed tools from Matilda's shed. Cleaned up all the spooky decorations meticulously till they looked worn, but clean. And now I was going to paint them—starting with the coffin at the back end.

Yeah.

That was a good place to start.

"It did *not* look like this when I was here on Halloween." Miles's eyebrows nearly climbed into his hairline. "This what you been doin' while I been workin'?"

"Yeah," my chest puffed up.

"Why?" Miles stared at me for a second like he didn't know who the fuck he was looking at.

My cheeks went hot all over again.

Truth be told, I didn't really know *why*. I mean…I did. Matilda and Beatrice had been talking. I'd found out Ben's daughters hadn't gotten to see the haunted house. I'd decided I wanted to give that to them—and Ben.

That I could fix this.

Maybe it was because there was little in my life I could fix now. Couldn't go back in time and change the past. Couldn't change anything about my physical health—at least…not the way I wanted. Despite the fact I'd told Miles I wasn't sick and needy, I totally fucking was.

And I guess…

I guess…when I heard about the haunted house I just thought—*finally*, this is something I can do.

Something I can fix.

I can make those little girls smile. Make Ben smile.

Pay him back for letting me borrow his arm—and maybe…maybe, when I'm gone, they'll miss me. I'll have done something good for fucking once. Made a difference, somehow.

I rubbed my eyebrow with my ring finger, shrugging again, because I wasn't about to crack my chest open like that, even for Miles, who had the softest, gentlest hands in the history of the world. My heart was brittle enough to shatter, even in his grip.

"You wanna help me paint?" I offered instead.

Miles, because again, he was an angel, nodded.

And paint we did, for hours, till the sun set and I followed him home like a lost puppy—desperate to find my place in this perfect little world he'd built.

ten

BEN

IT WAS ON WEDNESDAY NIGHT that I received an unexpected visitor. I'd just arrived home from picking up the twins and was in the process of wrangling them out of their winter gear—god, it was like herding cats—when there was a knock at the front door.

Mama had already fed them, thank God. So it was playtime, storytime, then bed.

Jane's coat was half unzipped, and Rosie still had one of her shoes on as I groaned in frustration and rose to deal with the door. "Do *not* run off to your room," I warned them both sternly, "*Please?* Papa is exhausted and does not have the energy to chase you down or clean your muddy boot prints off the floor."

I'd just deal with this really quick, and then I could finish taking care of the twins.

Maybe it was Baxter? Sometimes he popped by to bring us leftovers. He was sweet like that. I had no idea what he saw in my brother, Paxton, but enjoyed his pastries way too much to openly question it.

Without checking the peephole—because this was Belleville—I tugged the door open with what I hoped was a smile, but was probably more of a grimace.

Work today had been long and grueling.

I loved my job, I really did. I wouldn't have spent half my life in school for it if I didn't.

But that didn't mean that it wasn't exhausting sometimes. That having everyone and their dog show up all in a row wasn't enough to make me feel like my head was going to explode. It was Wednesday. Which was admin day.

Had I gotten any admin done?

No.

Not at all.

So fucking frustrating.

I maybe yanked the door a little too hard. Hard enough it slammed into the wall, making a horrible sound that made both twins startle, and…

Oh fuck.

Robin jumped.

Because of course it was Robin at my door after dark, dressed—again—in his ill-fitting winter clothes, his green eyes wide. He stared at the door, then me, then shrank a little. He looked scared. Of me. He looked scared *of me.*

Oh dear god, what had I done?

"No, no, no," I soothed without thinking. "It's okay."

Robin had taken a half-step back, and that made me want to die.

"Sorry!" Robin blurted, eyes wide like a skittish animal. "You're probably busy. I should've called—except I don't have your number. And it felt weird to ask Miles for it. Creepy kinda? I dunno."

We were both far too concerned about appearing creepy for our own good.

"I'm not busy," I said, pushing aside the day's frustration. I let it seep away, took a steadying breath, and reached out for him. He didn't flinch—thank God, but he did look nervous as I gave his shoulder a gentle squeeze. "Would you like to come in?"

"No," Robin blurted and then laughed. "I mean, yes. Of course I do." He peeked around my shoulder at the twins, gave a happy wave, and then his eyes narrowed as he took in the space behind them. The long wooden hallway. The grandfather clock at the end of it. The ornate rugs, and the kitchen island that was visible from the door.

"Then come on in," I pulled on him, but he resisted.

After ogling my home for another greedy second, Robin sucked in a breath, his heels digging in. "I finished the thing," he told me, eyes bright and manic. There was a smudge of something black on his cheek. Paint, maybe?

I ached to reach out and scrub it away with my thumb.

But I'd taken a lot of liberties already. I'd frightened him when he was supposed to be the one trying to frighten me. I didn't want to push too hard, for fear I'd send him running. Robin always looked like he had one foot out the door. Like he was one wrong word from disappearing entirely.

"You finished the thing?" My eyebrows rose.

Robin nodded. "Been working on it all week! Miles and Bubba helped." He nodded again, even more jerkily. The dark circles beneath his eyes were not better. In fact, he somehow looked worse. Skin sallow, a twitch to him that betrayed his exhaustion.

"That's very sweet of—"

"Are you ready?" Robin rocked back and forth on his heels, clearly excited. "To see it? Because it's ready. And up. And ready."

"I wanna see the thing," Rosie piped up from behind me, because of course she'd been listening.

"She wants to see it!" Robin pointed at her, like he was trying to convince me—and I wasn't already pulling my shoes back on.

"I…wanna see it too," Jane added, more quietly, her tiny hand clutching at my coat. I gave her a little pat to soothe her, took a deep breath, and tried to reroute my thoughts.

I had a hard time when plans got changed.

Had a harder time with surprises, if I was being honest.

It would take me a second to wrap my head around the fact that we would not be sitting down for our usual routine tonight. It'd be Robin's surprise, and then straight into the bath, and then bed.

Taking a steadying breath, I forced away my unease—knowing it was a product of my brain's betrayal—before I turned back to the kids to get them done up again.

I must've looked pinched because Robin stepped in like he had that day at the park.

"*Do* you want to see it?" he asked the girls, mock dubiously. "You don't *look* like you want to."

Both twins swiveled to stare at him, their honeyed eyes narrowing. "What you mean?" Rosie asked, just as dubiously.

"You don't have your clothes on properly." Robin's hands were on his hips as he eyed the missing shoe and unzipped coat. "No hats. No shoes." He shook his head. "You must not actually want to go."

Before I could blink, both little girls were tearing their winter gear back on. Their motor control wasn't the best, so I still had to help, but the willingness to get redressed made a huge difference in my efforts.

When they were done up like my little goth penguins again, I gently pushed them toward the door, surprised, when both girls latched on to one of Robin's hands, and he began to march forward. He flashed me a grin over his shoulder, all bluster, but I'd seen the look on his face when they'd grabbed his hands.

Seen the reverence there, the wonder.

The joy.

Swallowing the lump in my throat, I turned off the lights and locked up behind us. Then I headed down the steps in the back toward the parking lot where Robin and my children had disappeared.

"What is the thing?" Rosie asked. I could hear her tiny little voice from several feet away.

"Nun-ya," Robin replied.

"Nun-ya what?" Jane echoed, confused. Robin slowed down when it was obvious that Jane was stumbling. My heart ached.

"Nun-ya business."

The twins laughed, a high tinkling little sound—delighted, like Robin had just said the funniest thing in the history of the entire universe.

I died a little on the inside, warm, warm, warm.

Because they were right. He was.

The funniest, the sweetest, the most wonderful man I'd had the fortune to meet.

And he was *leaving*.

I couldn't keep him.

Even if I wanted to.

Robin was nothing if not dramatic. I realized this the moment we stepped onto the lawn of the B&B and I saw what he'd done to the place. Lights lit up the path—brand new, probably bought from the hardware store. Spooky, orange and red, they danced across the wilted fence and led the way around the back of the large, white latticed building.

"Go on!" Robin urged, passing the twins to me, and lingering behind us.

I held their hands tight, but didn't move.

Wasn't he coming?

My question must've been written all over my face because he replied without me having to utter a word. "This was for you," he told me, eyes crinkling. "Not me."

I didn't know what he meant until he turned to the girls, hand spread out, his painted fingers flashing. "Your dad has a surprise just for you," he told them, eyes wide, lips curled into a playful grin.

"He does?" Rosie asked immediately, always curious.

"He does," Robin nodded. "Just around the corner."

He's not taking credit.

The thought spun and spun and spun around inside my head as I stared at him, too shocked to have words to reply.

He's not taking credit for this.

Hours and hours of work.

And he's letting you take the—

"No," I jolted, turning back to him to try and communicate with my eyes that I didn't want this. I wanted him to be appreciated. I wanted my girls to know just how much work he'd put into this—even before we saw the damn thing.

Robin shook his head.

And it was only because of the respect I felt for him that my mouth clicked shut.

"Aren't you coming?" Rosie asked, twisting to look at Robin. "We can share our surprise with you if you want."

Robin wavered.

Clearly he'd wanted this to be a gift for me—for *them*. And I didn't know what to do now that the girls had decided he needed to be a part of it. When Jane latched on to his hand, offering him a shy little smile, Robin melted.

"I…" he glanced at me again, still conflicted.

"Onward," I declared in the silly way I often did when I played with the girls.

"Onward!" they parroted back excitedly, moving forward. There was no more room for hesitation. No more room for second-guessing. Taking charge felt second nature, which was unsurprising.

What was surprising, however, was how right it felt for Robin to be included in our little familial unit. Jane didn't say a single word to him, and he didn't try to push for more. And as we wandered through the decades old—recently repainted—foam cemetery outback, I couldn't help but spare Robin more than a few glances.

I stared at his expressive mouth. Stared at his unruly eyebrow and the way it twitched up with delight whenever Rosie pointed out something he'd done.

"Last year that looked way worse," she told him, and I watched with more than a little affection as his chest puffed up with pride.

"Did it?" Robin asked, green eyes dancing, flickering with the Halloween fairy lights that lit up the backyard just like they had in the front.

The new haunted house was spooky, yes.

Scary? Not so much.

But that didn't seem to matter. Not to the girls, not to Robin, and certainly not to me.

At one point Jane accidentally knocked into the very same skeleton I'd pieced together for Robin. And rather than get angry when the pieces fell to the ground, scattering wildly, he simply laughed, bent down and picked up one of the bones, and handed it to her.

Jane's eyes were wide, the waterworks that had been about to occur stalled by her confusion.

She watched warily as Robin picked up a femur for himself, and then jauntily tapped their bones together.

Delight spread across her face as rapidly as the sadness had.

She smacked him back.

Hard.

And for the last twenty minutes we spent in the backyard of the B&B I sat on the rickety fence and enjoyed the way Robin chased my daughters around. All of them smacked bones together, like a bastardization of fencing, and even Jane seemed to be warming up to him.

"Five minutes," I called, even though we probably should've gone home ten minutes earlier. It was past their bedtime. I was very strict about bedtime.

Circadian rhythms were important, especially for children their age.

"Ahhhh," both girls complained.

Rosie was hiding behind a tombstone—not well, because her little pom-pom-topped hat was sticking out. Jane was just behind her, even more obvious. Robin was pretending like he hadn't seen them, wandering around in "search of them" as my little hellions clearly planned to launch their very own attack.

They didn't seem to realize that the fact they'd spoken had given them away entirely.

Robin gave no indication that it had, either.

He was a good sport.

Silly, yes.

And a good sport.

"Oh, where could they be," he hummed to himself thoughtfully, hands on his hips. He took a long, exaggerated pause in front of the tombstone my darlings hid behind. He looked ridiculously cute like that. Though his cuteness was once again ruined by my very real concern that he was freezing.

I made a mental note to go through my closet and find him something warmer to wear to tide him over before I could take him shopping.

Riotous giggles escaped the girls, muffled by their gloves, but still ringing crystal clear despite that.

Upstairs in the B&B, the lights glowed yellow through the windows. There were several shadows watching us, but I paid them no mind. Belleville had and always would be the nosiest place in the world. I was not surprised that we were being watched. No doubt I'd get well-meaning, excited comments at work the next day.

Because no one had anything better to do than become incredibly invested in my non-existent love life.

Don't ask me why it didn't bother me that the whole town seemed to think Robin Johnson and I were an item.

And don't ask me why I hadn't corrected them.

Because correcting them felt like lying, and I wasn't ready to fully acknowledge that yet.

"Stay here." I made sure Robin was situated on the couch before doubling back for the girls and their winter gear. The grandfather clock tick, ticked and Rosie and Jane were so tired they barely complained as I tugged their coats and mittens off.

Half an hour later—a miracle, honestly, because normally it took far longer to get them bathed and into bed—the twins were sound asleep. Giddy, I took a deep breath and prepared myself for what was to come.

I'd insisted Robin come over.

It was only nine o'clock and I'd thought…perhaps a late dinner might be nice. When I'd asked him to come back with me he'd lit up like a kid on Christmas. Always eager to be included. It didn't take my degree, or even my general interest in psychology for me to read between those lines.

Robin was a desperately lonely person.

It was etched into everything he did.

Breaking his back for scraps of attention, and yet surprised when others gave him exactly what he'd been working for. As though he had stopped allowing himself to hope. How many times had he been disappointed?

How many people had ignored him till he screamed himself hoarse?

Till he decided he'd stop asking altogether.

It was dark aside from the light above the stove. Outside the front windows, Main Street was a ghost town of flickering fairy lights. Already the shops had begun decorating for Christmas. The hardware store had been the first, but the rest were quick to follow.

As I made my way down the hallway toward the living room, I wasn't sure what I was about to walk into. Half of me wanted to forgo dinner and conversation altogether. That half wanted to push Robin to the couch, to climb atop him, to kiss him till he was breathless and warm and his chilled cheeks were red for an entirely new reason.

The other half of me understood that things were more complicated than that.

The more I got to know Robin the more I wanted to care for him.

And if I kissed him—if I took what I wanted so freely—without having built trust first, I might shatter what little of his confidence there was left. Plus…part of me was terrified that if I pushed too hard, too soon he'd run.

I didn't need to worry, apparently.

Because when I took that last step out of the hallway Robin wasn't waiting, eager as a puppy on the couch for me like I'd hoped. Yes, he was on the couch. But there was nothing bright-eyed and bushy-tailed about him. He'd tipped over, his face squished against the cushions, body contorted in a way that made me cringe.

My back would have ached for weeks after performing a stunt like that.

Robin's white-blond hair was a mess around his face, his hands tucked tight against his chest like he had tried to make himself as small as possible. Like he was scared of taking up too much space. And most devastating of all…my coat—my still-chilly coat—was curled beneath his cheek, his sweet little face pressed tightly into it like he was seeking comfort from it.

Like something about me made him feel *safe*.

My knees became weak, and for a moment I had to lean against the wall so they wouldn't buckle. Because if there was one thing that had just become obvious to me it was the fact that Robin was my kryptonite.

Sleepily, with a muffled groan, Robin cracked one eye open, like he'd sensed my presence. "Were you scared?" he asked, his voice hoarse.

"Was I…" It took me a moment to remember the fact he'd made it his mission to frighten me. That day at the airport felt like it'd occurred years ago, not a few short days.

"At the haunted house?" Robin clarified.

"No, sweetheart," I countered, voice low and soft.

"Bah humbug," Robin sighed. And then, after *that* particularly adorable grumble, he fell right back to sleep again.

eleven

ROBIN

I WOKE UP WHEN A beam of sunlight poked me vindictively in the eye. With a quiet groan, I batted it away in the hopes of getting it to stop shining so fucking brightly.

"Is he dead?" a little voice asked.

"He just moved," another one replied.

I felt pretty dead, but I *was* moving, so I could only assume they were right. When I squinted my eyes open Rosie and Jane were standing creepily by my head, their big golden eyes wide. They were dressed in frankly the most adorable pajamas I'd ever seen. Looked like little Victorian dolls, all ruffly and sweet. Kinda like the twins from *The Shining*.

"Papa's making breakfast," Rosie explained.

I nodded, even though my brain was not online yet.

Coffee. I needed coffee.

"Papa's making breakfast," I agreed stupidly so that they'd stop staring at me like they wanted to poke me with a stick.

"Yes," Rosie nodded emphatically. "With chips."

"Chips?" I squinted, trying to figure out what the hell that meant. Potato chips? Tortilla chips?

Also where the hell was I—

This was *not* the living room.

I wasn't an idiot. And sure, I hadn't meant to fall asleep—even though that was honestly the best thing that could've ever happened to me—but I did, somehow, remember that I'd come to Ben's house.

I'd come to Ben's house and I…

Oh.

We were supposed to have a drink. Dinner? Dr-inner.

Dammit.

How had I ended up here? In a…I glanced around through gritty eyes…bedroom.

A bedroom. With pale blue walls, and little to no decor, a watch on the nightstand that looked very familiar and also expensive. There was a lamp beside it that was still switched on, despite the morning sun rays, and a whole stack of well-worn books.

Ben's room.

This was Ben's room.

How the hell had I ended up in Ben's room?

Panicked, I tried to sit up, but my body didn't want to. It wanted to sink back into the blankets and pillows and soak up Ben's scent now that I knew that was what the delicious smell was. Ahhhh, clean laundry. It smelled so lovely. Not like the mothballs at the inn, or the stench of man pits from the tour bus I had grown accustomed to occupying for great spans of time.

"Chips," I repeated dumbly. "Detergent." Damn. Probably some, "fabric softener."

"Did we break him?" Jane asked, her voice wavering.

"You can't *break* a person," Rosie countered like she was an idiot. "Can you?"

"Does he not like chips?" Jane asked her, sounding distressed.

They were so smart. So fucking smart. Knew way more than four-year-olds should know. I could only assume it was because their dad was a genius. And also…patient enough to teach them.

"Girls," Ben's voice rumbled from the doorway, silencing their chatter. "I told you to let Robin sleep." They made sounds in protest but those quickly died. Ben was probably making a sexy face. I wanted to *see* his sexy face. But…pillow and comfy…and oh my god, I hadn't slept this well in…forever.

Had he slept in here too?

Somehow I doubted it.

Where had he slept?

"He was awake when we came in!" Rosie lied.

"No, he wasn't," Jane huffed in reply, sounding mollified. Rosie gasped in outrage like Jane had just sold her out to the cartel.

"It's time to get dressed," Ben's voice quaked with laughter. "Grandma will be here in half an hour to pick you up for play practice. I expect you both to be ready in time for breakfast." How *bossy* of him. God, he was so hot. "Do you need help?" His voice softened, and the little girls scrambled away, their little feet thumping with a chorus of "no's!"

Bet he's making an even sexier face now.

Bet he's got his eyebrow twitching.

I should look—

I should…

Sleep.

Yes.

Sleep.

Sleep was good.

If I'd been less exhausted I might've noticed that a third, heavier set of steps didn't sound for a solid minute after the girls had left. That Ben was watching over me from the doorway, protective and sweet, and everything I'd never let myself dream I could have.

A little while later the front door opened and shut. I could hear its echo down the hallway, as well as quiet murmured voices. "Come along, angels," Ben said gently as he herded his kids down the hall. "Grandma's here."

"Are those Robin Johnson's shoes at the door?" Beatrice Montgomery's voice was high and strained with surprise.

"Shhhh, I'll explain later," Ben urged.

I caught a few more snippets of conversation but nothing that made any sense. And by the time the front door shut I was dead to the world once again.

This time when I woke, it was because I smelled something heavenly.

Roasted coffee beans, thick and delicious. Buttery somethings—and was that…oh god. Yes. Bacon.

Rising like a re-animated corpse, I groggily thudded to the chilly wood floor. My shoes were off, which wasn't surprising. I'd taken them off when I'd come inside last night, not wanting to be the kind of asshole who trekked mud into someone else's house.

Despite having toddlers, Ben's apartment was incredibly clean, and I didn't want to…you know, ruin it?

What was surprising, however, were the socks I was wearing. Because they weren't my socks. And they were unlike any socks I'd ever seen. Fuzzy and furry, thick as hell, the things went all the way up to my knees. I worried I'd slip, but when I took another step with a grimace, I realized the bottoms of the damn things had sticky pads.

Maybe that wasn't the right name for them?

But that's certainly what they felt like.

They were clearly idiot proof.

When I glanced down, my eyebrows shot up. My jacket was gone—that, I'd definitely not taken off—and in its place was another one of Ben's giant-ass hoodies. It had some sort of logo on it, looked like it was for college or something. When I pulled the hem up to my nose to sniff at it, more of Ben's delicious scent filled my lungs.

Damn.

Had Ben dressed me?

That was the only logical conclusion.

Groaning softly, I wandered out into the hallway, fabric still covering half my face.

I figured I'd tug it down before he saw me—but didn't want to give it up so soon.

Only that didn't end up working out because Ben was already standing at the other end of the hallway when I entered. And he got an eyeful of me molesting his hoodie.

"Good morning," he said, eyes dancing. His eyebrow twitched, and my face went bright red.

"Nose was cold," I lied, the hoodie still covering my face. Like a naughty kid, I yanked it down—only that sucked too because now my nose really *was* cold. And also my blush was even more obvious.

Ben's eyebrow twitched again, almost like he was waiting for something.

It took me a second, but I got it. Grinning, because this felt really domestic and kinda amazing, I shrugged a shoulder. "Morning, Bennifer." It was hard to look him in the eye, so I didn't. Instead, I made eye contact with his shoulder—so broad—and the expensive-looking sweater that adorned it.

"How did you sleep?" Ben asked, voice even warmer. He did not acknowledge his new nickname.

"Um," I licked my lips, my piercing slick against my tongue. "Good."

"I'm glad."

I forced myself to move, because I didn't want to act like a total weirdo—even though I just had. "Sorry for, you know…invading your fortress or whatever." Coffee. Damn. I really wanted that coffee. But I didn't want to impose.

Mom had taught me better manners than this.

I was from the South.

Being polite was bred into me.

"I didn't mind," Ben's voice crackled, bright as one of the Christmas fireplaces I used to watch in movies growing up. "I *don't* mind," he amended, lower this time.

"I'll be right outta your hair," I shrugged a shoulder. "Soon as I get your very warm…sock things off? And your hoodie."

"Keep them."

Right, okay. That was nice. But I couldn't help but feel disappointed that Ben hadn't asked me to stay. He must've seen me wilt because before I could speak again, warm hands were latching on to my shoulders and steering me toward what looked like a bathroom.

"Shower," Ben commanded. Only it was hard to pay attention to anything but his big-ass hands and how bossy they were—and how they were so fucking huge and strong and…fuck. My dick was perking up.

My dick was…

No way.

No way!

Elated, I glanced down at my crotch to confirm.

And yes. Yep. My dick was definitely at least somewhat hard.

"Shower," I agreed, because there was no way I was wasting this opportunity, even if I was at Ben's house. Especially because I was at Ben's house.

"I'll leave fresh warm clothes for you to change into."

"Warm clothes," I echoed again, shivering as Ben guided me toward the frankly fancy-ass shower he had. The bathroom was nice. As nice as his bedroom. The tile looked custom, and everything was homey and clean. It was one of those shower-bath combos. Probably for the kiddos. And a tub full of toys sat neatly in the corner as Ben leaned over me to turn the faucet on.

"I've got coffee and chocolate chip pancakes in the kitchen for when you're finished."

"Coffee and kitchens, yep," I bobbed my head. "Love this plan. Ten out of ten."

Ben rumbled out a laugh. I could literally feel it because his chest was brushing my back. "You are so fucking cute when you're sleepy."

He obviously hadn't meant to say the words because he stiffened for a second. I did too—because how could I not? It was like we were in tune. When Ben relaxed, so did I. Hot water blasted on, a few droplets spattering the both of us as he held very still behind me.

"You're *always* cute," I countered because it was true, and also I wanted to level the playing field a bit. Didn't want the poor guy to flounder.

Besides…he apparently thought I was cute.

And that was…yeah.

Damn.

Even my cheeks felt hot.

"Cute is not a word I often hear to describe me," Ben laughed, rising back to his full impressive height. His chest wasn't touching my back anymore, but I could feel how close he was. Feel the way his breath ruffled my hair.

"Bet you get sexy a lot," I blurted like an idiot. "Hot." That was worse somehow. "Gorgeous?"

"Says the man with eyes like sea glass and hair like snow."

"I see you, writer man," I joked. "You and your…*metaphors*."

"Simile," Ben corrected.

"Gesundheit."

"Oh my god." Ben laughed, this delighted chuckle that lit up the room. More water droplets hit my cheeks, and I had to fight not to twist around so I could see his face. Somehow that felt more intimate though, and I was having a hard time processing all of this already.

Ben's proximity most certainly did not make my dick go down, that was for sure.

"Take your time," Ben commanded, finally stepping out of my space. "You can grab a toothbrush from the basket beneath the counter."

"Thanks," I shivered, staring resolutely at the faucet.

"Use anything that's in there," Ben added, because he was psychic and somehow had known I was planning on using as little of anything I could—so as not to be a bother.

With his permission it was easier to relax.

His absence helped too as he retreated from the room and shut the door with a quiet click. Not thinking it through, I yanked his hoodie and my shirt over my head with one swift movement. Working on my pants next, despite his urging to take my time, I had no intention of dilly-dallying.

I'd get in, jerk off, and get out quicker than you could blink.

There were coffee and pancakes waiting for me.

With chips.

Chocolate ones.

I had my zipper undone, my naked upper body twisted toward the door when it slid open again. I froze, rigid, the root of my cock probably fucking visible—because I preferred going commando most days.

Ben stared at me from the doorway, his toffee-colored eyes wide as he took me in. A splotchy, ugly blush spread across his face as his gaze traveled across my bare shoulders and the tattoos there. His attention caught on my nipples—on the rings, probably—and he *groaned*.

"Did you forget something?" I asked because my mouth was faster than my brain.

"Clothes," Ben replied immediately, his eyes somewhere around my belly button and the crows that framed my hip bones. He licked his lips, voice hoarse. "I told you I'd bring you clothes."

"Oh." He had. He totally had. I'd forgotten. Oh shit. And then, because the face he was making made me want to shove him into the doorframe and beg him to touch my dick, I spoke, "What about now?"

Idiot, idiot, idiot.

"Hmm?" Ben's eyes were definitely on my hands now. On my zipper, and the way my happy trail crept upward.

"Are you scared now?"

Ben chuckled, eyes pinching shut as he shook his head. "Take the clothes, Robin," he said gently, making no move to step all the way into the bathroom. "Please."

I took the clothes.

They were warm, clean, and smelled like him, and I couldn't help the way I clutched them close like they were precious, because they were. When Ben opened his eyes again, his pupils had blown out, wide and dark.

"I'll see you at breakfast."

"Right," I agreed, because he totally would. After I jerked off in his shower and tried not to die a slow painful death of embarrassment. "Yep."

My pulse was thrumming.

Ben softened, like he could read how uncomfortable I was all over my face. "You're gorgeous," he told me like it was a fact. "You have to know that."

"I do?"

"Yes," Ben's eyes danced. "Now do as you're told."

And with that, he left me to my own devices.

I locked the door with shaky hands, put the new clothes down, and twisted back toward the shower. Not before making a detour to glance at the mirror though.

It wasn't that I was…necessarily insecure. I mean, I was. In a lot of ways. I knew I wasn't a super palatable person? I spoke too fast and too brashly. I didn't think things through. I ran. I always ran when things got hard.

But physically I knew I was…you know. Pretty okay? Symmetrical. Pleasing enough I'd never had trouble getting people to want to fuck me, or be fucked by me.

At least, I used to think that.

Until the sleepless nights caught up to me, and I kept forgetting to eat—and my ribs became Ribs with a capital R, and I stopped wanting to be naked in front of anyone at all, even myself.

Ben thought I was gorgeous though.

And for a second, I tried to see what he saw.

To see past the peppered scars I'd gotten from random accidents on set. To see past my protruding ribs. To see past the concave of my stomach, and the moles and freckles that my label always edited away.

I smoothed a hand over my chest and the nipple piercings I'd gotten when I was nineteen and sucked in a breath.

I looked tired.

I always did.

But I did look better than I had when I'd come to Belleville a week and a half ago. I'd had more sleep here than I had back home in months. Maybe my therapist was right? That getting away from the stress would help.

Maybe I hadn't been lying when I'd said it was?

Either way.

The permanent bruises beneath my eyes were still there, but the hollows were less…saggy? And I looked…damn. Despite my nerves, I looked pretty happy.

And that was as unfamiliar as my dick deciding it wanted to play.

Which was to say, very unfamiliar.

That had been one of the first things that'd stopped "working". My doctor said it was normal in cases like mine. That the libido would suffer. It was more than a little relieving to know that it maybe wasn't so permanent.

I brushed my teeth three times because I was terrified of my breath stinking around Ben. And when I showered, I jerked off quickly—even though I really did want to drag it out. Ben had said to use whatever I wanted, so I did. I soaped up my hair with his shampoo—sandalwood, yum. I scrubbed myself with his body scrub. Used his conditioner to get my dick nice and slippery, to fuck my fist till I sobbed into my shoulder and spilled down the drain.

Yeah, it felt weird to do that in a shower where there was a bucket of toys in the corner.

But beggars couldn't be choosers.

And I didn't know when the next time I'd get an opportunity like this would be.

When I was dressed and drowning in Ben's clothing, I felt quite a bit better. Water droplets slipped down the back of my neck from my wet hair as I made my way toward the kitchen and the scent of Heaven.

Ben was sitting at the table with his own plate in front of him. Beside him was an empty chair, and a second plate piled high—even higher than his own. Bacon, chocolate chip pancakes (not potato chips), and a giant mug with coffee called my name. A siren's song.

It was like he'd timed everything perfectly so that it would be ready for when the shower shut off.

"Looks delicious," I said eagerly, taking my seat with a happy thump. I wavered after a second thought, glancing at Ben to make sure I hadn't been too loud. "Sorry." I didn't want to disturb his calm.

"Sorry for what?" Ben arched an eyebrow. "You complimented my food. You haven't done anything wrong."

"I sat down loud."

"*You sat down loud,*" Ben echoed, like the words were in another language. He set his own coffee mug down, twisting to look at me with an expression I could only describe as fond. "Sweetheart, there's nothing wrong with the way you sat down."

"But the chair screeched."

"Chairs do that sometimes."

I was just trying to get over the fact that Ben had called me sweetheart and gorgeous all in one day.

"Mom didn't like loud noises like that," I tried to explain—because I was dumb, and my mouth wouldn't stop running. "One time Miles sat down too heavy and oh my god! You wouldn't believe the tongue-lashing he got later. It was at a party? She'd throw these parties. With her friends. Well…they weren't really her friends? More like acquaintances that all pretended to be friends because their families had money. You know? Fake friends. Like in high school."

Ben, to his credit, looked fascinated.

"Anyway. She didn't like that. Said it was impolite." I bobbed my head, cheeks hot. Then, because I'd been talking too long, I latched on to my coffee to shut myself up. Before I could bring it to my lips, however, Ben reached out and with one sexy-ass finger, pushed the rim gently till I set it down.

"It's still too hot," he admonished. "Wait a minute so you don't burn your mouth."

"I like a little pain," I said, because again—my mouth hated me.

The grandfather clock ticked and Ben's eyes fluttered shut for a moment before opening again, something indecipherable flickering deep inside them.

"Good to know." Ben cleared his throat and reached across the table. "Cream? Sugar?" Ben's hand flexed, knuckles turning white as he grabbed the creamer.

"Yes please."

He flashed me a little smile as he fixed my coffee up for me. "I didn't know how you liked it."

"I like it ninety percent sugar," I told him. "The sweeter the better."

"Also good to know."

Ben let me drink only after he'd decided it wasn't going to burn me. Which I appreciated, but also hated, because it meant my mouth kept running off without something to occupy it. I ended up shoveling pancakes in my mouth—then half-orgasming because holy shit these were good—just to shut myself up.

By the time my plate had been cleaned and my coffee was empty, I was a sleepy, happy pile of Ben's clean laundry. Leaning back in my chair, I watched Ben through pleased slits as he moved to rise from his chair. He made a face. A new face. A face he hadn't made before, and I frowned.

"You okay?"

"Fine," Ben rose to his full height with a hum and reached out for the dishes. But I beat him to it, slapping his hands away as I piled everything high and waddled my way toward the sink, careful not to drop anything.

"You cooked, I'll clean."

Ben was right behind me. "That's not necessary."

"Sure it's not," I agreed. "But it's happening anyway."

Ben laughed. He leaned against the counter to watch me for a minute. "You really don't have to do that. You're a guest."

"A guest that stole your bed and spent the night without being invited?" I arched an eyebrow. "A guest that is currently wearing your clothing, again stolen, and used half your bottle of conditioner to—" Oh no.

Oh no.

Ben's eyebrows shot up when my rambling screeched to a halt. "Used half my bottle of conditioner to *what*, Robin?" His voice was a quiet, amused rumble. There was heat in his eyes again, low and flickering.

My mouth clicked shut, further implicating myself.

"What did you do with it, Robin?"

"Ah hahahaha!" I twisted away from him. "Did I say something about conditioner? Because I didn't mean to." This was not going well. "I've never seen a bottle of conditioner in my life."

God, how embarrassing.

Especially when it'd been his face I was picturing as I stroked myself off. That eyebrow twitch. He was probably bossy in bed too, wasn't he? Super bossy. I licked my lips, staring at the soapy dishes blindly. "I mean—"

"I'm going to get ready for work," Ben said, cutting me some slack because he was an angel.

"Good plan," I agreed, splashing around in the water for something to do. My ears burned. My cheeks burned. My *everything* burned. That was happening to me a lot lately.

"Try not to use the dish soap the same way you used my conditioner," Ben teased. And then he was gone—leaving me to turn into a soapy, wrinkly-fingered puddle of embarrassment all on my own.

"He said *what?*" Miles choked on his slice of pizza.

"He said, 'don't use the dish soap like you—'" I repeated only for Miles to start coughing so loud he interrupted me.

"No, no, I got *that* part. I was just…surprised." Miles managed to not die somehow, though his face was red as he reached out for a glass of water. Bubs had left the dinner table and was upstairs playing with Jeremy. Who was *apparently* his, and I quote, "best friend in the whole world." Miles said the kid practically lived at their house nowadays.

Miles and I were in the kitchen. The ceramic cow on the table mocked me as I fiddled with my dinner and the clock above the table ticked.

"I had no idea Ben was such a flirt," Miles added, sounding just as surprised as he'd said he was.

"Well, I would hope not, considering the fact that you're married to his brother," I laughed, though my cheeks felt hot.

Today was a good day.

A *really* good day.

After eating breakfast with Ben he'd insisted I hang out with him before his first appointments of the day arrived. I'd sat on his couch and creepy-stalk-watched him while he did paperwork. And when his coffee had run low I'd offered to go get him more from the bakery across the street.

There was a cute kid in his early twenties manning the counter who looked vaguely familiar. He'd given me Ben's coffee for free—and one for me and the receptionist, Lynda, and a whole container of chocolate croissants.

Chocolate croissants that Ben later insisted I take to Miles and Bubba, as he said he had more than enough sweets at home.

Best of all though was the fact that when I'd delivered said coffee to Ben—after what I could only assume was a rough appointment with an old man wearing flannel—he'd pulled me into a side hug, ruffled my hair with his big-ass hand, and murmured right against my ear, slow and sweet, "You're such a *good boy,* Robin. Thank you."

Suffice to say I'd been floating on *that* particular cloud all day.

Despite the fact that he'd had appointments in the other room, Ben had never shooed me back to the B&B and its creepy floral sheets. And I spent the rest of the day cat-napping on his couch and re-reading his books on my phone when he had appointments so that I'd have new, fresh ideas to bug him about every time he returned.

Whenever he'd push the door open I'd grin from whatever new position I'd taken on the couch and wave. And one memorable occasion, I even hid beneath his desk so I could pop out and say, "Boo!"

It was the best day ever.

And the croissants made it even better! Miles had loved them. Bubba too. Even Trent had found them delightful. He'd snuck two with him as he'd run off to check on something at the farm. Apparently, he'd be vending at the Christmas market and he wanted to make sure the thing would go off without a hitch.

"You like him," Miles observed, eyes dancing.

I shrugged a shoulder, "I like a lot of things." I held up my pizza slice. "Like this pizza, for example. I like this pizza. In fact, I might even *love* this pizza."

"Flatterer," Miles laughed, eyes crinkling at the corners. He'd made the pizza, so he should feel flattered. It was good-ass pizza. Cheesy with fluffy dough and all the toppings you could imagine.

And then, because I was a glutton for punishment, I added, "I should've said something snappy in reply, right? Something clever. Like…" I played it cool like I hadn't been replaying that same interaction in my head over and over all day. "Fuck." The thought left me. I'd had a *perfect* comeback all planned out earlier. "Dammit. I forgot."

Miles snorted, reaching over to top off my glass of wine. He didn't drink, but I did—and he'd made sure to have my favorite kind stocked for my visit. I liked dessert wine. The sweeter the better, and this particular brand was my favorite because it had a skull on it and tasted just like grape juice.

"Why don't you ask him out?" Miles asked, because he was a nosy motherfucker.

"Because he's a serious kinda guy, dude." I glared at him, taking a sip of my overfilled wine, careful not to spill because I was still proudly wearing Ben's hoodie. "He's got kids. He's got a life here. And *my* life is back in L.A."

"You're here for Christmas," Miles wagged his eyebrows.

His eyes said, *anything can happen.*

"I'm here *until* Christmas," I corrected, nipping that in the bud immediately. "Which is what…?" I blew out a breath, my bangs puffing up. "A *month* away?"

"More than a month."

"Close enough."

"A lot you can do in a month."

"And break my own heart? No thank you." I took a longer sip, my own thoughts spinning. "Look…it's not like I haven't thought about it. I obviously have. A lot. I mean…Ben is *Ben*. Have you seen his smile? It's like…angelic or some shit. And the hands. Man. He's got big-ass hands. If you know what I mean." I couldn't help but leer.

"Right," Miles agreed, looking more amused than he should.

"But he's *related* to you—"

"No, he ain't," Miles immediately deadpanned.

"*Kinda*," I soldiered onward ignoring him and his sass. "And I'm not gonna fuck up what you've built here. You're happy. He's happy. I'm here temporarily. I'm not gonna be the Mento in your Coke bottle."

"That's a weird metaphor," Miles snorted again, amused, though his eyes now carried a sadness to them, amusement dampened.

"Simile," I corrected.

He laughed again, "Pretty sure it'd have to have the word "like" to be a simile."

I frowned because that felt correct.

I wrote music for a living, so I was no stranger to poetry. Music *was* poetry. Just with vibrations and a whole lot of extra soul. It could make you feel things with no rhymes and no words at all. It'd been a long time since I wrote something that felt like that, raw and real and honest.

Back in the early days, that'd been all I'd written.

I'd been young and bitter then.

Now what I desired to create had changed, less angry—less brittle. The music in my heart was silky and sweet. Love songs and longing. My label didn't want it. In fact, they'd half convinced me the world didn't want it either.

Robin "Trashmouth" Johnson was supposed to be all bark and bite.

There was no room for lace and loneliness. No room for regret and ache and love. No room for Christmas songs. No space for me to dream about coming home. Still though, a love song played silently along my fingertips every time I tapped against my leg. Because while they'd convinced me it wouldn't happen, my heart was stubborn, and it didn't want to listen.

I shrugged again.

"You know there's such a thing as a long-distance relationship, right?" Miles teased, taking another bite of his pizza.

"All of my relationships have been long distance," I countered. Miles stared at me, confused. "You know." I blinked. "Because I'm basically five feet tall."

"Jesus *Christ*," Miles cackled, choking again. When he was somewhat controlled a few minutes later, he softened all over again. His sweater was wrinkled. Cow print, like always. There was a hickey on his neck—good for him—and he looked happier than I'd ever seen him.

"You fit in here," I told him because it was true. "In your fancy lil kitchen. In this town. With these people who care about you. With your picket fence and your husband who adores you."

Miles smiled, lips twitching up. "You do too," he said, laying a large, warm hand across where mine rested on the dining table.

"You know I don't." My voice broke and I *hated* that it did. I was Miles's big brother. It'd always been my job to be strong, but lately I wasn't sure I could do it anymore. Like my battery had simply run out.

"You wanna know what I think?" Miles asked.

"No, but I think you're about to tell me anyway."

"I think…" Miles didn't remove his hand, and it burned. "I think that you're scared to be in love. That you're ready to run the second anyone gives you a reason to, whether it's a good reason or not."

"Scared?" I huffed, eyes rolling. "I'm not *scared*."

"I think you are." His voice remained the same smooth Southern drawl that felt like home, and I hated that the sound of it alone was enough to make my eyes burn. "I know because I was scared too. Hell, sometimes I still am."

I remembered the text he'd sent me. The long one from over a year ago. The text that had come through just when I'd needed it. That had reminded me that there was a place for me here, even if it was temporary, that somewhere out there I had a home—even if it was only borrowed.

"We had a fucked up childhood," Miles continued, voice quiet, like if he spoke too loud he was worried he'd scare me off. "I don't think I really realized that till I moved here and saw how many people *didn't*. Like Trent, for example—I mean—his mama and dad *loved* each other." His eyes were wide like that was a goddamn miracle.

I nodded, because it was.

"They were *good* to their kids," Miles added. "Left 'em wanting for nothing."

"Right." I didn't get the point of this. But it did give me some fun insight into Ben's childhood and what that might've been like.

When *I* thought of my childhood all I felt was untethered. So many memories, bitter sweet.

I thought of hands shaking as I picked Miles up from school. I thought of staying up late pricking my fingers till they bled while I sewed his Halloween costumes. I thought of begging for scraps of attention with my heart on my sleeve and tears in my eyes—and being sent away, like feeling the way I did was shameful.

I thought of pretty smiles and expectations.

A reputation to uphold.

"I think because of our mom, sometimes it's hard for both of us to realize that love, *real* love, has no stipulations." Miles sucked in a breath and his eyes burned holes into mine. "It doesn't come with strings attached. And it follows you, no matter how far you run. It's messy and sweet, and if you let it, it fills in all your cracks and crevices."

I had dozens of those, so many I wasn't sure even a love like he said existed could fill them.

My heart ached for Miles. It ached for me too. Because while I hated to admit it, there were years of heartbreak I still hadn't parsed my way through. Things I hadn't let myself process or even really feel *angry* about, even though I knew the second I did it might help.

I'd simply been too busy holding up the fort to acknowledge what I'd been through.

Miles didn't know the half of it.

He didn't know about my dad and the way he'd tricked me.

Didn't know about what he'd done.

Didn't know about the nights I'd spent on the streets in L.A. before I'd made it, praying to the stars that I could make it big enough my baby brother and his kid would never want for anything.

"I don't love Ben Montgomery," I told him, because that was what he was hinting at.

"No," Miles agreed. "But you could. If you weren't scared of him. If you weren't ready to bolt the second he said the wrong thing."

"I'm not *scared* of him either," I glared at him, my pizza growing cold and my wine mocking me. I kinda wanted to chug it, because a buzz might make this conversation go by easier. We didn't normally get all deep like this. But apparently it was just that kinda night. I didn't acknowledge his words about running, because it was too close to hitting the nail on the head. "He's the least scary person ever. Man's a giant teddy bear."

Miles stared at me for a beat, processing my words. A shit-eating grin split across his face. "A teddy bear?" He blinked. "You think *Ben* Montgomery is a *teddy bear?* Serious, grumpy, *cold* Ben."

My cheeks went hot all over again. "Fuck off." I flipped him off and his grin softened. "He's none of those things." Okay, so maybe he was *some* of those things.

"Maybe not to you," Miles waggled his eyebrows, then sobered. "When you're tired of running, this is a pretty good place to stop."

"You have croissants," I nodded toward the now-empty box on the counter.

"We do," Miles agreed, and then his tone lightened. "And for the record," Miles added. "Belleville's big enough for the both of us." It was almost like he'd read my mind. The way I'd wondered if there was room for two damaged Johnsons, just a few short days ago. Serious moment now over, Miles's eyes danced again. "Even considering all our baggage."

"Amen," I raised my wine glass in a salute and chugged.

twelve

BEN

THE REST OF THE WEEK passed in a blur. Some days Robin would stop by and bring me coffee at work but he never lingered. I could see in his eyes that there was distance there. Distance that hadn't been there before.

I wasn't sure how to cross that distance.

Wasn't sure I should, all things considered.

Sunday rolled around faster than expected. With the girl's play practice behind us, most of my paperwork done, and at least a dozen well-meaning but nosy comments about my new "boyfriend" I was ready for a break.

And to see Robin again.

When the twins and I arrived at the park—after we spent our morning watching the *Cask of Amontillado* episode of LilPoe fifty times in a row again—Robin was already there.

Part of me worried he wouldn't be, and I was glad to be wrong.

Once again, he was wearing all black. His feet were adorned in the same combat boots he always favored—*maybe because they gave him a few extra inches of height on top of a haunting aesthetic?* Beneath his long, thin jacket he did, however, have my hoodie on.

So *that* was at least an improvement.

And proved that he was as obedient as I'd hoped he'd be, considering the fact that I was the one who had told him to wear it.

Seeing Robin dressed in my clothing while out and about made something buzz warm and bright in my chest. And a grin spread across my lips before I could stop it. Jane and Rosie gave me a funny look, their little hands clutched in mine as we approached.

"So," Robin said by way of greeting. And then he paused, eyes widening. "I mean," he corrected himself, "Good morning, Ben-hilda and spawn."

I snorted, and the girls giggled along even though there was no way they got the joke. They simply liked to be included. And Robin was good at that. He made sure to give them both plenty of eye contact, and though he often addressed them, he never spoke to them like they were incapable of understanding.

Perhaps that was why they seemed to like him, even though they rarely took a liking to other people outside of their immediate family.

"Good morning, Robin," I replied, once again surprised by how low and warm my voice was. I couldn't help it when I was around him. He brought something out in me. Something protective and tender.

When he looked at me my insides lit up.

"I'm ready to be trained, O Captain, my Captain." Robin saluted, his heels knocking together. "Your loyal cadet."

I was pretty sure he had no idea what he was saying, but I was charmed anyway.

"Then let's get started," I replied, releasing the girls and pulling my satchel off my shoulder. Inside I had all the supplies we'd need. Props for the relay race, the most notable being a rope to tie our legs together, and the spoon and egg—a fake one this time—for the first portion of the race.

Robin, to his credit, was silent as I explained everything to him. Though that didn't mean he wasn't vibrating with energy as he stared between me and the girls, green eyes alight. He simply seemed excited to be invited. And it was that naive, almost childlike joy that made me realize, end date or not, there was no way I'd be holding back with him anymore.

The distance this week had hurt more than it should.

And I wanted every part of him I could get, for as long as I could have it.

If he noticed a change in me he didn't say anything.

Not when I brushed my fingers along the back of his neck when pulling the hat I'd brought him down over his ears. Not when I'd laced our legs together to practice the three-legged race, and spent extra time skimming my fingers across his calf. Not even when we fell to the ground in a giant, sunny patch when we tripped, his warm body atop mine, and the icy fallen leaves crunching at my back.

I was lucky I'd survived that fall, if I'm being honest.

Like God was watching out for me.

After going out for cocoa I invited Robin back to our home for dinner where we spent half an hour trading barbs and jokes in between the babbles of the girls whispering to each other, then us. He kept me company while I chopped, and after we'd eaten our fill of the pot pie we'd painstakingly prepared together—special thanks to Baxter and the dough he'd left me earlier—I'd left him alone on the couch for the second time since we'd met to get the girls ready for bed.

Robin didn't fall asleep this time.

He was wide awake when I returned, staring up at me with those green, green eyes, his hands clenched into fists over the jagged holes in his jeans. He'd ditched his jacket and shoes, his socked feet tucked up beneath him, my hoodie drowning him nearly to his knees.

"Spend the night," I said because it felt only natural.

Nervous, butterflies erupted in my belly.

Robin's eyes widened. His mouth dropped open for only a moment, betraying his surprise, before it shut with a gentle click. "I can take the couch." He didn't argue with me, which I appreciated.

"You'll take the bed," I told him immediately.

The stink face he gave me was truly legendary. "If you think I didn't notice you favoring your back after last time, you're dead wrong, methanpheta-ben."

Jesus *Christ*. I snorted out a laugh that quickly died when the rest of his words processed. "We'll share then," I offered, hoping my eagerness wasn't as obvious as it felt.

I'd written a scene like this in a book once.

It was a common trope in a lot of romances.

The only thing that would've made it better was if another snow storm had hit, fat white flakes blanketing the streets outside, and trapping Robin in my home where he belonged.

"I'm a blanket hog," Robin warned, obviously worrying about something he shouldn't be worrying about again.

"I'll survive."

"I might kick you."

"I have toddlers. I'm not afraid of a few accidental kicks."

"I snore," Robin countered.

"You don't," I replied, because he didn't.

A slow, happy grin spread across his lips. "There's nothing I can say that will make you change your mind?"

"No."

A beat passed.

"Okay." His voice was meek. Far meeker than it had ever been before.

"Do you want to spend the night with me?" I asked, because for a moment I'd seen him hesitate. "I can still take the couch." We weren't promising sex. Neither of us had even broached the subject, despite our flirtation-ship since the very start.

Not that I'd be opposed to it.

The walls were thick in my apartment, the girls were safely asleep. There was a lock on the door, and while I would never, ever, ever invite anyone else into my home for such a thing, Robin felt...well... He felt different.

He was my exception.

In most things.

I didn't make friends easily. I never had. Even back in high school when I'd been a die-hard eyeliner wearer and coated in buckles and black fabric of my own. I had friends because of how I looked, and not because I was particularly adept at making them.

I'd often wondered if I'd had a tendency to fall into cliques because of exactly that. A primal thing, searching for a pack by projecting where I'd like to fit because my words dried up and were easily misconstrued.

In a way, I admired Robin and his "trashmouth" as he'd put it.

He had so many words they spilled out freely. There was no hesitance, no doubt. I imagined if he let his walls down he'd have an easy time making friends. It was hard not to love him when he was so goddamn lovable.

Shaking away my thoughts, I crossed the last few steps between us and laid a hand on Robin's shoulder. "Would you like a drink first?" I asked, because while I was quite certain I did in fact want to share a bed with Robin tonight, a little liquid courage wasn't a bad idea for either of us.

We wouldn't be getting drunk.

That would be irresponsible.

But to share a glass of wine while curled up on the couch together sounded like the perfect way to end a lovely day.

"Yes please." Robin tipped his head back to watch as I moved past him. My fingers idly stroked through his hair on my way into the kitchen, the silken strands leaving a lingering sensation long after I'd released them.

If Robin was surprised when I returned to the couch with two half-full glasses of red wine in one hand, he didn't say it.

"Big hands," he observed, obviously impressed.

"A trick I learned I could do in college," I explained, sitting down and slinging an arm over the back of the couch. I beckoned him closer, watching him carefully for any signs of discomfort. The foot of distance between us closed as Robin crawled into the hollow I'd left for him.

He took his glass out of my hand with a happy sound, his sweet fuzzy head snuggled up against my shoulder. He was the perfect size to fit snug against my side, his socked toes brushing my ankle as he nursed his glass with both hands like he was holding a mug of cocoa, not a wine glass.

"Neat party trick," he agreed, voice echoing inside the glass. He took a long sip, made a face like he was expecting it to taste bad, then relaxed. "Oh." He was obviously surprised.

"You like your coffee sweet, I figured you'd like your wine sweet too," I replied by way of explanation.

"You figured right, big man." Robin took another sip, longer this time. He held himself very still, rigid against me. I didn't try to force him to relax. I figured this was like coaxing a wild animal close. Slow and steady was the way to go.

"So," Robin said, at the same time I took a sip from my own glass. I hummed in reply, biting back a grin when I felt him finally relax. His body grew pliant, the hard line of his broad shoulders, marshmallow soft. "How's your next book going?"

It was an out-of-pocket question, but I appreciated it all the same.

Not many knew who I was or what I wrote, and Robin and I had bonded the first time we'd met over our mutual appreciation for each other's art.

"My deadline is two weeks before Christmas," I said.

"But that's so soon!" Robin's eyes went wide. "How close are you?" He frowned. "Not that I know much about that stuff, but you have to be at least…kinda close, right?"

I made a sound to soothe him. "I've got a few days off after Thanksgiving. I'll finish then."

"You're evading the question." Robin's eyes narrowed at me, these grumpy little slits.

He was correct, I *was* evading the question.

Truth be told, I'd been spending all my free time with him lately. There hadn't been much time to write. I would figure it out though, I always did. And the last thing I wanted was to make him feel guilty. I'd had enough distance this week, thank you very much. "I'm on schedule," I told him, using the arm behind his back to gently tweak his ear. "Don't worry about me."

"Someone should," he snarked back, cheeks pinking up. I tugged his ear harder and he laughed.

"Is that your way of saying I'm incapable of taking care of myself?" I teased, thumb stroking along the fuzzy soft velvet of the shell of his ear. He'd taken his piercings out today aside from one at the top. I was careful not to tug for fear of hurting him.

"That's my way of calling you a lonely-ass loner," Robin replied.

That was something we had in common.

The loneliness.

He didn't really know me. He couldn't. We'd only just met. But his declaration was close enough to the truth that I didn't deny it. "I have a hard time with people," I explained instead of reacting. "My best friend lives in L.A. Aside from her, the only people I spend time and energy on are my family."

And you, I added, privately.

"I feel that." Robin nodded sagely. He bit his lip, his piercing clinking. "What about your kids' mom?" he asked, and then flinched like he'd done something particularly horrendous.

"The girls' mother is also my best friend that lives in L.A.," I replied, continuing to stroke his ear. I took a sip of wine to give my mouth something to do, even though I wanted to set the glass on the table and taste something far more tantalizing.

"Handy."

"Mhm," I agreed, watching Robin's mouth. It was a lovely mouth. Soft and pink. Expressive. I bet he kissed the way he did most things, voraciously and with little thought. Hunger curled hot, low in my belly. "We made a pact that if we both weren't married by the time I finished medical school we'd have kids together."

"Does she like kids?" Robin asked, curious.

"She does," I agreed. "Though she's always been more of an…eccentric aunt than a mother. The girls adore her, despite this."

"That's how I am with Bubba," Robin admitted. "Except I'm his uncle, not his aunt." His skin paled when he realized what he'd revealed, and he glanced at me through his lashes, a sad, sheepish expression on his face. I kept quiet, because I knew him well enough now to realize if I did he'd continue to speak. "He's my kid," Robin explained. "Biologically, I mean."

That did not surprise me.

Bubba looked exactly like him, down to the freckles and the swoop of both their button noses.

"Yeah?" I stroked Robin's ear again and he shuddered, lashes fluttering.

"I always wanted to be a dad," Robin blurted out, startling me. His eyes went wide. He wilted. "But…I mean…" The look he gave me was the saddest, sweetest thing I'd ever seen, like a puppy expecting to be kicked. "I wasn't ready? When Bubba was born. Didn't have any money. Didn't know what the fuck I was doing. I wanted to keep him but I just…I knew I'd just fuck him up. You know?"

Again, I stayed silent, though I made sure to maintain eye contact. To keep my gaze soft and sweet and indulgent, so he would know that I was listening.

I got the feeling he'd never shared this with anyone else before.

"I got no regrets. Miles is a better dad for Bubs than I ever could've been," Robin explained, voice quiet. "He came outta the womb like that,

I think. Some people do. You shoulda seen him the first time he saw Bubba. It was like he'd seen God or some shit." Robin's voice took on a fond tone. "He's always been emotionally mature for the most part— aside from when he was beatin' homophobic assholes' faces in." *Well, that had escalated quickly.* "Always gentle. Quiet. Patient. Good at listening. You know? The kinda dad a kid like Bubba needs."

Robin took a shaky breath. The wine had loosened his tongue, but he didn't seem to mind. He took another, longer sip, nearly emptying his glass, before he nuzzled against my shoulder. "I just wanted everyone to be happy. And honestly I was…scared."

"You did well," I told him because it was true, and I got the feeling he needed to hear it. He may not have been prepared to be a parent at that age but things had turned out the way they needed to. Miles was happy. It was obvious. And Bubba was probably the most well-adjusted kid I'd ever met.

"Thanks." Robin's smile grew more sure, more confident as he blossomed under the praise. "If there's one good thing I've done in my life, it was making Miles a dad." Robin finished his wine glass and removed himself from my body to set it down. Luckily, he returned right back to the crook of my arm the second it was settled on the coffee table. Only this time, he pulled his feet right up too. They curled between my legs, tucking under my thigh as he pretzeled into my side.

"Miles said you had good parents," Robin mumbled, muffled into my shirt. It was thin fabric, one of my favorite button-ups. I liked it because it was perfect to layer beneath sweaters when I went out. I could feel the hot puff of his breath on my pec, and my dick stirred as I slid my hand down his back in a slow, soothing manner.

"I did." I stroked again, embarrassed to find how much it turned me on that my hand took up so much space on his body. I could imagine tucking my fingers up inside him. The way he'd twitch and writhe, tiny legs sprawled wide while he fought to take me. "I do."

"We didn't," Robin's voice was still muffled. His toes wriggled beneath my thigh, and I bit my lip so I wouldn't groan. If he moved just a little up, he'd be wiggling right beneath my balls.

God, how long had it been since I'd been touched?

I forced aside thoughts of sex, and his charming little feet, trying to get my head back online.

"Miles said you never knew your father," I hummed, because he had. Or maybe…Trent had said that? It was hard to remember exactly who I'd learned the information from.

"*He* didn't," Robin corrected. "His dad fucked off to play pro football or something. We had different dads."

There was a lot packed into that little flippant statement. "But…you did?"

Robin froze. His wiggling ceased. Even the hot puff of his breath paused as he seemed to take a moment to process what he'd accidentally let slip.

When he relaxed again, I did too.

Up and down, back and forth, I stroked the long line of his back.

Robin took a slow, steady breath. "Fuck it."

I wasn't sure what he'd decided, but apparently it was important, because he wiggled his face so he could see me, his pointed chin digging into my pec. "My dad sucked."

I blinked, surprised.

"When I was…twenty, I think? I dunno. Twenty-one maybe. I got it in my head that I was gonna get Miles out." Robin's voice wavered. "My dad lived in a city north of where we did. I reached out to him to see if he'd help me apartment shop."

I had a feeling where this was going, but I didn't interrupt.

"I saved up for…fuck, I dunno. A year? Getting the first month, last month, the deposit, and yada yada. Enough for furniture and stuff. I worked myself to the fucking bone man. Because I thought—" Robin's voice was rough. "I thought I could surprise Miles? Figured we'd have a fresh start. It'd be easier to make music in a big city like that. He could go to college." He sucked in a breath. "I was gonna drive him up there one weekend, play it all cool, and then bring him inside our new apartment and be all, 'Surprise, motherfucker! Welcome home.'"

"I'm guessing that didn't happen," I murmured, my hand stilling on his back for just a moment before I began moving again.

"Nope." Robin shrugged a shoulder. "I knew…my dad was shit. Mama always said he was. But there was this time…when I was in high school that I'd *really* needed him, and he'd shown up when I called, and for hours…fucking *hours*…we'd sat at this diner downtown where Mama wouldn't see, and he helped me finish the project I was struggling with. I thought…*fuck*. I was such an idiot." Robin sucked in another breath. "I thought it'd be like that? That maybe Mama had lied about him or some shit, I dunno. He'd been so nice to me that one time. And Mama always had her own agenda…so I just…I gave him the benefit of the doubt." Robin's accent was thicker then. Probably the thickest I'd heard it, the warm croon of the South sneaking into the words.

"What happened?"

"I showed up to check the place out," Robin's voice cracked right in half. "We were supposed to move in a few weeks. I'd sent my dad all the money I had and he'd kept telling me and *telling* me that he'd get it all sorted, that it wouldn't matter if I checked the place out myself. Kept sayin' 'don't you trust me?' and all that shit. Sent me pictures of our place. Pictures I later figured out he'd gotten from a fucking magazine."

My heart hurt for him.

I couldn't imagine what that had been like.

"Thing was, I *didn't* trust him—even though I wanted to." Robin's voice was this quivery, wild thing as he stared up at me. "Call it instinct. But when I showed up a day early to double-check with my own fucking eyes and it turned out the building he'd told me we'd be living in was fucking full already, I wasn't even surprised." Robin's eyes never left mine. There was something raw and brittle twisting up inside them, like brambles and branches, covered in thorns.

His eyes said, *he hurt me.*

They said, *he lied.*

They said, *I'm scared everyone else will lie too.*

"He'd taken my money and was planning on running," Robin's voice was cold and dark. "So I went to his work, keyed his fucking car, and I just..." Robin trailed off.

"You just...?"

"*I dunno.*" Robin's fingers curled in my shirt, gently tugging. "I guess that's when I knew that people just...suck." Robin's words were dark and sad, but his actions betrayed him. He claimed not to trust people and yet, here he was, trusting me with his deepest, darkest secret.

Like he hadn't even realized that's what he'd done.

"Robin."

"He was my *dad.*" Robin's voice was shattered. "He was supposed to protect me."

"I know." I curled my hand around the back of his neck and squeezed. He glanced away, eyes lost. "He failed you."

"Maybe it's 'cause he knew I wasn't worth it." The words were muttered, quiet enough I don't think Robin meant for me to hear them. But I did. "A part of me has always been scared I'd end up just like him."

"*Robin.*" My heart thudded erratically as I waited for him to meet my gaze again. When he did, his eyes were hollow. "I may not have known you long, but I can tell you without a shred of doubt in my mind that if there is anyone on God's green earth that deserved better, it's you. You're nothing like your father."

"You *would* say that," Robin countered, cracking a little smile. "Because you're a teddy bear."

A teddy bear?

I squinted at him but didn't allow him to distract me, even though he made that difficult. "You are so incredibly sweet," I said softly— always soft because I didn't think anyone else had treated Robin gently. "You're loyal. You're thoughtful. You're talented." He flinched after each compliment like they were barbs.

Sweet, sweet baby.

How long had it been since someone was gentle with him?

Since someone loved him the way he so desperately needed?

"You're a ray of sunshine," I added, because it was true. "What your father did was not only an absolutely fucking horrible thing to do to a person, but also a literal crime. You didn't deserve that. He should've taken care of you, not stolen from you."

"I can take care of myself."

"You can," I agreed, because he could. I'd never met a more self-sufficient person. You didn't reach the level of fame he had without being incredibly competent. "But you shouldn't have had to."

He needed to understand that this wasn't his fault.

"Trusting your father proves what a wonderful person you are."

"I was naive."

"You were a *child*," I countered. "You didn't do anything wrong. Trusting people…choosing to believe in the good isn't weakness."

Over the years I'd seen a lot of things. Both personally and because of my profession. I'd met a lot of different people with different backgrounds. I'd heard stories—stories that *chilled* me, that hurt sometimes, that made it difficult not to believe the worst of people.

"The fact you still chose to give your father a chance, even after the lack of his presence in your life, shows how truly *strong* you are," I added, because it did. "Despite everything you'd been through, you still chose to trust him. That reflects positively on your character, not negatively."

"Even though he ended up fucking me over?"

"You can't blame yourself for a choice he made." My heart ached for him.

Robin sucked in a wobbly breath like what I'd said physically hurt. "Miles says there's room for us in Belleville despite our baggage. But even he doesn't know half the shit I've been through."

"You're a fighter."

"That's all I've ever done." Robin melted into me, the barbs in his eyes gone.

Robin amazed me. He truly did. Messy but kind. Scared, but willing to believe the best of people—just because that was who he was. I admired that, especially as someone who struggled to believe the best in people.

"You know what's weird?" Robin's voice was soft again, turmoil forgotten.

I didn't press, because it wasn't my place to. I'd said my piece, and he'd need time to process it, I was sure. Still though, I held him close, soaking him up like a dry sponge as I took a sip of wine so I could pretend like things were normal, even though they felt anything but.

"What's weird?" I echoed after I'd swallowed.

"*You.*"

"Me?" I laughed, taking another sip of wine before twisting to look at him.

"There it is."

"There *what* is?"

"My eyebrow." He reached up with one painted finger and gently poked at my brow. I snorted out a laugh, amused.

"I'm pretty sure that's my eyebrow."

"Nah. I adopted it. It's mine now." Robin grinned up at me. It was the cutest fucking grin. He was a little tipsy, but nothing uncomfortable. His toes wiggled beneath my thigh again.

Not rising to the bait, I spoke again, "What about me is weird?"

My heart thudded erratically, and I could admit I couldn't wait to hear what his response would be.

"Everything."

"Everything?" I laughed, incredulous.

"Yep." Robin's eyes crinkled. Lovely lines expanded as he did so, his dimples flashing. For the first time I could see the touch of age. He looked young, probably thanks to good genetics. But there was no denying that Robin Johnson's soul was old.

"Are you going to elaborate?"

"Nope." Robin's chin dug into my chest as he laughed, this quiet riotous thing. Because even now he was aware that my angels were asleep down the hall.

I wanted to kiss him.

Wanted to kiss his cherry red lips. To chase the wine along his tongue. To show him how much I enjoyed him, thoroughly, with my tongue.

Instead, I kissed his forehead.

Slow, sweet.

The skin was warm, and Robin shuddered beneath me as I stroked the back of his neck and lingered as long as I could.

When I pulled back there was a foggy expression on his face. I hadn't even needed to praise him this time to get him to respond like that, but that didn't stop me from doing it anyway. "You are so lovely," I told him, because it was true. "And so brave for sharing that with me."

Robin shivered, leaning into me with a muffled sigh.

"Are you ready for bed?" I asked him, gently rubbing the back of his neck and up into the fuzzy soft, shorn hair at his nape. "You can use my shower. I have pajamas for you."

"You're so good to me," he countered, like that was a miracle.

"You deserve to be treated well," I replied.

He didn't look like he believed me, but he didn't argue. That still felt like progress.

thirteen

ROBIN

BEN'S BED WAS SOMEHOW EVEN comfier with him in it despite how much space he took up. He was a cuddler. Which maybe should not have surprised me? But it totally did. Ben also was hot as a furnace—and grabby as hell, even when unconscious.

We'd gone to bed at either ends of the mattress. My fault, definitely. Ben had watched me with those serious golden eyes and I'd chickened the fuck out. Only that hadn't ended up mattering, thank God, because an hour after I'd fallen asleep—I was starting to think Ben was a miracle worker—he octopused that big-ass body around me and woke me up.

"Mmm," I whined into the pillow in complaint.

There was no reply.

Half asleep and groggy, I'd peeped one eye open to get a good look at my assailant. Ben was snoring beside me, drooling onto his pillow, his arm and leg slung over my body like I was the teddy bear I accused him of being. I could only see one of his tattoos from this angle, which was a shame.

I swear to god, when I realized that he had some, I'd nearly combusted right then and there.

Because being a hot doctor with a swimmer's body was one thing. Being a hot doctor with a swimmer's body and *tattoos*? Another thing entirely. They were swirling black ink and delicate lines. As floral as the undernotes of his cologne.

Ben made a cute little snort-y noise, sniffed, then went right back to snoring. He was heavy as hell. And sweaty. But in a good way. The kind of way that reminded me of sex and bare skin, and cocks.

I fell back to sleep quickly—again, a miracle—and the next time I woke I realized I had…maybe a bit of a problem.

If you could call it that.

I was flat on my belly, one of Ben's pillows hugged to my chest. His breath was hot at the back of my neck, his entire considerable weight plastered to my back. Ben slept mostly naked. Which was possibly the most amazing thing I'd ever discovered.

The only thing he wore were these frankly slutty pair of threadbare gray sweatpants that had a dick print obscene enough he belonged in prison. When he'd walked out of the bathroom after getting ready for bed, I'm pretty sure I'd swallowed my tongue.

"I can put a shirt on," is what he'd said, as if his dick wasn't taunting me, lying there all pretty and thick and long and *yummy*. I'd been half-tempted to fall to my knees, pull his pants down, and suck him as far down as I could.

But I'd been tired and full of wine and dinner, so I hadn't.

Other than being revealing as hell, Ben's pants seemed to have a second major flaw. They were so thin he might as well have been naked.

Actually, calling that a flaw was maybe too harsh.

And also inaccurate.

Because I had pretty much zero complaints right now about that. Especially considering the fact that Ben's dick was pushing hard into my ass, and I could practically feel every ridge and dip of it, the fabric was so threadbare.

"Christ on a cracker," I muttered into the mattress as Ben mouthed at the back of my neck, his cock wedged into the crack of my ass. I was wearing a pair of his boxers, and a hoodie that had rucked all the way up to my armpits, so there was pretty much nothing in the way of all that hot, hot skin smashed to my own.

He was still asleep.

I knew he was still asleep.

But I was currently being squashed into the bed and could not move whatsoever.

Not that I really wanted to. I had a god of a man grinding against me, and I wasn't about to pass up the opportunity to memorize what that felt like. Still though…Ben was my friend.

My friend.

And while sleepy Ben fucking me was seriously the hottest thing ever— new kink unlocked—I wasn't going to take advantage of him like that. Not without consent first.

"Ben," my voice was crackly raw with both sleep and arousal. "*Ben.*"

"Mmm," Ben whined, teeth sinking into my skin, his tongue liquid hot. Jesus fuck. Electricity shot up my spine.

"Ben," I tried again. "Benito. Beniciano. Bento box. Eggs and bake-ben. Cornish game Ben. A-Ben-Ca-Da-Bruh." The last one seemed to do the trick, because Ben stopped grinding. His teeth released my nape and he groaned, somehow sinking even deeper into me, his nose squishing into my skin. "You awake?" I asked, even though it was obvious.

"Unfortunately," Ben's voice was a low mumbling growl. Damn. Grumpy in the mornings. So he *did* have a flaw. I craned my neck to see the alarm clock, grimacing when I realized how early it was.

"You were fucking me with your dick," I informed him, muffled against the sheets. "Through your pants."

"I know." Ben laughed, the sound buzzing against my skin. He sounded embarrassed. Which was my job. "I'm sorry."

I froze, growing rigid beneath him.

He was…*sorry?*

So he really hadn't wanted it.

Mortification turned my skin bright red. I tried to wiggle out from under him, but gigantor wouldn't let me.

"Not like that," Ben apologized with his tone alone. "I'm still half asleep. Don't misconstrue my words." He curled his arms around me, his very hard dick still poking into me as he squeezed and squeezed and squeezed. I wheezed out the happiest breath I'd probably ever breathed. "I'm sorry because I didn't ask your permission first."

"Oh." The humiliation faded as happy-happy-happy chemicals danced all around inside my brain. I was surprisingly chipper this morning! For a dude up before the sun. Maybe it was because a big dick was poking me.

Probably.

"Does that mean you want to poke me with your dick some more now that you're awake?" I asked hopefully.

Ben chuckled. Chuckled! All sexy and low and amused. He stopped squeezing me like a dog toy, his teeth finding the back of my neck again. "Do you want me to do that?" he asked, always the gentleman.

"Does Mads Mikkelsen deserve another Oscar? Yes. Yes I want you to do that." My cheeks were hot as Ben laughed again.

He liked me.

I didn't understand why.

But he really did like me.

As evidenced by the fact he was always sweet-talking me. Always touching me. Always laughing at my jokes and finding joy in all the things I said.

My thoughts screeched to a halt when Ben ground his hips into mine again, slow and deliberate. This was different than the sloppy, sleepy ruts from before. This was a man on a mission. And that mission was to push his cock directly against my twitchy asshole, fabric barriers be damned.

Pulling back, Ben fucked forward with purpose again. A sharp snap of his hips that made me whine.

And then he was pulling away, taking all that hot, lovely skin with him. He flopped over onto his back beside me, sucking in a breath with a groan. When I glanced down I could see the tent his dick made. It twitched, and when I glanced back at his face, Ben was watching me.

"Why'd you stop?" I asked, because duh.

Why the fuck had he stopped?

"Show me your cock, little songbird," Ben's voice was low and sugary sweet.

Flames burst across my body, my own dick perking right the fuck up.

Like it'd never stopped working in the first place. I knew this was purely luck. That it had everything to do with the lovely night's rest I had just experienced—but still.

It was a gift.

I didn't need to be told twice, scrambling to get the comforter off my tangled legs. Scrambling to get the boxers I had borrowed from Ben down and off. Only apparently I wasn't fast enough for Ben, because while I was kicking around at the blankets he reached for the hem of the underwear with both hands and yanked them right down to my knees.

My dick slapped against my belly, sticky and hard, the skin flushed pink enough to see in the dark. The crows on my hips pointed toward it, framing the flushed skin as Ben growled, low and happy under his breath.

"So fucking pretty."

My cock flexed.

And then he was slurping me down, quick as that.

My hand tangled in the auburn waves on the top of his head, scrambling for support as my balls tapped his lips and bliss exploded behind my eyelids.

When he pulled off, spit clung from the tip of my cock connecting to his lower lip. Ben's eyes were *hungry*. "You've got the perfect sized dick," he told me. The praise lit me up from the inside out. His big hand fanned along my length, demonstrating without words just how *small* it looked in his grip. And then he stroked me, tight and rough, and deliberate— and my brain about fell out of my ears.

"Ben, Ben, Ben, Ben," I chanted his name, legs kicking out as my hole clenched tight. It'd been so long since the last time I'd been touched. And even then, it'd never felt like this. Electric all the way down to my bones. There wasn't a single thing I didn't like about Ben Montgomery.

Not a single fucking thing.

"Shhh," Ben urged, sliding up the bed so he was hovering over me, my cock clutched loosely in his grip. My legs trembled, balls drawn up tight. And then he winked. Because he was simply the hottest human to ever exist. I made a garbled sound and Ben tutted disapprovingly.

He hadn't even moved his hand again, but it felt like he was.

My hips stuttered, trying to fuck into him, but he kept his grip gentle enough my movements did jack shit. Like my dick was a leash, and he was holding me in place.

"You need to be quiet, little songbird," Ben purred, leaning down so our lips brushed with every word. "Can you do that for me?"

I didn't know if I could.

I didn't want to lie.

"Is that too hard?" Ben asked, voice low and sugary sweet. "Is that too hard for my pretty little bird? Can't stay quiet, can you, baby? You have such pretty notes to sing."

I nodded jerkily, once again trying to fuck Ben's fist and failing.

He released my cock as quickly as he'd grabbed it, hands gripping my hip hard enough to bruise as he shoved them into the mattress. "Did I say you could move?" he asked, voice still sugary sweet, though there was a threat laced within it.

"No," I managed, surprised by how croaky and needy I sounded.

"Are you going to stay still if I let you go?" Ben's lips brushed mine again.

"Yes."

He released my hip, long fingers playing at the sensitive skin that joined my legs and pelvis. They skimmed along the tattoos there, sliding low, a single finger tracing between my aching balls, up, up, up to the tip of my leaking dick.

"What a good boy," Ben murmured, still not kissing me. "So wet for me, aren't you?"

I nodded jerkily.

"Should we make you more wet?"

Again, I nodded.

"I think you can be quiet," Ben promised. "In fact, I know you can."

When Ben grabbed my dick once more his pace was relentless. Up and down, tight, slick, scratchy in all the right ways. I held my hips still because every time they so much as flinched Ben would tut at me again and slacken his grip till I apologized.

Staying quiet was half the battle. My eyes rolled back, my tongue curling as I gasped and shivered, so focused on not moaning that I forgot for a moment how this had even started in the first place. My dick leaked and leaked and leaked, growing wet just the way he'd promised it would. Like he was squeezing every drop to the surface till my skin was tacky and his hand was messy.

What felt like an eon later, voice low and thready, Ben murmured against my lips one final demand.

"Come," he said, like he fully expected me to do it on command. Like it was a trick and I was his puppy—and he'd trained me to obey. I sobbed quietly, balls drawing up tight as I did as I was told, hot cum spilling into his fist. He squeezed tighter somehow. Milking me through it, over and over and over till my skin was raw just the way I liked, and my eyes had crossed.

"You like a little pain, huh?" Ben cooed against my ear. "That's what you told me." *Schlick, schlick, schlick.* Ben twisted tighter around my cock. It hurt, it hurt, it hurt—and it felt...so fucking *good.* "Over coffee,"

Ben added, voice still sugary sweet and threatening. "Like you thought I wouldn't remember. Like I wasn't paying attention to every twitch of your expression. Like I wasn't thinking about pulling your nipples till you cried, or fisting your ass till it's pink and gaping and sore."

"Fuck," my voice cracked, a second orgasm building, building, building. I'd never come twice in a row before. Never knew I could.

"Looking at me with that smirk, and those eyes—" Ben bit my ear, his hot breath tickling in a way that made my blood sing. "Like I wasn't imagining torturing you till you made a mess all over the dining room table."

The second orgasm hit me like a freight train. No more cum came out. But it arched through me, over and over and over. And still, Ben toyed with me. Digging his thumb into my slit like if he teased me hard enough he could force a third out of my cock.

I sagged against the mattress when I was done, so oversensitive I didn't even have the energy to push him off my dick. Grip softening, Ben kept his hand curled loosely around my dick. Like he was simply keeping track of his property.

And then he kissed my cheek.

It was a chaste kiss, in comparison to what he'd just done to me.

My head felt heavy and my limbs were fuzzy as I made a garbled little sound.

"You did so good, baby," Ben promised against my skin, murmuring praise along my jaw, down my throat, and over the rucked up hoodie I still wore. "So *pretty*, aren't you? The prettiest. Look what a gift you gave me." I whined, cracking my eyes open—belatedly realizing they'd been pinched shut.

Ben's hand was in front of my face, cum-slick and messy.

"Next time, I'm going to finger you open," Ben promised, his sticky fingers slip-sliding across my lips.

"Mmm," I sighed, opening my mouth obediently as he fed me each finger, one at a time. Salty and bitter, the familiar taste made me groan.

"Clean them up," Ben ordered, as bossy as I'd hoped he'd be. "That's a good boy. Nice and thorough."

Lapping at the pads of his fingers and down between them, I felt safe and warm in a way I never had before. Like for the first time in my life, I'd found a place I really fit in. Because after this single, perfect sexual experience, there was no denying the fact that Ben Montgomery was everything I'd ever wanted and more.

He didn't let me touch his dick.

When I tried, he simply shushed me with another kiss to my cheek and rose from bed.

"Later," he promised, eyes glinting in the dark. "The girls are almost up."

I stared at him dumbly, eyes caught on the way his cock tented his pants. When he rose from the bed and headed for the bathroom, the light flicked on, and I flinched with a hiss, blocking its glare from view. "Get dressed, sweetheart," Ben hummed, leaning against the doorway, all that gorgeous tattooed muscle on display. There was a smattering of chest hair between his pecs. It was mostly gray, which I couldn't help but find... soooo fucking hot. "Then get some sleep."

Still bossy, even when his dick was pointing right at me.

"Mmm," I mumbled incoherently as I forced my own boxers back up. Ben had licked me clean at one point, though I wasn't sure when. It was a blur of muscles and warmth, and praise.

"I'll wake you up when breakfast is ready."

My dick twitched one last, final time, before Ben shut the bathroom door and I heard the sound of his electric toothbrush flick on. Staring blankly up at the ceiling, I allowed myself a single, solitary moment to freak the fuck out about what this might mean for our friendship, and for Miles—and for my stay here in Belleville.

And then I promptly fell back to sleep, blissed out and happy, with the knowledge that I'd been right.

Ben was one bossy-ass motherfucker.

Especially in bed.

fourteen

BEN

THE DAYS PASSED BY IN a blur after my night with Robin. And I found myself hoarding what little moments we had together as I waited desperately for Sunday to come. He'd tell me stories about Bubba when he'd pop in with coffee for Lynda and me. Apparently Miles and Bubba had both volunteered to help take down the haunted house, and in Robin's words, not mine, Bubba had been "a riot and a half the whole time."

Mama teased me over cannolis on Saturday. She'd already spent nearly twenty minutes last week interrogating me about Robin's shoes at my door. And this week was no different. In between bites of pastry she'd regale me with tales of what the twins had been up to while I'd been at work, in between teasing jabs about me finally finding someone and nosy questions about whether or not I'd read the werewolf books she'd bought me.

I was pretending to read them.

If only because she'd helped with my sledding mission, and I didn't think I could hold her off for much longer.

"You look happy," she said at the end of the night, her eyes dancing with mirth.

"Do I?" I blinked at her, then waved as a mother and her daughter I'd seen in my office earlier that week passed by. They smiled back, the little girl sporting a gap-toothed grin. Her name was Macy and she'd scraped her knee on her way to school and been so distracted by the blood she hadn't noticed she'd twisted her wrist when she'd fallen.

It was in a brace now, and her mother had told me earlier that week when I'd seen her again at Baxter's bakery, that the kids at school thought Macy was the coolest kid in the second grade now that she'd survived such an injury. She'd rolled her eyes and then informed me with a sympathetic grin that I might be seeing a lot more "wrist sprains" soon, on account of the trend her kid had started.

Truthfully, I wouldn't be surprised if that really did happen. In a town as small as Belleville the kids roamed in packs. I really, genuinely hoped that would not be the case, however. The last thing I needed was a flock of kids pretending to injure themselves so they could have braces of their own.

"You do," Mama said, interrupting my thoughts. I lowered my waving hand, sucked in a breath of cool, fresh fall air, and offered her what I hoped was a sincere smile.

"Have you ever tried a long-distance relationship?" I asked her, even though I already knew the answer. She and my dad, Charles, had been high school sweethearts. They'd been together their whole lives, pretty much, till the day he died. She was remarried now, and still happy, but there hadn't been much room for experimentation.

"I can't say that I have," Mama sighed, though her smile was gentle. "You really like him." It wasn't an accusation so much as it was a statement.

"I really do," I agreed. We continued walking toward my van, voices hushed. Another family walked by, probably to enjoy the lights that lit up Main Street, or grab a book from the book store. There was a fifty-percent-off sale going on, and it was only a few blocks down.

"I'm happy for you." Mama bumped her shoulder against my bicep and I sighed, tipping my head back to look at the glowing stars.

"I'd be happy for me too if it didn't feel like there was a timer ticking over my head."

"That isn't the way to live," she chided.

"I know."

"You know…" Mama paused, her hand on my arm. We were in the middle of the sidewalk but it was late enough the only families out and about were easily able to side-step around. "If I'd known one day I'd lose your father I wouldn't have changed anything."

My heart lurched, and I tipped my head down to see her, our eyes meeting. The sincerity in her gaze made me ache. "Even though it caused so much pain?"

"He was worth it," she said simply, giving my elbow another squeeze. "Good things are worth hurting for. He may be gone now, but his memory lives on. In each of you kids and the families and lives you build."

"Cheesy," I chided, lips twisting upward, because if I didn't joke, I might cry.

"Focus on the good," she said, tone soft. "*That's* the way to live."

It reminded me of being a little kid. Of my first panic attack. Of the way she'd held me and held me, and promised me everything would be alright. She'd been the one who'd taken me to a therapist. She'd been the one who'd always done her best to help me cope.

I was older now, but the anxiety hadn't gone away.

I'd simply learned how to cope with it.

It was a companion I'd never shake, and I was at peace with that now. At forty-five, I figured I deserved enough grace to allow myself that.

Mama's words followed me home that night after I dropped her off.

I kept them safe and protected inside my heart beside Robin's stories, Trixie's first tremulous hello, and the way I'd felt when I'd seen my little girls' wrinkled, red faces for the very first time. Precious memories. Good things. Memories that made the dark lighter, and the world a softer place.

On Sunday, after spending the morning playing with the girls, we returned to the park to train. Once again, Robin was there waiting for us. He was in my hoodie for the second Sunday in a row, and this time I didn't try to hide my grin.

Today I'd get his phone number.

He'd come home with me.

And I planned on snuggling him till those chilly pink cheeks were rosy warm, and his sweet little smile was protected by my bulk. Maybe if I was lucky I'd get to touch him again too. To see more of the faces he made. To make good on the promise I'd given him. To find out if he liked having my big hands tucked up inside him the way he'd hinted at the airport.

As usual, I made sure the girls were situated before emptying my bag. We only had one more training session until the festival, and I knew without a shred of doubt that we were going to lose. But that didn't mean we weren't going to give it our all.

Rosie tripped more often than she didn't, Jane was no better.

And I was somehow faster with the toddlers strapped to my legs than when I was roped up with Robin.

Still though…

I hadn't had this much fun in…maybe ever?

And I was going to enjoy every single second of it.

By the time we finished for the day, I was sweaty and flushed and had smashed Robin to the ground at least four different times, a fact that made my back more than a little angry. He hadn't complained though, and his flush was somehow worse than mine. He kept glancing at me through his lashes.

And I didn't have to be a mind reader to know what he was thinking about.

The way I'd pushed against him when we were in bed together.

How tiny his cock looked in my fist.

How badly he wanted to touch me—because I'd denied him the first time.

My little bird needed a lesson in patience, and while I too was eager to get to the "good stuff" myself, I refused to ruin what we had by taking things too fast. Maybe it was sadistic of me, but I enjoyed the way he squirmed.

After cocoa, we went out for dinner this time—pizza—from the only pizza joint in Belleville.

Slice of Heaven was packed despite it being a Sunday, and Robin kept twitching every time our thighs bumped beneath the table. The girls sat across from us, prim and proper, little napkins tucked into their dresses as they stared seriously down at their pizza like they expected the cheese to jump up and bite them.

I slid my hand beneath the table and up Robin's thigh, biting back a grin when he flinched, then groaned, sliding lower in his seat as he pressed into the touch. He peered up at me through his lashes again, his piercing clacking when he bit his lip.

"Eat your food," I commanded, giving his thigh a gentle squeeze. Even his legs were small. My hand took up quite a bit of space. Enough so that my fingers bumped his inseam, and I was able to cup the top half of it entirely. My eyes narrowed as a thought occurred to me, "Did you eat lunch?"

Robin glanced away, sheepish.

"Breakfast?"

"Matilda cooked," Robin blurted, obviously embarrassed.

"But did you eat it?"

"Yeees? Kinda."

"How do you *kinda* eat breakfast?"

The girls gave Robin confused looks. "Why didn't you eat?" Rosie asked. "Don't you know you're supposed to?"

"Breakfast is the most important meal of the day," Jane murmured quietly from beside her.

"If you don't eat you'll never grow," Rosie told Robin. "You'll stay like *that*, forever." She said the word *that* like Robin's current form was the most detestable thing she'd ever seen.

"Thanks for the advice." Robin smiled at the two of them, then turned to me with an expression that begged for *help*.

I nudged him with my shoulder, squeezing his thigh again, this time in commiseration. Because there was no help I could give that would protect him from toddler-barbs. They were simply too good at sniffing out one's weaknesses and stabbing right where they were squishiest.

"Maybe if you ate better you wouldn't be so short," Rosie continued, as if she hadn't just said that exact thing in a different way.

"Or look like you died," Jane added helpfully.

I snorted out a laugh and stepped in. "Robin looks tired because he's got a very hectic job."

"He doesn't have a job," Rosie pointed out. "All he does is walk around looking for you."

Robin chuckled and shrugged a shoulder as if to say "touche".

"He's on vacation," I corrected them.

Both girls eyed Robin curiously, as if learning that he did, in fact, have a job made him twenty times more interesting.

"Are you a emball-meer?" Rosie asked, because she'd recently learned about embalmers and now thought everyone should be one, as macabre as that sounded.

"A what?" Robin blinked. It took him a second, but then he laughed. "Ah, no. Nope."

"What about a funeral parlor director?" Jane added, sounding the words out slow and careful.

"Or a grave digger," Rosie chimed in.

"I don't do anything with corpses," Robin explained with a sympathetic frown.

"Oh," both twins said in unison, obviously disappointed.

"Their mother used to work in a funeral home," I explained to Robin under my breath. "They were on the phone with her earlier this week, and it's very much on their minds."

"*Oh*," Robin repeated, perkier this time.

"Robin is a musician," I told the girls, nudging him so that he would eat while I spoke. Rosie frowned, only half interested as she nursed her own pizza slice.

"I like music," Jane said in her tiny voice.

"I know you do," I grinned at her. "You have a beautiful voice." She had a child's voice. Pure and clear. Something that in my opinion, would always be beautiful. But she didn't need to know that. Puffing up with pride, Jane smiled at me, her sweet little teeth flashing.

"What do you like to sing?" she asked Robin, addressing him directly.

He choked on his mouthful of pizza in an attempt to finish quicker so he could answer. He looked honored to have been spoken to, which I couldn't help but find adorable.

"Robin's eating, darling," I said gently. "Give him a moment and he'll answer."

She nodded seriously, waiting patiently while Robin chewed. When he finished, he set the rest of his slice down and offered her a shy smile that almost perfectly mirrored her own.

"I..." he glanced at me, his cheeks growing pink, "Lately I've been interested in love songs." He seemed to realize what he'd just implied only after the words were out. The pink grew splotchy, traveling down his throat and across his ears as he ducked his head. "I mean..."

"*Love* songs?" Rosie made a gagging sound.

"Rosie," I admonished softly. "That's not very nice."

She wilted, offering Robin an apologetic smile. "Sorry."

"Um. That's okay," Robin replied, smiling right back. "I didn't used to like love songs either," he added. "Or Christmas songs. Or happy songs in general."

I gave his thigh an even tighter squeeze than before and the twins stared at him, enraptured as they waited for him to elaborate. I wanted him to elaborate too, so I didn't interrupt.

"I used to be angry," Robin said honestly, a regretful little smile twisting his lips. "Sometimes I still am. But…I try to…um. I mean…I'm trying to do things that make me feel happier now. Rather than things that remind me of the stuff I don't want to remember."

"I try not to think about the bug I stepped on," Rosie told him, looking remorseful. "It died."

"Oh," Robin nodded. "I'm…sorry for your loss."

"Me too," Rosie agreed. Then she did something I'd never seen her do before with anyone other than me. She leaned up on her tiny little feet, reached across the table, and gave Robin's hand a squeeze. Her chubby little fingers looked adorable wrapped around his. "I'm sorry for your loss too."

He looked flabbergasted, a slow grin spreading across his face. "Thanks." He squeezed her back.

As quickly as she'd doled out the affection, she took it back, sitting right back down with a dramatic plop. "You have really big feet," she told Robin, ruining the moment.

She probably meant the height of his shoes, but the comment was so out of pocket that I couldn't help but snort. Robin laughed too, his eyes crinkling at the corners as he nodded in agreement. "So true," he grunted, reaching for his pizza slice. "But not as big as your dad's."

I choked.

The girls eyed me like twin piranhas as they decided whether or not this was true. And then, unanimously, they both nodded. "Papa has the biggest feet," they agreed.

"He sure does," Robin agreed, eyes dancing.

And that was that.

Robin came home with me that night. We shared a glass of wine on the couch. He told me stories about Miles as a little kid, the beach they'd grown up visiting, and I regaled him with tales about my dad and the smiles he had never seemed to run out of.

It was odd.

I'd never felt this close with anyone other than Trixie, and even that was different.

There was no underlying current of sexual tension there.

I'd certainly never looked at her and wondered what her tongue tasted like.

Robin was my catnip. He made me laugh the way no one ever had before. He brought out emotions I hadn't even known I could feel. He made my heart feel light, my hands sweaty. He filled my belly with butterflies every time he smiled. And when he was sitting next to me, the rest of the world ceased to exist. All its what-ifs and worst-case-scenarios completely gone.

When I was with him, all the years before him melted away. Like there had only been him all along, I just hadn't known it yet. And for the first time in my life I was beginning to wonder if love at first sight existed outside of fairytales.

"Am I spending the night again?" Robin asked, voice mellow. He'd finished his glass of wine. It sat sentinel on the coffee table beside my laptop. This morning I'd woken up earlier than usual—before even the girls were up—to get some work done on my book.

"You are," I told him, and the smile he sent my way silenced any concerns I might've had that he didn't want to.

"Are you gonna do that thing to my dick again?" Robin's tone was sultry-soft.

Quirking a brow, I shifted closer. "I don't know," I hummed just to tease him. I loved how open and honest he was. I loved the way he held nothing back most of the time. The way he wore his heart on his sleeve. The way that beneath his bluster he was timid as a mouse.

I don't think he'd ever gotten a chance to be anything other than brave.

He was a fighter, I knew that.

But I didn't think he liked fighting.

And after hearing about his parents—the story he'd told me about his father in particular—I got the feeling that no one had ever taken care of Robin Johnson.

At least…not the way he deserved.

He looked tired.

Like he hadn't been sleeping again. Which was odd, considering how soundly he seemed to rest whenever I was around.

There were so many things I wanted to ask him. Questions about his past. Questions about his medical history. Questions about what he wanted to do after Christmas, and if there was room in his life for someone like me. If he still wanted to be a dad. If he didn't mind early mornings, and chocolate chip pancakes, and LilPoe reruns.

But I didn't ask him any of those questions. Because this was new, and he was warm and exhausted.

And I wanted to be a safe space for him.

Wanted to be where he rested his head after a long weary day.

I didn't want to cause the sleepy fog in his gaze to sharpen. I didn't want to wake up the demons that lurked in his pale green gaze. Didn't want to push too hard and frighten him off. So instead, I counted his freckles. I laced kisses along the shell of his ear, down his neck, and pushed him down, down, down, into the couch cushions. They squeaked a little at the same time he did.

"Ben?" Robin's voice was hoarse as he stared up at me. Sandwiched between my arms, he looked especially small. Breakable.

I wanted to wrap him in bubble wrap and keep him somewhere safe.

"Do you *want* me to touch your pretty little cock, Robin?" I asked him, feeding the hunger that curled liquid hot in my belly. "You've been giving me looks all day."

Robin gasped, eyes widening. Despite his incessant flirting, he seemed genuinely surprised that I could meet him step for step. "I promised I'd finger you," I reminded him.

"As if I'd forget." Robin rolled his eyes, and I snorted.

"I don't break my promises," I told him. That, in itself, was a promise. But it was also the truth. I had never, and would never, be the kind of person who went against his word. When I said I'd do something, I did it. No matter what.

Robin seemed to understand what I was saying because he relaxed beneath me, and his eyes went sweet all over again. "I told Miles that you're a flirt," he confessed, and I arched a brow in response.

"Did you tell him everything I did to you?"

Robin's cheeks went bright red. He shook his head. "No."

"Would you like this to be a secret?" I was okay with that. Not because

I didn't want to show him off, but because I could be patient. I could play the long game. And it wasn't as though everyone and their dog didn't already know how head over heels I was for the little blond stuck snugly between my legs.

Robin stared at me for a beat, his eyes swirling with complex emotion. When he shook his head a few moments later, it was deliberate and slow.

"Good," I replied, leaning down till our lips brushed. Up close like this, I could smell his cologne. Soft and musky. A sweet undertone that smelled just like the wine we'd shared.

When I kissed him sparks exploded between us. Liquid heat pooled low in my belly as our lips brushed, and I kept the pace controlled and slow. Robin kept trying to speed it up, these impatient little hiccups buzzing against my lips as he nipped and bit and tried to provoke me, but I never gave in.

Slow and steady, lick after lick, I coaxed his mouth to soften for me so that I could savor it. When he finally fully surrendered, it was with the most beautiful sigh. His breath ghosted against my skin and made me light up from the inside out.

Drugging, *lulling* kisses.

Robin's mouth was slack and needy, his sweet little tongue curling out every time I retreated. Like he wanted me back inside his mouth but was such a good boy he knew it wasn't his place to make demands.

When we parted I gave him one last peck on his cheek, then his nose, then his forehead. Lingering there, I soaked up the flutter of his breath before I pulled away, rising back to my knees to hover over him.

"Bed," I told him, ignoring my very hard dick and where it leaked, trapped inside my jeans.

Robin licked his lips, like he was savoring the taste of our kiss. I couldn't blame him because I wanted to do the same. His eyes were dark with lust as he stared up at me.

I'd never had someone look at me like I was the Second Coming of Christ before.

It was certainly flattering.

"Dick touching?" he asked, voice crackly warm. "And fingering," he added, head jerking eagerly. "Right?"

"Maybe," I replied because though I kept my promises, I could see how exhausted he was. I rose to my feet, grimacing when my back twinged. It'd been acting up today, though I'd done my best to ignore the dull, throbbing pain. If I'd been in New York I would've visited a chiropractor, but the nearest one to Belleville was over an hour away, and I simply had not had the time.

"Your back?" Robin frowned up at me from the couch. He wiggled onto his elbows, still spry and young—damn. Ten years, give or take a few. That was the gap between our ages. You'd think it was larger, considering how easily he still moved and the amount of energy he seemed to always possess, even when he was whittled thin with exhaustion.

"It's not happy," I agreed, holding a hand out to help him up.

Robin grimaced in sympathy. He accepted the help, though he looked wary, like he worried me pulling him up was going to make it worse.

"I'm fine," I reassured because I didn't need him to worry about me. "I just won't be performing acrobatics any time soon."

Robin nodded along, staring up at me from somewhere near my pecs, his green, black-lined eyes full of affection. "Ben..." he trailed off, voice intimately low.

"What?" I asked, waiting for him to gather his words.

"Can I rub your back?"

That had not been what I expected him to want to rub, but I wasn't about to say no.

"You want to rub my back?" I repeated, genuinely surprised.

"Yes," Robin nodded emphatically. And then he frowned, face pinching. "Unless you think that would make it worse? I'm not like...a doctor or anything."

"Good thing I am," I joked, pleased by how easy it was to play with him like this.

"Right," he agreed, grinning.

Robin's shy request did not prepare me for the absolute mindfucking pleasure that awaited me the second I lay on my belly in bed and he got to work. He did not give himself enough credit. His hands were strong and capable, his fingers stubborn as they worked out the knots along my spine and up beneath my shoulder blades.

I sank into it with a groan, the sound caught somewhere inside the pillow my face was buried against.

"One of the drummers that used to tour with me had a girlfriend that was a masseuse," Robin chatted away. He was sitting on my ass, his little legs spread wide, sweet little cock soft and brushing against me every time he slid up toward my neck. "I used to watch her sometimes because it seemed like a useful skill."

"Very useful," I agreed, blissed out and shuddering as he found a particularly sore spot up by my trapezius and gave it a pointed rub.

"Relax," Robin urged as I tensed up, pain buzzing as he pushed at the knot. "I gotta push to release it."

"Mmm," I replied stupidly as I finally felt the knot loosen, and the pain melted into pleasure. My dick was hard. It was impossible not to be hard in this situation. Robin was sexy as hell, especially when he was comfortable. "Harder, please," I instructed. "Harder than you think you need to push."

The tissue was damaged enough, even now, I needed a little extra push.

Robin didn't second-guess my words. His hands were capable and rough—guitar calluses probably. He dug in harder, just like I'd requested.

I was putty beneath him.

"How'd you hurt your back, anyway?" he asked, skimming his fingers up and down my sides and making me shiver.

I knew he wasn't asking about the night I'd spent on the couch or the falls we'd shared outside today.

"Car accident in my twenties," I explained, voice low. "Tore some ligaments. Fractured a disk. Most of it's healed but it still acts up. Especially when I—oh fuck." Robin found another knot. He pushed, his sweet thumbs working it loose as I groaned again. "It was worse when it first happened. Most days it's this annoying dull ache that never goes away. But on days when it gets bad, it gets…frustrating? Because I can't stop thinking about it. Thinking about the pain, and being annoyed that it won't go away."

I hadn't meant to say all of that.

I'd honestly never talked about my chronic pain to anyone but my physical therapist. But there was just something about Robin that made it easy to be vulnerable.

"It can make me irritable," I admitted, my most private, most intimate shame. "On the days it hurts the most." I sucked in a breath. "I like to think I'm a very calm person. But even I sometimes…break."

"That's okay," Robin said softly, hands still digging in. "It's okay to be frustrated, especially when you're in pain."

"It makes me feel like I'm not myself. Which is almost worse than the pain itself." Again, admitting something I'd never said to anyone but my therapist. I sighed, melting a little more as my secrets slipped free and Robin accepted them easily, as though they weren't dark and ugly at all.

"That has to be upsetting."

"It is," I agreed, because it was. And it was nice…to talk to someone about it. Someone who very obviously cared. "Staying active helps." God, that felt good. "And I'm usually good about doing my physical therapy but lately I—Jesus." Pleasure buzzed beneath my skin as Robin dug his fingers into my shoulders and rubbed. "I've been too busy."

"Too busy to take care of yourself?" Robin tutted like he wasn't a walking hypocrite. "For shame, Benzonatate." I coughed out a laugh, which was apt—seeing as Benzonatate was a drug used to help with coughing.

"Where did you learn that one?" I asked, amusement rumbling deep inside my chest. Robin seemed to like the rumble because he wiggled his narrow hips and his soft dick nestled against the small of my back.

"Google," he replied, sounding way too proud of himself.

"Did you Google 'medicine with the name Ben in it'?" I asked, already knowing the answer.

"Duh."

I laughed but my laughter quickly died when Robin's magic hands worked their way up my neck and into my hair. Scratch, scratch, rub. He wiggled his fingers, squeezing tight as shock waves danced through my body.

"Mmmm," I sighed, nothing but a happy puddle beneath him.

When he finished, he capped the lotion he'd borrowed and set it on the nightstand beside my pile of books. I was surprised he could reach, considering his size. I was always considering his size, if I'm being honest. There was something about how small he was that really did it for me.

I'd never thought of myself as a particularly kinky person.

But Robin certainly made me feel that way.

I'd never wanted to torture someone the way I wanted to torture him. To pull at his nipples till they were pink and puffy. To rub his sweet little cock till he spilled and spilled and spilled again. So oversensitive all he could do was dig his nails into my shoulders and beg. To pull his cheeks apart and spit on his hole. To play with it till he left drool on the mattress, and all he could do was twitch.

Most of all, however, I wanted to fuck him.

It was a primal thing, probably. Similar to the books I wrote, but different too. Because there was no beast inside me aching for release. It was simply me, sadistic—apparently—and needy, with a dick so hard all I wanted was to shove it inside whichever one of his holes was closest, and show him exactly who he belonged to. To breed him till his ass dripped.

Unfortunately for me, Robin's magic touch had relaxed me to the point of near incoherency. It'd been a long time since I felt this good. My body was relaxed, my bare back exposed as he ghosted his fingers up and down it, and my eyes began to droop.

I wanted to get him off.

Wanted to finger him like I'd said I would.

But first I…

First I…

First…

fifteen

ROBIN

BEN WAS ADORABLE WHEN HE was asleep. Super fucking adorable. It had taken me a while to understand what had happened, I was so distracted by scratching up into his thick red hair, and then down over the mole-speckled skin on his back. It was only when he started snoring that I realized the lazy lull of my touches had lured him to slumber.

I wasn't mad though.

Truth be told, I was grateful.

Because even though I had a giant—and I mean *giant*—delicious man underneath me, my dick hadn't wanted to come out to play. It had to happen eventually. I knew that. Wasn't like magic, where every time Ben was nearby my cock would wham-bam-thank-you-ma'am and start to work again.

Twice was enough.

Twice proved that after a good night and some solid sleep, my body was more than willing to cooperate.

But it was Sunday, not Monday. And I'd had a week of restless nights between me and the last time I'd dozed in Ben Montgomery's bed.

So yeah.

Ben falling asleep on me was a blessing, kinda. Because I didn't have to explain to him why my dick was soft, and why it probably wouldn't wake up at all.

Flopping over onto my back beside him, I couldn't help but find it funny that only a week ago he'd done that same exact thing beside me. Only *his* flopping had caused the bed to ripple, and mine barely disturbed the sleeping man beside me.

He mumbled something incoherent, squeezing the pillow in his grip tight, smacked his lips, and relaxed all over again.

And for several long, precious minutes, I let myself admire him.

I traced his wiry forearms and the fuzzy hair that clung to them. I stroked the bicep that had led me like Dorothy to the promised land of Oz. I brushed his hair away from his face and enjoyed his long dark lashes. Enjoyed the way they fluttered on his cheeks, spiky and soft. Enjoyed the wrinkles around his eyes and the gray at his temples that gave him a distinguished air.

I'd never thought I'd be into older guys, not that Ben was *old*—because he wasn't. Forties wasn't old. But he was still older than I was.

He'd seen more shit than I had.

And he had a family.

A family he'd chosen.

Kids he loved.

Kids that loved him back.

Miles said there was room in Belleville for the both of us. And I was starting to suspect he was right. But was there room in Ben Montgomery's life for a washed-up, fucked-up, Southern reject?

He made it seem like there was.

With every kind gesture.

Every time he included me.

Every warm smile, every laugh, every brush of his fingers.

Ben made me feel the way no one ever had before. When I was with him, I fit. Like we were puzzle pieces. Or harmonies. Two shapes, two notes, same tune.

I played with his fingers for a while, curled up next to him, my toes tucked beneath his meaty thigh. He was wearing the sweatpants again. The threadbare ones. And his ass looked almost as spectacular as his dick had inside them.

His hands were bigger than mine. Maybe veinier too? Though I'd always had particularly veiny hands. The hair on his arms stopped just above his wrists, and while his fingers were long and dexterous, his wrists were slender. I could loop my fingers around them—something that surprised me far more than it probably should.

Ben Montgomery was warm dinners, late nights, and laughter.

He was solid, and sure, and dependable.

He was the sun rising every morning, and the moon at night.

He was caring and predictable in the way only truly good people were.

And it was easy to love him in the blanket of night, with his snores a symphony in the quiet room. It was easy to tap out a love song against his knuckles, to soak up his warmth, to pretend—if only for a moment—that

I'd been lying that day I'd sat in the dark, eggnog in my belly, and shown Ben my blackened heart.

In his bed, I wasn't poison.

I was just me.

And he was Ben.

And for a moment, I let myself pretend that this could be forever.

The next week went by in a blur. I spent as much time with Bubba and Miles as I could. And when they were busy, I went on the hunt for Ben. Sometimes he'd be at work. Sometimes he'd be out with the girls. Sometimes he'd invite me for cocoa, and then bring me to his home. We'd play with the girls till they passed the fuck out, and on one very memorable occasion, Jane even asked if I would be the one to read her bedtime story to her.

Apparently they both got to pick one a night.

Which was…honestly a fucking *honor*.

And when I'd told Jane that, she'd grinned—at the same time Rosie's little voice piped up, sleepily from her bed across the room that I now, in fact, owed her more "monies."

After storytime when Ben and I had retreated to the couch to canoodle, I'd asked him about the swear jar. It seemed I was practically funding Rosie's entire illegal operation single-handedly.

"Illegal operation?" Ben asked, obviously amused.

"Well, yeah," I agreed, more than a little pleased with my life at the moment. I was in his lap. Which was somehow even better than being snuggled against his side. I could feel his dick beneath my ass when I wiggled—and he kept making this annoyed face at me like he knew I was doing it on purpose just to see if I could wake it up. "She's like a tiny Al Pacino." Putting on my best and worst Italian accent, in a low voice I added, "You owe me monies."

Ben cracked up.

Which was flattering as hell.

His whole face lit up, wrinkles exploding across it in the way they only did when he was truly overjoyed. I was more than a little proud of myself for making him snort like that. When I wiggled in his lap again to celebrate a job well done, Ben's eyebrow came back full force.

"Don't start what you can't finish," he warned, big warm hands finding my hips and squeezing tight enough to bruise. And then, like he hadn't just said the hottest shit in the history of the world, he went on to explain about the swear jar.

"She wants a cat," he hummed.

"A…" I was still stuck on the "don't start what you can't finish" thing. "Cat?"

"Yes." Ben's lips twitched.

"Not the kinda pussy I was thinking about, but okay," I replied, trying to make him laugh again. Ben's eyes widened at the same time his brow lowered. That was a new look. A Look with a capital L. Wow. Look at me go! Making him make new faces and everything.

"You don't *have* a pussy," Ben told me in case I'd forgotten. He'd seen all my bits up close and personal, so I figured it was fair he was confused.

"Fine, a bussy."

"A what?" Ben looked confused.

"Boy-pussy." I ground against his dick again, and he made this amazing little growly sound. "You know. Bussy."

"Robin—"

"I can make it real nice and wet for you, Ben Ben," I informed him. "I keep it snug." I was full of shit. There was no such thing as keeping your ass snug. At least…I didn't think so? But it was turning him on. And I could feel it. So I wasn't about to stop. "Keep it nice and tiny and tight for that big, big dick to goooOooo—oh-woah." My back hit the couch with a *thump*, the wind knocked right out of me.

"You have such a *mouth* on you," Ben purred, one of those gigantic hands squeezing my face and making my lips purse. I whined, low and soft, unable to help it.

Please, dick gods, let my dick wake up, I prayed.

"Such a pretty mouth," Ben added, staring down at my lips. "And it says the *filthiest* things."

"Trashmouth," I blurted, though it was muffled by the fact he was squeezing me. My cheeks went hot. "Comes with the territory."

Such a pretty mouth, Ben's words echoed around inside my head.

You're a good boy, Robin.

Gorgeous.

Sweetheart.

"Rosie wants a pet cat," Ben continued, like he wasn't looming over me. Like he wasn't holding me still. Like I wasn't imagining thirty ways I could take his dick in the next thirty seconds. "I told her if she can raise a hundred dollars that after Christmas we would go pick one up from the shelter."

Oh.

Oh my heart.

"I hope you know I'm going to be swearing up a storm around those kids," I told him. "How much do they have left? Twenty bucks? Thirty? That's easy. I can do that in less than a minute."

"I appreciate your enthusiasm," Ben replied dryly. He had the sexiest look on his face. Half grumpy, half amused. "But the *point* of making them earn it was to teach them patience and that there is nothing better than working hard for something."

"Listening to other people swear is working hard?" I blinked, confused.

Ben snorted. His brow furrowed. A grin spread across his lips. "When you put it like that, you have a point."

"This is why you need me around," I told him. "I've got fresh perspective."

"That's not the only reason I need you around," Ben said, sweeter than sugar. He leaned down and kissed my pursed lips. I could taste wine on his, familiar and musky sweet.

"You're after my bussy," I mumbled against his mouth, delighted when he jerked back so he wouldn't laugh right in my face. "I just know it."

"Jesus Christ, Robin," Ben cackled. He'd released my face, thank God. Because this time, he would not stop laughing. His hands went up, covering his expression as his shoulders shook and the most horrific, but beautiful, crackling kinda guffaw left him.

It was like watching a train wreck.

I couldn't look away.

"My bussy brings all the boys to the yard—" I sing-songed as Ben died of laughter, still straddling me. "And they're like—it's better than yours."

"*Robiiiin,*" Ben gasped out, lowering his hands and collapsing onto me. My song died as he smashed me into the couch, muffling his laughter into my neck now. Hesitantly, I reached around him, stroking a hand down the center of his back so I could feel his laughter vibrate through both sides of his body.

"Yeeees?" I replied, burying my nose in his downy, soft hair and trying not to die because I loved him. I loved him, I loved him, I loved him.

And it wasn't fair.

It wasn't.

Because I knew myself. I *knew* myself, and I knew the second things got too real—I'd run.

I always ran.

It was simply what I did.

Ben didn't reply. And I knew it was because he knew I wasn't ready to hear what he had been about to say. It was too soon. And I was too *me*. And my feet itched and itched and itched.

"Mmm," I sobbed, scratching at the pillows my face was smashed into as Ben licked the back of my neck and those big, lovely hands skated down my side.

"I told you I don't break my promises," he purred, teeth sinking liquid hot, just deep enough to sting as his other hand—his other very naughty, very sexy hand—uncapped the lube bottle on the bed.

I was naked. Well. *Kinda.*

Aside from the hoodie I'd borrowed—bunched up to my armpits—and the furry sock things that still adorned my feet because Ben had been "afraid I'd get cold without them".

His thoughtfulness knew no bounds. Especially when he was crammed up against my side and I knew without a shred of doubt in my mind that he was about to wreck my fucking ass.

At least, I hoped he was.

Equally as strongly, I hoped I'd get to touch him back today.

Knowing him though, he'd leave me hanging again without a chance to touch his cock at all.

It was early in the morning. Early enough the kids wouldn't be up for hours. Neither of us were morning people, as evidenced by Ben's sleepy grumblings when I'd rolled over and began to nibble along the back of his neck.

He'd woken up slow and grouchy—which, same, bud—but quickly perked up when he felt my dick push against his side. All it had taken was one little whine and Ben was wide a-fucking-wake.

And now here we were. The warm, dry skin of his abs brushing my back as he coasted his hand up and down my side, tracing my ribs and the dips of my hips as the slick, slick of lube coated his other hand.

How he was doing that with only one hand available was a mystery to me. I struggled doing most things even with both hands unoccupied.

"You want me to suck your little cock, baby?" Ben asked against the back of my neck, sending a shiver down my spine. My dick jerked. "Before I play with that sexy *tight* bussy."

To his credit, he kept it together for a solid five seconds before a low, rumbly chuckle buzzed along my nape.

"Okay, you're right—" I managed, muffled against the pillow. "No more talk of bussies." Though… "Calling my cock little is definitely good though. Super good. Fuck. Why is that so hot?"

"Because you *are* little," Ben murmured. "And if *you're* little that makes me…"

"Huge." My throat clicked when I swallowed, face hot. Then, because I couldn't help it, I added. "But um. Yeah. No need to use bussy. I'll survive without it."

I really *had* only been using it as a joke—and because I liked the way he reacted to it. But…even though it was honestly pretty hot when he said it still, Ben somehow managed to say it like an old man. Kinda slow and awkward, like he was sounding the word out for the first time. Which made me want to laugh. Even worse, every time he said it he wouldn't stop chuckling like the little shit he was. Which meant *neither* of us was taking it seriously at all.

"Are you sure?" Ben sobered a little. He laced a flickering little kiss behind my ear, his tongue sliding out to tease. Hot breath made a shiver run down my spine. "Because if you want me to tell you how badly I want to wreck your bussy I will."

"Oh, Jesus fuck," I gasped out, my dick twitching where it hung between my thighs. "I'm getting coal for Christmas this year."

"Naughty list?" Ben chuckled, amused.

"Always."

The warm, dry hand that skimmed my side slid down to my ass. It was easy for him to grip it. The size difference came in handy in this case as he dragged his thumb down my crack and pulled me open wide.

"This part of you is *definitely* naughty," Ben agreed, speaking conversationally, like my hole wasn't fluttering all over the place, and my dick wasn't drooling onto his comforter. He leaned back, made a quiet sound, like he was inspecting me, then slid back in close.

Hot breath tickled my ear the next time he spoke, "Just look at the way it twitches."

"Can't help it," I replied. "I'm a ho-ho-hoooo—" Ben cut me off when his dry thumb pressed against my hole, shoving hard enough I felt the skin give a little.

"When was the last time you were touched here?" Ben asked, tone still conversational. Slick fingers replaced the dry ones as his hand went back to holding my ass open.

"Um," my voice was crackly dry, all jokes forgotten. "Two years?" Fuck. Wait. No. "Three." That wasn't right either. When was the last time I'd been fucked? It'd been in Vegas. Not this last tour but the one before. Some guy who'd told me I was pretty in the parking lot at a rest stop. He'd tasted like cigarettes, left bruises I didn't want, and I'd said yes because the sky had been so empty, empty, empty, and yet somehow, my heart had been even emptier.

"I'll need to stretch you out first," Ben murmured. "Train you."
Jesus fucking Christ.

Ben training me brought visions of me on my knees with a collar and a leash to mind. He'd loom over me, that sexy brow twitch taunting me as he tugged on my leash, and told me that only good boys got treats.

"Yes please," I managed, shuddering as he pressed more insistently at my hole.

"I'm not fucking you tonight."

"Bah humbug." What a spoilsport.

"Even though you like it rough." Ben's thumb slipped in and I sobbed. Damn, I really *was* a whore. I couldn't help it. Because the second he was inside me I wanted more, more, more. It wasn't enough. It would never be enough. It couldn't.

Deeper he slipped, the scratch of his knuckle catching on my rim as he leaned back to watch himself disappear inside me again. When I glanced back, I wished I hadn't.

Because one look at the concentrated, almost pissed-off expression on his face made my dick threaten to spill entirely untouched.

"When the girls aren't in the other room I'm going to edge you," Ben promised, pulling his thumb out slow and easy, before fucking in with a snap that I felt all the way to my toes. The next time, he pulled out all the way. My hole twitched, begging for more.

"Edge me?"

"Edge you," Ben agreed, slipping his index finger in this time. It wasn't as thick, but damn, it was long. I clenched around it, and Ben rumbled his approval. "I want to see how long it takes to make you cry."

Well that was terrifying and also the hottest thing I'd ever heard.

"Won't take much," I admitted as he fucked in and out, the wet slap of his wrist echoing through the room. He slid his middle finger in with the other on the next thrust, and it burned so good my toes curled.

"Have you ever worn a cock ring?" Ben asked, keeping up the pace even though I was falling to pieces beneath him.

"Um. No."

"One day we're going to buy you one," Ben mused. "Bright red. So it blends in with your pretty little," he flicked my cock head and I howled, "Dick."

When Ben slid a third finger inside me I lost the game with my patience. I ground back against him, fucking onto his knuckles with a sob as my body trembled beneath him.

"Look at your toes curl," Ben cooed. "You *love* being fucked, don't you?" He twisted his fingers down, pressing hard against my prostate. I *sobbed.* "You give me these looks, you know?" Ben teased, the sound of his fingers fucking into me somehow growing louder as I moved back to meet his thrusts. I was surprised he even let me move, he was so damn bossy.

"L-looks?" I managed, even though I had no idea how my mouth was still working.

"Your eyes beg for it. For me to fuck you. I bet you'd let me pull your pants down and slip inside you anytime, anywhere."

He wasn't wrong.

"You…" Ben sped up, his fingers twisting, the pounding against my prostate too much for me to be able to survive. I lost my train of thought, head swimming with sensation. When I came it felt like I died. Pleasure exploded through my body, my cock spilling and spilling and spilling.

And it was good, it was *so* good.

It was so, so, so good.

"Oh fuck," I whimpered. "Oh fuck. Please. *Please.*" Ben kept his fingers inside me, shoving in hard now, his knuckles pushing against my rim so I could squeeze and squeeze and squeeze around him.

And then, because my teddy bear was clearly the devil, he leaned down, low and slow. And just like before, his warm breath teased my ear as he purred, "I wish this was my dick. That I could feel you squeezing around it. Milking me dry. Letting me *breed* this sweet little ass."

When my brain had stopped being broken and my limbs worked again, I made it my *mission* to touch Ben's dick.

When I told Ben that, he snorted out a laugh, gently removed his fingers from my ass, and gave it a parting rub. He did not respond to my stink face, other than to grin, lay on his back like a good sport, spread his legs, and gesture magnanimously at his cock.

It flexed toward me.

Like he was offering me a fucking treat.

Which…I guess he was.

"These sweatpants should be illegal," I told him, yanking down the fabric unceremoniously. "You should be in prison right now." He just chuckled, but otherwise didn't say a word.

When his dick slapped free—commando, damn—my brain broke for a second time. Because if I'd thought Ben's dick was hot when it was wrapped up in cotton, it was fucking *delicious* bare. I stared at it, mouth watering, my head spinning.

I'd always liked dicks.

Maybe it'd taken me till my early twenties to figure out that I was bisexual, but that had never changed my very real attraction to men.

Ben Montgomery was the epitome of a male specimen. He had hair in all the right places. He smelled clean and musky. He'd aged like fine wine, and his very large, very gorgeous body was made up of hard lines and compact muscle.

He wasn't as brawny as his brothers but there was no denying that he was strong.

"In prison?" Ben husked out, voice lower than before.

His dick twitched, the flushed skin making my mouth water. Thick and long, it listed slightly to the left rather than pointed directly at me. Like it was polite, for a cock, despite how hard it was. His balls were heavy and full, coated in a soft dusting of gray hair that I wanted to flatten with my tongue so bad, I nearly shoved my face down right then and there to do it.

Ben's cock was longer than mine was. Thicker too. Which only made sense.

Again, proportional.

"You know for being…" I trailed off, still staring at his dick. "*Indecent.*" I was very obviously distracted. He knew it, I knew it, his dick definitely knew it.

Ben's dick flexed at me again and I *whined*, reaching a tentative finger out to trace along the vein that ran up its length. Where to start first? So many options. The rosy head, all slick and soft…his balls, where I could bury my face and suck. The vein I was tracing, like a treasure trail to Heaven.

"You look hungry, little songbird," Ben murmured, slowly—confidently—spreading his legs wider. I could see the dusky dark skin behind his balls, and I ached.

I wanted to say something about looking for a "worm" to eat, but for the first time in ages the words simply didn't want to come out. Because Ben's dick was too pretty, and while his voice was hoarse and wrecked with arousal, I could see vulnerability flickering in his toffee-colored gaze.

I'd told Ben it'd been a while since I'd been fucked.

And I wondered…if maybe it'd been a while for him too.

"You have a really amazing cock," I murmured, surprised by how sincere and breathless I sounded. "Like…*really* amazing." I licked my lips, eyeing the flushed crown as a fresh drop of precum slid down his shaft. "I'd make a wax sculpture of it and put it on my desk—if I had a desk—just so I could look at it."

"Thank you." Ben's dick twitched again.

"Can I touch it?" My hands were shaking. I didn't want to fuck this up. I really, *really* didn't want to fuck this up.

Ben must've seen my anxiety because he softened even more, one of those huge, lovely hands reaching out to skim through my hair. "Of course you can," he murmured, affection evident. "You can do whatever you want to me."

My head spun and I whined again, sinking into the gentle scratch of his fingers as I lowered down close. Close enough I could smell the musky sweet scent of Ben's skin and those sexy-as-fuck thighs framed my face. I licked my lips, suddenly ravenous.

"Can I *lick* it?" I asked, voice low and wrecked.

"Anything you want," Ben countered again, keeping his tone gentle.

There was something about his constant patience that really did it for me. In a sexy way, yes. But also in a…softer way too. Like he was bubble wrap and I was glass—and he knew just how tight to wrap to keep me from breaking.

His skin tasted just as good as it smelled. With a hungry mewl I tucked in, running my tongue up his shaft to the tip, where I dug into his slit to taste him directly. The texture was velvety soft, almost silky right around the crown.

"Fuck," Ben swore under his breath, the hand in my hair tightening, then loosening, his balls pulling up tight. "That's it, baby." His voice was a husky, half-purr. "Just like that."

Lashes fluttering, it only felt second nature to continue to tease his slit. To rub and rub at it, chasing all the slightly salty cum the moment it surfaced.

"Such a hungry little thing," Ben murmured, still petting my head. When he tightened his grip again, gently urging me to take more, I was quick to comply. The deeper Ben sank into my mouth the more at peace I felt.

I'd wanted this.

I could admit that now.

I'd wanted to be full of him. To have his complete attention. To suck and lick, and sink low, low, low. He cursed again, stroking his fingers through my hair, over my cheeks, and thumbing where my lips stretched wide.

When I glanced up again, the expression on his face made my skin feel hot.

He looked *wrecked.*

Completely fucking wrecked.

The way he'd wanted to wreck me.

His legs were shaking, like he was doing everything he could not to snap up into my mouth and choke me. The sadistic gleam in Ben's eyes made it obvious he'd thought of doing just that. And that was…fuck.

That was *so* hot.

I latched onto his hips, gently urging him deeper, trying to convey to him just how badly I wanted him to give in to his desire to fuck me. Ben was a bit of a bully when he was horny—and that paired with his normally serious and soft demeanor was simply the sexiest discovery I'd ever made.

He was exactly what I'd always wanted.

Ben hesitated, but after the second time I tugged on his hips, he gave in.

Snap went his pelvis, sinking till his crown was snug in the back of my throat and his balls slapped against my chin. I choked. And it wasn't even on purpose. He was simply that fucking big. Gagging, my eyes burned as Ben pulled me off his dick.

"No," I whined, when it slipped free, slapping sticky-wet against his tight belly. "I *want* it." My voice was fucked-out and hoarse. Sounded like I did when I was on tour after back-to-back performances.

Ben arched his eyebrow at me, waiting for a solid—painful—ten seconds to see if I'd change my mind, before a sly, evil smirk spread across his lips and he was shoving me back down onto his fat cock. Slow and easy, every time I tried to speed up or take more than he wanted me to he'd pull my hair till it stung and force me to comply.

And every time he did, pleasure would zing up my spine, zipping through my body all the way to my toes.

I'd told him I liked a little pain, and fuck—he was perfect—because rather than make me beg for it, he simply gave me what I wanted.

After teasing me for what felt like forever, but was probably only a few minutes, Ben let me have what I wanted. With my face smashed against his pelvis and his cock down my throat, I found the peace I'd been searching for.

The world was quiet aside from the steady swoosh of his breath and my own needy grunts. My mind drifted, my lashes fluttering as Ben pressed into me, grinding against my mouth like I was nothing more than a sleeve for him to fuck.

My dick wanted to wake up again. I could feel it, twitching back to life, as I pulled up then pushed down, urging Ben to move. He grabbed my face with both hands, the molten hot skin causing more tingly buzzing to dance through my body as he followed my lead and began to fuck my face in earnest.

Smack, smack went his balls against my chin, the skin soft and prickly in a way that made me feel *crazy*. I couldn't breathe. Couldn't think. There were no sleepless nights, there was no trip to L.A. looming over me. My contract didn't need to be signed. The world didn't feel too big. There was just Ben, and his monster cock, and the way he pounded me like I'd been desperate all my life to be pounded.

When he came it was so far down my throat I couldn't taste it.

Once, twice, three times he fucked me, rhythm stuttering as he rode out his high. His eyes were darker than coal, his face flushed. Sexiest of all, however, was the way he bore his teeth at me, pearly white and flashing,

"Fuck," Ben swore again, using his grip on my hair to pull me from his dick. I made sure to give it one last, lingering suck on my way off. Ben's eyes rolled back, and I shuddered, aching to make him make that face again. He cracked a smile, eyes drifting shut. "Maybe *you* should be the one in prison," he teased.

"Because of my superior cock-sucking skills?" I asked, voice scratchy and quiet. I eyed his balls thoughtfully, debating if he'd let me sink down to suck on them like I'd wanted.

"*Goddamn*," Ben shuddered, like the sound of my voice like this was enough to get him going again.

And then he yanked me up the bed, hauling me into him, all our sweat-sticky skin pressing together as he fluttered kiss after kiss against my lips, my cheeks, my ears, my throat. His hands smoothed down my body, finding my ass, and slip-sliding along my still-lubed crack.

"*Ben*," I whined, my hard dick jutting out at him.

I couldn't believe it'd managed to get hard a second time in one night.

"Up here," Ben's voice was a low command. My limbs were fuzzy and my head was full of cotton so it took me a second to respond. "*Now*, Robin."

Up I went, straddling his face as his big hands cupped and squeezed my ass cheeks and he pulled my hips forward to feed my dick into his mouth.

Wet, hot, and tight, he swallowed around me.

I didn't last more than a minute, my hips twitching, my hole fluttering as Ben snuck a finger inside me again and crooked till he found that spot that made me sing. When I spilled, he swallowed every last drop. He nibbled at my thighs, at my belly. He pinched my dick and lapped the salt from the skin, sucked my balls into his mouth, and toyed with me till I was scratching at his hair weakly and sobbing quietly.

"Shhh," he murmured, still teasing my now-softening cock. "You like this."

He was right. I did.

So I let him continue to torture me. Till my eyes burned, my cheeks were wet, and I had bite marks up and down my thighs. I thought it was over then because my dick couldn't rise, and I doubted Ben's could either.

But it wasn't.

"Up," Ben urged again, his finger still in my ass.

"Mm?" I shuddered, dick limp and aching so, so good. I loved this. Loved how raw and used up I felt. There was no room for sadness or self-consciousness like this. And for the first time in my life I truly felt like I didn't have to take care of myself.

Ben knew what I wanted before I even knew it.

Ben knew how to take care of me.

Ben was the comfort I'd never known I needed. He was strength and home and trust. He was laughter, shared wine glasses, and belonging. He made me want to stay.

"Up," he urged again, voice rough and full of affection. "Do you need help, baby?"

I whined.

The sadistic gleam was gone now as Ben wiggled my hips up till my soft cock pushed into the pillow above his head. It was nice that he'd helped, even without me having to ask. Though I still didn't get why he *wanted* me like this. "Hands on the headboard," Ben murmured from somewhere beneath me.

I grabbed on, still shaking, my head fuzzy.

And then his tongue was there. Hot and slick and lick, lick, *licking* at my asshole. Stretching my rim as he wiggled his tongue beside his finger.

"Oh fuck," I gasped out, head dropping down.

We didn't have a lot of time before the girls would wake up. I didn't want to be too loud. But it felt almost impossible not to gasp and shudder as Ben made room for himself inside my body. When he pulled his finger out, my ass clenched and clenched and clenched, trying to coax it back in.

"Empty," I complained without meaning to, my voice unrecognizably soft.

"I know, baby," Ben's voice crackled, low and husky. "I know your pretty little hole is lonely, isn't it?" He cooed, pressing a kiss right over my ass. "I need you closer," he urged, forcing my hips down.

"You won't be able to breathe," I argued—even though I really didn't mean to.

"Sit on my face, little songbird," Ben replied, tone flat and demanding.

I sat on his face.

He groaned, running his nose and lips all over my perineum, and then up against my hole. His hands felt impossibly huge as he clutched my ass tight, squeezing and squeezing—like he loved the give of it, as he gave my hole a filthy suck.

Like he was kissing it.

The same way he kissed me.

There was no way my dick was managing a third orgasm. But in an odd way that made me like this even more. Because Ben was simply doing it because he wanted to. Not because he was trying to get either of us off.

He simply wanted to start his day by eating me out.

And I was…absolutely not complaining.

Flick, twist, flick.

Ben rubbed and kissed and slurped around my hole. His beard scratched. It was barely more than stubble, but it was enough to make my already sensitive skin burn. He pried my cheeks open wider, teeth gently worrying my skin as his tongue lick, lick, licked where I was sticky and empty.

For ten glorious, sloppy minutes Ben feasted on my ass. He got his fingers back in at some point. Three this time. Probably part of his "training". And by the time he was done, his wrist had to have been sore from the way he'd pounded into my oversensitive body.

When he withdrew, I felt cold all over.

I only knew he was done because he gave my hole one last, chaste kiss, and then tugged me down the bed and into his arms. Ben massaged my hands—somehow understanding that I'd been gripping the damn headboard for dear life. He fluttered kisses along my cheekbones again. His lips were cherry red and abused as he told me what a "good boy" I was.

"So good," he murmured, kissing along my cheek and stroking over my flank. I was shaking. I knew I was. But I couldn't seem to stop. "Such a good, *good* boy." Ben's praise made me light up from the inside out.

No one had ever been this sweet to me.

"So pretty, so obedient," Ben continued, pulling me till I was snuggled into all that warm, sweat-damp muscle. "You're *my* pretty little songbird, aren't you?"

I wasn't sure how I felt about the nickname, since I'd never had one before. But in that moment it was good, good, good. I wasn't Robin "Trashmouth" Johnson. Wasn't famous. Wasn't the kinda guy who dreaded his everyday existence, didn't know how to talk to people without putting his foot in his mouth, and was tired, tired, tired.

I was Ben's pretty little songbird.

And I was a *good boy.*

"Yes," I managed, voice rough and sugary sweet.

"So pretty," Ben murmured, stroking over my cheeks, across my eyebrows—which was a little weird but nice—and into my hair. "You're tired, aren't you, sweetheart?" Ben whispered as his thumbs curled beneath my eyes, pressing gently at the dark circles.

"Tired," I agreed, voice cracking.

"I know, baby," Ben kissed me to reward my honesty. "You work so hard, don't you?"

"Y-yeah," my voice cracked again, hot tears burning beneath my lashes.

"You just want to rest," Ben's voice was gentle, calm. I leaned into his touch, tears leaking down my cheeks. "You've been so strong for so long."

"Yes," I agreed, because he got me. He fucking got me the way no one else had.

"You just need someone else to take care of you for a change." Ben kissed me gently and I cried my agreement against his mouth, a wet little hum that I knew was probably more gross than sexy, but Ben didn't complain. "That's okay," Ben murmured, unfazed by the tears. "That's okay. I'm here. I'm here now, sweetheart." He kissed me again. "I'll take care of everything. So that you can rest."

The weird thing?

I believed him.

Ben held me till I fell asleep not long after.

I knew he had to get up to take care of the girls so I wasn't offended when eventually the bed next to me was empty. At one point he'd redressed me, but I'd barely noticed that either as I slid into the warm space he'd left, curled around his pillow, and dreamed.

Dreamed of a world where I was Ben's songbird forever.

Where he could care for me.

Where I was well and rested, had a family of my own, and the future was bright, bright, bright.

When I woke up later, there were pancakes and coffee awaiting me—just the way I liked it. Ben kissed me good morning, stroked his hands up and down my back, and made me promise to eat both lunch and dinner.

And I let myself love him.

Quietly.

Happily.

Because I knew my time would be up soon, and I thought—just this once—I'd let myself forget what I was.

sixteen

BEN

THE BULK OF NOVEMBER PASSED by in a beautiful autumnal blur. I spent any time I wasn't at work or playing with my daughters with Robin. Coffee dates snuck into the middle of the day between my appointments. Matinees at the theater, playing Christmas movies. Little walks after dark, with each of us holding one of the girl's hands. We checked out the lights down at the pond, all of us puffing in the chill.

I did my best to give Robin everything on his Christmas to-do list.

On one rather lovely night right before the last leaves fell, Robin accompanied us to a bonfire in the woods. We'd filled up on apple cider and craft beer, and he'd somehow gotten Rosie to agree to do the Macarena with him. Which was as silly as it was impressive.

Watching them wiggle their butts in the same direction while Jane curled up against my shoulder was probably my favorite memory in the world. It felt right. To share that with him. For Robin to have so easily slipped inside my world. He was as stubborn as a thorn, and I knew one day if he left, I'd feel that ache forever.

Like Mama had said though, some things were worth the inevitable pain.

And if there was one thing I was coming to recognize about Robin Johnson, it was the fact that knowing him—for however long I would be blessed to know him—would be worth every resulting heartache.

Maybe *that* was love.

Accepting that one day you might lose the person that made your heart full, but choosing them anyway. The deeper I sank, the harder it would be to heal, but I was at peace with that.

On Sundays we'd all train together, Robin would spend the night, and *I* would spend as much time as I could inside his body. Fingers, tongue, whatever he'd let me. I learned him, inside and out, and on the nights when he was simply too tired to do anything but curl in my arms and rest, I held him.

Because that was perfect too.

It was a pattern. A beautiful, glorious, wonderful pattern. Like a patchwork quilt, different squares, all sewn together to make what would one day be the stories I told my grandchildren. They'd ask me if I'd ever been in love, and Robin's eyes would come to mind. His laugh. His smile. The way he was more open than anyone I'd ever met, and yet more guarded too.

Like his heart was under lock and key.

Like he had one foot out the door, even as he gave me everything he had to give.

He was…

He was the kind of man that inspired sonnets and love songs. Which was fitting, considering what he did for a living. I found myself shifting, my world brighter than ever before, my smiles more freely given.

Well-meaning folk on the street commented on my changed demeanor. And Mama asked me when the wedding was going to be—she was joking, obviously—but still, that only inspired more ideas. Fantasies that made my heart flutter and my world a brighter place.

My books took a positive turn.

A turn I hadn't expected.

Even seeing the women I'd been raised by giggling about the rimming and felching I'd written could not dampen my newfound joy.

And as the last of Belleville's autumn leaves withered and fell away, I felt myself falling with them.

I never wanted it to end.

But even I knew something needed to give. At least...if Robin and I were going to figure out how to make this work between us after Christmas had ended and he'd gone back to L.A. I wasn't opposed to a long-distance relationship. I visited California often enough because of book signings that we could see each other. And I had more than enough money to make those visits more frequent.

After watching the way he'd bonded with my daughters, I was more than a little inclined to foot the bill to have him more permanently in our lives. They loved him. Adored him, really. Even if they teased and prodded and poked him.

"Your hair looks bad," Rosie had told him one day as they'd sat across from each other at the breakfast table. Robin had blinked, slow and sleepy, the way he did for the first half hour after waking up. His hair truly had looked bad, sticking up in every direction, white and fluffy. He'd had a pillow crease on his cheek, which I couldn't help but find endearing.

He'd barely reacted to Rosie's barb, other than to flick a blueberry at her.

To which she'd stared at him, and stared, and *stared*.

And then started giggling so ferociously it should've probably made him frightened. For the rest of the morning, she'd followed him around, chucking blueberries at him in revenge. And Robin, gamely, would simply laugh and bat them off.

I'd put a stop to it, of course.

And we now had a rule that throwing food was prohibited. But still. Watching them play together, comfortable and happy, made me feel warm in a way I never knew I could.

I'd never seen my children take to another person the way they had with Robin.

And while he knew exactly when to bluster to make them laugh, he was gentle with them too. Once, when I was cooking dinner—Jane was crying in the corner, and Robin came to the rescue. I'd been trying to get her to open up about what had happened, but she'd been tight-lipped and red-faced, and retreated to lick her wounds in private.

I'd decided to give her space until she was ready to be comforted.

But apparently the person she'd wanted hadn't been me.

Because when Robin had showed up, pushing through the front door using the key I'd given him, she'd immediately made a beeline right for him. Her chubby hand had cupped his, tugging him into the corner where she'd hidden earlier. He flashed me a single, concerned glance, but happily followed along.

He'd sat down beside her, silent and careful, and gingerly offered her a shoulder to cry into. And after twenty minutes of whispering back and forth both of them had come into the kitchen with matching smiles on their faces. Robin had told me later that she'd been upset about play practice earlier that day, and he'd offered to help her practice.

After that…there was no stopping the torrent of feelings inside me.

I'd never expected to find a partner. I'd never *looked*. And yet, one had stumbled upon my little nest and found me anyway. It seemed the universe was looking out for me because Robin was the happiest accident I'd ever made.

Which…was *why* I'd asked Mama to watch the girls on a weeknight—which I never did—so that I could take Robin out on a date. A real one. I didn't give it a name. Because I could see Robin's wings spread any time I got even remotely serious, ready to take off.

Maybe he just needed more time.

Needed to decide he wanted us as much as we wanted him.

Me: Does seven work?

Robin: Hi, Ben-nana bread

Robin: Also, duh

Robin: I mean yes

Robin: Sorry

Robin: That was rude

Robin: I think...?

Robin: I got excited!

Me: You're fine. Wear comfortable shoes.

Robin: What does that mean?

I could picture his face so easily then, the little scrunch between his brows, the way he bit his lip piercing when he was confused. He was probably worried I wanted him to wear something less flashy so that we wouldn't stick out, though that was not the case at all.

Me: It means we're walking and I don't want you to get blisters.

Robin: Please tell me we're not going hiking

One of the girls was eyeing my mother's walls critically, her markers clutched tight.

"Rosie, don't even think about it," I said, soft but stern. She slumped, disappointed to have been thwarted.

"But—"

"Don't you think Grandma will be sad if you draw on her walls?" I arched a brow, waiting patiently for her to come to the same conclusion I had. Nodding sullenly, Rosie sighed unhappily. I grabbed a piece of paper out of my work satchel, passing it to her with a smile. "This will be better," I reassured, watching as her little face stared at the paper dubiously, as if to say—how in the world is *this* better? "Then I can hang it up at the office."

That got her attention.

Rosie's eyes widened and she immediately clutched the paper close to her chest. Then she beamed at me and scurried off to make me a masterpiece.

When I turned back to my phone, I discovered that Robin was panicking.

Robin: ...

Robin: Ben

Robin: Ben Ben Ben Ben

Robin: Ben please tell me we're not hiking. I hate hiking. Oh god.

Me: We're not going hiking.

I put him out of his misery, crossing an ankle over my leg and leaning back as I texted him again.

Robin: Thank god.

Me: Walking shoes, Robin.

Robin: what if I told you I only have one pair of shoes?

Me: I would ask if they're comfortable.

Robin: they are

Me: Then you're fine, baby.

Robin: I love that you text like an old man with perfect grammar and shit

Robin: this is my new favorite thing about you

Robin: second only to the way you say bussy like you're eighty years old

Me: Jesus Christ.

Robin: I also love the way you say Jesus Christ. All grouchy and amused. You're cute, Ben Ben.

Robin: The cutest

Me: Try and wear something somewhat warm, please.

Robin: so now you're ignoring me

Robin: I see how it is

Robin: ignore my love, Ben Ben

Texting was getting me nowhere. Robin was clearly excited, and because I wanted to hear that excitement for myself, I called him.

Mama walked into the room at the same time the call connected. She tilted her head curiously at me as the twins marched right past her and toward the counter and where the snack I'd prepared them sat in matching black bowls. Chopped apples and peanut butter to dip it into. It was their favorite.

They shuffled away once they'd acquired their food, returning to their now-shared art project across the room like they were returning to battle.

"Hi, sexy doctor man," Robin's voice was way too loud because Mama's head snapped toward the phone, her eyebrows shot up, and a wicked grin spread across her lips.

"Hi, baby," I hummed, tilting away from her knowing gaze, my cheeks burning as I spoke more quietly. "I'll be there to pick you up at seven thirty. Wear my hoodie, okay?"

Oh god. She was *listening*. I could feel Mama's eyes boring a hole into the side of my head.

"Aye, aye, Captain," Robin said in the way he always did. Then he lowered his voice conversationally. "I have a surprise for you."

I didn't like surprises.

I never had.

Everyone knew this.

But I wasn't about to tell him that.

"I love surprises," I lied, immediately very aware that Mama would see right through that statement. She laughed, proving that I was correct, and I shrank even lower. I should've taken the call outside, I realized belatedly.

"No, you don't," Rosie said, because she always had something to say.

Mama laughed at her too, and I prayed to God that Robin hadn't heard.

"You don't like surprises?" Robin had, in fact, heard because he sounded concerned.

"I do," I quickly reiterated. Rosie opened her mouth again, her little teeth flashing, and before I could think it properly through, I rushed to speak, "I like them if *you're* the one planning them."

Robin was silent for a solid ten seconds.

When he spoke again his voice was hushed, reverent. "That's super fucking sweet, Ben." It was hoarse. The way his voice only got when he was overwhelmed. "Fuck. You're just…fuck, man. What am I even supposed to say to that?"

I smiled, unable to help myself.

Mama continued to stare at me like I'd grown a second head.

"You're perfect," I promised, because he was—and he sounded self-conscious. "Seven thirty. Okay, sweetheart?"

"Seven thirty," Robin agreed, all his joking forgotten for now. "I'll wear warm socks and the hoodie you gave me."

"Good boy."

"See you soon, Ben."

"Pack an overnight bag."

"What kinda girl do you think I am?" Robin gasped in mock outrage. Quicker than I could blink he was back to serious again. "I'll get it all ready. Tell the twins I said hi?"

"I will."

"Cool. See you soon, Ben Ben."

"Goodbye."

When I set my phone down, Mama was leaning against the doorway, still staring at me. Behind her, the girls had moved on—feigning disinterest even though I knew they were eavesdropping on our every word.

"I've never seen you act this way," Mama said, sounding giddier than she should've. "I *knew* you could do it!" she declared, like seeing me in love was the most impressive thing I'd ever done. She said it in the same tone she'd told me she was proud of me when I'd graduated medical school. I wasn't sure if I should be elated or offended.

"I *told* you I like him," I countered, cheeks hot.

"Hearing about it and *seeing* it are two different things," Mama said wisely. "Happy is a good look on you, Benjamin." On her way past, she squeezed my shoulder before stopping behind me, turning the sink on, and filling a glass with tap water. She took a sip, and I watched her, cheeks still impossibly hot.

"*Mama*," I complained, ready to die because this was so *embarrassing*.

I couldn't just walk out. She was offering to watch the girls. Besides, she was my best friend, and even though the teasing was nearly painful, I figured she'd earned it.

"You make the *cutest* faces!" She cackled, a smile hidden behind her water glass. "I can't wait to tell Matilda."

"*Weird* faces," Rosie piped up, proving once again that she was listening. I covered my face with one hand, horrified and amused all at once.

I supposed they *were* weird faces.

At least where the twins were concerned.

I'd never looked at anyone like I looked at Robin.

I never wanted to.

"Stop being so freakishly tall," Robin complained when he realized that he was still too short to kiss me without my help, even while standing a step above me on an escalator at the outdoor mall.

"Watch your step," I said, instead of giving in to his flirting. There was a time for flirting. And it was not at this moment, when one misstep could lead to injury. Escalators were one of the things I hated most in this world.

I eyed it distrustfully as Robin stepped off of it—confident, despite being the kind of man with two left feet and no sense of self-preservation. My own step was measured and careful, less of a flounce, as I made it onto solid ground and tried to calm my racing pulse.

Robin, to his credit, must've noticed how nervous I was because he reached out with one hand and curled his mittened fingers around my own.

"Don't worry," he said softly.

I'd been told not to worry many times in my life. And it had always, in turn, caused me to worry more. Weirdly enough, in this case though, Robin's magic words somehow worked. Because his "don't worry" wasn't an empty platitude.

It was his way of keeping me present.

His way of promising to be more careful in the future.

I squeezed his hand back, tightly, and he grinned, bumping our shoulders together.

A chilly breeze danced through the walkway, cutting through the open air. It was dark already. A fact that felt like home, and yet I'd always hated. Hated when the winter nights crept in, the world went dark, dark, dark, and time seemed to work on a shorter schedule.

"Now that we're away from the scary escalator," Robin tipped his head up, eyes dancing. "How about that kiss?"

I leaned down, grinning as I took his mouth in a searing, lingering kiss.

A camera flashed, and I flinched, pulling back in surprise.

Robin froze, his smile wobbling as he twisted around, the loose posture he'd had only moments prior now stiff and uncomfortable.

"What's wrong?" I asked. The family that had been posing in front of the North Pole display we'd stopped by, continued taking photos. *Flash, flash.*

"It's nothing," Robin said, despite the fact it was obviously not nothing.

I didn't push.

But Robin didn't relax. As we shopped for winter clothes for him, he remained stiff and curled in on himself. He continuously glanced around us, as though he was scared to be out in public.

As if he was…

As if he was scared to be out in public…*with me.*

I stiffened too.

I tried to push the thought to the side. Because I knew that wasn't like Robin at all. Not the Robin I knew. But this icy, paranoid, uncomfortable person beside me didn't feel like my Robin anymore. He tried to pay for the clothing I'd selected for him, but I refused, carefully pushing his credit card to the side.

It was a black card.

His wealth had never been more obvious than it was in that moment.

It felt like a cavern had opened up between us and I hated it.

This was the first time we'd felt off when we were together. And I didn't…I didn't know how to fix it. Robin said thank you and smiled at me when the clerk handed me back my own card and then the now-full shopping bags, but his smile was a hollow ghost of the smile he usually gave me.

And that was…god.

It was awful.

Rather than let the rest of the night go on like this, I urged Robin toward a private space inside the outdoor mall. It was my favorite spot to take the girls. Sometimes they'd get overstimulated in public and need a moment of quiet.

Off the beaten path lined with shops, there was a tiny little grove. They usually set it up for Santa's Village, or the Easter Bunny in the spring, but it wasn't late enough in the year for that. Which meant it was empty as we arrived, and I gently steered Robin toward the solitary bench near the back end of the little cove. I urged him to sit, hovering over him as I debated what to do.

The echo of the mall was still behind us, but it was quieter now. Quiet enough I could hear the panicked uptick of Robin's breath as he did as he was told without complaint, his broad shoulders shuddering.

What was—

What…

Oh.

It had taken me far too long to realize what was going on, considering the fact I had panic attacks myself. But there was no denying what exactly was happening to Robin now as he quaked and quaked, sitting in my shadow, his green eyes half-lost.

"Oh, darling," I sighed, sinking down to my knees, despite their immediate protest. They ached as I hovered my hands over Robin's cheeks, pausing before touching him, because I didn't know if it would be welcome. "Can I touch you?"

"Just…just a little, okay?" Robin nodded jerkily, his breaths still ragged, his body still pulled in tight. Fight or flight. I could see it now. See the way he itched and itched to run. "Just my face."

His skin was icy cold as I cupped his face in my palms, gently stroking over it.

"It's okay, sweetheart," I promised quietly.

We sat there for a long time.

Long enough I wasn't sure my frozen legs would be able to cooperate. My back protested the odd position, but I fought through the pain, waiting for Robin's eyes to clear and his body to soften. When it did, I could finally breathe again.

"I'm sorry," Robin said, his voice crackly and low with remorse. "Sometimes I just—"

"The camera," I murmured, continuing to stroke his cheeks.

"I thought someone took a picture of us," Robin replied, confirming my earlier fear. The one I'd tried not to think about. I must've made a face, because he was quick to assuage my fears. "I don't want to ruin your life," he said, voice wavering like it only did when he was hurting.

I remembered the way he'd been recognized at the airport.

The way he'd held himself then, uncomfortable but earnest, as he'd done his best to give advice to the little boy who had approached him unsolicited.

Icy clarity washed over me, and I sat up a little taller.

"You hate it," I said, genuinely surprised.

"Hate…what?" Robin echoed.

"You hate being famous." It wasn't a question so much as it was an observation. It was odd. Normally someone with Robin's background would've thrived on the attention he never received as a child. He was a walking contradiction.

"Yeah," Robin admitted, like he had just given me nuclear launch codes. "I do." His face pinched. "You can touch me more now. I'm okay."

Forcing myself up—Jesus god, that hurt—I slid onto the bench beside him. It felt second nature to stretch an arm behind him and pull him in close. Just as naturally, Robin wiggled till his chin was sandwiched on my chest, his green eyes blinking up at me.

"That must be hard," I said, staring down at him as he picked at the seam on the side of my jeans without noticing that was what he was doing.

"I didn't realize," he admitted, nervously *pick, pick, picking* away. "Not until it was too late to take it back."

"You're more relaxed in Belleville," I realized, stroking up and down his back just the way he liked. He melted into the touch every time, like he'd never been touched before in his life. Not this way, gently and without expectation.

"No one knows me there," Robin shrugged. "It's like…an alternate dimension or something."

"Why didn't you tell me?" I asked, continuing to stroke. "We could've done something else—"

"You wanted to take me shopping," Robin protested, sitting up straighter, his chin really digging in. "It was so sweet. No one's ever wanted to do that for me before."

"We could've shopped online."

"It's not the same." Robin sucked in a breath. "Look," he said, softly but firmly. "I'm tired of missing out on being a real person." There was nothing but sincerity in his eyes. "And if I didn't want to come I would've told you."

They said, *believe me.*

They said, *I know my limits.*

They said, *don't take this from me.*

And what was I supposed to say to that?

"It's not that I don't want to be seen with you," Robin said, somehow reading my mind. "Except that it kinda is?" he added, shrugging one shoulder self-consciously. "Because if they see us together—if they take pictures, and find out who you are—your peace is shattered, just like mine has been."

"Oh, *Robin.*"

"I don't want Rosie and Jane to be recognized by the fucking vultures out there," Robin continued. "I want you all to live normal, happy lives. Without what I am…corrupting them."

"*Robin,*" I rumbled again because I got the feeling I'd just stumbled upon a landmine. "I've known who you were from the start."

He opened his mouth to protest, so I shushed him softly.

"It's my turn," I said, keeping my tone gentle. "Let me finish."

Robin nodded jerkily, mouth clicking shut as he melted into my side. His eyes were doing that thing again. Growing far away, like he was imagining the best path to take as he ran.

"Robin," I murmured a third time. I waited till his eyes focused again, and I had his full attention. "I have known since our very first conversation that one day someone might see us together, might take a photo, might expose me and my secrets."

"Everyone will find out about the werewolf porn, Ben," Robin's voice was high-pitched, like he was trying to sound like he was joking when he wasn't. "They'll dig up everything. There's no such thing as true privacy. After a certain point, you're not a person anymore. Good or bad, everyone will have an opinion about you."

I understood what he was saying, but he didn't seem to understand that I already knew that. "*Sweetheart*," I murmured, my hand squeezing the back of his neck tight. He fought at first, growing stiffer, harder—until abruptly, all at once, he melted, slumping into me gratefully.

"The camera flashed and I just—" his voice was quaking. "I saw your life flash before my eyes. All the things you'd miss out on because of me. All the sacrifices you'd have to make—just because we were together."

So *this* was why he always looked ready to run.

It made sense, in a sad, cosmic way.

That here Robin was, beloved by thousands—maybe millions—and in his head he was still the scared little boy whose father had tricked and hurt him. The same little boy that was constantly ignored by his mother. The same little boy who had never felt like he was enough. Who had turned away his chance at a family because he was terrified he would fail the people he loved most. The same little boy who had been conditioned to expect the worst from everyone and everything.

Except...

Apparently me.

Otherwise he wouldn't be here clinging to me. Wouldn't be showing me his exposed heart like he knew I'd protect it more fiercely than he ever had. Robin had not only just given me the keys to his heart, he'd opened the lock himself.

It was humbling to be privy to Robin's darkest secrets.

And I vowed to myself to keep them—and him—safe.

And maybe, just maybe, if I could make him realize the roadblock in his own head, it would mean that there was a future for us outside Belleville and its walls. Like a stray cat, he needed coaxing. Needed to be shown, rather than told.

Still though, there had never been a time in my life when I'd regretted hearing a kind word or reassurance. So I figured I'd start there.

"Robin," I tried for a fourth time, this time lacing a quiet command in my words. He remained relaxed like it was my bossiness that allowed him to settle. Which was…good to know. "I am well aware of what could happen," I reassured him again, keeping him close. "And I can tell you right now, that there is nothing that could scare me off."

He stared at me, like he was looking for a lie, even though there wasn't one.

"I know because of what you've been through, it might be difficult to believe that I'm not lying," I reassured, because he needed to hear this. "I know that trust for you is hard won. I told you once that I don't break promises—which I know again, might be hard to believe. It might take a long time for you to understand that I am sincere. That I am not like your father, or your mother, or any of the other people that have wronged you. But I am patient and you are worth the wait, however long it takes. I am a very difficult man to frighten. Especially considering the fact that since the day that I met you all you've done is make my life better. And in the meantime, if my secrets are the price I need to pay to keep you, then I will gladly give them away."

"Good things are worth hurting for."

Mama's words came rushing back to me as I pressed a kiss to Robin's forehead. His skin was no longer quite so cold. He'd stayed quiet the entire time I spoke, listening to me with his heart still hovering vulnerable between us.

"You're not *poison*, baby," I promised, lips still pressed to his skin.

Robin inhaled sharply, a panicked little sound. "Damn. I hate that you remember that I said that."

"Of course I remember." I gave him a squeeze. The trees around us rustled. Off in the distance I heard a child's excited chatter. "How could I forget that my favorite person in the entire world said something so awful about himself?"

"I'm your favorite person?" Robin asked, voice tiny and sweet.

"Of course you are," I said honestly. "You're my Robin."

"Oh," Robin said, warmth flooding his voice. He wriggled, grinning up at me, the lost look in his eyes gone. "You're my favorite person too."

"Don't lie," I teased.

"I'm not lying!" Robin replied, aghast.

"You'd pick Mads Mikkelsen over me every day."

It was a joke, to make him laugh. To shock the last of the chill from his limbs and the ice from his blood. It somehow worked, because Robin cackled, smacking my chest with a happy jerk.

"Shut up," he snorted, eyes dancing.

And I had to kiss him then, because he was perfect, perfect, perfect.

And he deserved to be loved.

Deserved to be kissed.

Especially in public.

Especially where people could see.

Robin was a little on edge, but for the most part, he remained mostly relaxed while we finished up at the mall. He'd stopped offering to pay after the second time I stared him down, and so, I was more than a little pleased with the wide selection I'd bought him—and his compliance. Everything was in black, because while I wanted him to be warm, I certainly had no intention of changing him.

"Babe, you bought me like an entire new wardrobe," Robin laughed as I hauled his bags in my arms. Normally the weight wouldn't bother me, but I really had irritated my back a bit earlier, and the strain was making my arms begin to shake. I was doing my best to ignore it, but it was hard not to be frustrated when the last thing I needed right now was my back acting up.

Robin, once again, to his credit, immediately reached out and snatched the bags away from me. We were halfway to the escalator, which made me nervous in general. The idea of accidentally blocking my view with the bags, therefore making it difficult to know when to step off, made me incredibly uncomfortable.

Robin sensed this, clearly, because he went on ahead with a chipper hop to his bow-legged step. When he stepped onto the top step, he twisted to grin at me. "Coming?" He waited expectantly as I took a hesitant step onto the moving steps.

"Thank you," I murmured, cheeks a little hot.

Robin shrugged, arms laden with bags, his solid body brushing against mine as he leaned back fractionally to comfort me. "No problem," he said, tipping his head back even more so he could grin. He righted himself quickly though, so as not to make me more anxious.

When he carefully leapt off the steps he was quick to shift out of the way so I'd have time to move as slowly as I liked.

My heart fluttered as Robin stepped into line with me the moment we were both on solid ground. It felt second nature to slow my pace so he could keep up as we headed toward the parking lot where my van awaited.

We were only half an hour from the Christmas Market.

It popped up in November each year and stayed till the week before Christmas. Robin had mentioned wanting to visit it the first day he'd come to my office, and I was more than a little giddy at the prospect of taking him.

Tomorrow was the Pie Festival.

Which meant it would be unwise to stay up too late.

Not that I was going to let that stop me.

The girls were with Mama till tomorrow morning and the relay race—and I had…*plans.* Plans that I was more than a little excited to see Robin's reactions to.

On the car ride to the market, Robin had about a thousand adorable questions.

He asked me about college. About New York. Asked me about my favorite foods, my favorite book I'd ever written, my favorite TV show.

He said the most brilliant, most hilarious things sometimes.

Especially when he was telling me stories, like…the time that he'd seen a guy cut someone off at a red light—and the stranger had nearly gotten rear-ended because of it, then gotten out of his car and thrown a fit. "Some dudes are assholes," Robin told me with a pumped-up, angry little frown. "I mean—I'm small. I can't be small and have small dick energy. Fuck that."

And.

"I think I'd be a bridezilla if I got married."

And.

"You ever wonder what that pole that kid licked in *A Christmas Story* tasted like?"

We'd recently seen that movie in the theater, so I understood why it was on his mind.

My favorite little tidbit of conversation, however, was when he asked me another adorable question. It wasn't anything anyone had ever asked me before. It felt poignant in a way none of the others had.

"What's something that makes you irrationally angry?" Robin asked. It was an out-of-pocket question, and I had to fight back a laugh.

"When people don't use their blinkers," I responded immediately—because that had literally just happened.

"Tell me another one," Robin wheedled, wiggling excitedly in his seat.

"Shouldn't it be your turn?" I replied. We were getting close to the market, and I mourned the fact the conversation would have to end.

"No way," Robin replied immediately. I snorted out a laugh and tried to come up with another one. It was surprisingly easy. Easier than telling him things I liked, anyway.

"I hate when Trent calls me Doc Ben Ben."

"Huh." Robin blinked. "Why?"

Snow glittered on the ground, crunching beneath the wheels of the car as we rounded a corner at a glacially slow pace.

"It feels derogatory," I said, surprised by my own answer. I'd never really thought about it before. "I'm the only member of my family that went away for school. It's always made me feel like a bit of a black sheep. I guess when he calls me that it only reminds me of that."

"Why don't you tell him that it bothers you?" Robin asked, frowning in commiseration like he understood what I meant. Like he understood not quite fitting in, especially when you desperately wanted to.

"Because I know he doesn't mean to hurt me," I replied. "And for me…

intentions are everything."

"Even if the person that has good intentions does stupid shit?" I got the feeling we weren't talking about Trent anymore.

"Of course," I replied evenly, meaning every word.

"I'm not like that," Robin replied. "Like you. I'm not all…magnanimous or whatever."

"That's a lie if I've ever heard one."

Robin laughed, reaching over to smack my leg—gently though, because he'd figured out pretty easily what would set off my anxiety, and being distracted at the wheel absolutely made that list.

"Alright, your turn," I hummed. We turned another corner, and I waited, more than a little eager to hear what he had to say.

Robin hemmed and hawed for a moment before answering.

"I hate…*pillow talk.*"

"Pillow talk?" I blinked. "*Interesting.*"

"Okay, Hannibal Lecter, what does that say about me?" Robin teased. I could feel him watching me, and when I glanced over briefly, I was right. His eyes were bright and full of affection. He looked so fucking cute all snuggled up in the passenger seat it made me ache.

"I think…" I kept my tone light, heart thumping. "I think you hate pillow talk because you feel like you're putting on a show."

"Fuck." Robin stared at me for a beat, the frankly cutest look of amazement on his face like I'd read his mind. "I think you're right."

"You're a performer that hates to perform."

"Damn." Robin's eyes were wide when I turned back to the road, wishing I wasn't driving so I could watch him indefinitely. "You know…" his voice was softer. "I think that's why talking to you doesn't bother me."

"Yeah?"

"Because I've never been anything but real with you. It's easy, you know? Easy in a way it's never been easy before."

That had to be the sweetest thing anyone had ever said to me.

I made Robin dress up in his new coat and mittens—not borrowed from me, this time—in preparation for heading into the large warehouse-like building that the market was hosted inside. It was wedged deep inside the mountains, and the switchbacks that led to and from it had always given me the heebie-jeebies. The lighthearted conversation in the car had greatly distracted me from that, however, and I was more than a little grateful for that.

"Where are we?" Robin asked, swinging his door open with gusto, his new black puff coat clinging to him as he leapt out of the car. His boots crunched on the gravel underfoot. Above us, the sky was indigo, stars winking between the gaps in the trees.

We were catching the tail end of the day at the Market, but I figured neither of us would care. An hour and a half was plenty of time to knock off another thing on his Perfect Christmas To-Do List.

Robin had confessed to me once, wine glass in hand, that he'd never had the kind of Christmas he'd seen other kids have. That he'd thought the movies were liars—at least till the year he was given time off for the holidays and saw how much effort Miles put into Bubba's Christmas.

And that was the day he realized it wasn't a fantasy at all.

It was possible.

You just needed someone to care about you enough to make it happen.

I was going to do my damndest to give him that this year.

I'd already been buying and wrapping presents. They sat hidden in the closet, ready to go out beneath the tree when I set it up. Normally I'd let the girls decorate while I watched, but this year I planned on inviting Robin to join us. I had a feeling that would mean a lot to him.

Robin's hand clutched mine tight as we made our way inside the building. Warmth immediately flooded forward, making the fact I'd forced him to wear a coat, mittens, hat, and scarf pointless. Still though, he shivered too much in Vermont's weather for me to feel comfortable allowing him to wander practically naked.

Robin's eyes were wide as he stared at all the vendors. His chest puffed up as he inhaled greedily the scent of roasted nuts and wax melts filling the air. It was always hectic here. Too many people. Too many things.

I hated it.

But at that moment I loved it. I loved it so fucking much because the look of wonder on Robin's face was worth any overstimulation I was about to experience.

"Oh my god," Robin said, voice reverent. "It's like a fucking movie, man."

"Are you surprised?" I asked, more than a little proud of myself.

"Super surprised," Robin beamed. "Luckily for you, I *love* surprises," Robin told me, smacking my chest with one mittened hand. "Omg." He smacked me again. "This is like, exactly what Hallmark made me think it would be."

"Yeah?"

"It smells like Christmas in here, Ben!" Robin smacked me a third time. "I think I had a candle that smelled like this one time." He laughed, head tossing back. "I was on tour." He flashed me a grin. "I sat in my bunk on the tour bus on Christmas that year and sniffed the fuck out of that thing. I think we were passing through…Kentucky, or something? I dunno.

Made me feel less alone."

That was the saddest thing I'd ever heard.

"Why don't you pick whatever you'd like," I hummed, nodding toward the first row of vendors. "My treat."

"Is everything going to be your treat today?" Robin asked, squinting up at me.

"Yes."

"Well, okay then, Daddy Ben-bucks." He snorted out a laugh at his own joke, squeezed my hand tight, and leaned into my side. Glancing up at me through his lashes, shy and all grumbly masculine deliciousness, he added, "You do know I'm loaded, right?"

"Your wallet is no good when I'm around," I informed him.

"Good to know," Robin's eyes crinkled, and something inside them settled.

"And for the record, I, too, am 'loaded.'" I cracked a smile so he'd know he wasn't making my wallet hurt by allowing me to take control financially. It gave me a thrill of satisfaction to know he was wearing the clothes I'd bought. That even when I wasn't around, I was providing for him.

Robin's eyes widened as he tilted his head and gave me a calculating look. "I *knew* your cologne smelled expensive," he muttered under his breath.

And that was that.

We shared a bag of roasted nuts, a styrofoam cup of cocoa—not as good as Belgian cocoa, but still passable—and a cinnamon roll. I said a prayer for my blood sugar, but didn't complain as Robin led us down each and every aisle on the hunt for gifts for all his favorite people.

It didn't escape my notice that he didn't buy anything for himself.

He hesitated when I first brought my card out, probably concerned that my offer to treat him did not extend to all of his purchases today. That was completely incorrect however, and I quickly soothed those fears.

With every purchase I made on his behalf, I stood a little taller.

It was easy to get swept up in this. To feel like I mattered in his world. And it was more than a little satisfying to know that I could take care of him, even at moments like this. The truth was Robin could provide anything and everything for himself, which was why the fact he was allowing me to do this for him meant so much to me.

He eyed a booth full of Christmas ornaments, one in particular that was full of ravens. When he wasn't looking, I purchased it, careful to slip it into one of the other bags so that I could surprise him with the gift later. So that he'd have ornaments that represented him up on our tree.

Robin carried the bags again, which I appreciated. I needed to lay down at some point, or pop a pain pill or two before I was ready to carry anything heavy. I could feel the foam roller I kept under my bed calling my name, but I didn't complain.

And despite my irritation that my back was affecting me, I was able to push through. Robin's smile helped more than he probably realized.

We bought cow sweaters for Miles and Bubba. A small fake tree covered in baubles for Trent. A new e-reader cover for my mother. Art sets for the twins. Furry socks for every one of the kids in Miles's classes. (That bag was the largest, and lightest somehow).

"Sweetheart," I murmured softly when we were halfway through the venue. Robin stopped his eager hopping—trying to see over the shoulders of the couple in front of us—and turned his attention to me.

"Yeah?" he asked, arms laden with bags, and yet, one of his hands always remained free to stay snug inside my own.

"Aren't you going to pick something for yourself?"

Robin blinked at me, brow furrowing like he'd truly forgotten that was his mission in the first place. There was icing on his lips from the cinnamon roll and I reached out to gently brush it off, licking the pad of my finger while he watched.

His cheeks went hot, his *fuck-me* eyes returning.

Immediately my dick twitched to life.

"It's hard to pick something for myself," Robin admitted, instead of beating around the bush. "Will you…pick something for me?"

"Only if you pick something for me," I countered.

Robin grinned, as if I'd just issued the most amazing challenge he'd ever heard. "Deal."

He leaned up, waiting expectantly for me to bend so he could smack a kiss against my lips.

"Ew," a small voice sounded behind us.

I startled, twisting a little at the same time Robin did. Laughter burst free when we both saw who had interrupted us.

Bubba Johnson was staring up at us, face scrunched, his hand clutched tight in Jeremy Collin's grip. They were sharing a bucket of nuts of their own and eyeing us curiously.

"Bubba!" Robin said, immediately forgetting about me as he tried to surreptitiously hide the bags of presents he'd bought just in case Bubba could see inside them.

"Are you guys on a date?" Bubba asked, eyes gleaming.

"Are *you*?" Robin countered, only for Bubba's eyes to go wide and confused. Jeremy's face was bright red. For a twelve-year-old he sure looked grown up. Reminded me of what I'd been like as a kid, quiet and large and serious.

"Ew, Duncle Robin," Bubba laughed. "I'm too young to date."

"Damn right," Trent's voice popped up from behind the two. He was nursing a thermos, probably with the powdery cocoa crap he stocked at his house. I grimaced at him. "Mama didn't tell me you guys were coming to visit the booth," Trent said, a knowing glint in his eyes.

"Mama didn't know," I countered, eyes narrowing. "No one knew."

"*I* didn't even know," Robin piped up, grinning at me. "It was a surprise."

Trent stared at Robin, then me. He was silent for a beat, processing this. "So you're here…to surprise Robin—and *not* to visit the family booth?" He blinked. Trent knew better than anyone how much I hated it here. I avoided it like the plague, I always had. Last year I'd helped out when he'd gotten sick, but that had been out of love for him, and not because I enjoyed this place whatsoever.

My cheeks felt hot as he pieced together what was happening.

The second he did, to his credit, his eyes went round and he jumped to my rescue.

"Alright kiddos—" Reacting quickly, Trent grabbed them both by the shoulders, turned them right around, and steered them in front of him. "Let's leave the two love birds alone." He flashed me a grin and a wink. And then he ruined his good brother moment by adding, "Your Uncle Ben's never been on a date before. We don't want to mess it up for him." Trent made sure to speak loud enough I heard.

And I wanted to die.

And also punch him in the face.

"Shithead," I muttered, and Robin laughed.

"You owe me monies," he told me in his best Rosie impression. The annoyance Trent's interruption had caused bled away as quickly as it had come. I leaned down to kiss Robin, aching to taste his laughter.

"You can have all the monies you want if you keep looking at me like that," I murmured, kissing him softly—the way he'd always deserved to be kissed.

"Teddy bear," Robin accused against my mouth, muffled and awkward and perfect.

"Only for you," I promised, because it was true.

Robin fell asleep in the car on the way down the mountain. He had the present I'd picked for him clutched tightly to his chest. I'd caught him eyeing the large round stuffed crow more times than I could count—and covertly, while he'd been distracted sniffing wax melts, I'd nabbed one.

I knew I'd done well, because when I'd presented it to him, his eyes had misted up—and he hadn't said a word. Just simply tucked into my chest and hugged me as tight as he could.

His present for me had been a pen. It was a fancy pen, made of marbled wood and gold. And I had immediately fallen in love with it. Especially when I realized just how well he'd grown to know me in such a small period of time. This was the kind of gift I would've picked for myself. And when he'd tucked it into the bag he'd informed me cheerfully that a "sexy doctor like you needs a sexy-ass pen."

I didn't wake Robin.

I let the crunch of gravel beneath the wheels and the fat snowflakes that had begun to fall comfort me as we made our way down the mountain.

The van was good in the snow, and it was drifting leisurely enough there was no need to worry.

Still though, I made sure to take each turn slow and steady—both to avoid any icy patches, and so that I wouldn't jostle Robin while he rested.

It was only after we arrived back in Belleville, traveled down Main Street and past my office to the parking lot behind it, that Robin finally woke up. He snuffled, jolting wide awake only seconds after his first sleepy sigh.

"Oh shit."

"Shh," I murmured, gently stroking a hand through his hair as the heater blasted hot air at us both. It ruffled the hair on my arm, but I ignored the odd sensation. "It's okay."

"I fell asleep!" Robin stared at me, horrified. "During our *date*."

"That's okay, sweetheart," I promised. "It was a big day."

I didn't point out the fact he'd just acknowledged that it *had* been a date. It was enough to know that he understood what it'd been. Despite knowing that that had been a slip up on his end, for sure. He was very careful to only ever refer to me as his friend, and our relationship as temporary.

A fact I hoped in time I could change.

Especially after our talk at the mall.

"But I didn't *want* to sleep," Robin tried to explain. "Which—I mean… is crazy, considering how much I've wanted that for like…forever. But today I just…I didn't want to miss a single second." He stared at me, conflicted.

"The night's not over," I murmured, tracing the curve of his cheek and enjoying the way he shivered. "Don't look so sad."

"But—" Robin's voice cracked. "What if this is our only one? And I just…"

"It won't be," I promised, leaning over and kissing the frown right from his lips. He hugged his crow plush tighter, and the fluff of the stuffed beast brushed against my flannel as I sank back into my seat.

It took a couple trips to get everything up the stairs. I tried to help, but Robin gave me the grouchiest, most adorable face I'd ever seen, and commanded me onto the couch with a point of his painted finger and a scowl.

"No way, asshole. Sit your gigantor ass down."

I'd done as I was told, because truthfully, my back was still protesting. When Robin returned after neatly piling all his presents up safely on the kitchen counter, he eyed me with concern.

"What do you need, babe?" he asked, gaze snapping to the cold sweat at my temple.

"Pills in the cupboard, please," I replied. Normally I'd get up and get them myself. But normally…I was alone.

Robin proved himself to once again be an incredible partner.

Because thirty minutes later, my meds had kicked in, my back was loose and warm, and he was kneading the muscle with his talented hands on my bed.

I'd wanted to take him apart piece by piece.

Wanted to edge and tease and torture him.

I'd had a plan, dammit.

But my body fought me once again—and I had no choice but to concede to it. Robin didn't seem to mind though as he settled into my side and his fuzzy toes skimmed my thigh. "You wanna watch a movie?" he asked, voice soft.

"Mmm?" I cracked an eye open to look at him.

He had his phone out, one already loaded up.

It was an old film. *White Christmas*? Maybe. When the title popped up, I hummed thoughtfully, realizing I'd been correct.

"I like the music," Robin confessed, his phone propped up so that I could see it without straining my back. He tangled our thighs together on the bed, and my heart warmed as I soaked him up greedily. His little socked feet kept brushing my calves and shins, legs as short as ever—and I couldn't help but find that adorable. "This is the kinda shit I wanna make, you know?"

"Why don't you?" I asked, as the sweet crooning from the microphone filled the room.

"I can't." Robin's brow ticked down. "Label won't let me."

I blinked, then frowned. "*Baby*." I twisted to look at him better, noting the unhappy tilt to his lips as he shrugged a shoulder.

"They said it's not part of 'my brand'," Robin admitted, like he was directly quoting someone. "They won't even let me sing Christmas songs for the *Christmas* party they're making me host on *Christmas* Eve."

"What party?" This was the first I was hearing of it.

Did that mean he wasn't going to be home for Christmas?

My heart lurched, some of my fuzziness fading as that realization washed over me like ice water.

"Every year my label does this *big* Christmas party. They pick an artist, and that artist hosts." Robin sighed, the movie continuing to play as he pressed his lips into a flat line. "It's supposed to be this prestigious thing? You know, to be *selected*."

"Right," I agreed, my heart still thumping erratically.

"This is the last year my contract is active before I have to renew it. So

I should be happy they asked me to host?" Robin sighed. "But it feels *weird*…that all these people are going to be at my house. *Strangers*. And I know that it's supposed to be this super cool, *wonderful* thing and yet… they've made it clear that I don't even get to fucking sing what I want to."

"What if you did it anyway?" I asked, because even though I was still trying to process this new information, I wanted to be here for him.

"Did what?"

"Sang Christmas music."

Robin blinked, like that thought had genuinely never occurred to him. Then a slow smile broke across his lips—only to fall more quickly than it had arisen. "I dunno," he sighed, looking pleased but conflicted. "Could get me blacklisted. Make it so that they don't want to renew my contract. Would be career suicide."

"Would that be a bad thing?" I wished I could take the words back the second they came out. Robin flinched, like he'd been struck. So I had no choice but to explain myself. "I mean…maybe there are other labels out there? That would allow you to have the freedom to do what you want."

Robin nodded, like this thought had genuinely never occurred to him before. "I *have* built a name for myself…" he agreed, pensive.

"You have," I reached out to stroke his hair out of his face. "Maybe… putting your foot down wouldn't be such a bad thing?"

"Would people even…want that?" Robin asked, voice wobbly. "I mean. I'm like…a one-trick pony. Except the pony does the same trick over and over—instead of just the one time."

He was so fucking cute I wanted to bite him.

So I did, sinking my teeth into his shoulder and enjoying his little cackle in reply. "Don't bite me, motherfucker," Robin snorted, shoving my head back. His eyes crinkled at the corners.

"Then don't say mean things," I replied.

"That's rude you know," Robin pointed out. I grinned, wide and unrepentant, and he grinned to mirror mine.

"Think about it," I replied, trying not to be biased—and failing. "Maybe you could have a different home base too, if your label changed. Somewhere…snowier."

Robin grew stiff all over again, his eyes narrowing as he stared at me. It was the same look he always gave me when I pushed too hard, too fast. But I couldn't stop myself. I was running out of time, and I needed him to know I wanted him here—even if he wasn't ready to process that yet.

"This bed is awfully big for one person," I wheedled, keeping my tone light.

"*Yeah*, right," Robin snorted with an eye-roll and the gentlest shoulder-shove known to man. "You're the size of three people combined. *I* can barely fit in here, and I'm like a quarter of your size."

I bit him again and he cackled.

"Belleville needs more emo-punk musicians," I added, sweetening the pot. Robin looked pleased that I actually knew the correct way to label his music. "More Christmas songs," I added, tone softening even more. "Love songs too."

"Your mom wants me to be a wedding singer," Robin informed me, cheeks pink. "She told me at the book club that your cousin is getting married. Tried to hire me."

Christ.

I laughed, shaking my head. "I'm sorry—"

"Don't apologize," Robin waved me off. "I like that she doesn't know who I am. I like that no one does." He shrugged again. "It's nice to just be…me, you know? Miles's big brother. Bubba's uncle. Your—" Robin cut himself off, eyes widening.

"Tiny goth shadow," I finished for him, even though we both knew he hadn't been about to say that.

"Yeah, *exactly*." Robin bobbed his head.

"Who would bring me coffee when I'm tired if you moved all the way back to L.A.?" I asked, once again trying to entice him. It was silly, bribing him with something that clearly only benefited me. But it definitely worked, because Robin nodded along, like his coffee deliveries were the most important part of his week.

"Who would teach Jane to sing?" Robin fretted, not realizing that he'd been caught in my web.

"She's worried about the play," I agreed. "She needs your expertise."

"But that's over by Christmas," Robin frowned. "She won't need help for long."

"There are other plays," I told him, my heart still beating erratically. "She wants to be a performer. But she's shy—"

"Miles was like that too," Robin informed me, dark brow still knit seriously. "He needed a lot of help socially."

"You could help her the way you helped him." I was playing dirty, and I knew it. Robin loved the twins. Probably more than he liked me, if I'm being honest. "You're better at that than I am."

"And *Rosie*—" Robin groaned, mussing up his own hair as he stressed. "Who's gonna help her with the cat?" Rosie was only five dollars away from meeting her goal, thanks to Robin and his sneaky enthusiasm. "You're too busy being hot and smart," he added seriously. "You don't have time to learn to be a cat dad."

I bit back a grin. "You would make a *great* cat dad," I told him just as seriously.

"I know!" Robin wailed, twisting to look at me again, his pale green eyes fraught with emotion. It took him a second, but it seemed he'd finally caught on to my evil plan. His eyes widened, and then softened. And then his cool, scratchy palm was cupping my cheek. "You are one sneaky bitch, you know that?" he hummed before pinching my cheek to punish me.

I shrugged a shoulder, copying his signature move.

"Hey, Ben?" Robin asked a few minutes later after he'd snuggled into my side and turned his attention back to Bing Crosby.

"Yes?" I asked, sleepy and quiet, tucked up beside him.

"Would you really want me to stick around?" Robin asked, his voice wavering. "I mean…not that I *can*. But *if* I could. Would you…would you want that? Not for the girls, or—the coffee or whatever."

"Of course I would," I told him honestly. "You're my sunshine."

Robin melted, muffling a swear against the pillow and a groan.

He twisted around, phone forgotten completely this time, and as he flung his arms around me he kept his grip gentle so as not to further twinge my back. The fact it was this sore did not bode well for the relay race tomorrow. But I'd already come to peace with losing, and I was fine with that.

"I'm sorry I couldn't fuck you tonight like I wanted," I apologized against his downy soft hair. Robin made an angry sound—his head whipping back so he could glare at me.

"Shut up."

"I *wanted* to," I told him, voice more vulnerable than I'd let it be with anyone else. "It's..." I sucked in a breath. "It's unfortunate that my body gets in the way sometimes." I tried to smile, but it was pained. Not because of my back this time, but because I hated that the night hadn't gone exactly to plan.

It had been a *good* plan.

The best plan.

And I felt cheated.

"Believe me, I know how that feels," Robin admitted, voice quiet and hushed. I didn't think he did. He was young. And he'd never had an injury like the one I'd had.

I must've looked confused because he explained, voice shaky, "I dunno if you've noticed, but I have pretty severe insomnia?" Robin cracked a smile, trying to keep his tone light even though the topic was very heavy. "It started when I was on the road. There'd be these nights where I was so amped up from performing my eyes just...wouldn't shut. I'd just lay there—and the harder I tried the worse it became. And then the anxiety started to kick in. And then the late nights got later. And everywhere was *unfamiliar*, and *new*—and I was so fucking *lonely* I just..." he made a soft, frustrated sound.

"After a while, I stopped sleeping at all. And the more desperate I got to fix the issue the worse I made it. Like stressing out about it was actually hurting me more." Stress was killer on the body, especially for someone who felt their feelings as strongly as Robin did. "When I fell asleep on your arm it was like fucking nirvana," Robin admitted. "I *knew* you were special. Ever since then. Like there was just something my body recognized about yours that made you...I dunno—" he cut himself off, obviously embarrassed. "It's cheesy."

"Tell me," I demanded, tone still soft.

"You make me feel *safe*," Robin admitted. My heart ached. Then, because he realized he'd gotten off track—he continued explaining. "Anyway. Sometimes, because of the lack of blood flow and yada yada yada—doctor speak—my dick just doesn't…"

Oh.

Oh.

It took me a second to understand what he meant. "But you jerked off with my conditioner." I didn't mean to say it out loud like that—it simply came out. Robin made a sound like he was dying and hid his face in the pillows.

"That was a *celebratory* jerk off!" he whined. "Because it'd been a really long time since I'd rested enough that my dick decided to wake up."

"Robin," I sighed, melting into him and lacing a kiss against the flushed skin at the back of his neck. "Thank you so much for sharing that with me."

So he *did* understand.

Even if our situations were different, they were close enough.

"It made me feel broken for a while, you know?" Robin's voice was muffled. "But…" He twisted to peep one lovely green eye at me. "I'm not." He said the last two words with enough confidence that it caused a slow grin to spread across my face. "You taught me that, you know?"

"I did?"

"Yeah. Just now. And before—when you told me about your back." Robin shifted, peering at me, his cheeks bright red and his expression sheepish. "Made me realize how stupid it was to beat myself up over something I can't control, when here I am—not mad at you at all for pretty much the same thing."

"A double standard," I agreed, so fucking proud of him I wanted to bellow it from the rooftops. I was distracted. Distracted enough, that I hadn't noticed Robin had not given me the surprise he'd promised.

"Soooo…*yeah*," Robin nodded, making sure I was making eye contact before he spoke again. "You're perfect the way you are. And there will be other dates—" It was my own words, thrown right back at me like he hadn't even noticed that's what he'd done. "So don't feel bad." His words were soft and sweet, and as the blanket of snow fell outside, peace fluttered around inside my belly.

Somehow, I knew, deep down, that things were going to work out for us.

I wasn't sure how.

But they would.

And it was with *that* confidence that I drifted off to sleep—content that tomorrow we'd be losers together—and I'd get to prove to Robin once and for all that I wanted him, "poison" or not.

seventeen

ROBIN

THE SNOW HAD MELTED BY the time we arrived at the fairgrounds that hosted Belleville's Annual Pie Festival the week of Thanksgiving. I'd never attended before. Miles had never taken me—which was apparently a motherfucking shame. Because the second I arrived, I was both shocked and delighted by how bright and lovely the whole place was.

This was *nothing* like any of the events I attended in L.A.

The closest I'd gotten to anything this lively was the one and only time Nancy had taken me to the Santa Monica Pier for my birthday, and even that paled in comparison to the event that unfolded at the Belleville fairgrounds. It hadn't helped that the paparazzi had found me there, but I was trying not to think about that—and them, and the way they affected my life back home.

It seemed like every member of the entire community had decided to attend. There were colorful booths, similar to the market Ben and I had just attended. Vendors that sold fall treats delicious enough to make your mouth water. Signs, jauntily painted and arranged, pointed to various areas of the fair grounds. And hilarious depictions of apples were thrown up everywhere.

There was soul in everything here. In every handmade product. In every pie booth. In every stroke of paint and fabric tent.

People laughed and grinned at each other. They shared treats back and forth. The air was full of cheerful chatter and the sweet smell of apple cider donuts. There was this odd sense of camaraderie, like friendship itself had a scent.

Before, I'd thought the oddest part of Belleville was the fact that no one recognized me.

I'd since changed my mind.

The weirdest part about Belleville wasn't its penchant for decorating for Christmas too early, its tiny population, or the fact that everyone seemed widely invested in each other's lives. No. The weirdest part about Belleville was the fact that every single person here seemed to genuinely be nice.

They *helped* each other.

They were quick to throw compliments—barbs, sometimes, in good fun—but everything was done in good faith.

I could see why Miles loved it here.

Why he fit in.

This was the kind of place he should have always lived.

"Robin, look!" Bubba's voice was loud and cheerful, muffled a little because he had a fucking apple in his mouth. I'd seen him bob for apples about fifty times—and holy fuck, it got even more impressive each time he did it.

The kid should be in the Guinness Book of World Records or some shit.

"Dude," I replied, just as shocked this time as I'd been the first time. "Holy fuck."

Rosie's little hand immediately shot out, bumping into me. I laughed, fumbling around in my pocket for a dollar bill without having to look. I pressed it into her little palm before she retreated back to her spot by my side, her other hand clutching my coat.

I'd offered to hold her hand and she'd refused.

That didn't mean she hadn't stuck to my side like a goth barnacle though. Cutest little barnacle I'd ever seen.

Ben was off somewhere…being sexy and dad-ish. Jane had wanted a donut. So Papa Ben Ben was finding her a fucking donut. Because he was just, you know, *perfect* like that?

We'd been up late the night before, but neither of us had complained.

Neither of us had complained about our early morning together either.

I mean…what was there to complain about? Wasn't like I was anything but pleased with the way Ben had eaten my ass till I made a mess of the sheets, and then tucked his cock between my thighs and rode me like a goddamn champion. He'd made me sticky enough we'd spent half an hour in the shower cleaning up.

Okay fine, *an hour*.

Because he apparently had not been done with my ass yet.

He took his plan to "train" me quite seriously. No matter how much I assured him that I could take his gigantic-monster-dick, he simply ignored me. I didn't mind. Ben knew better than I did, anyway.

And it was nice to trust someone else like that.

Lord knew, I never had before.

You know…it's funny?

Really.

All of this was.

Standing here, with Bubba grinning at me. With Rosie clutched close. With the world full of orange and red and happiness.

It was funny because I hadn't expected it. Because even though I'd come home hoping to spend time with my family, I'd never let myself dream that my reality could be so bright. That the world could be soft. That I would be welcome.

That I would feel like I belonged.

There were times I felt a shadow of this happiness out on the road. When the lights were bright and the crowd was loud—and then quiet. When they waited, patient, phone flashlights dancing in the dark—and I opened my mouth and sang. When their words mirrored mine, and my music became theirs, and the world felt like a small, perfect place.

But those moments were few and far between.

And Nancy's words had been rattling around inside my head—especially after Ben and I had talked the night before.

"It would be okay for you to quit, Robin," Nancy had said the last time we'd spoken. "I mean, I'd miss you. You're my favorite boss. But even I can see you're slipping. And if you keep going down this path, you might fall too far to get back up again."

I was tired of feeling off balance.

Tired of having one foot out the door.

Tired of living the way I had.

And as I stood there, in a crowd of people that weren't family but felt like they were—I wondered if I'd feel that way if Belleville was my home. If I'd be so exhausted if my days were full of Ben's smile, the girls' laughter, chocolate chip pancakes, werewolf book clubs, and Miles's homemade pizza.

Maybe there *was* room for me here.

Maybe I'd be *happy* here.

In Vermont—with its watercolor falls, with its bonfires, with its Pie Festivals, and early snow storms. It was a slice of heaven tucked tight in the mountains and farmland. An oasis in a world that was too big, too empty, too full all at once.

I wished then that I hadn't chickened out the night before.

That I'd given Ben the surprise I'd promised.

But I figured…there was time for that later.

"You okay, Robin?" Ben asked, his voice startling me out of my thoughts. Bubba had run off. I could see him showing Trent and Miles the apple he'd just won, his hands gesticulating wildly as they smiled at him, indulgent and fond.

The perfect parents.

In the perfect town.

My hands squeezed into a fist, the pair of gloves Ben had bought me creaking.

"Robin?" Ben asked again.

And then he was in front of me. His dark red hair was windswept, his cheeks flushed from the chill in the air. His lips twisted into a smile, but there was a worried quirk to his dark brows. A lock fluttered free from his usually perfectly styled hair falling across his forehead.

Rosie's hand found mine and I squeezed her gently, warmth flooding my body.

"I'm good," I told him, surprised to find it was true.

"Yeah?" Ben hummed, watching me carefully. He had Jane attached to one arm, and a box full of donuts in the other. His back was much better today. My stomach rumbled.

"I'd be better if you shared some of that with me," I nodded toward the box, and Ben snorted out a laugh.

"Mmm, I don't know," he teased. "There might not be enough."

"There's like six donuts," I pointed out, mock outraged. "You're telling me you're going to eat all of them?"

"Big feet, big appetite," Ben replied with a teasing twist to his lips.

"You're greedy," I complained. "Greedy, greedy."

"*Hey*," Jane said, voice quiet and as close to angry as I'd ever heard her. "You said they were for *me*."

Ben's teasing smile softened as he turned to look at her. He crouched low to speak, tone gentle. "I was just flirting with Robin," he promised, like she was a little adult.

So fucking cute, oh my god!

I seriously doubted Jane knew what "flirting" meant, but she seemed to settle regardless, nodding seriously up at her dad, her little pigtails swinging. "I want *two* donuts," she negotiated—because he'd made her sad.

Apparently Rosie wasn't the only evil mastermind in their family.

"How about a donut and some cider?" Ben negotiated right back, always aware of the twins' sugar intake. He'd already promised them cider—earlier, when we'd first arrived. But Jane didn't seem to realize she'd been tricked because she nodded along, excited about the idea of not just one, but *two* different kinds of treats.

Ben broke the box open, handing a donut to both of the girls with a napkin each. And then he made one up for me, his eyes crinkling at the corners as he passed it over. I accepted the donut with a grin, then groaned, because damn—it smelled like fucking nirvana.

"You Vermontinarians don't fuck around when it comes to apples," I told him around my mouthful of chewy, delicious goodness.

Ben snorted, lips quirking up. "I think that word gets longer every time you say it."

"What word?" I played dumb as he reached out to gently brush the sugar from my lip with the hand Jane had abandoned so she could double-fist her own donut. "Vermontinarianarians?"

"Jesus *Christ*," Ben laughed. I fluttered a kiss against his gloved fingers, simply because I could—even though he wouldn't feel it.

His eyes were the color of honey when the sun hit just right, and for a second, I was lost in them. Lost in the way he looked at me like I was something good, and right, and precious. Lost in his smile, the prettiest smile in the whole wide world.

No one had ever looked at me like that.

His eyes said, *I adore you.*

They said, *I adore you.*

They said, *I adore you, I adore you, I adore you.*

My throat felt tight all of a sudden. My eyes burned. I shoved more donut into my mouth and pretended like I hadn't read the sonnet in Ben's gaze. Pretended like my heart wasn't racing. Like my hands weren't sweaty. Like I wasn't two seconds from bolting the moment he turned his back.

Because Ben was Ben, he didn't push.

He never did.

He was more of a coaxer, that one.

Like I spoke a secret language and he'd figured out how to translate.

Always patient, even now.

"It's okay, Robin," Jane told me, leaning heavily against my side, her tiny voice sweeter than ever. "Don't worry."

We'd lost the race. Which…shouldn't have come as a surprise despite our training. I was slow and uncoordinated. The girls were better than me—but only by a bit. And Ben, despite being pretty fast, hadn't been able to make up for the lack of skill on his team.

Still though, he was grinning, like he wasn't mad at all.

His smile was brilliant as he spun Rosie around in lazy circles on the dance floor. The way he was bending had to be hurting his back, and I made a mental note to make sure to give him a rub later to help ease the ache.

The sun had set, fairy lights twinkling in arcing loops above us. Other families littered the shoddily put up, temporary dance floor. But the chaos of the day had softened, and the crowds had begun to dwindle. Jane hadn't wanted to dance, and I'd lied and told her I didn't either—so that we could hang out together.

"Thanks, baby," I said softly, leaning down to kiss her fuzzy head. I hadn't thought the kiss through—probably should've asked first. And for a second, I just froze, worried I'd crossed a line that I shouldn't have. Apparently, I hadn't needed to worry, because instead of pushing me off, Jane twisted and smacked a kinda slimy but perfect kiss against my cheek in return.

Jane seemed to think I was torn up about losing.

And I was—in a way—because I would've loved nothing more than to help my favorite little gremlins win.

Honestly, if the race had taken place even two months ago I would've been devastated. Would've been beating myself up. Would've been dissecting every move I'd made to try and figure out where I could've been better.

But instead, I just felt…peace.

Because despite the fact we'd lost because of me—despite the fact Ben had bet on the slowest pony on the track—things hadn't changed a bit. He was just as gentle, just as flirty, just as Ben-nish as before.

His smiles were wide and bright and unrepentant.

He handed them to me freely.

Like it cost him nothing.

Like they were *mine*.

And I didn't feel like a loser. I didn't feel like a waste of space. I didn't feel like a nuisance, or a problem. I didn't feel like it was my fault. And the girls didn't treat me like it was either. They simply told me that we would keep training and try again next year.

Next year.

Like they expected me to be around that long.

Ben swayed to the beat, Rosie's little feet on top of his as he led her in a looping, graceful circle. And as Jane leaned into me, and I curled my arm around her, settling my cheek on her warm, fuzzy head, I watched him.

I watched him because he was a miracle dressed in cashmere and a tan flannel coat.

I'd spent a lot of time wondering about Ben lately. Daydreaming about what he liked to do when he was bored. About his emo days in highschool—because oh my god, Ben in eyeliner? *Fuck me!* About where he chose to shop. About his favorite foods, his favorite color, his favorite place to go when he was sad.

And now, I wondered where he'd learned to dance.

Where he'd learned to *smile* like that. All wrinkly and soft and beautiful.

I wondered how someone so wonderful could be real at all.

And how he could love me.

Because he did.

I'd have to be blind not to see it.

Eventually, Jane changed her mind and decided that she *did* in fact want to dance after all, so we joined Ben and Rosie on the dance floor. Some twangy country song was playing over the speakers. And though it wasn't my jam, I could appreciate the ambiance. Especially when Ben swapped me for Jane and I got to enjoy swinging Rosie around, her riotous giggles carrying through the air.

That night, both twins wanted me to read them bedtime stories.

Both of them.

Which felt like a gigantic fucking honor, man. And I was so excited I couldn't help but stumble over my words. Especially because the picture books they wanted were all Edgar Allan Poe remakes—and used words I'd often read (in books) but hadn't really used aloud.

Reading and speaking were two different things.

But neither twin seemed to mind when I stumbled, they simply corrected me when I fucked something up.

Ben leaned against the doorway the whole time, listening silently in the dark like the giant teddy bear he was. And when both little girls had collected kisses from their dad, he led me to his room and undressed me slowly and deliberately, with flickering little pecks against my cheeks and ears, precious and gentle and perfect.

"Spend the night," Ben requested, even though I'd already spent the night before.

"Okay," I agreed, breaking my own personal rule not to cross that line as if I'd never made it at all.

I gave him the back rub I'd promised myself I would.

And Ben curled around me, protective, and warm—and the scent of sandalwood and blossom lulled me into sleep. And once again, I didn't bring up the surprise.

Thanksgiving Day came and went. It was as hectic as I'd expected. Mama Montgomery was a fucking matchmaker, oh my god. Put me right next to Ben with a knowing glint in her eyes—like she knew just how whipped I fucking was and wanted to help me out.

I'd stopped sleeping at the B&B altogether.

Ben would text me—even on the days I hadn't seen him. He'd make sure I ate, checking up on me when he decided was the "proper time" for meals to take place. In turn, I made sure he kept up with his physical therapy.

Dude lived on a fucking schedule, and though I found it kinda hilarious and annoying in an endearing way, I loved that about him too.

He was structure, safety, and warmth.

He had therapy appointments on Thursdays. Had physical therapy once a month. Had his Saturdays with his mom. His Sundays with the girls. He worked out in the mornings. His shift started at ten on the dot. And he left work at exactly the same time every day.

And despite how busy he was, despite the fact that there was always something he had to be doing, Ben somehow made time for me. Like I was important. Like he wanted me around. Like he was willing to adjust his carefully put-together life just so he could fit me inside it.

Like clockwork, every night without fail, he'd invite me over.

And I'd come.

Because what else was I supposed to do?

When my time here in Belleville was almost up, and I couldn't sleep without him anyway. I didn't pretend to put distance between us anymore. We practically lived in each other's pockets.

We'd spend sleepy, happy mornings together, with and without the twins. And instead of training on Sundays, I got to spend the day playing with Rosie and Jane. Counting their now full swear jar, and rewatching the same fucking episode of their favorite show with them over and over again.

On the days Ben had taken off to finish his book, I spent all day feeding him snacks, and entertaining the twins. His mom had been the one that was supposed to watch them, but she'd come down with a cold right after Thanksgiving.

Not that I minded.

I liked helping.

Liked when Ben leaned on me.

And even more than that, I *loved* the twins. Loved the way they laughed. The way they sassed me. The way they watched me with wide, toffee-colored eyes—just like their dad's—staring at me like they thought I was as wonderful as I thought they were.

It was on the last day of Ben's time off that the truth about my surprise finally came out. But not before I accidentally terrorized Ben first.

Rosie was building a wall in front of me with pillows, blocking me in the back corner of the room. As far as I could tell, we were reenacting the *Cask of Amontillado*—which again, was their favorite episode of LilPoe.

After the second time the pillow wall collapsed, Rosie's face went red, her mouth opened—and a horrible cry escaped.

"Hey, *hey*—" I gently pushed the pillows aside and reaching for her. "It's okay, sweetie—"

She made another garbled noise, angry and wet, and I glanced around the room desperately to try and figure out what to do. Ben had already begun wrapping gifts and putting them beneath the tree that we'd decorated together—motherfucker had surprised me with ornaments of my own, the big softie. And as my gaze raked over the baubles, it landed on an empty cardboard box that was stacked in the corner ready to be recycled.

Distract the gremlin.

"Why don't we make a better wall?" I offered, trying to redirect her attention.

Despite the fact I'd been the primary caregivers for the girls for the last few days, this was my first time witnessing a true freakout. For the most part, they were incredibly chill kids. But…they were still toddlers.

And Rosie had reached her limit.

"You can even tape me in!" I declared, already leaping over the pile of pillows and toward the giant fucking box. "It'll be like building a wall, only better." I had no idea what Ben had bought that was that fucking big, but hey! Didn't matter at the moment.

Rosie sniffed dubiously, her face still as splotchy red as Ben's became when he was embarrassed. I could see the resemblance then, because her eyebrows twitched the same way that his did as she debated whether or not I was full of shit.

"I want to trap Robin in a box," Jane replied helpfully from where she'd been sitting quietly on the couch watching the same fucking episode of LilPoe they always did. It was turned down low, and she'd still been able to mouth every word.

"Um." Well, this had escalated quickly.

But hey! What was the worst that could happen? I'd just kick the box open if I got stuck.

Twenty minutes later, I could hear the girls giggling and whispering and the sticky sound of tape being smacked on the box I was inside. They were downright chipper, all ire forgotten.

"Can you breathe?" Jane double-checked, her voice muffled by cardboard.

It was dark in here, and I was hunched in a tiny little ball, but that didn't seem to matter.

"I can breathe," I promised, loud enough to make sure they could hear.

"I love this game," Rosie told me, slapping another piece of tape on. Her evil laugh returned, and I choked on a laugh of my own.

It was only when the very top flap of the box was completely shut that we got caught.

I heard Ben's feet enter the room and pause. He had heavy steps, probably because he was one heavy motherfucker—*believe me, I know*—dude smashed me into surfaces like ninety percent of the time I was with him.

"Where's Robin?" he asked, sounding genuinely concerned.

The girls giggled evilly.

It was getting a little sweaty in the box. And I didn't want to freak Ben out, so I called out to him so he'd know I was fine. "I'm in here!"

"In where?"

"In the wall," Rosie cackled.

"He's in the wall!" Jane echoed, sounding slightly less evil than her sister.

"He's in the..." Ben somehow sounded more concerned than before.

"In the box!" I answered.

"*What?*" Ben's voice was flat, true confusion flooding his tone.

"Robin's in the wall," both girls told him unison. "We put him there."

"Oh Christ." And then the top of the box was being torn open, light was flooding in, and Ben's concerned face was lingering right above me. "Robin, are you okay?" he asked. He was gorgeous as always. Different than normal because there were dark circles beneath his eyes, and his beard was longer than usual.

"I'm fine, baby," I replied, leaning up to smooch him. "We were just playing."

"In a box?" Ben's voice went high.

"Yeah!" He didn't kiss back. Which made it obvious that something was off. I frowned, popping the rest of the way out of the box like a fucked up magic trick, game forgotten. "Hey," I hummed, following him when he retreated. My fingers curled in the hem of his sweater, giving it a gentle tug. "I'm okay."

It was a testament to how tired Ben was that he'd been this freaked out by an innocent game. He was normally a very controlled person. I knew he had anxiety like I did—it would be impossible to miss it, even if he hadn't outright told me about it and the therapist he'd been seeing since he was in school.

But…damn.

It hurt to see him so upset and to know that I'd inadvertently caused it.

This was way worse than the escalator.

"I'm sorry, Papa," Rosie's little voice was small and sweet.

"I'm sorry too," Jane agreed, crowding around his legs.

"Me too," I tacked on, still searching his gaze, noting the flicker of concern still there. He stared at me like he was searching for injuries, only relaxing when he saw none.

"It's okay," Ben's voice was rough as he squeezed an arm around me and pressed a kiss into my hair. "It's okay," he promised again, kissing me one more time before leaning down to gather the girls up in his arms. "I just got worried."

They curled up against him, murmuring sweet little apologies against his collar as Ben kissed their heads.

I thought he'd be mad at me.

But he wasn't.

"C'mere," he commanded, still looking exhausted and hot and amazing. "I only have two arms."

I stepped out of the box, tripping, then righted myself before tumbling into Ben's embrace.

"We won't play Amontillado anymore," Rosie promised, her sweet voice pressed to Ben's throat.

"You can play," Ben replied. "But with an open box, please?"

"Of course." I squeezed him tight, more than a little pleased when he melted into me. "I didn't think."

"It's fine," he said softly. "It's fine."

And it *was* fine.

Because he was warm again, warm the way he always was. And despite the fact that I'd somehow fucked up—it was his reaction to that mistake that made it obvious what a very good, wonderful man Ben was.

Because he was patient.

And he was kind.

And he forgave me—even when I was stupid.

Later, in bed, Ben explained to me why he'd been so worried. Apparently, it wasn't the safest thing in the world to be taped inside a box. Even one made with something as flimsy as cardboard. Something about air flow and cardboard dust particles, and allergens.

I'd never known that.

I'd always just figured cardboard was cardboard, you know?

And maybe it was.

Maybe it hadn't actually been dangerous at all.

But to Ben…it had certainly felt that way. And I wasn't about to write off his feelings like they didn't matter, especially when it was easy to apologize for scaring him and promise not to do it again.

"You didn't do anything wrong," Ben promised, when I did just that. He stroked a hand over my cheek, fingers curling in my hair. "I swear."

"I know," I agreed, because I did know. "But I'd rather not freak you out again, if I can help it."

"Sometimes I get…" Ben shrugged a shoulder—something he'd only recently picked up after spending more time with me. "Sometimes all I can see is the worst case scenario," he tried to explain. "I've been this way since I was a kid. But after medical school, and working as a doctor, it's only gotten worse. Nowadays, I mostly see people for little ailments. Colds, sprains, the flu." He frowned, eyes growing darker. "But when I was a resident at the hospital I'd see the most horrible…*random* things. Especially on the nights when I worked the ER." I kissed his palm and his lips quirked up, the faraway look in his eyes fading. "I don't think I've ever quite shaken the fear that something like that could happen to someone I love."

"I'm a pretty tough guy," I promised him, and Ben's eyes crinkled.

"I know," he agreed, pressing in close. "And most of the time, I can rationalize with myself. But I've been so…"

"Tired," I finished for him. "You've been so tired." It was easy to give him grace, to understand that he might not be functioning the same way he always did, while running on little to no sleep.

You should give yourself the same grace.

It was a random thought, but poignant.

"I'm so close," Ben murmured, sliding in to kiss me slow and sweet. "Only the epilogue."

"And then what?" I replied against his mouth.

"I edit it," he laughed, kissing me again. "And I send it away."

I perked up when something occurred to me. After returning his kiss, I then pulled far enough away that I could speak, "Did the cardboard box thing *scare* you?" I asked, sounding way too excited about the prospect.

Ben snorted out a laugh. "You *worried* me," he corrected.

"Damn," I sighed, then kissed him again. "I wanna know what happens to Beckett."

"We have a deal," Ben reminded me, as if I could forget.

"I'm starting to think this was an unfair deal," I countered against his mouth as he grinned. "You're impossible to scare."

"Not impossible," he teased, curling those big, lovely arms around me and squeezing me in close enough my ribs ached. I wheezed, just to make him laugh. "Just difficult." His eyes sparkled, like a fucking cartoon or something.

"I've tried everything," I complained.

"Mmm," Ben agreed noncommittally. "Jumping out at me and yelling 'boo' isn't 'trying everything.'"

"*Boo*," I pouted, grinning when he snorted out another laugh.

I'd miss him.

I knew that.

I'd miss him a shit ton after Christmas too—but mostly I was referring to the dress rehearsal I was required to attend in just a few short days. The dress rehearsal that was *supposed* to be my surprise. The surprise I hadn't had the guts to give him…at least…until now. "Hey, Ben?" I asked, shifting back so I could look at him. "I know it's a long shot but… would you wanna go to L.A. with me?"

Ben's eyes widened, but other than that, he didn't react. "Go to L.A. with you?" he asked, keeping his voice neutral. I could see a thousand thoughts flitting in his eyes. And it took me a solid ten seconds to realize how my question might have sounded.

"Oh shit. I mean for the weekend!" I laughed, face bright red. "Not like…permanently."

"Oh," Ben replied, sounding oddly…disappointed?

No.

No.

There was no way.

I was reading way too much into this.

"I know you've got the girls, and you're super busy, and it's really late notice?" I rambled, cheeks still hot. "But I have to go back home for the dress rehearsal and I just thought…um." God, what had I thought? That he'd want to drop everything and join me?

Christ.

He had a life here.

That was ridicu—

"Of course, I'd love to come," Ben replied immediately, fingers tightening in my hair. It stung the way I loved, and my lashes fluttered, wandering thoughts skittering to a halt. "When? I'll need to book a ticket."

"Um, about that—" My pulse thrummed, and for a second it was hard to meet Ben's gaze. "I kinda already got you one? You know. Um. Just in case."

Ben was silent for a moment as he processed this. And then he was forcing me to look at him, and when our gazes met heat flooded my body. "That was so sweet of you," he rumbled, lips curved into the private, special smile that felt like mine and mine alone. "Thank you, baby."

"Um. Yeah," I stuttered, feeling hot and achy—my hole twitching. He normally only looked at me like that when he wanted to fuck his fingers into me. I licked my lips, and Ben chased the movement with his gaze.

"When do we leave?" he asked, still staring at my mouth.

"Friday," I stuttered. "We'd be back by Monday." That wasn't even the worst of it. I might as well confess. "I already asked your mom, and she said she was feeling well enough that she could watch the girls." That had been an awkward fucking conversation. But only because Beatrice had grinned at me the entire fucking time like a fucked up old-lady version of the Cheshire Cat.

"You thought of everything, didn't you?" Ben purred, low and sweet.

"I figured I could show you my place," I squeaked, shuddering when his teeth sunk into the side of my neck as I spoke. "A-and the—um. The taco stand I like." Sounded stupid when I said it out loud. It'd been way more romantic in my head. "We could fuck—"

"Now *that's* a good idea," Ben bit harder and I moaned, pleasure zinging up and down my spine.

"No interruptions—" I managed. "And then we'd—"

"Mmm," Ben dragged his tongue over the skin he'd just bit, sending shockwaves through my body.

"We'd—" I twitched.

"You know what I think?" Ben asked, syrupy sweet.

"W-What?"

"I think if I'm going to fuck you on Friday, we better get some more training in, don't you?"

Oh fuck.

Oh fuck yes.

His hand slipped into my pants easily bypassing both layers of fabric, nails scratching down my thigh. "You owe me a surprise," Ben hummed conversationally. "I feel cheated."

"This *was* the surprise!" I laughed, cheeks hot. "I just…got distracted and forgot to tell you." More like I chickened out.

"I expected something a little lacier," Ben replied, point blank. Graciously allowing me to be a coward.

"You are a greedy monster," I gasped out, shocked.

The idea wasn't a bad one though. I'd never worn lingerie. It'd never occurred to me as something I could do—as a dude. But now I definitely was thinking about it. Ben would like that, wouldn't he? Seeing my ass cupped in lace. Those big fucking hands pulling on the edges of the thong, smoothing them flat so they lay just the way he wanted.

"You like it," Ben purred, fingers slipping around my now very hard cock. I groaned, the tight dry warmth of his grip making the heat that had pooled low in my belly simmer. Bucking up, my lashes fluttered as Ben pushed between my legs, his fingers moving slow and dry and easy. Not tight enough to sting. Not tight enough to be anything but a tease.

"I...do," I agreed, because it was true.

"You wish I was meaner," Ben teased. His thumb traced the seam between my balls, and I quaked.

"I like the way you are," I replied, honest—and distracted—because his big hand was still on my dick, stroke, stroke, stroking. "You're perfect."

Ben was quiet for a moment, and when I met his gaze again his eyes were full of heat. "You're perfect too," he replied, kissing me soft and slow and sweet. "So fucking perfect."

Because Ben was actually the best man in the world, he grabbed the lube.

Slick, tight, and hot, he wrung my cock. I was two seconds from spilling when he released me, and the ungodly whine that escaped simply made him chuckle.

"Give me a second," he murmured, fumbling with his own pants. When his dick slipped free, the tip flushed red and wet, I groaned. "There we go," he murmured, pressing his length against mine, his fist squeezing us tightly together.

"Jesus," I gasped out, head lolling back.

"*That's it*," Ben urged, stroking us up and down, tighter than before. He liked it tight. Liked it to hurt a little, just like I did. "Let me take care of you, just like I promised."

I shuddered, a sharp sob escaping when Ben's free hand came up to pull hard on one of my nipple piercings. "F-fuck" He pulled again, and my toes curled. It hurt so good, the pleasure-pain making my blood sing. Three more times he tugged, timing each pluck with his other hand, so I was squeezed and hot, and flushed.

"So close—I'm so—"

Again, he brought me right to the edge before backing off.

"You *sadistic* motherfucker," I gasped out as my approaching orgasm ebbed and then faded. My balls ached. My everything ached, more accurately.

"Shhh," Ben murmured, low and soothing. He had that mean glint in his eyes again. The glint he only got when we were in bed together, and he was enjoying making me squirm.

"Whyyyy?" I gasped out, twitching toward him when he wrapped his fingers around us together again and began to stroke once more. Slower this time, nice and easy. It wasn't enough. It wasn't enough, and he knew it—and I knew it—and I ached and ached.

"You're so pretty when you suffer, my little songbird," Ben murmured, leaning down to kiss me. The hard bite of the kiss was in sharp contrast with the slow, steady glide of his hand—never tight enough—never enough.

My hips flexed, trying to force him to tighten, but he didn't.

He knew exactly what he was doing to me.

"Fuck," I whined, nipples hard and flushed puffy red. Ben plucked at them again—the right, then the left—twisting the rings just enough to make my blood sing.

"Beautiful," he sighed against my lips, pulling back, his eyes black with lust. "So fucking beautiful." The praise made me feel hot all over, like I'd been dropped in a vat of honey. "You're so good for me. Allowing me to tease you like this. Whining for me. Making my cock hard enough to burst."

My hips twitched again, and Ben's hand went slack in response to punish me. He tutted disapprovingly against my lips, then moved again, dragging kisses across my cheek, down my throat, and then up behind my ear. His breath was hot when he spoke again, "You're *my* good boy, aren't you, Robin?"

"Fuck," I whimpered.

"Say it," Ben's breath was hot against my ear. "Tell me what you are."

"*I'm your good boy.*" My voice broke.

"And you're beautiful, aren't you?"

"I'm beautiful." I ached and ached and ached.

Ben had so much power over me then, because of my unspoken feelings for him. Because of the way he was cradling me. Because of the pleasure he held, just out of reach. And yet…he was using that power to heal me, rather than hurt me.

And I loved him, I loved him, *I loved him.*

And I was scared, scared, scared.

"Do you see how hard you make me?" Ben whispered. I glanced down, groaning low when my gaze fluttered over the slick, fat head of his dick. In and out of his fist, slow and easy, he wrung our cocks together. "Do you *feel* how hard you make me?" Ben squeezed us tighter, and I shuddered, balls pulling tight.

"Y-yes," I managed, because I knew if I didn't reply fast enough he'd make me anyway.

"You're a blessing, Robin," Ben promised, nipping at my ear and finally, blissfully, tightening his grip. I sobbed, hips threatening to twitch again, even though I knew better. Ben wanted me to lie back and take it, so I would. "You're *my* blessing."

Tight, slick, rub, rub, rubbing, Ben twisted our cocks together.

His dick was much larger than mine was. A fact that was seriously fucking hot, and made more obvious with us pressed length to length like this. Even his balls were bigger, hanging low as he rutted our hips together, the *schlick, schlick* sound his hand made making my blood sing. Every time our balls tapped it felt like nirvana.

"You're going to come for me," Ben informed me, like it was a fact. I nodded jerkily, because he was right. I totally was. My fingers dug crescents into his biceps—the same lovely biceps that had started all of this. "You're going to come for me and you're going to thank me afterward." Ben nipped at my ear again.

"Y-yes," I agreed, because he was right—I was.

"*Now.*" Ben's hand tightened at the same time that quiet rumble bounced around inside my head. He'd toyed with me for long enough I felt like I was drowning. And when I finally came, my dick spilled and spilled—and it felt like it went on for ages.

"Thank you," I gasped out, wet ropes of cum slicking his big, hot hand as he squeezed, squeezed, squeezed us together. "Thank you," I managed again.

"So pretty," Ben drawled, smooth and soft. He'd twisted to watch my dick spill, and all I could see was the cowlick on the top of his head, the slope of his nose, and those lovely dark lashes. "So fucking pretty."

Ben pressed my dick flat against my belly with his palm. His hand was bigger than it was, a fact that sent a thrill through my body and threatened to make me spurt again. He pressed harder, and I sobbed, my balls twitching.

Ignoring his own dick, Ben wiggled the tip of his finger inside my slit, rubbing, rubbing, as his breath came out in low, greedy pants.

"Christ," he groaned, cock pointing right at me, heavy between his legs. "You're perfect." It was the second time he'd said that tonight, and it made me light up even brighter.

When he stopped staring at my recently tortured dick, Ben kissed me again. It was sweeter than before, less teeth this time. I was drowning in him, and I never wanted to find the surface again.

I wanted his dick inside me.

Wanted it so bad I could barely breathe.

"On your belly," Ben murmured against my lips, voice husky and scratchy with arousal. "I want to see that pretty little hole."

I was on my belly faster than I could blink. Ben laughed, this low, almost *dangerous* chuckle that made the hair on the back of my neck stand on end.

"Elbows and knees, Robin," he commanded, shuffling between my legs. His dick brushed my ass cheek, leaving a sticky trail in its wake.

I wiggled onto my knees, feeling weirdly vulnerable with my ass up, and my hole winking at him. It wasn't like he hadn't seen it before. Hell, Ben was more intimately acquainted with my asshole than I was. He'd had every part of his body in there pretty much—except his dick.

A fact that we were about to rectify. *Rectum-ify? God, that was awful. Why did I do that?*

"Arch your back for me," Ben instructed, voice crackly soft. I arched. What else was I supposed to do?

"*Fuck*," Ben's voice dropped even lower, somehow. His big hands came up to frame my ass cheeks, digging in the center way he liked, and spreading them wide so he could really stare. Exposed and vulnerable, my hole shuddered.

Ben made a sound in the back of his throat, and I only had a split second to react before he was spitting on my hole and working it in with one of those thick, lovely thumbs. "I've never wanted to wreck something as badly as I want to wreck this pretty little hole," Ben promised. The sadistic murmur to his voice made my spent cock twitch.

"B-Ben," I complained, shuddering when he spat on my hole again. Hot dry hands pinched my cheeks together so I'd feel the sticky slide of his spit cling between them.

God, that's filthy.

"What?" he replied, tone flatter than before. Bossy Ben had made his epic return. "You don't think this hole is pretty?" His thumb pressed harder, and I sobbed.

"I—" No matter what I said, I was going to put my foot in my mouth. "I guess it is." There, that's what Ben wanted to hear.

"Everything about you is pretty," Ben stated, like it was a fact, at the same time his thumb sank inside to the first knuckle. He spat on my hole again, and I shuddered, feeling weirdly exposed and hot all over. I knew for a fact there was lube underneath the pillow. I also knew that he'd be grabbing it any second. Ben wasn't the kinda guy to think spit was a substitute for real lube.

But he was also dirty as fuck, and ridiculously hot.

So the fact that posh, hot Doctor Mc Ben Ben was rubbing his spit inside my hole was just—Jesus fucking Christ.

It was filthier because it was *him* doing it.

Because I'd never expected him to do, or be anything like this. I guess maybe I should've—considering what kind of books he wrote. But…still.

I'd never been more happy to be surprised in all my life.

Ben's hands left my ass, his thumb gently slipping free—and just like I'd anticipated, the quiet snick of the bottle of lube opening echoed through the room. It was dark in here, the lights off save for a small night light in the corner that Ben kept on in case the girls came in in the middle of the night.

The door was locked now, of course—but later, after we'd cleaned up and dressed, I knew he'd open it a crack. Always wanting to be available to the people he loved most.

It was one of the things I appreciated the most about him.

How emotionally available he was.

He didn't play games with me. Didn't toy with my feelings. Maybe he teased, but he respected my limits. Limits I hadn't even known I had, and yet somehow Ben knew them before I did.

"Relax, baby," Ben's voice was sugary sweet. My hole twitched, and warm slick fingers pressed snug against it, simply rubbing, not even asking for entrance.

I tried to relax, I really did—but the harder I tried, the less relaxed I became.

"You're doing so good, Robin," Ben hummed, gentler than before, like he'd noticed my internal struggle. "So good," he repeated, fingers rubbing around, then against, then around my hole again. "Are you gonna let me in?"

He could've pushed in anytime.

But instead, he was waiting for me.

For me to *submit* to him.

The second I realized that, it was like a switch flipped in my brain. I stopped fighting. My legs stopped shaking. I sank down from my elbows to my chest, face pressed to the mattress, and my fluttery pink hole went slack beneath his touch.

"That's it," Ben cooed approvingly. "That's just what I wanted, sweetheart. So obedient, aren't you? Such a good, *good* boy." His fingers pressed in and it burned. Two at once—because he knew I liked it that way.

Slow and steady, Ben pushed deep, deep, deep. Till he could tap against my prostate with every thrust. Till my body was shaking for a new reason, and my hips were fucking back to meet him.

"I'm going to hold still," Ben warned me, wrist angled so his fingers made stars explode behind my eyelids. "Because I want you to ride me." Low and gravelly, Ben's voice grew deeper. "I want to watch your ass bounce as you fuck yourself on my fingers." And then, less mean than before, sweet all over again, he added, "Is that okay, baby? Can you do that for me?"

"Yes," I hardly recognized my own voice.

When his fingers stopped moving, I did as I was told. Bouncing back and forth, seesawing on his hand, grinding hard into his knuckles to feel him as deep as he could go. He snuck a third finger in at one point and it burned so much worse than the other two.

And I loved it.

I loved it so fucking much.

"Pull your nipple rings," Ben's voice was breathy and hoarse. "Keep fucking yourself."

A slick sound was coming from his hand—the other one—not the one

I was grinding into. And I knew without having to look that he was getting off on watching this. He groaned, this low, animalistic little grunt.

When I reached up and tugged at my piercings, a broken gasp escaped me. It was probably the most pitiful sound I'd ever made.

"*Harder,*" Ben commanded. I didn't know if he was talking about my hips or my nipples, so I simply responded with both. Grinding back into him, fucking myself as I pulled and pulled. "Fuck yes," Ben's voice went higher for a second, breathier, the slick sound of him stroking himself off picking up the pace. "Fuck."

He was close.

I could hear it in his voice.

"Still baby, hold still—" Ben urged. For a second, I thought he was going to cum on me or something. But instead he did something infinitely better. He snuck his pinky in beside the other three fingers. And this time, when I sank back, I sobbed. "Fuck," Ben repeated. "Fuck, you have no idea how good you look."

It ached so good.

It was slow going, but I took him in to the knuckles again. I didn't think I'd ever been stretched so wide in my life. It burned and burned—in the best possible way. There was no room for doubt in my mind. No room for insecurity in my heart. I was too full of Ben to be anything but satisfied.

"Fuck," Ben repeated as I began to experimentally pull off, then sink down again. Greedy little swivels of my hips that made my dick swing. It wasn't hard again, but it didn't need to be. I enjoyed this far too much even without the promise of more wet orgasms.

Faster his hand worked, the bed shifting as Ben began to pound his fist in earnest. It was loud. Louder even than the squelch of his fingers inside me. I wanted him to pull them out. To stick his dick in where I needed it most.

And I knew he wanted it too.

But he was *Ben*, so our first time had to be perfectly planned to his satisfaction.

A fact that was overwhelmingly endearing, but frustrating all the same.

"I'm going to cum on your hole," Ben informed me, still humping his fist. "I'm going to smear it into your tattoos." Oh Jesus fuck. "And then, I'm going to scoop up what's left, and make you clean up the mess you made me make."

That was all the warning I got before Ben was painting my stretched hole with his cum. Hot pulses of pleasure splattered my flushed skin. I continued to fuck myself on his fingers, pulled hard enough on my nipples they felt like they might fall off—and sobbed.

It felt like I was cumming, but nothing came out of my dick.

Just this never-ending wave of pleasure that I never wanted to stop.

Ben, *because he was Ben,* kept all his promises.

But on top of painting my tattoos with his fingers and making me lick his fingers clean, he did something far filthier. He murmured praise against my skin, against my ribs, against my hair. He fluttered dozens of kisses along my body, my protruding ribs, the crows at my hip bones, and the bony tops of my knees.

He kissed my toes, and my shins, and my fingers, one by one.

And after he'd cleaned me up with a warm, fluffy towel, and bundled me in pajamas, he rose from bed, opened the door, and returned to bed, sleepy soft.

His arms were as octopus-y as usual as he curled around me, his nose pressed to my throat. "Have sweet dreams, Robin," he said, like the giant teddy bear he was. Like he hadn't just spent the last hour practically fisting me and making me dry orgasm.

One of Ben's big hands slid over my chest, warm enough I could feel its heat even through the hoodie I'd borrowed. His breath came slow and easy, body succumbing to rest after a week of non-stop working. When he tweaked my nipple, hard, I whined—and he laughed.

Before immediately falling asleep.

eighteen

BEN

"PAPA?" JANE ASKED OVER BREAKFAST at my mom's on the day Robin and I were due to leave for the airport. She had syrup on her chin, and her little blonde pigtails were slightly crooked. I'd thought I'd gotten them perfect, as usual, but apparently I'd been distracted.

When I'd offered to fix them she'd leveled me with an entirely unimpressed stare, and that had been that.

"Yes, angel?" I replied, sipping my coffee, a thousand and one thoughts buzzing around inside my head. Like: what would we eat for lunch? Should I pack a lunch in my bag for us to avoid the crowds at the airport? What was the best way for me to protect Robin from the paparazzi he hated? Could I hide him so he wouldn't feel uncomfortable?

The girls often asked me random questions, and normally I was more present. But my anxiety was at an all-time high because I wanted this trip to be perfect. I wanted to prove to Robin that he could let me into his life. That the fact he'd opened up to me was a good thing. That we could make this work.

I wanted to show him what our life could be like, if he decided to let me be a permanent fixture. I wanted to show him that I was capable of handling everything he needed me to, and more, just like I'd promised.

"Why doesn't Robin have a home?" Jane asked, stabbing her French toast like she was trying to kill it.

It took me a second to process her words, and when I did, all my swirling thoughts halted—frozen still.

"What?" I asked, hollow.

"Doesn't anybody love him?" she asked, carving my heart right out of my chest with her sweet little hands. I stared at her, unable to find the words to respond.

"What do you mean?" I asked again a moment later, even though I knew what she meant. I was stalling. Trying to get my heart to work again, when all I could think of was sad green eyes and a boy whose parents had trained him to think the people he loved would always hurt him.

"Robin was helping me sing," she explained. "And he said he wishes he could sing what he wants to—like how I can." She frowned. "And I asked him why he can't. And he said that if he does he'll lose his home."

"But Robin doesn't *have* a home," Rosie tacked on. She'd been oddly silent this whole time. Normally she was the chatterbox, so this was out of character for the both of them. "If he had one, he wouldn't be so sad. And he wouldn't be at our house all the time."

Jesus *Christ*.

Mama's voice echoed somewhere deeper in the house, probably yelling at one of the older grandkids that were over. But I could barely hear her. Could barely hear anything over the pounding of my own heart, and the whoosh of my breath.

This felt like a *big* moment.

The kind of moment that carved paths through ice and shattered icebergs. That shook foundations. That cracked through stone.

Before I could open my mouth and ask the girls if this was their way of asking for Robin to stop spending so much time with us—they beat me to the punch. Eviscerated me, with their tiny blonde pigtails, and their honey-toned eyes.

"Can't Robin's home be with us?" Jane asked, quiet and pure.

"We love him," Rosie told me matter-of-factly. "He can have my bed if you don't want to share yours anymore."

I stared at them both for a beat, trying to figure out what the fuck I was supposed to do in this situation. I'd genuinely never thought I would ever date. But meeting Robin had thrown that right out the window. Since then, I'd made a plan in place for this, for the day I'd tell the girls that I wanted to keep him, that Robin would be coming home permanently—if he wanted to, of course. But that plan had not included the girls bringing it up first or so soon.

I was floored in the best possible way.

"That's very sweet of you," I told Rosie, warmth flooding my chest as she sat up taller, looking very pleased with herself. "But not necessary. If Robin moves in with us, I would prefer he continue to share with me."

"Why?" Rosie asked, like I'd just shat in her cereal.

"Because they're in love," Jane explained, like she'd explained this a thousand times. She frowned at her sister. "People who love each other share beds and kiss and stuff."

"I hate that," Rosie told me, but then frowned. "But…I would hate it more if Robin left."

"He has to go back for his job," I explained, voice soft. "But maybe he can have a home with us whenever he comes to visit? Would you like that?"

"Can't he quit his job?" Jane asked. "I don't want to share him."

Rosie hesitated, but ultimately opened her mouth too. "I have almost a hundred monies. He can have it."

They understood the concept of money. At least in relation to jobs. I'd had to explain it to them as they got older. And it was part of why they were so proud of my medical practice, and acted like little warlords every time they came to visit.

"What about your cat?" I asked, my heart in my throat.

"Robin is kinda like a cat," Rosie replied, shrugging. "And I don't have to clean up poop."

"And he sings too," Jane interjected. "And he's funny."

"And he makes you smile," Rosie added on, like *that* was the highlight of it all.

I hugged them both then, because I wasn't sure what else I could do when my heart was full, and my eyes were burning, and my world felt whole. When I released them both they went back to eating like nothing at all had happened.

And it was with new confidence and determination that I kissed their little faces and headed off to pick Robin up for our trip.

Now that the girls were on board there was nothing stopping me from making him permanently mine.

Well, except for…Robin himself.

"So, fair warning," Robin mumbled where his face was smashed against my bicep, "things might get a little…weird."

That ended up being the understatement of the century. Unfortunately, for both of us—but for Robin especially—someone had let it leak that he'd be arriving in L.A. today. Which we only knew because when we stepped off the plane, fingers tangled, there was a group of paparazzi already waiting.

I wasn't so much surprised as I was…sad.

For him, at least.

Because the second he saw them he shrank. Not his body, but his soul. I watched it wither and fade inside his eyes as he stood tall, shoulders back—like he was putting on armor all over again. He donned his sunglasses, his eyes hidden from view, and I ached for him.

Before that moment, I hadn't truly realized just how at ease Robin was when we were alone. Because this felt like an entirely different person, this stiff, perfectly grinning mannequin beside me. Even worse than the day we'd gone to the mall.

He tried to drop my hand but I wouldn't let him.

And as we shouldered our way through the crowd, dodging questions, cameras flashing—I understood for the first time why Robin was so worried about 'poisoning' Belleville.

I could understand feeling terrified after living a life like this for god knows how long. He'd explained to me, yes. He'd *warned* me. But nothing prepared me for the reality of Robin's world.

His world was full of people asking inappropriate questions. Of people trying to touch him without permission—of eyes, and eyes, and *eyes*. Eyes everywhere. Comments thrown out like yesterday's trash. Invasiveness treated like it was normal and okay, when it clearly was not.

Like he was a prop, not a person.

There was a cab waiting for us near the curb outside the LAX airport. Robin made a beeline for it, his sunglasses perched on his nose, his smile never wavering. He'd told me, shy and nervous before we'd landed, that he preferred to ride around in cabs because they brought less attention.

Truthfully, I was a little shell-shocked by what was happening. Which was why it took me a second to react when one of the paparazzi that had been following us reached out and latched on to Robin's shoulder.

I stared at the hand for a beat, genuinely flabbergasted that someone would have the audacity to touch him without permission. Robin tried to shrug the man off, and it was that little motion that made me snap out of the crowd-induced fog I'd been in.

I grabbed the man's wrist, tight. Twisting, I yanked him off of Robin, using my bulk to shield Robin from the rest of the hungry, hungry eyes as he slid into the cab.

The man released a pained hiss, but I didn't release him. Not until Robin was safely inside the cab, our backpacks abandoned for me to deal with. It was a testament to the trust we'd built that he'd allowed me to handle this.

"You have *no* manners," I told the handsy man, shocked all over again by the vicious growl in my voice. I released him, but not before he stuttered out an apology. The apology should've been for Robin, but I wasn't about to force him out of the relative safety of the cab to hear it.

Jerkily, I grabbed our bags and forced them into the trunk. All the while, I ignored the murmurs behind me. Ignored the fact that no doubt someone had caught me grabbing the man on camera. The worry of future assault charges burned in the back of my mind—but I pushed the thought aside.

When I slid into my seat in the back beside Robin, my heart was pounding. I shut the door, locked it, and turned to him, my heart in my throat.

"I'm sorry I brought you here," Robin said immediately, back to being my sad, small little songbird. He picked at the holes on his jeans, shoulders slumped. His sunglasses were still on, shielding his eyes from view.

"Don't be." It was easy to reach for him then. Felt as easy as breathing to cross that distance. To kiss him soft and sound and gentle. "I'm so glad I'm here."

"You are?"

"I am." His lips felt cold against mine. Icy. I made a quiet sound, coaxing him to open so I could lick inside and warm him up. When I pulled away after several long minutes, Robin was flushed, and his eyes weren't nearly as hollow. I pulled his sunglasses off and set them safely inside my pocket so I could see him properly.

"I've got you," I promised him, because I did. "I'm here now." He nodded, a horrible little sound escaping as tears blossomed in his eyes. He squeezed them shut, his whole face pinched. I didn't make him look at me again, simply slid into the middle seat, buckled up, and pulled him into my side. "What's your address?" I murmured, listening intently as Robin replied, voice trembling.

"He knows it."

"Fucking vultures," the cab driver said in sympathy. Apparently, Robin worked with him often—at least, often enough that the man had his address memorized. As we made our way out of the busy terminal he regaled me with a few adorable but concerning stories about Robin and previous trips just like this. "One time, he dropped his coffee on a handsy guy," the man laughed, sounding amused. "Accidentally, of course."

"Good for you," I hummed, knowing that had not been a fucking accident. Robin may be clumsy, but he wasn't the kind of clumsy to drop a hot coffee cup.

Robin warmed up the longer he remained tucked against me. I murmured reassurances against his hair, fluttering gentle kisses wherever I could reach as he scrubbed his wet cheeks against my coat.

He was dressed in the clothes I'd bought him. They fit in when he was in Belleville, but out here they felt odd. Like he was an alternate version of the man I'd met all those weeks ago. I hoped they gave him strength the way his sunglasses seemed to.

If I'd thought the airport was bad, the entrance to his apartment was worse.

This time, I was more prepared though, so it went better.

I handed Robin his sunglasses back and he donned them with a grateful smile. It felt like I'd passed a test I didn't know I'd been taking. And I was more than a little relieved.

I grabbed our bags first, then blocked Robin from view as we made the quick trek across the sidewalk to the entrance of the high-rise building. It was a nice building, all glittery black glass and steel bars. I would've appreciated it more if I wasn't growling at people.

It felt second nature to protect him.

It always had.

But here that need was even more prevalent.

When we were through the large glass doors of the lobby we both relaxed. The paparazzi stayed outside, blocked by the one-way glass. The door man gave Robin a smile that was wide and friendly as he offered to take our bags.

"I got it!" a sharp feminine voice called, accompanied by the click of heels and the scent of bergamot. I swiveled to face the newcomer, more than ready to fight off another person. I moved Robin gently behind me, facing the threat head on, my jaw tensed.

"*Nancy!*" Robin's voice was warm, muffled a little because he was behind me. He didn't stay where I'd put him for long, wiggling happily against my back, his head popping out to stare at the severe woman in black as she approached.

She had a short dark bob, all straight lines and hard edges. Her makeup was impeccable. Her lips painted crisp sharp-edged black. Dressed in head-to-toe business casual, she had a rather impressive silhouette. Tall, vicious, with a coldness to her.

It only took me a second to recognize the name and relax. Nancy. Robin's assistant. He'd told me about her.

We'd had a lot of time to talk on the plane, and in between naps Robin had told me stories and given me warnings about our time here—always a worrier, that one. It hadn't taken much to realize that Nancy was the best part about his life here.

He adored her.

"Honey, you look absolutely *dreadful*," Nancy said as I stepped to the side so Robin could greet her. "Flannel, *really?*" She arched a perfectly manicured brow. "Are we fucking cows now too?"

All of the clothes I'd bought Robin were black, the flannel included. I wanted him to be warm, not to erase who he was.

"Oh my god," Robin laughed. "You can't just say that!"

"You can't come home looking all lumber-jack-y and expect anything different," Nancy replied, leaning down to smooch his cheek. "Who's this?" Nancy twisted to assess me, rising up to her full, impressive height.

I stood taller, surprised that for the first time in years I felt like I was in grade school. She gave off the same energy my third grade teacher had. Strict but kind.

"This is Ben," Robin twisted his head back to beam up at me. His tears had dried, though his eyes were red rimmed. "You'd know about him if you hadn't told me I wasn't allowed to call you."

Nancy rolled her eyes. "If I hadn't told you not to call me you'd be bothering me every day when you were supposed to be resting. Besides, he's *birthday* Ben. I remember." *Birthday Ben? What did that mean?*

Nancy took a step back, hands on her hips, her eyes sweeping over me. "Have you ever thought of modeling?" she asked, point blank.

"Modeling?" I blinked, confused. My cheeks went hot. "No—I…"

"He's tall," Nancy nodded toward me, talking to Robin now. "Good bone structure."

"Hot like fire," Robin agreed, making my cheeks burn even more.

"I'd like to see him in a tux," Nancy hummed thoughtfully. "If we gave him a trim, shaved off the scruff, I think he could be a good candidate for a men's magazine. He's got that aged like fine wine look about him."

"Ben doesn't like that stuff," Robin replied, because he was the sweetest man in the entire world, and knew that about me, even without me having to say a word. "He doesn't even have his picture in the back of his books."

"His books?"

"Yeah," Robin chirped, getting excited all over again. He launched into a happy tale about how we first met, embellishing my charm—Jesus god, I'd been awkward—and updating Nancy on every single thing we'd done together from that point onward.

Nancy took hold of the bags, before I could, and marched us toward the elevator as she listened.

Robin's hand found my own, squeezing, squeezing, squeezing.

It centered me as we launched toward the sky, my belly left somewhere down on floor one as we climbed and climbed. By the time we reached the top of the building—because of course Robin lived in the penthouse, why was I surprised at this point?—Robin had just finished telling Nancy about how I hadn't gotten mad at him when he'd made us lose the relay race at the Pie Festival.

"He didn't make us lose," I interrupted for the first time.

Nancy twisted to look at me, dark eyes flooding with warmth.

"I tripped you," Robin squinted at me, like I was lying.

"We tripped together." I smiled at him, and he melted, this sweet little grin spreading across his lips. "Mutually assured destruction."

"I guess we shouldn't have expected anything different," Robin laughed, surprising me—and proving how far he'd come with that simple statement. "I mean, your legs are like twice the length of mine."

"It was inevitable," I agreed, leaning down and kissing the top of his fluffy hair, because I could. Nancy's eyes burned a hole into the back of my head, but I tried to ignore it. I wasn't about to start acting weird around Robin just because we had an audience.

I'd already promised myself that nothing would be different out here.

And I wasn't about to break that promise.

Robin's apartment was pretty much what I'd expected after seeing the lobby, and figuring out he lived in the penthouse. The wide open floor plan made the place feel cold and sterile, white walls climbing nearly thirty feet into the air. The back wall was made entirely of glass that led to the city below. I could see the cars piling up for rush hour down on the street, small as ants.

A large white couch sat in the center of what was supposed to be a living room, but was more similar to a warehouse with its concrete floors and metal support pillars. Beneath it was a white and black rug, something cold and artsy, that I got the feeling Nancy had picked.

There was no sign of Robin anywhere.

And that made me…so incredibly sad.

Robin and Nancy were chatting while I wandered. I could hear them discussing the dress rehearsal that would be hosted here tonight, and all the people that would be coming to set up—only to take everything right down immediately after.

The cupboards in his kitchen were mostly empty aside from a half dozen different kinds of teas. All seemed to be supposed to promote sleep, and my heart hurt for him as I slid the cupboard shut and eyed the white island distrustfully.

Did he even know how to cook?

Did he have pans? Pots?

I ducked beneath the counter, movements even more careful than usual. I refused to hurt my back again. Not when we had plans this weekend.

Inside the cupboard there were a few pots and pans, but they looked brand new. Frowning, I straightened. Robin had wandered his way over, apparently done chatting with Nancy. He was back to his usual self, his eyes bright as he hopped up onto the island beside me, his cute little feet kicking as he reached out to reel me in.

One of his painted fingers pushed against the furrow between my brows. "Why so serious?" he asked in a horrible Joker impression.

"Baby, when and *how* do you eat?" I blurted.

Robin blinked. His finger stroked over my eyebrow before he cupped my jaw and grinned up at me. "Ever heard of this thing called takeout?"

"You can't eat takeout every day," I replied, immediately concerned. "It's not good for you."

"I don't have a Ben in L.A. to cook my meals for me," Robin countered with a laugh.

"Maybe you need one," I muttered, betraying my own truth.

Robin blinked again, eyes going wide. He didn't seem to know what to say. And I knew I'd pushed a little too hard, so I backed off, leaning down to press a kiss against his forehead as I processed all the new information I'd just learned.

If Robin truly wasn't ready for me to at least be a more permanent fixture in his life down here, the least I could do was hire him a personal chef, right? Or a food service?

I had enough money.

Between my salary as a doctor and my book royalties I was set for life.

"I'll figure it out," I promised him, so he wouldn't stress about something new. When he released me I went off to figure out where he slept. If he didn't have a proper bed I was not going to be happy. I wouldn't put it past Robin to sleep on the couch simply because he was too tired to head up to the loft.

I was more than a little relieved when I entered his bedroom and discovered he did, in fact, have a bed. A very nice bed. With a thousand different kinds of pillows, and at least five blankets all with varying Halloween prints.

Robin was right behind me when I paused, taking it all in. The night stand with a bunch of abandoned mugs on it—probably from the tea downstairs. The pile of books at the base of the bed, most of which were mine. The guitar in the corner of the room, older and more well-worn than the one he used on stage. The tiny little knick knacks and trinkets that sat in the windowsill. Probably momentos from his travels.

What was most telling of all, however, was the book shelf against the back wall. It was full of photos. Most of which looked like they'd been shoddily shot on a cell phone. Pictures of Bubba and Miles—at varying ages. All carefully, delicately printed and stuck into a variety of mismatching frames.

The rest of the apartment was bland. It looked like something out of a catalog and not somewhere that someone could call a home. But this room…with its black curtains, its character, and nest of a bed—yes.

Yes, *this was* the kind of place Robin should live.

He reminded me of a crow in a way, collecting small shiny things for later. I had no doubt every rock, every shell, every penny had a memory attached. It was fitting that crows were his favorite animal.

"Sorry, I didn't get a chance to tidy up," Robin apologized from behind me. "I don't like having someone in here to clean. Feels weird, you know? Like I'm Bruce Wayne or some shit, when I'm not."

"Don't apologize." I twisted, opening up my arm so that he could settle into the hollow there just like he did at home when we snuggled on the couch. Robin hummed, wriggling in close, making a happy little sound in the back of his throat. "I like your room."

"It's way messier than yours is," Robin laughed, self-consciously kicking a leg out to try and hide a stray pair of underwear on the floor beneath a wayward blanket that lay bunched against the wall near our feet.

"I don't mind," I told him honestly. And I didn't.

"I'm usually really tired by the time I get back here," Robin tried to explain. "I kinda just strip and then flop down…and…*try* to sleep?"

There was emphasis on the word try, and again, my heart ached.

Robin had told me about his insomnia. He'd told me about all of the little things he'd struggled with since it'd steadily been worsening. Including the times he feared he'd pass out like he had on stage. The concrete floors concerned me, as did the idea of putting him here— leaving him alone, where things could get bad all over again.

It hadn't taken long for me to figure out that Robin slept far better with me than he did on his own. He told me once that I was like a narcotic. I wasn't sure if that was an accurate comparison, but I hadn't argued.

It wasn't my place to tell him what to think of me. I was just happy he thought of me at all.

He shone so bright sometimes, all I could do was bask in his light.

Robin made his way past me, flopped onto his bed with a quiet groan, his legs sticking straight out like a goth starfish. I grinned, following after him with a chuckle. Carefully sinking to my knees, I reached for his boots. He didn't kick me off, simply holding still as I began to unbuckle them, one buckle at a time.

"My feet probably stink," Robin complained, still not moving.

"That happens when you wear shoes and walk all day," I replied, gently tugging one shoe off before moving on to the other.

"You're so nice to me." Robin's voice was quiet, muffled. I was quiet for a moment as I finished getting his other foot free. Pressing my thumbs into his now-socked insole, I gently pushed till he groaned.

"Of course I'm nice to you," I countered, the unspoken *I love you* sitting heavy in the air. It was hard not to say it. It'd been hard not to say it for weeks.

Which was kind of cosmically hilarious in a way.

I'd never loved anyone but my family and Trixie.

And yet here I was, so freshly into a new relationship, and I was ready to make all the declarations I'd never wanted to before.

I could distinctly remember a conversation I'd had with my dad when I was a kid. It was about the same age all the boys in my grade were discovering that girls weren't so awful after all. And I'd been…confused. Because I didn't feel anything like they felt, and I hadn't wanted to pretend.

"You don't need to be anything other than what you are," my dad had said, laying a big warm hand on my shoulder and giving it a tight squeeze.

"But…" I'd trailed off, because even I had known that being different sometimes meant receiving attention that I didn't want.

"Benjamin," he'd cut me off, crouching to his knees, and talking to me like I was an adult. Like I was smart and this was important. Like he expected me to listen. His eyes had met mine, the same color as my own, his dark hair curling around his ears. "There's always gonna be people that'll make you feel like you gotta change so that you can fit in." His hand squeezed again, so impossibly large and gentle. "And you're gonna have to make a choice. Whether you'll be the kind of man who is who he is—or the kind of man who is who *they* want him to be."

I'd nodded seriously, and he cracked a smile, slow and sweet. "You're smart," he said gently. "Only one path leads to happiness. You'll figure out which to pick."

He'd released me then and waited for me to follow—and off we'd gone, finishing our work at the farm for that day. And the whole time, his words had rattled around inside my head. They'd felt like a splinter, stuck deep inside me as I ate dinner with all my brothers, quiet as a mouse.

Mama had asked me what was wrong, and Dad simply told her I was "thinking."

He'd always been in my corner.

He'd always known what to say.

It wasn't until I'd woken up the next morning, after a fitful night, that I decided that I knew what kind of man I was gonna be.

I'd made my choice at nine years old, and I'd stuck to it ever since.

I'd never pretended to be something I wasn't.

Never minced words when I could've said the truth.

Never lied about my feelings, or lack thereof.

So holding back…holding back was *difficult*. It was a weight I wasn't used to. A weight I'd never been equipped to carry. And yet…somehow, I managed. Because Robin deserved my patience. And I knew with just a little more time, just a little more loving, I could show him that the kind of man I'd decided all those years ago that I would be, was worth staying for.

That *I* was worth it.

That he could run to me, rather than away.

And my arms would be open, always.

Just for him.

nineteen

ROBIN

I DON'T KNOW WHY I expected Ben to start acting weird the second we were in L.A. Maybe it was the part of me that was still used to being disappointed. It didn't take more than an hour for those fears to be put to rest, however, as Ben made a place for himself in my life as easily as I'd made a place for myself in his.

He was always there.

Always helping.

Taking care of me, chatting with Nancy, standing stoic and quiet in the back of the room while he let me do my work. He didn't get in the way, and his lips were always twisted into a proud little smile. Like looking at me shine made him happy.

It'd been a long time since I enjoyed being watched, and I found myself melting into it now, as I stood on the temporary stage that the crew had constructed, running through the musical numbers that had been selected for me.

This was just the dress rehearsal. It was the only time we'd be running through everything before I returned for the party on Christmas Eve. I already had an idea of how my home would be decorated—Nancy had a binder full of pictures that she and the event coordinator had decided on. There'd be a caterer with ridiculously tiny plates full of ridiculously expensive food. An open bar. A giant black and white Christmas tree that was tall enough to tap the ceiling.

Now, the room was bare, aside from the crew, the performers, and Ben.

It was a skeleton of what it would be, and yet…I felt high, almost.

My skin was buzzing.

Energy burst through my body, the excitement of the performance—despite the fact it was only practice—making me feel worth my weight in gold. *This* was how I'd used to feel when I was on stage, before the nights went dark and the eyes became too much. *This* was the reason I wanted to be a musician. To feel the music move through me, to feel it's throb and ebb. The zap of electricity that shot through my veins every time I hit a note just right.

It was nice to feel it again.

I never wanted it to end.

"That was your best yet," Nancy praised when I finished the last set, gently giving my shoulder a squeeze. The band was already packing up. They were new people. No one from my previous tour. I didn't even know their names, and normally that would bother me—but right now, I was too excited to care.

Ben clapped, as did the rest of the crew. I said my thanks, then stepped down, letting Nancy bark orders as I made my way toward Ben and his spot in the corner.

"You were *amazing*," he promised, his eyes sparking with heat.

"Oh?" My eyebrows shot up as Ben pulled me in close. Close enough his very hard, very delicious dick pressed against my belly. "Oh," I repeated, lower this time. "I didn't know my singing did it for you."

"I didn't either," he admitted, leaning down so his breath was hot against my ear. I licked my lips, piercing clicking against my teeth when I bit down with a groan. "You do this thing…when you're playing," Ben hummed, voice crackling like fire. "Your hips push forward, and your pants pull tight—"

"Jesus fuck."

"Your pretty little cock has been teasing me all night."

Suddenly, I could not fucking wait for everyone to leave.

The L.A. city lights spread out beneath our feet as Ben and I peered down black glittering glass into the streets below. My belly swooped the way it always did when I got this close. Despite the thickness of the glass and its safety, my body was still convinced I would fall.

It was past dark now. The crew had cleaned up and Nancy had given me a parting kiss on the cheek before leaving with a wave and a click of her high, high heels. I wouldn't see her again until I flew in on the twenty-third.

The goodbye was as bittersweet as it'd felt when I'd first left L.A. to go to Belleville over a month ago. Only this time…something inside me felt more settled.

I wasn't ice cold and praying for mercy. Wasn't operating on half an hour's rest and six cups of coffee. I hardly felt like the same person, even though I knew I was. Like the skeleton Ben had put back together for me, I had all the same pieces—only now that Ben had arranged me I was fundamentally changed.

The moment we were alone at last, Ben and I had poured ourselves congratulatory—in my case—glasses of wine before we meandered our way toward the window. And now here we were, what felt like miles above the city streets, and I was floating—but that had everything to do with Ben's proximity and the promise of what was happening tonight, and nothing to do with the height of my penthouse apartment.

"You had fun tonight," Ben said, and his voice was soft and sure as always. I made a sound in agreement, sipping at my wine and tipping into his side like it was second nature. Even though I wasn't sure it ever truly would be. There would always be a little part of me that was grateful for his warmth, that was made reverent by how solid and sure he was.

He'd coaxed me forward, gently, patiently.

He was careful with his words, with his gestures, never giving too much—always more aware of my boundaries than even I was. Like he had wiggled his way inside my brain. Like he was a part of me now.

We were different.

In fact, we had more differences than similarities.

Ben was everything I'd always wished I could be. He was steady and strong, dependable and loving. And yet being with him never made me feel like I was lacking. He was the first person in my life that I had let truly see me. The first person that I had no walls up with.

"Robin?" Ben's lips were against my temple now, gentle and sweet. I realized too late that I hadn't replied. He sounded worried. Which was fair, usually I was a chatterbox when I was with him. "We don't have to—"

"I am hopping on your dick tonight. Taking a one-way ticket to pound-town. Eating a full plate of eggs Ben-ad-dick." Frowning, I added. "Ben-addict?"

Ben snorted, amused, and I was honored to experience one of his snorts against my skin. Felt weirdly tickle-y and very pleasant, if I'm being honest. "We can postpone," he hummed. "If you're not feeling well."

"Why are you trying to cockblock me?" I twisted around, grabbing on to his face with my free hand and giving his cute little cheeks a pinch. His lips pushed out as I squeezed, and his eyes danced—though his concern was not gone entirely.

"You're quiet," he said, like me being quiet made him worried.

Again, proving that just like I'd suspected, he really fucking paid attention.

"It's a good kind of quiet," I replied, relaxing my grip enough that he could twist and press a fluttery kiss against my palm.

"Yeah?" Ben's voice was low and softer than snowflakes.

"Yeah," I agreed, my own voice just as husky. "It's like…for the first time in my life I feel like I'm exactly where I'm supposed to be." My heart skipped a beat, and my eyes burned. "And I'm…enjoying it. Being here—with you."

It might be the only time I had this.

Except…now that we were here—I didn't think I could stomach that anymore.

A life without Ben Montgomery was not a life at all.

He was the click of a metronome. He was C major. He was lilting notes and revelation. He made my world quiver and shake, like the last tremulous notes of a love song. He was peace and longing, and happiness, all rolled into one tall, serious, but kind man.

With his sweaters. And his chocolate chip pancakes. And his daughters, who he was so, *so* good with. With his snort laughs. With his gentle hands. With his brilliant, wicked brain. And the way he could bring me higher than anyone ever had before, but held me when I was at my lowest just as easily.

Ben was the kind of man who deserved sacrifices.

He was the kind of man who deserved to be *chosen*. To be chased. To be cherished. Bright as the winter mornings I'd seen in the Christmas movies I'd grown up coveting. He was childlike laughter, tearing open wrapping paper, and home—idealized in one, lovely, cologne-wearing person.

"I don't think I was ever happy till I met you," I admitted, voice cracking down the middle. "Like the 'me' from before, and what I felt, was duller somehow."

"Robin," Ben's voice was low and crackling with warmth. And yet his eyes were warmer. He curled me in close, our wine glasses clinking.

"No," I interrupted him, for once in my life not overthinking what would happen next, or who I was, or who I needed to be. "I need to finish."

Ben nodded, watching me with such affection it normally would've made me freak out. But right then—I wasn't afraid. I wasn't afraid of losing him. Because right then there was nothing in the world but us, the lights below us, and this moment—and how precious it felt.

"I've never brought anyone here," I told him, voice serious for once. "Not even Miles."

Ben nodded.

"I see the way you look at me," I added, heart thumping erratically. "I'd be blind not to."

Again, Ben nodded.

"You've been so patient." My eyes were burning. "And I just…want you to know that this—this thing we have—is the best thing that's ever happened to me." I gestured between us. "And I…" I wanted to tell him I loved him. I wanted to so badly, but the words still wouldn't come. "I can't imagine my life without you." That was better, right? Closer.

Closer than I'd ever gotten to being truly vulnerable.

"You know that scene in your book?" I added, palms slick with sweat. "Beckett." Ben nodded. "I told you when we met about the part when Beckett left his pack and his brothers behind." Ben nodded a third time, kind as ever. "And we made our deal." I sucked in a breath. "I always thought…I always thought that was like me, you know?"

Ben made a quiet sound, urging me to continue, but he didn't speak. My giant, silent teddy bear.

"I always thought—everyone was better off without me. That I…have a tendency to complicate things." I bit my lip, piercing clinking. "And when I read about Beckett I thought—here's a guy who gets it. A guy who understands what it's like to put the safety of the ones he loves above himself, even if it means he ends up alone."

Ben's eyes were encouraging.

They said, *go ahead.*

They said, *I'm listening.*

They said, *it's okay.*

"I think your book broke me a bit," I admitted. "I was on tour. Sat in my bunk and blubbered like a baby for like an hour till Nancy came to get me for dinner." My lips twisted into a wry little smile. "It was the first time I really felt seen, you know?"

This was a different kind of communication.

It was the kind that made you feel cracked open, your rawest most vulnerable bits exposed. And yet, here I was, trusting Ben with all the things that hurt. Because I knew he'd protect them, even better than I had.

"I think for most of my life I've been so scared of hurting the people I love that I've kept them at a distance. I told myself it was because I was being protective. That I was doing right by them." It was hard to get the next words out, hoarse as my voice was. "But I think that's just a lie I said so that I could hide behind my choices." Ben's eyes were fathomless, the warmth in them never fading. "The person I was actually protecting… this whole time…was me."

I'd never admitted that to anyone, not even myself.

"Because I thought—if one more person—" My voice broke. "If one more person lets me down, I don't think I'll make it."

"*Baby*," Ben's voice was a rumbly, crackly murmur. Hot tears spilled down my cheeks. I reached up, dashing them away, the city lights nothing but a blur.

"When I love people—" I hiccuped, "they hurt me."

"*Shhh*, I know." I don't know how, but Ben magicked our wine glasses away. And then he was curling around me, blocking out the lights and the world. And all there was left in my peripheral vision was cashmere. There was only his cologne. Only his biceps, and how lovely they felt huddled around my body.

His breath ruffled my hair.

"I'm so scared of being hurt."

"I know." Ben kissed my head. He kissed it again. And again. He squeezed me tighter, and I broke—let all my pieces fall loose. "*I know.*"

"But you won't hurt me," I managed, surprised by how sure I was as the words come out. "You won't."

"I won't," Ben agreed—a promise.

"Because you're Ben Montgomery."

"I am."

"And you *always* keep your promises."

"I do."

Ben's mouth tasted like happiness, which sounds cheesy, I know, but it's true. His breath was warm, and his tongue was warmer—and his body felt impossibly large where it squashed mine into the mattress.

We hadn't started out here.

First we kissed against the window. We'd tested Ben's nerves as syrupy sweet kisses turned harder and rougher. The glass had been chilly against my back—if only because Ben's body had been so, *so* warm. I'd clung and clung, and he'd clung back just as fiercely.

Like he was worried if he stopped holding me I'd simply sift right through his fingers.

I've had sex loads of times. Years ago, when I'd first started out and moved to L.A. with no money in my pockets, and no friends—one-night-stands were the easiest way to find a place to rest at night.

I'd slept in hundreds of foreign beds.

Done the walk of shame what felt like a billion times.

Given pieces of myself away with every encounter.

This was the first time I'd been with someone and I felt like they were giving back. Like…this was one of those silly, dopey love movies from the 90s. Like we weren't fucking at all. Like it was deeper than that. I was Julia Roberts and Ben was the sexy man who had decided that despite my flaws, maybe even because of them, he was going to keep me.

Making love.

That's what *this* felt like.

Especially as Ben very carefully, very slowly—because no one wanted him to get hurt, thank you very much—oh my god, carried me up the stairs to my room and laid me on the bed. He always treated me like I was something fragile and precious. Like I was a delight, no matter what I was doing. He asked me *again* if this was what I wanted—and I'd laughed, because he was so annoyingly sweet it made me want to scream sometimes.

And then we kissed.

And kissed some more.

And we kissed and kissed and *kissed*.

And it was slick, and warm, and home, home, home. It was happiness and comfort. It was lulling and delicious. These almost drugging, languid swipes of his tongue that made me feel like I was melting.

The world could've been ending outside and I wouldn't have cared.

"Yellow if you want me to slow down," Ben murmured, kissing my forehead, my lips tingling the second he pulled away. "Red to stop." He kissed my cheek. "Green if you like something and I'm checking in." He kissed my ear.

I shuddered, fingers bunching up in his sweater. I was wrinkling it.

Maybe stretching it out too—to the point that "Robin" fingers would remain inside it forever.

Ben didn't seem to mind.

"I'm going to take *such* good care of you," Ben murmured, this quiet rumbly murmur that made me light up from the inside out. And then he added, as if what he'd already said wasn't sweet enough. "Thank you for trusting me with this. With…you."

I was fully clothed and yet I felt naked.

"Thank *you* for listening," I replied, voice rubbed raw, like my feelings had given it a rug burn. "Thank you for *seeing* me."

"I adore you," Ben said, the words his eyes had been telling me for weeks. "*I adore you,*" he repeated, because once would never be enough for either of us.

"I adore *you*," I replied, because it was true. It was true, and at that moment, I wasn't too scared to admit it.

Ben was quick and efficient as he stripped himself of his clothing. All that gorgeous tan muscle on display. I fanned my fingers across the flowers that ran up his forearms, skipping over the scrawl of the twins' names, etched delicately between petals.

The veins danced beneath my fingertips as Ben's chest heaved, his free hand fumbling between his legs to get his button and zip undone. He shucked the rest of his clothing off quickly, dick slapping free.

And god, was it a lovely fucking dick.

Thick, and long, and—fuck. *Yes.*

I'd never get tired of staring at it.

Never.

He'd been patient until this moment. Always biding his time, like a crocodile lying in wait just below the surface of murky water. But now he was exposed, his feelings written all over his face as his cock rose from a nest of auburn curls, veiny, hard, and delicious.

It was an honor to see Ben so open.

He had more walls than I did.

And as he worked his fingers under the hem of my mesh shirt, I shivered. Ben was more gentle with me than he'd been with himself. And it was hard to think about anything but the sexy cock swinging between his legs. Flushed bright red, the crown leaking obscenely. It brushed my thigh, skimming the hole in my jeans, and I groaned.

Together, we pulled my shirt up and off.

And then Ben's mouth was on my chest. Liquid hot, his tongue laved my nipples, teeth sinking in like he was as ravenous for me as I was for him. Weirdly enough, my explosion of honesty hadn't poisoned this. In fact, it somehow made it better. Made me feel raw and open and needy in a way I never had been before.

Trust was the elephant in the room.

"You're so beautiful," I croaked out, shivering when Ben's hands froze, his head swiveling to look up at me. His eyes were nearly black with lust, the honey color swallowed almost entirely.

"Thank you," his voice was hoarse. "So are you."

I didn't think anyone had ever told Ben that he was beautiful before. Because the splotchy flush on his cheeks was telling.

"I've never met a more wonderful person," I added, because it was true. Ben made a hurt little sound, head sinking down as he fluttered a grateful little kiss against my sternum. My pants and boxers were the only thing between me and all that warm, lovely skin. Normally I'd be impatient. I'd be swearing and pulling and begging.

But this…moment was too perfect to ruin with haste.

If this was all I ever got, I was going to make the most of it.

I would memorize Ben's moles, memorize the cowlick on the top of his head, memorize the sounds he made when he finally, blissfully lost control. I'd keep him safe inside my heart beside all my darkest secrets. Because Ben had proven to me that he was far more precious than all the things that made me brittle, and it was as he pressed one more final kiss against my sternum that I realized I cared about him more.

Cared about him more than my carefully guarded heart.

Cared more about him than protecting myself.

Cared more about him than I cared about myself.

"Lift up," Ben's lips skimmed my throat as his fingers found my zipper and tugged it down. I did as I was told—because duh, when Ben tells you to lift up you fucking lift up. He wiggled my pants down, pausing for a second, a sharp exhale escaping him. "*Robin*," his voice was a low growl.

"Surpriiiise," I replied, heart skipping a beat.

Ben's fingers fanned along the lace that hugged my hips, a quiet groan escaping him. "I *knew* I liked your surprises," he murmured, an almost reverent tone to his voice. When I glanced down I nearly came. Because the juxtaposition of Ben's big ass hands on my hips, paired with my cock, pressing insistently against see-through black lace—

"Didn't want to disappoint you," I replied, going for teasing.

"You couldn't," Ben stated like it was a fact. "Not even if you tried."

And then he was sinking that delicious mouth down, placing greedy, wet kisses along my hip bones. His tongue flickered out to taste the lace and my head fell back. Flick, flick, Ben worked his way down toward my dick.

When his mouth closed around the tip I moaned, spreading my legs as far as they could spread, while still trapped by my jeans. It was the immobility that kinda did me in, actually. Because I couldn't fucking move and that was…Jesus, that was hot.

"Ben," my voice cracked right down the middle. "Ben, *please.*"

His mouth slipped off my cock and he made this adorable grumpy sound, like I was pissing him off by taking my dick away.

"I'm stuck."

"I know," Ben laughed, biting my hip almost punishingly, before he ripped my pants off so fucking fast it felt like a magic trick. When I could spread wide, I groaned again, my balls pulled snug against the lace as Ben dropped his head back to my cock and suckled at it through the fabric. Already the panties felt sticky.

Hell, if I was being honest, they'd been sticky since the first time Ben had kissed me against the glass. He made these happy little growly sounds, like the flavor of my cum pleased him. It was honestly fucking filthy. The way he slurped through the fabric, flicking his tongue to catch every drop.

By the time he pulled my panties off, they were soaked through, and my dick was aching.

"How do you want this?" he asked, voice low as he wiggled back to gently extricate the panties from my ankles. They looked impossibly small in his hands.

"Let's go vanilla," I replied. "Wanna see your kinky-ass face."

"Ass-face?" Ben teasingly arched an eyebrow, and I laughed—only that laughter died pretty damn quick, because when my gaze fell to Ben's cock again, I was gifted with the fucking obscene sight of him fisting my panties around it and giving it a long, lingering stroke.

A drop of cum pooled at the tip of his dick, leaking onto the fabric and mixing with his spit.

"Jesus fuck," I whimpered, my dick twitching, and my hole clenching around nothing.

"Missionary it is," Ben hummed. "To start."

"To start?" I echoed, still staring at his dick. Staring at how fucking huge it looked, the strappy lace of my panties wrapped around it. He stroked again, and I felt electrified, ready to do just about anything to feel that dick inside me.

"If you think I'm only fucking you once tonight you are about to get a surprise of your own."

I laughed, though it was really more of a moan.

I reached down, legs pushing up toward my chest, my fingers spreading my cheeks to give Ben a flash of where I wanted him most. "Are you gonna fuck my bussy, Ben Ben?"

"Jesus fucking Christ," Ben replied, fisting his cock again as he laughed—my jokes obviously doing it for him.

He pulled the panties off his dick and flicked them at my face. I snorted, batting them away, though I was quickly distracted as the quiet click of the lube opening echoed through the room. It was like fucking Pavlov's dog or some shit, because that sound immediately made my hole twitch, and my balls draw up tight.

Ben leaned over me, the length of his body pressing into mine as he leaned on one elbow—somehow able to support himself entirely on the single arm as his other hand slip-slid between my cheeks. Slow and searching, he gave my hole an exploratory rub.

"F-fuck," my voice broke and Ben's response was low and sweet.

"Relax, little songbird." His fingers continued to pet at me, teasing me into submission as he fluttered an almost innocent kiss against my cheekbone. At least…it felt innocent—in comparison to what his hand was doing. "Push out when I—"

I did as I was told, groaning as Ben slipped inside, the pad of his finger wiggling experimentally deeper.

"You're acting like you've never fucked me before," I complained as he moved impossibly slow.

"I haven't."

"I—" I guess I didn't have anything to say to that. Because he was right. Sure he'd had his fingers inside me more times than I could count, but this was different. Because there was a condom wrapper beside the lube bottle tonight, and Ben and I were going to be joined for the first time.

"What, no snarky comment?" Ben teased, kissing my temple affectionately. "No silly nickname? Not going to try and boss me around again?"

"Wouldn't work even if I tried," I agreed, shuddering as he pushed deeper, and deeper still. "We both know you're the one in charge."

"Fuck," Ben's voice was back to that quiet little growl. He slid a second finger in with the first and I whined, fingers biting into his biceps.

"What, you like that?" I teased, squeezing around him and enjoying the slight burn. My lashes fluttered. "You like being the one in control?"

"Of course I do," Ben replied, fingers twisting and then—oh fuck. Jesus. It was my turn to swear now. I whined softly, the bite of my fingers growing slack as all my focus was redirected to the pleasure zinging from where Ben was brutally pushing against my prostate. "When I'm in control, you're safe."

I gasped out, squeezing around him, eyes rolling back as he pushed in and out, the wet sound obscene.

"When I'm in control, you're spoiled and stuffed full—" Ben continued, still fucking me, his wrist snapping a little harder. "You're happy."

He was right, so I didn't argue.

I just spread wider and arched my back to take him better.

Ben's third finger burned more than the first two had, but I didn't mind. I'd never minded. I liked that even more than if I'd felt no burn at all. It reminded me of how big he was. Reminded me that this massive monster of a man was inside me.

His dick was most definitely bigger than three fingers.

And when he was focused on my ass, his dark eyes full of lust, gaze trained on where he pushed in and out of the hot-wet-pink, I wiggled my foot down to press against his dick.

"Fuck," Ben groaned, hips bucking. His gaze snapped up to my face, brow arched almost threateningly.

"*Ben*," I begged. My snark was noticeably missing, voice plaintive and sweet. "Please."

I knew he'd continue to stretch me for hours if I let him. Knew he would edge me. He'd bring me to the brink over and over—like he loved to do.

But I needed him.

I *needed* him, and I knew he needed me too.

Ben—because beneath all that sadistic deliciousness, he was a giant teddy bear—immediately complied. He rose up my body, the crinkle of the condom wrapper sounding as my now-empty hole gaped.

He didn't make me wait long.

"Green?" he murmured against my lips, his sheathed cock bumping against my hole. I clenched in invitation, and Ben groaned.

"Green," I agreed, because I was. I was green-green-green.

And then he was pushing in. And it ached and ached—so fucking good. Made me feel split wide. Like I was forced to evolve to accommodate his girth. And I loved every fucking second of it. Loved the way every inch caused new little zaps of electricity to skate up my arms. Loved the way Ben's chest heaved, and his breath left him in an overwhelmed swoosh.

"You feel so good," he gasped out, the words hot against my temple. "Fuck, baby. You're so tight."

I didn't have words, so I just nodded, whining softly, my ass giving for him. Steadily, he pressed inside. Inch by inch. I wanted to force him to move faster, but even I knew that wasn't the best idea.

When Ben bottomed out we both released a groan. And then laughed. Only the laugh made me tense up—and Ben made this delicious sobbing sound, his hips grinding in deeper—like he simply couldn't help himself when I squeezed around him.

God, he was big. So fucking big. I could hardly breathe I was so full.

"Ben—" I managed, somehow, voice wobbling.

"Fuck, you feel so good," Ben repeated, lower than before. He slid out a little, testing the give of my ass. "Can I…?"

Always polite, that one.

"Please," I replied, shuddering. "Please. I need—I need you." It was hard to say those words, even in a setting like this—with the person I loved most in the world. But I managed. I managed, because Ben was worth leaving my comfort zone for.

"I need you," I repeated, and no truer words had ever been spoken.

Ben's mouth was liquid hot as he took me in the kiss to end all kisses. Teeth, tongue, nipping, biting. He owned my mouth as greedily as he owned my ass, slipping out all the way with a gasping whine—only to shove back into me with a harsh snap.

I raked my nails up and down his chest, up his back, into his hair— holding on for dear life as he pounded into me, all his carefully controlled walls turning to dust.

Snap, snap, Ben's hips drove into me, sending me higher and higher and higher.

I whined, a high brittle sound, sucking on his tongue, my body giving for him.

He made these delicious little growly sounds every time he pounded inside me. My hole gave, loose and wet, squeezing around him with every delicious snap of his hips. Close, so close, I shivered beneath him, desperate to make this last as long as possible. Ben had different plans, however, because one of his big, lovely hands closed around my cock. He squeezed once. One single time—and that was all it took.

I spilled with a broken sob, my entire body bowing toward him as Ben milked every last drop out of me, still thrusting in earnest.

He followed soon after, two, three, four sharp ruts of his hips as he spilled inside the condom with a quiet groan. He collapsed onto me, his cum-stained hand smearing across my hip as he held me close, face pressed to my skin.

"You're perfect," he promised, quiet enough I wasn't sure I was even meant to hear. "You're so perfect."

I clenched around him and he groaned, hips giving another aborted thrust—like he simply couldn't help himself.

When he tried to pull out, I dug my heels into the backs of his thighs, forcing him to stay put.

"Stay," I begged, kissing the gray at his temple the way he always kissed me. "Just a little longer." Ben nodded, curling tighter around me, his big warm body squishy and slightly sweat-sticky. "Wanna be full of you just a little longer."

Ben groaned, grinding into me again, his big ass flexing. I could feel it beneath my heels when I skimmed upward, enjoying the happy little sounds he made as he fucked me the way he'd promised he would.

"Next time we're gonna do that without a condom," I promised, voice dropped low. "And you're going to breed my ass."

"Fuck yes," Ben fucked forward a third time, a sharp enough snap that for a moment there I thought he'd gotten hard again. But he hadn't. Not yet. "Gonna breed you full, my little songbird," Ben murmured, sounding half drunk and sated. "Gonna make your sweet ass gape as it leaks my cum."

My big, gorgeous teddy bear.

"Hell yeah, you are," I agreed—because holy fuck did I want that.

"Good boy," Ben hummed, voice a sleepy rumble. "You're such a good boy, Robin." He fluttered a kiss against my neck where he was nestled. "Such a good, *good*, boy."

It wasn't the first time he'd said those words and yet it warmed me just the same.

My eyes burned and I grinned, letting my lids drift shut.

Because this was a *perfect* moment. And I wanted to memorize every bit of it. Wanted to memorize the way Ben's leg hair prickled. Wanted to memorize how it felt to have him inside me—all that hot, thick length rearranging my insides. Wanted to memorize the hot brush of his breath, and the way he held me close like I was precious.

I felt precious then.

I felt *good*.

But even more than that…I felt loved.

All my wiry, sharp edges. All my freckles, my moles, my frown lines. My protruding ribs, and mistakes I'd made nothing but things that made up the person Ben Montgomery adored.

Because as I lay in Ben Montgomery's arms, the world no longer felt like a scary place. I wasn't afraid of being disappointed. Wasn't scared about what the future might hold. I was full, in more ways than one, and for a man who had lived his entire life starved—that was…

That was pretty fucking awesome.

twenty

BEN

L.A. WAS A FEVER DREAM. For nearly three days I had Robin all to myself. After his dress rehearsal we were left entirely to our own devices. After fucking Robin for a second time that lovely, wonderful night, I made my way down to the street to find us tacos.

He'd told me where to locate his favorite taco stand, and I'd literally manhandled him back into bed so he wouldn't follow me.

I wanted him to be sleepy-soft and sated, his hole gaping, his body lax.

Didn't want him coming down to the street only to be bombarded by well-meaning fans, and less well-meaning paparazzi.

Luckily for me, the same doorman that had been there before was still on shift. He grinned at me, waving and directing me out the right way toward the taco stand. And when I returned thirty minutes later with my arms full of paper bags full of food, he'd given me the code to head upstairs.

I'd honestly forgotten to ask Robin for it, so I was more than a little grateful—and made a mental note to give him a hefty tip later when I had the hands to reach my wallet.

Robin was asleep by the time I'd finished depositing the takeout on the nightstand beside the bed. Like a dog, his nose twitched, however, and only a few seconds later his eyes drowsily blinked open. He zeroed in on the food, his stomach gurgling, and I laughed.

"Hi," Robin said, groggy and happy as he wiggled slowly—his ass had to be at least a little sore, despite my preparations—toward the food. "Hi, gorgeous," he said directly to the food and not me.

"I see how it is," I laughed, settling onto the mattress and easily manhandling him into a sitting position. Normally I wouldn't allow eating in the bed. It wasn't something I tolerated at home—and we were about to sleep here, so I didn't want to cause a problem in case either of us spilled. However…Robin looked exhausted. And the rest of the house was so fucking cold and unwelcoming that I didn't want to make him leave his happy little nest.

I figured I'd deal with any crumbs or spills should they happen. Even if it meant I needed to go out again to buy us sheets.

"Oh, you're here too," Robin joked, throwing his arms around me and giving me a grateful squeeze. "Did you get me—"

"I got you a torta." I kissed his cheek.

"With extra limes on the side?"

"So many extra limes," I agreed.

"Ben Montgomery, you are a fucking catch." Robin smacked a kiss against my chin, before he pushed me away so he could make grabby hands at the tacos.

"Hold still," I urged, before crossing the room to gather up the blanket that sat on the floor discarded. I figured it could work as a kind of barrier beneath the food. Carefully, I tucked it over his lap, then worked my way through the take-out bag to find his food for him.

Robin made the happiest slurping sound when I handed him his drink, lashes fluttering as he groaned.

Reminded me way too much of the groans he'd made when his slick pink hole had opened for my cock, and for a moment, my movements halted entirely as visions of him taking me—split wide—assaulted my senses.

This was going to be a problem.

I could easily foresee myself losing focus at the randomest times, recalling just how perfectly Robin's body took my dick. I had more than a few delicious plans to plow that pretty little hole. Plans I was quickly realizing would need to be enacted soon, if I wanted to keep my sanity.

"Ben?" Robin blinked, and I jolted back into action, handing him his torta on a little styrofoam plate as well as the limes he'd requested. "You okay?"

"I'm great," I grinned, because I was. My stomach growled, and I reached for my own burrito, sinking onto the mattress at Robin's feet to dive in myself. Normally I was a slow eater. Careful about taking enough bites and chewing properly—but damn, fucking apparently took a lot out of me, because it felt like I blinked and my burrito was gone.

"Here," Robin said without pausing. His torta bumped against my lips and I took a bite, sighing after I swallowed because it was fucking *delicious.*

"You don't need to—"

"Open up, gigantor." Robin pushed his food against my lips again. I wanted to protest, because this was his food, but…I figured if he was offering it to me he wanted me to have it. I took another bite, and Robin made a pleased little sound.

When he tried to feed me a third bite, I ducked away, however, dabbing at my lips with a napkin, my heart thumping unsteadily.

No one had ever fed me before.

It was intimate in a different way than pushing inside his body had been. And I found myself floored by it, all over again.

"You want more?" he asked, only halfway through his food. I shook my head. "You suuuure?"

"Thank you," I replied softly, enjoying the way he took a bite of his food, his cheeks puffing up. "I'm good."

Robin ate like he perpetually thought he only had five minutes to get his food down. So it was funny how slow he was moving tonight. Like we'd switched places.

When he'd finished, I cleaned up, enjoying the way he watched me, those green eyes dark with heat. And then we showered together, the hot water pressure was ridiculously good. I made a mental note to have a shower head just like this one installed at my place—because it was heaven on my back.

Robin and I fell into bed together with a groan, clean and satisfied.

And for the rest of the weekend we repeated that pattern. We'd fuck, eat delicious food, and sometimes pop in a Christmas movie or two. Robin seemed to really like the ones that had snow—which was unsurprising after seeing his first reaction to it back home.

It was heaven.

Truly.

But on the last night, as we lay in bed, my heart fluttering, Robin curled up against my chest, I realized just how homesick I felt.

Like he'd read my mind, Robin's voice echoed through the quiet, groggy and sweet. "I'm excited to go home tomorrow," he admitted innocently, like he hadn't realized what he'd just said at all.

"Yeah?" I murmured, stroking my fingers through his hair.

"I miss the girls," Robin admitted, squeezing me tighter. "Not that I don't love the manic sex-fest we've been having, because I do—like…so much." His ass was well-fucked, cum slick between his cheeks, so I knew he was telling the truth.

Apparently Robin liked being bred as much as I liked breeding him.

"But I miss my lil mob bosses," Robin wriggled and I squeezed him tight, pressing a kiss to his fluffy head.

"I miss them too," I agreed, because I did. So much.

"You think Jane's been practicing?" Robin asked quietly. "I gave her a bunch of tips, but she was still worried about the play." The performance was on the twenty-third, right before Robin's plane was due to depart back to L.A. It was a Christmas play, something the elementary school had thrown together with open doors for kids—even the ones too little to be real students—to participate in.

"We can go over her lines again when we get back," I agreed. "She'll appreciate that."

"Rosie's no help," Robin sighed. "All she wants to talk about is her cat."

"She's almost to a hundred," I informed him, because I'd forgotten to tell him earlier.

"No shit?" Robin perked up, his chin digging into my chest. "Oh my god. I bet she's so excited."

She was.

Her words came back to me, however—the innocent offer to give away all the money she'd earned and the opportunity for a pet, so that Robin would stay.

"Would you want to go pick one out with us?" I asked, stroking through his hair as his pretty lashes fluttered.

"When?"

"It'd be after Christmas." We'd been so careful not to talk about what was happening after Robin returned home to L.A. I'd been terrified of scaring him off. But now…that fear was fading. After these last few days together I simply couldn't fathom my world without him in it.

I would make it work, no matter what that took.

Even if it meant giving up Belleville and its peace.

"I…" Robin wavered, his face scrunching up sadly. "I'm not sure what my schedule will be like."

"We can wait," I promised, warming even more when he simply melted and offered me a big smile.

"You sure?"

"I'm sure," I said, making room for him in my life because it was simple. Making room for him in our lives—because it was what the girls and I wanted. "They want you there."

"Okay," Robin grinned, eyes scrunching up happily. "Then fuck yeah, I'll come."

It was effortless to kiss him then, to imagine a world where all of this was easy. Where we got to keep him. A world full of Christmases like the movies, haunted houses, and pets. A world where Robin Johnson was ours forever, my missing other half.

December twenty-third crept up on us a lot sooner than I would've liked. Robin never went back to the B&B, aside from the single time to gather his remaining things and officially move them into my bedroom. I made room for him inside my closet and dresser, and he was so excited by that simple gesture that he'd fallen right to his knees and blown me.

Our mornings were a perfect mix of pancakes, toddler barbs, and Robin's stories. He played with the girls like he always had—and now that he was officially unofficially living with us, had even more time to help coach Jane for the upcoming performance.

It was adorable watching him from the kitchen as he ran lines with the twins. Rosie had an easier time remembering hers, so she usually abandoned them only a few minutes in, but Jane remained just as stoic, just as serious as always.

"And Santa came down the chimney," Robin repeated one night, waiting for Jane to echo him.

"And Santa came down the chimney," she replied, voice quaking.

"With a big—"

"With a big THUD!" Jane maybe screamed the last part, a little too loud, but Robin was not deterred. He clapped riotously, more than a little proud that she'd remembered her lines on her own—and spoken so loudly.

She had a hard time with that.

The speaking loudly part.

When Robin wasn't coaching Jane, he was on the couch scrolling through humane shelter websites with Rosie. We all knew it was unlikely the pets they were looking at would be available come time to pick them up, but Rosie appreciated the time he took despite this.

It was an honor to watch Robin bond with my children.

And one night, only a few days before Robin was due to return to L.A. for good, I bit the bullet and asked him if I could tell people about us—Trixie first. He seemed surprised, probably because of our earlier conversation when I'd asked him if he wanted us to be a secret, and he'd said no—but otherwise just gave me a double thumbs-up and told me, "fuck yeah."

"You're dating someone?" Trixie's voice was as soft as ever, quiet enough that even with the volume turned all the way up it was hard to hear her.

"I am," I hummed.

I'd opted to call her on my last full day in office before the holidays. Obviously things happened, and as the town doctor, it was possible I still might get called in—but I liked to at least try to pretend my time was my own.

"What's his name?" Trixie sounded as excited as I'd hoped she would. She'd always been my number-one fan. I missed her—especially hearing her voice like this—and I made a vow that the next time I went to L.A. I'd make a point to introduce her to Robin.

After I'd finished explaining the magic that was Robin Johnson, Trixie's voice was somehow even softer.

"I'm happy for you," she said, sweet as ever. "I really am." She didn't tell me how difficult it was going to be. Didn't tell me about all the negatives of long distance—or lecture me about the age gap. All she asked was if he loved the girls, and when I answered yes—and told her he'd been more open with affection with them than he even had with me—she'd simply laughed. "I always wanted this for you," she told me, cheesy as it was. "You deserve to be loved, Ben Montgomery."

"I want it for you too." My heart was fuller than it had ever been. "And ditto."

"Wish granted," she replied, an awkward lilt to her words that had me perking up.

"Trixie—" I jolted, more than a little surprised. "Are you seeing someone?"

"I am," she said. "She's lovely."

"Oh my god. *Bitch*, why didn't you tell me?"

"Why didn't *you* tell *me*?!" she countered.

I laughed.

For the next hour we chatted about our lovers, and it cooked up a scheme that I hoped would end well for me and Robin.

Because if there was one thing I wouldn't tolerate, it was splitting up our family on Christmas. Performance or not. L.A. or not. And Trixie told me she would do everything in her power to help my plan come to fruition.

"THUD!" Jane's voice echoed through the auditorium, tremulous but stronger even than it had been at home when she practiced. Robin was sitting beside me, a literal armful of bouquets at the ready for the girls. He was dressed in the clothes I'd bought him. A black ensemble, a big puff coat, fluffy black collar.

It was supposed to snow tonight.

Which made me nervous because Robin would be heading to the airport—and I worried about him. I'd wanted to drive him but he'd told me no. He wanted me to spend time celebrating after the performance with the girls, and assured me that he was more than happy to spend the trip with Miles and Bubba.

I didn't have an argument for that.

Even though it felt a little like he was running.

I figured I'd be chasing him soon enough, however, not that he knew that—so I didn't worry too much. Even though the thought of being without him even for a few days made me scared.

When the play was over, a line of kids—of all sizes and ages—dressed in varying elf, Santa, and tree outfits stood in a row on the stage. They held hands and bowed, the roaring of the crowd impossibly loud in the quiet space.

Belleville wasn't a big town, and yet it seemed like every single member had come out tonight to support the kiddos. People lined the walls, all cheering and clapping. Jason, from the grocery store, stood at the back of the room, whistling—and beside him, Leanne, the bookstore owner, was grinning. She had one of my books in her hand, like she'd been reading during the intermission—and my cheeks burned.

Soon enough everyone would find out that I was the author. It was inevitable now that I'd been spotted with Robin and posted online. But I was…at peace with that. I only spared a single thought for my impending doom, before turning my attention back to the stage.

The twins hunted the crowd for us, the same way they had every time they'd marched their cute butts on stage. Rosie saw me first, her eyes going wide as she stood taller.

Jane spotted me next, her little eyes as wide as her sister's as a sunny grin split across her face. She didn't often smile like that, and it always made my heart hurt when she did. Warmth flooded through me as I beamed back at them, so fucking proud of what they'd just accomplished.

"That's my girls!" Robin screeched from beside me, somehow the smallest, and loudest person in the whole room. I glanced down at him, half-tempted to kiss him just because he was so damn cute. He didn't have eyes for me though. His attention was solely focused on our girls. "Fuck yeah!"

Rosie grinned, her eyes gleaming like she'd somehow heard his voice above the din of the crowd. She dropped the hand of the girl next to her and made a come hither motion with it—the same way she did every time Robin pulled money out of his pocket for her.

Robin cackled, his giant bouquets crinkling as he jumped up and down, and then he was racing through the aisle, and I was chasing him. The second we neared the stage, the twins were running too, leaping across the floorboards toward us, their sweet little red elf outfits bouncing. Robin dropped the flowers, ready to catch them as they neared the edge.

I grabbed Rosie before she could jump, trusting Robin to catch Jane. The girls were giggling like crazy, their sweet little laughs lighting up the air as Robin struggled to pick up the bouquets while still holding Jane. He managed somehow, and gave one to each of them, accompanied by an adorable cheek smack and a, "congratulations on being badasses."

And then he handed Rosie two dollars, and she was wiggling in my arms, trying to get to him.

It didn't even bother me that both the twins seemed to want Robin more than they wanted me.

And why would it?

When my world was a beautiful, wonderful place.

When I had everything I'd ever wanted.

And my heart was full, full, full.

twenty-one

ROBIN

I MISSED BEN BEFORE I even left Belleville limits. Felt like there was an empty hole beside me as I sat silent in the passenger seat of Miles's truck, my suitcase gathering snowflakes in the truck bed. I hadn't wanted to be without the things Ben had bought me, and therefore my backpack hadn't cut it this time around. Miles, because he was an angel, was quiet as we drove through the dark, snow crunching beneath our tires.

I would've been excited about the snow, except I knew I wouldn't get to benefit from it.

"I'm going to miss the sledding," I sighed, leaning my head against the chilly glass as the flakes came down harder, and farmland and trees blurred by.

"Miss the sledding?" Bubba echoed from the back seat. He'd gotten a bouquet of his own—and was rather proud of himself, sniffing at the flowers where he sat beside Jeremy. I swear to god, I hadn't seen Bubba without Jeremy attached to him the entire time I'd been visiting.

They looked especially cute today. Jeremy was dressed like a polar bear in all white with his nose painted. Bubba was an elf just like the twins had been, though he wore green and not red. Both of them had winter gear over their outfits, thank god.

"You know, *the sledding*," I reminded him, surprised he'd forgotten. "The sledding all the Montgomery's do? Every time it snows?"

Bubba made a confused sound, and Miles snorted—amused.

"*Darlin'*," he said softly, his big hands at ten and two on the steering wheel. "Ben's a lying liar that lies. That ain't a thing."

"What?" I blinked, confused.

"He only said it was because he wanted to take *you* sledding," Miles snorted. "Called his mom in a panic, got her to help orchestrate the whole event."

"Why didn't you tell me?"

"And ruin the gesture?" Miles slanted me a look. "I ain't a snitch."

I felt blindsided by this.

"Why would he—"

"Because he loves you," Bubba interjected from behind us. "Obviously."

"Oh." My heart skipped a beat. I stared out at the snow for another beat, trying to process this. "He…"

"Ben's been head over heels for you since day one," Miles added, sounding very pleased. "Everyone knows it. You'd have to be blind not to see it. Could barely keep his eyes off you the entire welcome party. He's obvious as hell." He snorted out a laugh. "He smiles…so much when you are around. It's like he's a totally different person."

Suddenly all of Miles's meddling made even more sense.

"Roben," Bubba chimed in, self-importantly. "That's your ship name."

"You gave us a ship name?" I twisted around to squint at him before returning my attention to the road and Miles's sly grin. In the past, I'd read fanfiction about me and my ex-band-mates, so I was familiar with the terminology. That had been a freaky but enlightening experience—and also super fucking hot, if I'm being honest.

I'm pretty sure I'd read at least sixty different iterations of my old drummer fucking me in about a hundred different positions.

I definitely hadn't looked at him like that when we'd been working together—and when I'd found the fanfiction I'd felt that loss keenly. But that was years ago, and I had Ben now—so my thoughts of fanfiction remained chaste. Mostly.

Except for now that Ben and I had been spotted together it made me wonder if fanfiction for us would start to pop up? That was a fun thought.

"*Actually,* Matilda's the one that gave you a ship name," Bubba replied, sounding miffed that she'd beaten him to it. "And Grandma B heard and shared it with me." Grandma B was Beatrice Montgomery. It'd taken me a second to get that, but after spending several weeks bonding with Bubba I was used to his fun little nicknames for everyone. Mine was still somehow the worst. Duncle Robin was an atrocity. An adorable atrocity—but an atrocity all the same.

Without missing a beat, Bubba continued, "Oh, and she told Becca. And Uncle Baxter. *And* Uncle Paxton."

"And Trent," Miles piped in helpfully. "Who told me."

"And Jason," Jeremy tacked on from where he'd been sitting silent in the back seat in his giant hand-me-down coat.

I didn't know who "Jason" was, but Miles's reaction to the name made me think the fact that *Jason* knew was a pretty monumental thing.

"And if Jason knows—" Miles started.

"The whole town knows," Bubba and Jeremy finished for him, in unison.

When I twisted to look at the boys in the back seat again, they were grinning like hyenas.

"You're telling me that an entire town has shipped me and Ben for weeks?" I snorted, surprised. "That feels like a lie."

"Well, it's not," Bubba shrugged. "Also, more like *months*."

"They did it to me too," Miles commiserated. "On a smaller scale, but still." He grinned, eyes crinkled at the corners. "At least you didn't have them placing bets about when you'd get together."

"No shit?" I stared at him, somehow still surprised after hearing this new information just how unhinged this entire town apparently was.

"I won," Bubba declared like the evil—adorable—shit he was.

"He got a big ole wad of cash," Miles shook his head affectionately.

"I spent it all," Bubba declared. "Got a marine biology encyclopedia."

"And we took him to the aquarium," Miles laughed, eyes crinkling. "He spent the rest of it buying stuff from the gift shop."

"They had a sperm whale," Bubba pointed out—like the fact they had a whale named after cum meant he had to buy it. "I bought two."

I had no doubt that the second whale had been given to Jeremy.

This whole conversation was weird—but not in a bad way.

It was…enlightening to know that Belleville was invested in Ben and my relationship. Certainly explained all the "congratulations" that had been thrown my way lately. It was different from the attention I got anywhere else. It really felt like people here wanted…the *best* for us—for me too. And while everyone was certainly *nosy*, they were all also well-meaning. Like they cared, even though they didn't have to.

And it wasn't like when we'd been kids—the fake pleasantries that had been handed out like candy in the little town where we'd grown up in North Carolina. These people were genuine. They said they cared, because they did. They said good morning, because they wanted your day to start off right. They said congratulations because they were glad that you were happy.

They weren't like our mom.

Not at all.

Still though, even Belleville's nosiness couldn't distract me from the fact that Ben, as early as when we'd first hung out, had *lied* to me. Had pulled together a fucking *Ocean's Thirteen* of his own just to take me sledding. I still didn't get why he hadn't just *told* me he wanted to take me.

Except…that I did.

Because me at that time would've run so fucking far and fast he never would've seen me again. I'd been ready to bolt, even though what I really wanted was to spend as much time with him as possible.

It's why I'd always found a way to him. Why I'd been full of excuses as I wormed my way into his life, one awkward encounter at a time.

I maybe hadn't been ready then. To admit that I wanted him more than I'd ever wanted anything else, in all my life. But I could admit that now, in the privacy of my heart—with the snow and wind blowing chilly—and the people I loved most in the world giggling because they wanted to see me happy.

Finding out about Ben's secret had to be the sweetest fucking thing I'd ever learned. In my *entire* life. It made me wonder just how many random little things Ben had done to make me happy. How many hoops he'd jumped through, just to see me smile.

Did he even like going shopping? Or the Christmas Market? Or the movies? He didn't like crowds, didn't like places that felt overstimulating. The answer hit me like a slap to the face. It didn't take a genius to come to the obvious conclusion that Ben had done all those things because he loved me.

No one had *ever* treated me like that before.

No one.

My heart hurt.

"Hey," Miles sobered, reaching out to give my shoulder a squeeze. "You okay?"

Normally he double-fisted the wheel like he was trying to strangle it into submission—so the fact he took his hand off the wheel meant a lot.

"I…didn't know." My voice broke, and Miles squeezed me tighter. "That he'd done that. The sledding thing." All the other things too, though I didn't say that.

The light turned green and off we went. Miles removed his hand, and I missed it the moment it was gone.

Everything felt different now.

Leaving felt different.

I'd said my goodbyes to Ben and the girls—as briefly as I could, because I hated goodbyes. I'd promised I'd come back to visit when my schedule permitted it, and I'd meant it. Ben and I hadn't broken up. But it felt wrong, leaving—wrong in a way it'd never felt before.

I was running in the wrong direction.

Snowflakes blurred by, and my heart stayed somewhere behind us, in the dark—stuck in the snow.

I was supposed to be spending Christmas with them. I could feel that now. I was supposed to be with them when they opened the presents I'd bought them. We were supposed to be together, like the families I'd seen in Christmas movies growing up.

And yet…here I was—speeding off toward the airport and the chilly, bare apartment that awaited me. To a concert I didn't want to perform at, for people I didn't care about, to feed a career that didn't feed me back—not anymore.

My contract renewal was going to happen after the concert was over. Nancy had already drafted it up. All I needed to do was sign. It would be years of tours. Years of money. Years of traveling the world, of adoring fans, of padded pockets. And it should've made me happy—seeing as for the longest time this was all I'd ever wanted.

This had been my dream.

Only…I was realizing that I had a new dream now. I had a new dream and he was tall as a mountain, smelled like sandalwood and blossom, and had frankly magical fucking biceps.

"Miles?" I said softly after a minute of quiet, my thoughts spinning.

"Yeah?" Miles kept his tone light, though I could tell he was doing that on purpose—probably could tell from my silence that I was thinking. We'd been through a lot together, Miles and I—and though I hadn't been the best about communicating with him in recent years, he still knew me better than just about anybody.

"Do you think I'm stupid for wanting to…" I sucked in a breath. "For wanting to leave everything I've built behind—because Ben fucking… orchestrated a sledding expedition?"

Miles was quiet for a minute, a minute that felt like a century.

"You know…Gram told me something last year that really struck a chord with me," he admitted, voice far away. Bubba and Jeremy were quiet, aside from a few rustles. Miles sucked in a breath, similarly to what I'd just done—my giant, dark-haired mirror. "She said: How long are you gonna tell yourself you're not worthy of the kinda love you want?"

His words echoed around inside my head, twisting tight around my heart.

"I…" My throat clicked.

"Relevant, yeah?" Miles replied. "You remember Margie?"

"'Course I fucking remember Margie."

"Sweetest dog in the world," Miles sighed. His hands flexed on the steering wheel, a far off expression on his face. "I told you over and over I'd never have another dog." My heart thumped wildly. "Now I have two."

My eyes burned.

"Things change," Miles said softly. "And when you love someone… losing them is inevitably gonna hurt." He shrugged. "But…you can't live your life with one foot out the door. Take it from me—that's *not* fuckin' livin'." Miles's voice was sad. "I wish sometimes that I'd wasted less time worrying." His eyes were warm as he flashed me a smile. "But then I wouldn't have met Trent when I did. And he came just when I needed him—but only when I was ready to take that leap."

The car was quiet, the kiddos in the back probably listening intently.

Miles didn't often talk this much. It was an honor to witness the kind of man my little brother had become. He was stronger now than ever before, and more sure of himself. I was so damn proud of him.

"You're allowed to grow, Robin," Miles added. "To change. And sometimes to grow there's gotta be hurt along the way."

It *would* hurt, losing the career I'd built—even if I didn't love it anymore. But it would hurt more to leave behind the only happiness and peace I'd found. I loved Ben more than I'd ever loved the lights, and the stage, and the music.

I loved our quiet, peaceful moments.

Loved being a source of strength for the twins.

Loved feeling like I had someone to count on.

Loved being someone Ben could lean on when the weight on his broad shoulders grew heavy.

And I couldn't do that if I wasn't here. Couldn't do that if all I gave them was the occasional holiday and scattered FaceTime calls. Couldn't be the kind of partner—the kind of man—I had always longed to be. Since the day my dad had shown me a cookie-cutter shape of what I didn't want to become.

I don't think I'd taken in a full breath since then. Don't think I'd ever let myself truly relax, knowing what kinda monsters were out there— parading around as people that said they cared.

But that perception had only hurt me, even after the barbs of what my parents had done had been pulled free. I'd let them injure me, over and over, let the wound fester till it consumed me entirely. Till it tainted all my actions. Till I became scared of everyone, good and bad.

Living a shadow life, with only the empty nights for company.

I never let people close because it was easier to run if I didn't.

Miles was right. That wasn't a way to live.

And he may not know the extent of what my dad had done, but his words were still applicable. Maybe one day I'd be ready to share that with him. But today was not that day. My thoughts were too full of Ben and the girls—and the what-ifs the future held.

"Good things can be scary," Miles added. "And sometimes they can be downright *painful.*"

"Like growing pains," I nodded, a hot tear dashing down my cheek.

I felt small, cold, and warm—all at the same time as Miles broke me apart one last time. "And it's okay for growth to be uncomfortable, hell, take it from someone who knows." He cracked a smile, and another tear slid down my cheek. "I ain't good with words, you know that—I ain't never been good with them," Miles added, even though he'd literally just been shooting poetry out his ass. "So, instead of answering your question outright, I'm gonna finish lecturing you by asking you one of my own."

The joke fell flat, but I appreciated it all the same. Miles's lips were twisted into a gentle little smile that fell as quickly as it had risen.

"Okay," my voice was raw.

My heart continued to thunder. Snow fell.

The world was quiet, quiet, quiet.

My cheeks were wet.

"You been running all your life, Robin. *Aren't you tired?*"

I *was* tired.

I was so fucking tired.

Even more so now that I was about to go back to the place I hated most in this world, instead of spending Christmas with the people I loved.

Another lonely Christmas.

Only it was worse this time, because I knew what I was leaving behind.

I nodded and it hurt so fucking bad to admit how weary my soul had become. But Miles said good things sometimes hurt. And those words were a balm on my heart as I sniffled.

"*I'm so tired,*" I admitted, voice rough and wet.

"Then maybe it's time you let yourself rest."

Then maybe it's time you let yourself rest.

Then maybe it's time you let yourself rest.

Miles's words spun around inside my head. I pinched my eyes shut, more tears spilling free. His big hand lay on my shoulder again—probably another red light, judging by the color of my closed lids.

"And Belleville's big enough for the both of us," I repeated the words he'd spoken to me all those weeks ago.

"Sure is," Miles agreed.

My pulse was racing as I opened my eyes and peered out at the dark, snowy roads. So different from the world I was used to seeing. An alternate reality that could be mine if I simply chose to keep it.

The snow fell and fell and fell.

My lungs opened up.

I breathed—and as easily as it had filled me, all those years ago, the poison in my lungs melted away. And I knew without a shred of doubt in my mind where I wanted to lay my weary head to rest.

The party was raging. Lights had been strung across the ceiling of my apartment. They dripped, glittering icicles sliding down the walls and making the space feel far more lively than it ever had before. A giant tree just like the one Nancy had showed me on her vision board sat in the corner. Probably twenty feet tall, the thing was coated in white and black bulbs to match the decor.

Everyone was mingling. They'd been mingling for hours, drinking champagne, munching hors d'oeuvres, and gossiping.

It all felt so…pointless.

Schmoozing.

People with enough money they could grind it up and gargle with it and never notice the loss. I missed Belleville fiercely and its madness as I sat on the window ledge near the back wall, watching, waiting for my turn to perform.

A few opening acts had sung already, smaller fish—bands that had just joined. I'd been like that once. Hungry for any opportunity I could get to move forward.

Nancy had been fighting off reporters for me all night. Especially after I'd pulled her aside earlier that afternoon and told her what I wanted to do. She'd been sad, yes, but she'd been happy for me too. And despite the risk to her own career, she'd helped me arrange everything the way it needed to be for me to move forward with my life.

Miles had said it was time to rest.

And it was.

But first…I had to end the cycle I'd begun.

And as soon as the loose ends were tied up—I planned on running toward my future, rather than away from it.

Despite the large size of my apartment, the space managed to feel claustrophobic. I was just glad the stairs were fenced off so I didn't have to worry about anyone finding their way up to my bed. It wasn't *that* kind of party, true, but that didn't make me any less glad to have my privacy maintained.

"You ready?" Nancy hummed, approaching me, the click of her heels somehow louder than the chatter bouncing off the walls. She paused in front of me, her dark eyes soft. "There's no going back," she added, voice quiet enough only I could hear. "Are you sure this is what you want?"

I let my decision spin around inside my head. Let the thoughts settle. Let my future dangle in front of me, brilliant and brighter than the lights that decorated the tree.

If things went right, this would be my last Christmas away from my family.

If things went right, I could have the holidays I'd always dreamed of. I'd have my birthday off, Bubba's birthday off—Miles's too. I'd have every Pie Festival, every Valentine's Day. I'd be there to help pick out Rosie's cat. I'd be in the front row for all of Jane's performances. And every night, sleep would come easy, because I'd be settled safe in Ben Montomgery's arms, in his bed he said was big enough for the both of us.

There'd be no eyes.

No harsh comments.

Only Ben's biceps, his snort-laugh, and the way he made me feel like I was ten feet tall.

I'd be his songbird, and no one else's. And maybe one day I'd learn to love music again.

"I'm sure," I said, the muscle in my jaw jumping as I bobbed my head. "I've never been surer-rerer of anything in my life."

"Good," Nancy replied, her eyes a little wet. I'd never seen her cry. Not in all the years we'd worked together. She offered me a hand up and I took it, my pulse skittering, my palms sweaty as she gave it a squeeze.

"Nancy?" a quiet, sweet voice echoed from somewhere behind Nancy's shoulder. An adorable petite woman dressed in a head-to-toe black lacy dress approached. She looked oddly familiar, her dark eyes full of warmth as she smiled at me, blonde head bobbing.

"Hi, baby," Nancy pressed a kiss to her cheek, before gesturing toward me. "Robin's about to go on."

The woman stared at me for a beat, a demure smile gracing her lips. She had the same kinda energy as a doll, almost. But not in a "Chucky" way, more like a goth fairy godmother or some shit. Like she was built from porcelain and good vibes. "Good luck!" she said enthusiastically, her eyes dancing like she knew something I didn't.

"Thanks," I smiled at her, annoyed I didn't have time to ask her name— or properly introduce myself to Nancy's girlfriend. Because holy fuck, apparently Nancy was dating someone now? Who knew!

What a mindfuck.

The crowd parted for me, quieting somewhat as I made my way to the stage. Nerves fluttered around like mad inside my belly. I'd never done something this risky. Never done something this goddamn *terrifying* in all my life. I was about to throw everything I'd built away.

This was scarier than when I'd moved to L.A. on my own.

And I'd thought *that* had been bad.

I took a breath, fingers slipping easily along the microphone's surface. I'd opted not to play my guitar tonight. Normally I would—but I didn't…want a shield between me and what I was about to do, even though it might make things easier.

I was tired of picking the easy route.

And I…well…

I was ready to start pursuing the things that made me happy.

Ready to grow, even though it might hurt.

I was ready to make that leap.

Because for the first time in my life I trusted that there would be someone there to catch me.

And I knew that at the end of this terrible jump I'd find that Ben's arms were still wide open. That his chest was warm, and his heart was thumping, and he'd do what he'd done since the day we met—and give me somewhere safe to call home.

Nancy's phone was pointed toward me—for my personal social media. And the group of reporters that had been added to the guest list—per my request—were equally armed with cameras and phones of their own. *Go big or go home, right?* Some of them had both, probably live streaming, if I had to hazard a guess.

Which was good.

Really good.

Exactly what I wanted.

Except that it was still fucking *scary* to be scrutinized like this. Especially considering what I was about to do. What I'd been psyching myself up to do ever since Miles had dropped me off at the airport with a final hug and told me I was required to open my present when I came back home.

You've done this a thousand times.

It's fine.

You're fine.

Everything is fine—

Eyes, eyes, eyes. So many eyes. So many that the room felt small. So fucking small. I couldn't breathe—I couldn't—I searched the crowd, looking for something familiar in this space that I'd owned for years, but had never felt like mine.

It was only when I spotted a man with auburn hair that I was able to suck in a real breath.

I knew that my eyes were playing tricks on me.

That there was no way that Ben was here. It was Christmas Eve for god's sake. Even if he'd scored a plane ticket, it wasn't like he could just drop everything and fly across the country on a whim.

But for a moment, as I closed my eyes, I let myself believe he had. That he'd flown out right after me. That he'd made his way here, just to be with me on Christmas Eve. That he'd chased me, even though I wasn't running anymore—at least…not from him. That Ben Montgomery had performed a Christmas miracle.

The crowd went quiet as the first wispy notes of guitar filled the air. I squeezed the mic tight, tapping my fingers against it to count the beat as I waited for my turn to join in. It was my first song—one of my most popular. Sad and angsty as the rest of them.

When I'd written these I'd been in my early twenties and my heart had been a gaping, open wound.

I opened my eyes, searching the crowd for the redheaded man I'd seen earlier. I couldn't see him though, but that was fine. It let me believe the illusion that Ben was here just a little bit longer.

When the song ended the room erupted into a chorus of applause. I smiled as the next song began, and I melted into my stage persona like I always did. This song was less haunting—a little more revenge-fucky.

And as I bounced around the stage, belting into the mic, I let the reality of the situation finally set in.

If all went well, this would be my last time performing these songs.

I said goodbye with every warbling word. Said my thank-yous as I slid across the stage, Christmas lights flickering high above me. The city lights winked below from the view through the window, the same way they had when Ben had been here—when he'd entered my world without hesitation, despite the implications it brought with it.

By the third song the audience was really feeling it. It was hard to get celebrities to join in. A lot of them liked to "play it cool" but tonight they played along. Bobbing their heads, grinning. A lot of them even mouthed the words along with me as another song began to play and I amped up the performance level even more.

I was sweaty and grinning—the leather I wore clinging to my skin as tightly as the glitter my makeup artist had painted on. Louder I sang, higher I climbed, saying my goodbyes to the stars I couldn't see, to all the places I'd toured—to the world beyond them.

If this was going to be my final performance, I was going to make it count.

Go out with a goddamn bang.

I finished my set, and by the time I was done the crowd had moved in close. They'd kept their distance at first, but by the time the last twang of the guitar sounded, they were pressed tight to the stage like glittery sardines. Nancy stood at the back of the room—beside the reporters. Her phone was still up, and I could see tears glinting in her dark, expressive eyes.

She knew what this was, even though no one else did.

I blew her a kiss, and she grinned.

Her girlfriend whispered something to her, and she made a frankly disgustingly squishy face down at her, all blatant affection. The crowd murmured in confusion when I didn't step off the stage even though my set was finished.

And then it happened.

What I'd been plotting and planning.

The last part of my final goodbye.

The crowd quieted again, as my bandmates picked up their instruments one last time. Soft and soothing, the quiet croon of the first whispering notes filled the air.

Familiar notes.

Notes they'd all heard, year after year, when the nights were cold—and people sought home. When the streets were lined with fairy lights. When the world was just a little kinder, just a little more hopeful.

I pressed the microphone to my lips, listening to the loop of notes as I searched the crowd one final time.

This was it.

The moment I couldn't take back.

It was growth, and it was scary, and it would hurt—

But…

I was okay with that if it meant I got to keep Ben Montgomery.

"I'll be home for Christmas," I sang out, sweetly—the way I'd wanted for years. Into Nancy's camera I sang, directing the words to the man who waited—probably asleep in bed, biding his time till his alarm went off so he could become Santa for my favorite kids in the world.

Nancy's free hand covered her mouth, her eyes continuing to glisten.

The crowd was silent, reverent.

My heart was full.

"You can count on me." The next line was choked and somehow even softer than the first.

I'd told Ben once that I wanted to sing love songs, and that's what this felt like. It was a promise to him, just like the promises he always gave me. I hoped, even through the video, he'd be able to see in my eyes what this meant to me.

What he meant to me.

No one spoke the entire time, like they understood what this was without me even having to say it.

Peace settled over me as I murmured the last line of the song, my heart full and warm. "I'll be home for Christmas." I searched the crowd, briefly—when my eyes caught on the redheaded man I'd seen earlier. When I saw his face, I was so startled I nearly missed the last and most important line of the song.

He was a few rows closer than before.

The gray at his temples caught the light.

His eyes were honey.

They said, *I missed you.*

They said, *I'm here.*

They said, *you'll never spend another Christmas alone.*

"If only—" at the last moment, I switched the words, my heart cracking right down the middle as Ben Montgomery smiled at me from the center of the crowd. "In our dreams."

The song ended, and with it, so did my career.

Silence echoed through the room as the notes petered out.

"Thank you so much for coming tonight to my last performance," I said as the crowd remained quiet, and my eyes were all Ben's. "It means the world to me."

Ben's smile grew broader. He had a twin in each arm, despite the late hour. I had no idea how the hell he'd managed this. It felt like magic. The miracle I'd hoped for.

"I want to dedicate that last song to the man who owns my whole-ass heart," I continued—heart fluttering like wild as the speech I'd prepared flew right out the window. I sniffed, throat tight. "I'm so grateful to be here. I'm so grateful to have been able to dedicate my life to music, which has always been my passion."

Murmurs filled the air, the quiet shattered as the crowd stared at me almost like they were one entity, not a billion different people.

"It has been my blessing and honor to get to do this for as long as I have," I hummed, eyes still all Ben's. "To get to meet you. To perform for you. To get to share with you my heart."

His eyebrows pinched together, like he was confused.

"*This* was my dream," I said softly, ignoring the murmurs, and staring Ben down. "But I have a new dream now. And while I'll miss all of you—so much," that was directed to my fans, the people who had built me from the ground up—people who truly felt like my friends, my family. "I want to give *him* my heart now. So I'm going to be taking some time to rest."

The peace broke, shattered by my words.

After I dropped that particular bomb, Nancy did what she did best.

She worked the crowd, climbing onto the stage and directing the attention away from me. She'd put her phone away, and the livestream to my social media was over. I couldn't catch a single word she said.

I couldn't.

I couldn't look away from Ben.

I was worried if I did I'd discover that I'd imagined he was here.

"Let's give a round of applause for Trashmouth!" Nancy clapped, urging the crowd to do the same, though they all looked shocked. Applause was slow but erupted quickly, a domino effect. There were a few whistles, and I did my best not to worry about my label or the fact that I knew my rep was somewhere in the crowd.

Nancy would handle it.

She always did.

She gripped my shoulder, leaning in close as the applause grew louder. "I'm so proud of you." Ben's smile never wavered. Not once.

Nancy's words wrapped warm around my heart as she released me, and I made my way to the edge of the stage.

"Robin?" a tiny voice sounded. I blinked, shocked when I glanced down and saw Rosie's sweet little head peeking up at me from the bottom of the stage. The strange blonde woman from before—Nancy's girlfriend—was with her. Her fingers gently stroked Rosie's hair with affection, as my sweet lil goth angel peered up at me.

It took me a solid thirty seconds to realize why the fuck Nancy's girlfriend looked so familiar. And why the hell she was with Rosie.

This was Trixie.

Holy shit.

What a small fucking world.

Before I could properly freak out, Rosie was talking again. "You didn't tell me," she complained, frowning at me like the fact I had been secretly famous and the singer of her favorite band was an epic betrayal.

"I'm sorry, sweet pea." I sank to my knees, and Trixie laughed, helping lift Rosie up onto the stage so we could talk better. For a second, I was concerned about the vultures in the crowd—about the cameras—but Trixie didn't seem worried, so I didn't either. "I didn't know how."

Because she was the sweetest, best kid in the whole wide world, it only took her a second to forgive me. "I liked your song," she said as I opened up my arms and curled them tight around her. "But your hair looks bad."

I snorted out a laugh, breathing in her sweet-baby scent, my eyes pinched shut tight.

"Did you wear heels because you're worried people will think you're short?" Rosie continued to roast me as I squeezed her close.

"Yes," I agreed, because I had.

"Oh." She obviously hadn't expected me to admit that.

"Thank you for coming," I said, pressing a kiss to her head, my eyes burning.

"You came to *my* play," she countered, twisting back to stare up at me. "I wanted to come to yours."

Right. Because that's what this was to her. A play. I cracked a grin, unable to help myself.

"You sounded beautiful, sweetheart," Ben's voice was a welcome, quiet rumble. I heard him over the crowd, my heart thudding unsteadily as I twisted to find his voice. "I'm so proud of you."

Jane was sitting on his shoulders, staring at me awestruck, her little eyes wide. She was wearing the same delightful black ensemble that Rosie was. I squeezed her twin tighter, flashing her a smile of her own, before turning my attention to Ben.

"I…" I didn't know what to say. Didn't know what to do—now that he was here—now that he'd made my life into a Hallmark movie. "I was coming home for good," I blurted, voice cracking right down the middle.

"I know," Ben said, voice just as hoarse.

Like he *had* known.

Even though I hadn't.

My heart fluttered.

"I love you," I said, because it was true—and because he deserved to hear it first, after being so patient, for so long.

"I know," Ben replied, making me laugh hard enough Rosie made a grumpy sound and decided that being snuggled by me was no longer comfortable. She pulled out of my arms and I let her go, watching in amusement as she flopped onto her butt, her little black Mary Janes thudding against the lip of the stage as she turned her attention back to the woman I was certain now was her mother.

I stood up after I double-checked that Trixie had Rosie handled. This was the first and only time I'd ever been taller than Ben Montgomery. Grinning down at him, I couldn't help it as a few hot tears slipped down my cheeks.

I'd been crying a lot lately.

But that was okay.

I figured after living my life as repressed as I had, it was okay to let loose every once in a while.

"I love you too," Ben promised, making sure I was listening. "I have—"

"Since the day we met, pretty much," I finished for him, leaning down, our breath mingling as Jane eyed us eagerly and Rosie's face pinched. "I know."

Ben grinned, wide and unrepentant. I wanted to taste it, so I did.

He tasted like home. Like new dreams. Like peppermint gum.

Like Christmases, the way they should be. Like trust, warmth, and solid foundations.

His lips were soft, just like I'd remembered. He kept his tongue to himself for the most part, which was a shame—but something I totally understood. We were in front of the girls, after all, and the fact that he was a dad at all times was something I loved about him.

When we parted, I felt better than I had in years.

"Give me Jane," Trixie demanded—surprisingly sassy for a woman with the energy of a willow tree.

Ben laughed, but didn't argue, passing their daughter down so she was sitting next to Rosie on the lip of the stage. Trixie smiled at the both of them, flashing me a wink, before distracting them to give us some semblance of privacy. The crowd had left us alone, probably because Nancy had redirected their attention—she was a badass like that.

Ben held his arms out, and I toed the edge of the stage, leaning down to curl my arms around his neck.

"C'mon," he urged.

"Your back—" I protested.

"Is fine," Ben finished for me. "Just…move slowly."

"Okaaay." With a sigh, I very, *very* carefully let him take my weight, settling into his waiting grip, and laughing as my belly swooshed and Ben squeezed me in close. Dangling in the air I could feel the rapid thump of his heart as his familiar scent filled my lungs.

He pressed a kiss to my ear, and then my cheek, and then my forehead. His stubble tickled. My skin buzzed—and for the first time in a long time, it felt like there wasn't a noose hanging over my neck.

I was free.

"I quit," I told him, even though he already knew that.

"I'm proud of you," Ben hummed. Somehow coming from him it felt different than when Nancy said it. I'd loved it then too—I didn't think

I'd ever tire of hearing those words, I'd received them so sparingly in the past. But still.

When Ben said "I'm proud of you" it was because he understood what I'd done.

Not only that I'd picked him—but that I'd picked myself.

He knew better than anyone what I'd been struggling with.

He was the keeper of my heart, after all.

"I'm so happy you're here," I told him, the emotions bubbling up as my arms tightened around him. "On Christmas Eve too—" My throat was hoarse, and my eyes burned, a great hiccuping sob escaping. "What about Santa?" My voice cracked right down the middle. "What about the presents under the tree—and the cocoa you have in the cupboard? And all the plans we made? And the—and the—"

"It's not Christmas without you, baby," Ben's lips were against my ear, his breath warm as he made a soft shushing sound as I blubbered. "I was never going to let you spend another Christmas alone. The girls and I decided we needed to come take you home. Besides..." I pulled back a little, grinning when Ben winked. "When I called Santa he said he didn't mind postponing the holiday one more day so you could be there."

I couldn't stop crying. Once the waterworks had begun I was fucking *done-zo,* motherfucker. My makeup ran, but I couldn't be assed to care. Not when Ben was here. And the girls were here. And even though I was embarrassing myself in front of Trixie—ohmygod—I was so *happy.*

So fucking *happy.*

The rest of the night was a blur of well wishes. Nancy tried to help me with my makeup at one point—and I only let her because I didn't want to look like a hot mess parading Ben around the rest of the night.

The girls spent a long time at the window with their mom, staring out at the city below, their chubby little hands leaving prints. Ben and I mobbed the refreshment table, feeding each other tiny little bite-sized potatoes and cuts of steak. And by the time the last of the guests left, the girls, Ben, and I were ready to fucking go to bed.

I spared one last thank you to Nancy—silently of course—when we entered my room and I realized that the sheets and blankets had all been washed, the bed remade. The girls eyed it with wide grins, all its pillows piled high—and launched themselves at it like the wild hyenas they were.

We bundled up, the four of us, squashed together in my bed as the massive Christmas tree below the loft winked at us.

The girls were asleep the second their heads hit the pillows, but Ben and I stayed awake for a few more precious minutes. Smoothing my hand over Jane's hair and her crooked pigtails, I leveled Ben with a look I hoped conveyed all my excitement—all my gratitude—all at once.

"I love you," I told him quietly, because it was true. "I love you so much."

"I love you too," Ben's palm was warm and scratchy as he stroked over my cheek.

"I never want to be away from you again."

"Me neither."

"Is that…is that okay?" My heart wobbled, my eyes wet—again—despite the fact I'd spent the last two days crying, it felt like. "Because I literally mean never. Like. People can pry you from my cold dead body."

"Jesus *Christ*," Ben laughed, my favorite sound in the whole wide world.

"Was it worth it?" I asked, because I needed to know. "Was waiting… for me worth it?"

He'd been patient. So fucking patient.

And I just…

"Does Mads Mikkelsen deserve another Oscar?" Ben countered, voice lilting with warmth. I sobbed out a laugh, smooching him hard enough our teeth clicked. He softened the kiss, urging me to slow down, his fingers bleeding heat against my skin. "Of course it was worth it," he finally murmured. "I was waiting for *you*."

I felt like I was dying. Like my skin was on fire, and my heart was full-full-full. Breathless out of happiness. Excitement burning hot in my chest. Anxious for the future rather than because of the past.

"I have one more question," I teased, our lips brushing, my heart in my throat.

"Hmm?" Ben waited, sleepy-sweet.

"Did I scare you, Ben?" My heart stuttered. "When I left?"

Ben laughed, a quiet, sweet little sound. He pressed another kiss to my lips, and instead of answering my question, gave me the last piece of the puzzle I needed before I could rest. "Beckett gets to go home," Ben replied, voice husky and gentle. "And he's sickeningly, deliriously happy."

"He is?"

"He is," Ben whispered, kissing me again, and then again—just because he wanted to. "He gets married." My eyes burned.

"He does?"

"He gets to be with his brothers."

"Y-yeah?"

"He heals," Ben's voice was a quiet, soothing rumble.

"He gets his happy ending," I echoed, kissing him back as my heart stuttered, one last, lovely time.

"He does," Ben agreed—a promise.

I'd made a lot of bad choices in my life.

Choices that hurt.

Choices that changed who I was—and not for the better.

I'd had fears and doubts. Poison that bled black in my veins.

But there was none of that now as Ben Montgomery gave me the happy ending I'd always wanted, but never thought I deserved. Because just like Beckett, I was going home. I was going to have the Christmas I'd always dreamed of with the family I adored, and the people who loved me just as fiercely as I loved them.

And while I knew that life would always have its obstacles, and that falling in love wasn't a cure-all for the past I was still healing from, I was no longer scared to move forward. My feet didn't itch.

Not anymore.

And I wasn't poison.

In fact…I'd never been poison at all.

epilogue

BEN

"TAKE ANOTHER HANDFUL, KID, YOU know you want to—"
Robin waggled the cauldron full of candy that he was holding like he
was offering the lineup of kids drugs. I tried not to laugh—and then
stopped trying, because some things were impossible and there was no
point wasting my energy.

The kid made a happy sound. I recognized him from a few weeks back.
It was good to see he'd gotten over his ear infection and was feeling well
enough to be out trick-or-treating. He grabbed a second entire handful
of candy—before shoving it into his bowl with a grin, and a lisped out
"thank you", before tearing down the street, his dragon tail swinging.

"Fill up," Robin commanded the next kid, looking way too fucking
pleased about his giant four-foot cauldron. The entire thing was full. It'd
taken us nearly an hour to dump all the bags of candy into it—and while

it was maybe, definitely overkill—I couldn't help but find it cute.

This was Robin's first Halloween in Belleville and when I'd informed him that trick-or-treaters didn't often come up to our door because it was around the back of the building, he'd been *devastated*.

Which was whyyyy we were out on the street, freezing our balls off, with Robin's cauldron attracting flocks of kids as they ran by with their parents.

The girls were in bed already.

We'd taken them out earlier, and they'd tuckered right out after we'd wrangled them out of their matching Wednesday Addams costumes and into bed. Neither of them had wanted to be Pugsley. Robin and I were still dressed up as Gomez and Morticia, and I had no idea how he was managing to stay out here wearing…*that*.

His body was cupped by a floor-length black velvet gown that hugged every curve. It dipped down the center, and every time he leaned over I got a glimpse of those perky little nipple piercings.

I'd done my best not to stare—because being hard while handing out candy to children was a goddamn nightmare I did not want to live, thank you very much—but it was difficult.

He'd even done his makeup. Though I was more than a little glad that he'd abandoned the black wig only ten minutes into taking the girls out trick-or-treating earlier. Robin claimed it was itchy. A fact that I could empathize with, as my Gomez mustache was uncomfortable itself. It was relieving to know that he could choose comfort, even if I couldn't.

"You're going to single-handedly be responsible for ninety percent of the cavities these kids get," I laughed as Robin waved at another group of kids. These ones looked closer to their teens and were dressed up as the cast of *Stranger Things*.

"Pshhh," Robin waved me off, though he looked adorably giddy about the prospect. He and Miles hadn't had big Halloweens like this when they were kids. He'd told me the saddest, most adorable stories about making Miles's costumes for him when he was a kid—only for most of the houses to close up early, and their bags to remain mostly empty.

We were healing his inner child, one cavity at a time.

And I couldn't be mad about that.

Especially when he made sure to give all the kids with beat-up sneakers the king-sized bars.

Robin's therapist had urged him to do things like this. To allow him to work through some of the darker moments of his past by making brighter memories. Which was also why he'd randomly come home with giant stuffed animals (friends for the plushie I'd bought him), fake realistic crows (because omg, they're so cool, Ben!), and enough Halloween decorations to choke the corners of our normally plain kitchen.

I didn't mind though, I never had.

Seeing Robin's chaos made me happy. Almost as happy as knowing that he was healing, that he was nesting, in his own way.

Two hours into our candy pedaling, the chill was beginning to get to me. I wasn't the only one affected. Robin was hopping around on his feet, back and forth, his hands stuck into his armpits to keep warm.

"Robin?" I was about to suggest we go upstairs and warm up—but then I saw the look on his face and the words died.

Without another word, I peeled my suit jacket off and slung it over his shoulders.

Robin grinned brightly.

And I subjected myself to another hour of the cold because seeing that smile was worth any discomfort autumn might bring.

Robin waddled as he tried to haul his cauldron upstairs—only for me to gently urge him to the side and lift it myself. I moved slow and careful as always. Up the stairs we went, and he ducked around me to open the front door with a happy hum. His boots clomped on the floor as I set the cauldron down by the couch and rose up, twisting from side to side to stretch my back.

A lot had changed since last Halloween.

For the better, most definitely.

Robin was the best thing that had ever happened to me—and that had only proven to be even more true as the months blurred by, and we got to spend more time together.

He'd moved in right away—something that made me grateful as I was far too old to want to play games that way. He'd opted to keep his apartment in L.A. for when we visited Trixie and Nancy, another fact I appreciated—and something that proved to me once again just how thoughtful my little songbird was.

When the building next door to my medical practice had put up a for-sale sign in the spring, Robin had bought it immediately. He'd been so damn excited it was contagious. And I'd watched enraptured as he turned the downstairs into the recording studio of his dreams so that he could continue to create the music he wanted to, without the threat of labels or money hanging above him.

It was one of my new favorite things to curl up on the couch in his studio with the girls and listen to Robin play. He'd fiddle around, heaven-like notes dancing through the air, make an angry sound like it wasn't good enough, only to immediately begin again and make *more* heavenly sounds.

He chewed through a pack of pencils every week, writing sonnets out on note pads, and abusing every utensil that came near his lovely mouth. And it was an honor to witness the evolution of his creativity, as Robin found his footing and began to make the things that made his heart happy.

The upstairs apartment above the studio was something else entirely. Robin had paid my brothers a pretty penny to renovate—only to politely kick them out when the walls and carpets were up and hire a new crew entirely.

None of them had been offended, which made me think that they must know something I didn't.

A fact that was only proven on the night, sometime that summer, when Robin had brought me upstairs to show me what he'd built us.

"Is this weird?" he said, sounding nervous as I stared at the space, my heart fluttering like crazy. "It *feels* weird. It is weird, isn't it? Dammit."

What could only be described as a sex dungeon was laid out in front of me. There was a wall full of paddles and other miscellaneous tools for our pleasure, as well as a rather plush, rather large bed pushed to the back of the room. A leash hung beside the paddles, taunting me. There were other furniture pieces as well, things I glossed over as my gaze fell to the bed and the restraints that were already attached to each of the four posts.

In the back of the room, adjacent to the bed, was a gorgeous mahogany desk. It housed what had to be the most amazing chair I'd ever seen. Cushioned, with back support—lumbar specifically. Buttery leather that looked softer than sin.

"I figured this could be our space, you know?" Robin said, staring at me. "That desk is for you—when you're writing." He continued to talk, overselling the room, obviously nervous. I didn't mean to not react—my mind was simply…imploding. "There's a massage chair back there—" he gestured to the only corner of the room I hadn't stared at yet. "For your back!" Robin added. "Because I love giving you rubs, and I'm definitely going to keep doing that—but I figured on the days that I'm not here, or you need a little extra—mmmmph."

Robin's mouth tasted as good as it always did.

His body was warm and pliant as I marched him right over to the bed. He bounced a little when I pushed him down into it, a quiet whine escaping as I made quick work of the buttons on his jeans and shoved my hand inside to curl around his dick.

"Jesus fuck," Robin gasped out, hips pushing into my hand, his eyes rolling back. "I take it you like it?"

"I *love* it." I squeezed him tight enough to hurt—just the way he liked it—and Robin sobbed.

And then I proceeded to show him just how much I loved the oasis he'd made us with my hand, and my tongue, and then my cock. Shoving into him fast and hard from behind as he bit the pillows and sobbed, the sweet pink of his hole giving for me.

I dug my teeth into the back of his neck, tight enough to bruise, forcing him to lie down and take it as the bed frame smacked against the wall, and for the first time since we'd gotten together—I didn't have to worry about making him make too much noise.

That wasn't the only surprise, however.

Robin was full of surprises.

Like the fact he apparently hated musicals.

A musician…that hates musicals.

And the fact that he loved long socks—but only a very specific kind of long socks. They had to be, and I quote, "thick enough I don't feel the boots, but not so thick that my toes are pinched."

He loved French toast in the mornings—not as much as my pancakes, but still.

He loved taking care of me—especially on my "bad back" days. He'd spend hours watching the girls, rubbing my back, and making sure I had my muscle-relaxers, my foam roller, and anything I needed.

He loved doing dishes—which I hated doing.

He loved putting leftovers away—another thing I hated.

He loved stealing my sweaters and hoodies. Loved parading around town broadcasting to everyone whose bed he was sleeping in, and whose home was now his. Robin was very loud about how much he loved me. Sometimes to the point that he'd embarrass the hell out of me—make my cheeks go splotchy red—as he told the little old women at my mom's book club that he'd joined, just how much he enjoyed my hands.

"They're good hands," he'd said, eyebrows wagging—always feeding the townies and their curiosity.

My mom cackled. She loved him. I'd known she would—but I hadn't anticipated just how much. "Oh dear," she said, shaking her head like she didn't know what to do with him at all.

"How good?" Matilda asked, still holding her signed copy of my newest book.

Robin just grinned, wide and wicked, and wagged his eyebrows some more. And said, "Wouldn't *you* like to know?"

Even after discovering that I was the author, my mother's book club had continued to read my stories—a fact that both horrified and amused me. They got a kick out of "Little Benjamin Montgomery and his smutty tales." And now a lot of them would make comments about the books during their check-ups. Trying to wheedle trade secrets out of me so they could use them as bargaining chips against each other.

It was humiliating and hilarious, all at once.

And I found I didn't mind.

Especially because Robin got such a goddamn thrill out of it. Lording the fact he knew insider information over all of them like he held nuclear codes, and not knowledge over which werewolf couple would get a book next.

I had learned a lot about Robin over the last few months.

I learned that he loved going to the drive-in theater. Loved it when I forgot to shave and I scratched beard burn all over his neck. He loved the Christmas presents I'd bought him—an entire collection of soft, bat-covered things, and plushies. He loved decorating our house like it was Halloween, months in advance. We'd had bats hanging from our doors since June.

Robin loved being bitten, and grabbed, and pinched, and fucked.

Loved when the girls were at my mom's and I could edge him for hours and hours and hours. Edge him till he sobbed and cried, hot tears spilling down his cheeks at the same time his little dick burst.

He loved the cock ring I bought him—red, just like I'd promised.

Loved it when he was still asleep and I'd slip it on him, then finger him nice and slow and take him from behind. Loved waking up stuffed full, with his nipple piercings tugged tight in my fingers.

"Jesus fuck," Robin had gasped out, the fifth or sixth time I'd woken him that way. "Fuck yes."

He'd been so tired after another sleepless night in the studio. After spending all day playing with the girls and taking them on adventures around town. He'd passed out before we'd even had our usual shared glass of wine—and right before he'd fallen asleep, he'd told me a single, lovely word. A word that meant this was a definite go, and I was welcome to do whatever I wanted.

"Green, Benisaurus Rex," Robin had murmured, sleepy sweet and rough.

And then he'd promptly passed out.

He'd been so cute I hadn't wanted to disturb him. But when the early hours of the morning hit and I woke up before him—I could no longer contain my hunger.

His skin was sleep-warm as I kissed the back of his neck, enjoying the prickle of his new haircut and the way the buzzed hair was shorn soft. Slowly, I slid kisses across his shoulders, and down the center of his spine, keeping my touch gentle, but firm enough not to tickle.

He made a sleepy sound, wiggling with a smack of his lips, his ass snug against my crotch.

Lower I kissed, down, down, until my lips skimmed his boxer briefs, and I was close enough to my prize I could feel anticipation burning bright in the air.

My cock was aching, the tease of the perfect globes of Robin's ass making my head spin. With a hum, I buried my face between his cheeks, grinding my nose and lips in so I could suck at his sweet little hole through the fabric.

Robin shivered, but otherwise didn't wake up.

Fuck.

God.

My dick hurt.

I reached down, squeezing it tight as I nosed at his hole through the fabric again, head swimming. The trust it took for him to allow me this was just—*Jesus*.

It really fucking did it for me.

Especially knowing Robin's past and what he'd been through.

I slid his underwear down inch by inch, notching my lips at the top of his crease, my tongue lapping the sensitive skin as the fabric slid lower and lower. The moment the boxers slipped down past his knees, his pretty hole winked at me, hidden in dusky shadow between his cheeks.

Unable to help myself, I grabbed one, spreading him wide so I could get a better look.

Fuck, he was delicious. A dusting of pale hair circled his sweet pink hole, taunting me as I rumbled a pleased little sound and dove in to lave kisses over my favorite part of his body.

With every swipe of my tongue, Robin's hole softened, like he was welcoming me in.

I checked periodically to see if he'd woken up, but he hadn't—

He was still completely unconscious.

It wasn't long before I was too impatient to do much more than slick up my fingers and stick them inside where he was liquid-hot and tight. Robin grunted, his hips shifting a little as one finger became two, and I worried the back of his neck with my teeth, my dick hard enough to drill a hole into the mattress.

I wanted to stick it inside him so fucking bad.

Wanted to shove in and in and in, and wake him up with him knowing exactly who he belonged to. Wanted to fuck him till my cum filled him up, then fuck him again just to drive it deeper.

When he was ready, I pulled my fingers free, marveling as his hole gaped. It tried to shut. A valiant effort that was fruitless, it was too well-fucked.

"Fuck." I hardly recognized my voice as I slicked up my cock and pressed the flushed crown to his loose rim. His hole gave easily, sliding like butter as I slipped in, one inch at a time—slowly, slowly.

It wasn't until I was fully seated that Robin finally woke.

He made this startled sound—my favorite sound—and then whined, his hips shifting wider to accommodate my girth. Already, he was grinding into the mattress, then back against me—even though his brain wasn't awake enough for words.

"Fuck yes," Robin finally managed, voice low and sleep-scratchy. "Fuck me, big guy. Give me that big ole—"

I pulled out and slammed back into him, eyes rolling back as the hot-pink of his ass gave beneath my dick. Fuck, it was heaven. Molten lava just clutching, *clutching* at me. So fucking tight. I loved the way our balls tapped when I sunk in deep. I loved the way his tiny body struggled to fit my girth. Loved when he was still half asleep and relaxed. Loved feeling him wake up around me, his body twitching to life.

"Breed me," Robin begged, voice quaking. "That's it, Ben-Ben—I need it."

In and out I rutted. Over and over. Smack, smack, smack—until Robin's words dried up and all he could do was sob. His waist felt tiny in my grip. The perfect handle to force him onto my cock.

When I finished, I groaned low, unable to help myself. I'd wanted to hold on longer, but Robin had been furiously humping the mattress— and he'd made the prettiest sound when he'd come. Clutched my dick nice and tight and made me see stars.

I flexed my hips, fucking my cum back into him a few more, glorious times. When I was done, I settled my hips against Robin's, cock nestled as deep as it could go so it could soften up while still inside him—just the way he liked.

"Fuck, I love you," Robin sighed. He twisted to give me one last happy little smile before he promptly fell right back to sleep—stuffed full and sated.

"Ben—" Robin's voice interrupted my thoughts, as he wandered toward me from the kitchen, the slinky black fabric of his Morticia outfit clinging to his frame. "You okay?" He frowned, concerned. "You didn't hurt your back with the cauldron, did you?"

I shook my head. "Just thinking."

"Thinking?" Robin arched an eyebrow, and I reached for him, tucking him easily under my chin.

"Thinking about how pretty you are when you take my dick."

"Oohhhh, I like this train of thought," Robin laughed against my chest, snuggling his arms around me and squeezing me just as tight. "Sounds like I'm getting some vitamin B tonight." Robin blinked. "Vitamin D?" He waggled his eyebrows. "Filling up my prescript-Ben."

"Thinking about how I want to do this forever," I murmured, my heart fluttering, the sweet expression on his face undoing me entirely if his jokes hadn't.

"Hug me?" Robin squeezed tighter. "Fuck me? Listen to my superior jokes?"

"All of the above." I pressed a kiss to his head, the thoughts I'd been having for months dangling on the tip of my tongue. "Robin..." My voice was warm, my pulse racing anxiously as I pulled back a little so that he would too.

"*Benjamin?*" He tipped his head up to meet my gaze, a question in his eyes that I couldn't help but answer.

"How would you feel about a spring wedding?"

"A spring—" Robin's eyes went wide. He shoved me away from him faster than I could blink. And then his feet were thundering down the hall and he was running from me—and I only had a split second to realize I'd fucked up before Robin's voice was echoing from the back of the house and soothing all my fears.

"Go, go, *go*!" he yelled.

There was a clatter of tiny feet hitting the floor.

"This is not a drill!" Riotous giggles danced through the air. It was a testament to how excited the girls were, and how obviously this had been planned, that they weren't grumpy at all at being awoken. "Code red!"

"I wanted it to be code black," Rosie's quiet voice complained.

"I wanted code purple," Jane added.

"Code whatever the fuck you want!" Robin's voice yelled again. Meowth, our black cat, sat on top of the grandfather clock staring at me, obviously unimpressed by our shenanigans. His tail swooped lazily, back and forth, almost in tune with the *tick, tick* of the clock.

I snorted out a laugh, my heart thumping as I heard more rustling, more muttered yells, and waited for whatever my loves had in store.

Rosie was the first to enter the hallway. She was wearing her pajamas, and her hair was a mess. Twin pigtail braids disheveled. In her arms, she had a poster—covered in glitter—probably courtesy of Bubba, who had dubbed himself the king of poster-making. I did my best not to read it because I was certain it would ruin the surprise if I did.

"Close your eyes!" Robin yelled at me as he burst into the hallway, herding Jane and her matching sign in front of him.

I closed my eyes.

More rustling, more whispered words.

"Okay!" Robin hummed. "Open."

When I opened my eyes the sight that greeted me nearly took me to my knees.

The twins were grinning, as was Robin, standing directly behind them, his own sign held high above his head. Spelled out across the three posters in looping, glittery font were four, beautiful words.

Will you marry me?

My heart was racing as I took it all in, taking a mental snapshot so I'd never forget this moment—or the expression on any of their faces. The girls looked incredibly excited, their eyes bright, matching grins on their faces.

"So?" Robin waited, his sign wobbling.

"So?" I teased, eyes dancing.

"Yes or no, motherfucker?"

The girls snickered.

"Yes," I agreed, because what else was I supposed to say? When faced with the cutest fucking proposal I'd ever seen.

"Fuck!" Robin swore, nearly dropping his sign. "*Dammit.* Where's Meowth?" He dropped his sign and pointed at the girls with one painted finger. "Wait here. We forgot the cat."

"You forgot the—"

"There he is!" Robin skittered over to the grandfather clock, hopping up and down, up and down, trying to catch him. Meowth stared at him, just as unimpressed as he'd been with me, before he finally let Robin pull him down. "One sec!" He wagged a finger at me, and then dug around in his pockets—he'd insisted his dress needed pockets, and now I knew why—before pulling out a handkerchief and a ring.

"Stop looking!" Robin glared at me, and I twisted my head away, sharing a snicker with the girls as he swore some more and got Meowth ready. "Go!" he commanded the cat. I turned to look because I couldn't help it.

Meowth did not go.

"C'mon!" Robin gestured toward me. "Go to Papa Ben-Ben." The cat again, did not go. "Jesus *Christ*. You're ruining my proposal," Robin wailed, obviously distressed. "I'll give you a treat," he bargained. "Two treats. Three?"

"Baby—"

Meowth moved, slinking toward me, the handkerchief around his neck winking as something shiny hung from it, near his throat.

"Thank God." Robin was beaming at me again, practically vibrating in excitement. "Go on!" He waved both hands at me, bouncing on his heels. "Surprise!"

I was definitely surprised, that was for sure.

Bending down, I carefully unwrapped the handkerchief from around Meowth's neck. I tried to pet him but he swiped at me, then trotted off, back to the grandfather clock, which he climbed like a goddamn ninja before settling to watch.

The ring that hung from the fabric was gold. Simple. Just the way I liked.

I swallowed the lump in my throat as I gently wiggled it free.

"What do you think?" Robin was right in my space. I'd been so distracted that I hadn't even noticed him approaching. "Look on the inside. It's engraved." He wiggled in excitement, so pleased he might as well have had a tail to wag.

"I love it," I replied honestly, throat tight and eyes burning. I twisted the ring around, shifting it in the light so I could see what was etched inside.

"You're my…" A snort escaped, my heart expanding as I finished reading the last few words, "Happy Ben-ding?"

"That's right, motherfucker. You're my—"

I kissed him, slipping the ring on, safe and snug. It fit perfectly, just like he did, as I swung him in the air, and the riotous cheers of the twins echoed. I kissed Robin then. Kissed him like the world was ending. Kissed him like he'd always deserved to be kissed.

And I was grateful then, to the universe for putting me in his path.

To the airline for giving me the seat next to his.

And to Robin most of all.

Because he was the best gift I'd ever received.

And I knew my future would be filled with joy because of him.

My precious little songbird, my sunshine, and the family that we'd built.

Blissfully, gloriously, ridiculously happy.

Forever and ever.

The End

Robin's Perfect Christmas to-do list

- ~~see a movie~~ 1 go **SLEDDING!!!**
- see a holiday movie
- go to the market thing
- see a *REAL* snow storm
- make snowmen with Bubba
- drink hot cocoa

thank you!

THANK YOU SO MUCH for reading and happy holidays to all of you! This project was genuinely such a joy to create. I was kicking my feet and giggling the whole time. Robin, especially, is near and dear to me and there were a few moments within the story that felt like they broke my heart just to mend it right after. This year has been a hard year and it was such a delight to be able to dive back into Belleville again and get to experience the magic of this fun little holiday series for a third time.

Rest assured, that this will not be our last trip to Belleville, though what direction the muse flows is your guess as good as mine. This series has become such a comfort to me. It feels like a hug for my heart, and I cannot wait to visit this silly little town with all its lovely people again. Thank you so much for all your comments, messages, and motivation. It has meant the world to me as I was creating this book to know how many of you were excited to read Robin and Ben's story.

Special thanks to Molly for making my books look like magic. To Kat for all the beautiful 'Southern-isms'. To all my wonderful alpha readers for keeping me sane and motivated as I wrote! I love you all to bits.

Thank you to everyone who contributed their time, energy, and love to this project; you are all my dear friends. And most of all, thank you to the reader, because without you, the creation of this story would have been meaningless. I write the words, but you are the ones who bring the story to life. Each and every one of you is priceless. Thank you for falling in love with these characters alongside me. I love all of you so much.

If you'd like to keep in touch with me and get access to exclusive mini-fics, character art, author updates, and more, you can sign up for my newsletter at **faelovesart.com/newsletter**. Or join my Facebook group, **Fae's Faves**! You can also find me on Instagram **@fae.loves.art** and on Patreon.

All shares, comments, reviews, and discussion of *If Only in Our Dreams* are encouraged and appreciated!

Happy Holidays! I'll see you in 2025.

about fae

FAE IS OBSESSED with anything romance. From a young age she realized she had a passion for falling in love over and over again. She loves to tell stories through both her art and writing. With a passion for classical monsters, meet-cutes, and contemporary romance, you can often find her with her nose stuck in a book and her pet corgi, Champa, on her lap.

She currently resides in Utah with her amazing husband and her collection of squishmallows. When you read one of her books you can expect to find love stories between humans, monsters, and loveable assholes that will make you laugh (and cry) as you get lost in their worlds for just a little. Every story comes with a happy ever after guarantee.

Find her online at:
WWW.FAELOVESART.COM